DIVINE PORTALS

An Epic Last-Days Adventure
Through Time, Love and
Deliverance

J. E. GUNTHER

Divine Portals—An Epic Adventure Through Time, Love and Deliverance, by J.E. Gunther

Printed and distributed by Lulu.com

Published by Second Advent Life ©2025

ISBN: 979-8-9934132-0-4

Cover design: J.E. Gunther.

Cover image: Charles Thonney a.k.a. SummerGlow on https://pixabay.com

The views expressed within this work are the sole responsibility of the author, and do not necessarily reflect the position of, nor does it possess the approval of, the Church of Jesus Christ of Latter-Day Saints.

This is a work of fiction and is not affiliated with any existing literary or entertainment property. Pop culture references are made herein, but no attempt is made to endorse, defame or infringe on those properties. The characters merely mention them in passing. Characters, names, incidents and dialogue are either products of the author's imagination and are not to be construed as real or are used fictitiously. Some songs in the public domain are quoted. Songs not in the public domain are only mentioned by name and not quoted. Many cities and places are real, and some are invented.

Dedicated to all ADHDers out there who know how terribly difficult it is to finish anything we start unless there's a deadline, and the awe and surprise when we actually do.

If I can do it, so can you.

Time is like a bayou
Flowing either way
Murky forward, dark behind,
languishing today.

Heavy is the air here,
Slowing every breath.
Tell me never, tell me true,
Tell me after death.

I will listen, I'll return,
Any moment, now.
Time is like a bayou,
Come discover how.
JEG

~Preface~

This novel explores the very last days before the Second Coming of Jesus Christ and beyond, but we will also visit Louisiana in the 1800s, chiefly in Sainte Jeanne (suhnt ZHEHN), a fictional village in Terrebonne parish. I named this village in honor of Joan of Arc (*Jeanne D'Arc*), who listened to the Voice and obeyed. She died as a martyr and was later dubbed a saint by the Catholic church. Joan symbolizes strength in the face of severe opposition, torture and death.

In the 1800s, folks in the Louisiana Bayou country spoke French. They were descendants of the French Acadians (Cajuns) who were kicked out of Nova Scotia in the early 1800s, or the high-born French, who migrated to the area in the early 1700s, some of whom intermarried with the Spanish and were called Spanish Creole, or mixed with "free people of color" from Haiti, as well as some of the indigenous Amer-Indians, mainly the Chitimacha, Houma (HOH-muh) and Choctaw, and were called Black Creole.

Southern Louisiana history is much more complicated and diverse than this simplistic micro-summary. So, for now, just know that our heroine spoke Cajun French. But in this book, it's mostly English, similar to how older Louisianans speak currently. I have not closely mimicked the bayou accent, since that would be nearly impossible to do and make it tedious to read. Just for fun, search for "Cajun accent" on the Internet. That accent didn't exist until they were forced to speak English in the early 1900s and is spoken at a faster pace than a Southern drawl.

I have included the occasional Cajun, Creole or Standard French term, to remind you that the Louisianans are speaking French, as are the Talbot party when in Stella's presence. French words and phrases are italicized and are in the Glossary and Pronunciation Guide following the last chapter, but you can probably figure out from the context what they mean. Fair warning—I'm from Texas, not Louisiana, so I hope genuine Louisianans will forgive me for throwing a little "Texican" into the mix.

Explanatory Notes follow the glossary. They provide attributions and more information in case something puzzles or interests you. They are organized by chapter and page. (My author buddies insist that novels should not have footnotes, so I took them out.)

Do read the Chronological Timeline after you finish reading the story. (Thanks for the suggestion, Kim!) It may help some pieces fall into place for you, since the storyline moves back and forth freely between the future and the past, and events change. But don't peek ahead of time. It will ruin some surprises for you.

As for the time-travel element, for God all time is now, (See Explanatory Notes), so I can accept time travel for translated beings, but I don't think our mortal bodies can do it in their present form. Perhaps I'm wrong, and the events in this book could, indeed, happen. Someday, we'll know.

Sensitivity alert: There is plenty of goodness and many miracles within these pages, but this is not a book for children or youth. References to incest, rape, child abuse and cannibalism are made, though not graphically described. Some violence does occur, some in self-defense, some with malice. There is no sex beyond the implied incest nor vulgarity beyond "hell." Doctor Grant uses, in one instance, a mild profanity common in the 1800s, and Stella smooths it over.

JEG

~CHAPTER 1~

The Plan

"Before I formed thee in the belly I knew thee…"
Jeremiah 1:5, *The Holy Bible*

2054, New Jerusalem, America

Oliver Talbot paused in the quiet, light-filled hallway before entering meeting room number two. He caressed the arched walnut door, running his hand over it with reverence. This fragrance of fresh-milled wood took him back to before the wars and desolation.

Hundreds of fires he had witnessed on his journey here still burned in his mind's eye: millions of trees, buildings, rubbish, books, bodies. Piles and piles of bodies. Traces of that horrific stench clung to him, despite his recent shower.

This exquisite wood embodied the promise of better times to come here in New Jerusalem, in what used to be Missouri. He opened that magnificent door and stepped into the room, startled to find his own dad as one of two men present, with JoAnne, his stepmother, radiating a surprising vitality.

"Hello, son," said Rick Talbot. He, too, seemed younger and more vibrant.

JoAnne hugged Oliver and said, "I'll be out in the hall. Good to see you."

"You, too. You look amazing."

"Thanks." She winked and whispered, "Have faith," before exiting.

1

His dad came forward with an outstretched hand, pulled him into a handshake with one hand and a firm hug with the other. *Maybe someday, I'll be the spiritual giant he is, but he's a lot to live up to.*

"Oliver, how long has it been? Five, six months?"

"I lost track, but that sounds about right."

"Tired?"

"Yeah." Oliver said, though "tired" fell far short. *Depleted, stomped on, missing brain cells. Missing half my soul. That comes closer.*

"I'm sure you have a lot to tell me, and I want to hear all about it, but we'll catch up later." Rick released his hand and indicated the other gentleman. "You remember Elder Wilson?"

"Welcome back to New Jerusalem," said Theodore Wilson, a tall, lanky man of undetermined age with white hair, a white suit and unmistakable self-possession. They shook hands. "Have a seat."

"Thank you," Oliver said, curiosity mounting.

The three of them perched on metal stools in an otherwise empty room, creating a perfect triangle. The luminous cloud over the city shone through a frosted skylight, washing the white plaster walls and polished floor in an ethereal glow, hinting that past and future met right here, radiating beyond the shadows in the distant corners of the room.

Eerie thought. Focus, Talbot.

The two elders sat in companionable silence, watching him. He bounced his new sandal in nervous anticipation, ankle resting on the other knee.

Why am I here? Another rescue mission? Another trek? He needed rest, renewal. Still, he trusted in the Lord and would go and do, regardless of his preferences or exhaustion.

Without any preamble or embarrassment, as though this happened every day of the week and twice on Sunday, Elder Wilson laid out this new assignment.

"Say what?" Oliver slapped his twitchy foot onto the floor and stared, brows knit together. *Incredible! Is this a joke?* He relaxed his face into a good-natured grin, masking his disbelief. "Sounded like you said I'm being sent back in time. Guess I forgot to clean out my ears."

Scrubbing months of grunge off in the shower felt great, but I'm ready for sleep. Maybe I'm already in bed, dreaming strange dreams.

"Your hearing is fine, son," Rick said. "If you need some time to wrap your head around this, we can meet later… after your last consultation?" he asked Elder Wilson, eyebrows raised.

The straight-faced counselor lifted his chin in affirmation.

Oliver held up a hand. "No, no. I just need to get this straight: I'm going to the year 1879 to pick up a wife because no woman in *this* century would have me?" He gave a skeptical snort. "Seriously? Men are outnumbered at least five to one. It's a pretty safe bet that *someone* could tolerate me for eternity. I haven't had a chance to check 'em all out yet, so gimme a sec."

Dad raised an eyebrow. "There is no need to 'check them all out,' son. The Lord in His infinite wisdom knows that you and this particular young lady are a great fit. For eternity."

Too surreal. Must be a prank. "So, why doesn't He bring her here? What, is the Tardis stuck? Only goes one way?" He snickered. "I wouldn't have to stay in 1879, would I? I just got here."

"Oliver…" Rick's inflection held a gentle warning.

"If you're finished," said the unruffled Elder Wilson, "maybe you could cut the snark and listen. Of course, you want to stay here in New Jerusalem. It's the safest and cleanest place on this continent. However, keep in mind that this opportunity is a privilege from the Lord, not a prison sentence."

Oliver's shoulders dropped. "I'm sorry. It's just that I'm exhausted and I've been through a lot. This is difficult to absorb." *Or believe.*

"Of course. You conducted yourself well, by the way, on your first trek here and on your recent mission to bring the West Virginians here."

"Well, thanks," said Oliver, uncomfortable with praise he didn't deserve. He had captained a company of seventeen stalwart sisters who had not all survived, and neither did his mission companion, which weighed on him. *Dad probably told him about the first trek. But how could he know anything about the second one? He couldn't. He's assuming. And now they're expecting me to buy into time travel. No possible way. I need sleep.*

Dad said, "Remember when I told you it was the Lord's will that I marry JoAnne? You protested and questioned my sanity. You're doing the same thing, now."

Elder Wilson, fingertips connecting over his lap, said, "How do you think Jesus feels when we don't trust Him to guide our lives and keep His promises?" he finished with a pointed look.

"Sounds an awful lot like our family motto, doesn't it, son?" Rick asked. "Our Savior is *all powerful*. He really can do anything, and we really can trust Him."

Oliver had been asking himself that skeptical question from scripture: "How is it possible that the Lord will…?" Doubters fill in the blank with whatever they cannot imagine an all-powerful God producing. His version varied only in detail: *How can the Lord take me back to the nineteenth century and match me up with a woman old enough to be my great-great-something-or-other? So not happening.*

The guidance counselor droned on. "Our Lord has directed us to bring you two together in her time, to give you the chance to experience trials so that you will bond, and grow in love and—"

"More trials?" Panic rose in his throat and crawled up behind his eyeballs. "I haven't had enough, just getting here? Twice?"

"So, now you think it's time to sit back and watch other people have trials," his dad said.

Ouch. He preferred to believe he had the faith and obedience required of people expecting to greet Jesus at His Second Coming. *But time travel? Gimme a break. So bogus.*

Rick gestured in a wide arc. "This new city is a mere taste of what is coming. It is the *inception* of a Terrestrial state. Not even close to Celestial. It is a mere glimmer of what you might one day enjoy, if you submit your will to the Lord and trust Him."

"Sure, Dad, but seriously, time travel? Is there a hidden camera in here? Somebody gonna jump out and yell 'Gotcha'?"

"Tell you what," said his dad as he rose to his full seventy-one inches, "we'll give you a chance to process this. Let us know what you decide."

"One more thing," added Elder Wilson as he unfolded his six-four-ish frame from the stool. "Time travel is not bogus," he said, and exited through a side door.

Oliver's mouth dropped open. *I did not say that out loud.*

Dad gripped the handle on the door to the hallway and paused before leaving the room. "I would have expected such resistance from your sister, but you? After all the miracles you've witnessed?"

Left alone in the meeting room, Oliver had an animated argument with himself.

"It's crazy, right? On the other hand, it's kind of intriguing. Still, there's no way. I mean, Dad might be pranking me, but I can't picture Elder Wilson doing that. Of course, they *are* friends. But how did he know what I was thinking? Coincidence? JoAnne said to have faith. Is the Lord really directing this? I want to believe, but this is *too weird.* Impossible."

Upon leaving the meeting, Rick closed the door and reached a hand to his wife, JoAnne.

"How did it go?" she asked. Fingers entwined, they strolled down the creamy white, sunlit hallway, reminiscent of an art gallery with lovely paintings between the doors on the left and windows on the right.

"He's struggling both to comprehend and accept time-jumping," Rick said with a sigh. "Plus, he's having trouble picturing the Lord as his matchmaker."

"I battled that last one, myself. Twice."

He squeezed her hand before opening the outside door. "The question, of course, is one of trust and faith. And I assumed Oliver had both. But now... I'm not convinced." He inhaled the fragrances of flowers, sunshine and sawdust. *Peace, peace.* It grieved him that Oliver doubted, but it grieved him more that his own translated state did not preclude a wrestle with frustration.

She patted his arm. "Give him a little time. He has always risen to any challenge. And don't fret over your parting words. You weren't impatient, you were 'reproving with sharpness.' He must have needed it."

"I thought you said you wouldn't listen in."

"I heard enough to know you were practicing patience," she said.

"Hm." He wished he had already achieved flawless patience and didn't need to practice. "Guess I'm not quite perfect, yet. Come on. Let's walk over to the cottage."

7

"Or," Jo said, her eyes sparkling, "We could teleport."

He grinned at her playfulness. "Let's just act like normal mortals and stroll over there. It's a pleasant walk. Oliver will take a while, I think, to come to terms with his destiny."

⁓⁂⁓

After hashing out his doubts and questions to the point of exasperation, Oliver left the room, oblivious to the elegant door and the fine artwork in the hall. Once outside, he wandered past gardens and buildings with people working in them and on them, laughing, talking, and singing.

This Zion-in-progress has blossomed. His joy in its birth rushed over him. *They've made quite a bit of progress since I left for West Virginia. It's shaping up.* Whitewashed adobe buildings had sprung up everywhere, sparkling in the bright light of the heavenly cloud over the city.

Mm. Love the clean air. No putrid smoke and ash or dust kicked up by earthquakes. His mind calmed, and peace settled over him.

The Holy Ghost chose that moment to whisper, *~Read your patriarchal blessing.~*

Oliver hesitated. *I don't have a copy anymore, but it's probably on file, somewhere. The library, maybe? If they don't have it, they'll know where to find it.*

Arriving at the library, he found shelf after empty shelf. The few available physical books huddled in pitiful clusters. Gravitating to a room full of people on computers, Oliver found an unoccupied sister missionary and asked about his blessing and about the empty shelves.

"I can help you find your blessing," she assured him. "And we encourage people to fill up the shelves by writing replacements for the millions of books burned in the last two decades. We'll receive more scriptures, too, as additional records are recovered and translated. I'm so excited to read more."

"That *is* exciting," he said, and sat down at the computer she pointed him to. "Maybe we'll get the backstory of Aminadi, Amulek's ancestor. All we have is a teaser." He ran his hand lightly over the keyboard. *This is like coming home. I haven't used one of these since before the call-out.*

"Aminidi? Oh, yes, he's the one who interpreted the handwriting on the temple wall. I've wondered what it said. Was it the same thing that Daniel saw on the king's wall?"

"Maybe. That would make sense."

She indicated where to find the correct digital files and helped him retrieve his blessing. "You can print this out if you wish."

"Great, thanks," he said, as he clicked on the appropriate icon. "I'm surprised at all this equipment. Even the paper's pretty rare."

"Yes, our Church leaders prepared well. This way to the print room." She indicated the door on the left, then led the way. "They stored these electronics and many tons of paper in vaults during the destruction and war, so we can continue the work for all those who still need their ordinances done."

"About a bazillion?"

"More or less," she agreed. "This your first time to visit New Jerusalem?"

"I was here for a couple of weeks and left on a trek mission."

"Welcome back," she said as another sister missionary joined them. Oliver acknowledged the new arrival. "I'm curious," she added. "Is it still bad out there?"

Their expectant faces blurred, while images of violence and destruction pushed their way in, but he slammed a mental door on them and threw the deadbolt. No sense in dwelling on it. "Yeah."

As the first sister handed Oliver two printed sheets, the most significant line in his blessing popped into his mind, as if holding the paper on which it was printed unlocked his memory.

He thanked the missionaries and headed to a bench in a little park. Basking in the light, beauty and peace of his surroundings before turning his attention to this treasured message from God, he read the key passage aloud: "'Be patient in waiting for your eternal companion, who will only appear across a great chasm of time. Cherish her...' A great chasm of time... I thought it meant when I was old, or in the next life or something. This was predestined!"

His outburst drew the attention of nearby people, but he ignored them. His gaze fixed on the horizon across that meta-physical breach of time and space, he imagined the nebulous form of a woman waiting for him. Saturated with the Holy Ghost, his mind opened to a vision. He and an incandescent woman, her features unclear, knelt in a light-suffused realm before the dazzling Lord Jehovah, who spoke first.

"It is not recommended for eternal companions to request different earth times."

"I cannot be content," she pleaded, "to have all the privileges of living in the End Times if my dearest friends are lost."

"I will provide for them," Jehovah said with mild reproof.

"Please use me for that purpose. I want to be born sooner to help them."

"Master," Oliver's spirit-self added, "*my* mission is to build Latter-day Zion and prepare others for your return to earth. Is there no way to reconcile our differences?"

"I am The Way. This scheme of yours will be costly in mind, body and spirit. Are you still willing?"

The woman communed with pre-mortal Oliver without words. "We are."

"Then rise, my children, and fulfill your mutual desire to bring others home to me."

The scene faded. His skin prickled as he rose to his feet, a clearer path before him.

~~~

~CHAPTER 2~

Rough Start

"But thus saith the Lord, Even the captives
of the mighty shall be taken away, and the
prey of the terrible shall be delivered..."
Isaiah 49:25, *The Holy Bible*

Late January 1880, Memphis, Tennessee

Oliver reflected on that fateful, somewhat embarrassing day when he had received this great gift of going back in time to meet the woman of the vision. Her tug on his arm jolted him back to reality, and he chuckled at the irony. *Can I call this 1800s world "reality"?*

His sweetheart pulled him to a bakery on their stroll through downtown Memphis, its inviting aromas jostling with the stench of the gutter and the heady, flowery fragrance she favored. The welcome sunshine warmed his back on this brisk winter day. *All this appears pretty solid, but if my senses deceive me, may it never end.*

"Would you like a brioche, Ruby?"

"Oui, merci, Oliver."

He couldn't help it. Delight in her expressions and how she pronounced his name in her Acadian French bubbled inside him. It sounded like Oh-leh-vehr. *I'm tempted to kiss her right here on Main Street, just to goad her into saying it again. But besides coaching me in the formal speech of this century, my instructor nixed public displays of affection for the 1800s, so I'd better not.*

Oliver purchased the treat for her, instead, and guided her back out to the sidewalk.

They had been shopping for a wedding ring, and now as his future bride enjoyed her bread-like cupcake, his thoughts wandered to their beginning.

When I first came through the portal, I thought the woman in the vision would be on our steamboat, but no one fit the picture. It took a trip to shore in Plaquemine, Louisiana, to find her at the doctor's office. Two months of persuasion convinced her that I am trustworthy, sincere and good marriage material. But why were her defenses so slow to melt? Abuse? Betrayal?

Her fascination with steamboats gave me the perfect excuse to invite her aboard the SS Infinite. She lit up when I offered to give her a tour, but wouldn't commit to a definite date, at first.

"Ruby…?" The alias, born of necessity, had become so natural to Oliver that her true name seldom crossed his mind.

"*Oui?*" Finished with her brioche, she spared him no glance before urging him to the nearest window display.

"Why did you hesitate to tour the *Infinite* with me that first time? You delayed your acceptance for days."

"*Beaucoup* reasons. One, I didn't know you well enough to trust you, Oliver. I thought, 'Could this be a trap?' I wanted to be on a steamboat, but not as a landed catfish."

"Touché, my love." *Thank the Lord I served my mission in France, so I can understand her... Mostly. Cajun expressions are unique.*

"Reason two, my pitiful wardrobe. I owned nothin' but two much-mended calicos."

"You were wearing those when I fell in love with you, Ruby. You could wear rags, and my pulse would race." She did turn heads, even with a scar on her forehead that interrupted her left eyebrow.

"That is sweet, *merci*. But to wear such rags in public? And with a fine gentleman? *Non et non.* I had to acquire a suitable dress, though it pained me to use my savin's. My sole desire was to escape Henri, and I wanted that money for a ticket upriver."

She laid her free hand on his upper arm. "Which brings me to reason three: I need protection on main streets and I do treasure havin' my very own defender." The ardor in Ruby's gaze intensified.

"My distinct pleasure," he said, nearly undone by an immediate flare of sparks.

"God alone knows where Henri is. We cannot assume he has given up."

"True," he said, brushing a crumb off her chin.

"*Merci.*" Ruby swept the street with a cautious glance. "But my *chapeau* helps to hide this face, does it not?" Impishness masked her concern as she resumed her inspection of the novelties behind glass.

"I suppose that bonnet does deflect most public scrutiny, since you spend so much time pasted to store windows. But he wouldn't be this far north, would he?"

"Ooo. What a lovely settee."

15

Distracted again from the subject at hand. It would be frustrating if she weren't so adorable. Such expensive things probably didn't exist in her little bayou village. Of course she's ga-ga over all this stuff.

As Ruby explored the displays, he admired her reflection in the glass. Her dark-brown, wavy hair boasted a white streak that, though not extraordinary in his time, drew attention in hers. Today, though, her bonnet covered most of it.

"So, what changed your mind?" he asked, as they reached a window of Goldsmith's Department Store, set with a cheerful montage of the latest in home goods.

"Oh... a little voice pushed me to accept your invitation. And during that visit, I fell in love with that steamship *par excellence* and your parents, in that order. Ahh, the porcelain. And the crystal," she said with a sigh. "*Très beaux.* So beautiful."

"And finally," he said to himself, since she wasn't listening anyway, "you fell in love with me." Soon after that initial boat tour, she accepted his parents' invitation to leave the doctor's employ and join them in their mission. They visited cities up and down the Mississippi River, bringing relief to the destitute.

I wish she had enlisted because of me, though I love her enthusiasm for the work of the Lord. She'd make a great missionary. Gradually, her interest in him grew, and culminated in his proposal of marriage and her acceptance at the Christmas gala aboard ship.

Was it a whole month ago? No way. A single moment in time. Well, all right, many perfect moments, despite the danger. Her alias fits. She's a jewel. I hope she chooses a ring with rubies. Once she's ready to decide, we'll make the purchase and take the portal back to New Jerusalem. Easy breezy. She'll love it there, and I know everyone will love her.

Gratitude flooded him, and he admired the two of them in the window glass. She wore a dress of rich greenish blue that accentuated her curves, and a matching cape. His black suit and top hat coordinated with her outfit perfectly. Back in New Jerusalem, he shaved his beard but kept his mustache and traded his blond ponytail for a period style.

"Let's find a photographer," he said. "We'd make a handsome picture."

She tore her gaze from the collectibles in the window, surprised. "With my scars?"

He whispered, "You're beautiful," and in front of at least thirty passersby, he took her in his arms, inhaling her scent. *I thank Thee, Father, for Thy generosity. I know I don't deserve her, and it's true I didn't believe this was possible, but I'm so grateful.*

"Oliver?"

Acknowledging her embarrassment, and with a silent apology to his instructor, he released her to resume their walk, drawing her hand back into the crook of his arm.

"Those scars hardly show, my love," he said. "Just that quirky eyebrow of yours. The photographer will think you're flirting with him."

Her laughter bubbled up, erasing the worried lines between her brows. As her head tilted back and her sparkling gaze met his, she jerked, gasped for air and froze. Women screamed.

"Ruby?" Confused, he caught her as she crumpled, encountering stickiness on her back and the ivory handle of a knife. *No!* "Help! Help me!" he cried, his heart threatening to exit between his ribs. That beloved glint in her eyes faded, leaving her staring at him, sightless. Empty.

"Ruby!" He shook her in his desperation for a response, causing her bonnet to fall back and hang around her neck by its ribbon ties. *Oh God, why?*

Onlookers yelled, "Fetch a doctor! Somebody!"

"I'll go!" a young boy shouted, taking off at once. Oliver had more faith in his dad's portion of the Lord's power than he did in 1800s medicine, but at this point *any* aid would be comforting. He spotted his father and another man restraining a black-haired, unkempt individual who fought like a madman.

"Dad, help Ruby!"

"That's Stella Rubidoux, you fool!" the man yelled in French as he attempted to jerk himself free from his captors. "She kilt my woman, and now she pays!" The man craned his neck in all directions. "Lefroy! Teasdale!"

No one claimed those names or came to the murderer's aid. *He's whacko. She couldn't have killed anyone. That must be Henri Boudreaux, the man she's been so afraid of. I should have protected her better. I should have...* Oliver tightened his arms around Ruby, or rather, Stella, and buried half his face in her hair. *I failed her. Oh, God, please help me.*

His stepmother appeared from behind the men controlling the furious perpetrator. She hurried to Oliver amid the growing crowd of shouting people.

"Mama Jo," he choked out. "She's... She can't be... Get Dad. I need him. Now." Cradling Stella's upper body in his arms, he sat down on the cold granite curb, shaken and incredulous. *This can't be happening!*

"He's coming, dear boy. He must find someone else strong enough to help hold Henri."

"So it *is* Henri."

"Yes." JoAnne bent to remove the dangling bonnet and set it aside before sitting beside him. With one arm around his shoulder, her other hand reached to close the girl's eyes. "Oh, Stella."

The doctor arrived with the winded messenger boy. Conducting a brief examination, he pronounced her dead and sent another young teen to fetch the undertaker before disappearing, claiming an urgent case to attend to.

Rick squeezed through the crowd of sympathetic onlookers and crouched beside the tragic little cluster. "Henri's in custody, now."

"Turn her around, lad," said a burly policeman as he approached. "We must claim the murder weapon." Oliver complied by pulling her into his chest. The knife hurt her going in and it hurt him to watch the cop yank it out. He puked into the gutter, and his dad handed him a handkerchief.

"Dad," he said in an urgent, tense whisper as soon as the police left with the weapon and the defiant, shouting Henri. "You have to heal her. You've done this before, so I know you can. You can bring her back."

At that moment, the crowd parted for the hearse.

"Not now," said Rick in an undertone.

"You have to do it now before they take her."

"Can't do it at all, son."

"Why not? No. You can!"

Rick laid a cautionary hand on Oliver's arm. Shaken to his core, Oliver wiped his nose on a clean corner of the fouled hanky and stuffed it into a pocket. Remembering his own handkerchief, he pulled that out and finished the job. Shadowy wolves of despair circled, nipping and growling, hungry for his soul.

Suck it up, Talbot. Don't give in. Don't give in. Don't... He pulled her closer. *Why? Why doesn't Dad fix this?*

A fine, black funeral coach with the words "Canaday & Co, Undertakers" emblazoned on the side in white script arrived. A paunchy, unremarkable man in a black suit and top hat secured the reins and descended from the driver's seat. Releasing the latch on the back double doors, he removed an oblong rattan basket, leaned it back against the hearse and opened the lid.

His dad stood up and encouraged him to do likewise, but Oliver refused. The pain of losing his love gripped him in an iron vise, body and spirit.

The driver introduced himself as Mr. Canaday and waited to assist. And waited.

"Oliver."

The tenderness in his dad's voice touched his mind with clarity and resignation. Clutching Stella's limp form with one arm, Oliver allowed his dad to help him up by the other. He clung to her for another tortured moment, wherein he memorized her face and kissed her crooked eyebrow before releasing her into his dad's arms.

The undertaker guided Rick in laying Stella into the oversized basket, closed the domed lid and buckled the straps, before the two of them pushed it into the coach. JoAnne wrapped an arm around Oliver's waist. In anguish, he returned the embrace, arm around her shoulders, as his dad joined them. Mr. Canaday fastened the double doors and prepared to take notes, pencil at the ready.

"Name?"

"Rub—" started Oliver, throat catching. Head down, he tightened his arm around Jo in a silent plea for help, biting his lips.

"Stella Rubidoux," JoAnne said.

"Date of birth?"

"May 29, 1857," Oliver whispered.

"Speak up, please," came the brusque directive.

Oliver swallowed and repeated the date a little louder.

"Coffin?"

What else would she be buried in? A body bag?

His father answered for him. "Perhaps it would be best for me to come by your place of business later today to settle the details."

"Very well," came the cool reply. "I require a deposit of ten dollars."

JoAnne dipped into her handbag and produced the necessary funds. A murmur arose from the crowd, expressing shock over a woman casually dispensing so much silver.

Could we get a little privacy? Don't these people have somewhere to be?

The expressionless businessman dropped the coins one at a time into a small drawstring bag, presented his business card to Rick and tipped his hat in their general direction before mounting the driver's seat and flicking the reins.

Oliver's pain threatened to swallow him whole as he watched the retreating hearse turn left and, for all he knew, roll off the edge of the world. His empty world. *God go with you, my love, since I can't. I wish I could have saved you. There's nothing left for me here, or anywhere else.* "I can't believe you let him take her away," he said. Two sets of arms encircled him. The crowd dispersed like ashes in a draft.

"Let's return to the carriage, son," said Rick, picking up Oliver's top hat off the street and brushing it off. "We'll talk about it there."

Listless, Oliver trailed behind his parents to the horse-drawn conveyance, barely aware of his legs moving or the smudges of dirt, vomit and blood all over his fine suit. *I don't understand. We didn't change the outcome. She still died. Why are we even here?*

No one spoke for the remainder of the solemn ride back to the docks where the *SS Infinite* waited. JoAnne held Stella's bonnet on her lap; Rick held Oliver's hat.

Unwilling to move, anger building, Oliver remained seated after the carriage crossed the stage—a bridge from dock to boat—and rolled to a gentle stop. Typical noises of labor and conversation hummed outside.

"So, explain to me why you couldn't bring her back," he said, not bothering to keep the edge out of his voice. "You've done it for other people. Why couldn't you do it for me?"

The driver opened the door for them.

"Give us a moment, please," JoAnne told him.

"Of course, ma'am," he replied and closed the door.

"Dad."

"It's not allowed, Oll. It's not the plan."

"Not the *plan*? You said the *plan* was for us to go through the trials of mortality. *Together.* And now she's gone. Why did you even bother to bring me here if she was just going to die, anyway?"

He strangled a frustrated yell before it could escape and stared out the window at the city he had come to love before it all soured. He had enjoyed dressing the part and learning all about Ruby's—Stella's—time, but now, he felt foolish. Cheated. The short vision he experienced back in New Jerusalem flitted across his darkened mind, but he pushed it away.

Probably wasn't an actual vision. Just something my over-excited mind conjured up. Some grubbies, a jumbo bag of chili-lime chips and a video game would hit the spot, right now. Too bad those last two aren't available. How do I veg and escape in New Jerusalem? Or pretend a trip to the past never happened? Maybe it didn't happen. Maybe it's all an illusion.

"It isn't over, yet," said JoAnne.

"What?" Oliver, overcome with pain, lashed out. "She's dead. *I'd* call that 'game over'."

Jo's soothing voice held no reprimand. "Trust in the Lord with all the pieces of your broken heart, even when you don't understand. Even when it appears impossible."

"It's *completely* impossible." He clamped his jaws shut with taut muscles and returned to staring out the window at nothing. Not nothing. He watched the cherished scenes with Stella play out as if in a movie. *How can she be gone?*

"I know it doesn't make sense now," said his dad, "but someday, I promise it will. With God, all things are possible."

Oliver stared at him in disbelief, until one tiny molecule of hope revived as he studied the assurance in his father's eyes.

~CHAPTER 3~

Her Beginning

*"Behold, I have refined thee, but not with silver; I have
chosen thee in the furnace of affliction."*
Isaiah 48:10, The Holy Bible

June 1874, Five Years Earlier, Sainte Jeanne, Louisiana

"Nettie! Nettie, where *are* you?" *Please Lord,
don't take her yet. I can't go back home. Not ever.*
Frantic, Stella Rubidoux searched all around Nettie's
garden and the tired, old cabin, her mind racing. *Will I
have to risk a trip to the store to get help?*

Jacques down at the general store would be
happy to put himself between her and danger. But what
if her tormentors found her before she secured
protection?

Blood pumping in her ears, she twitched her
faded brown skirt up a bit, leaped over the two steps to
the gallery porch of the cabin and checked inside. A pot
of something savory simmered in the fireplace, so Nettie
couldn't be far, could she?

Maybe she's gatherin' eggs. Stella grabbed
Nettie's stubby shotgun, checked for cartridges and sped
out the door, scanning the trees as she ran. She hoped to
find Nettie and feared encountering someone else. Or
two someones.

Nettie, or Antoinette LeBlanc, the local
traiteuse—female healer—in this southern Louisiana
village of Sainte Jeanne, cared for her as her mother

would have, had *Maman* lived. Stella gravitated to anyone who would treat her better than her remaining relatives did.

Nettie offered the bonus of teaching Stella all she knew about plants and potions, methods and mixtures. She planned on Stella taking her place one day. According to tradition, a "treater" or healer passed the gift to a family member of the other sex. Because her son had passed and left no progeny of his own, Nettie would have taught her nephew Jacques to be a *traiteur*, had he not declared a decided aversion to the prospect.

Stella, as René's step-granddaughter, received Nettie's gift instead, and did her utmost to learn all she could about the healing arts, for she hated to disappoint her beloved godmother. Feisty but kind, the old woman had invested over ten years into teaching, clothing, correcting, and defending her, easing the horrors of life with *Père* and her brother Georges.

"Nettie!" she hollered, desperate after finding an empty henhouse.

"I'm over here, *chère!*" Nettie emerged from the woods behind her home with an armful of herbal treasures. Relieved to the point of weakness, Stella ran to her godmother on shaky legs.

Nettie eyed the gun. "You huntin' varmints?"

"They might be huntin' me." With a trembling hand, she scooped up what Nettie dropped. "Ooh! What's this?"

"A prime specimen of *Manglier.* Most rare 'round here."

"Don't recollect ever seein' one."

"Found it up on the rise. I ain't seen it before, neither, but it's in one of my books. A prime bruise you got there, Stella. We better git a poultice on that."

"Naw, I'm all right."

"What's it for, this time?"

"Same as all the others, dear Nettie. Nothin' atall." Her fingers stroked the narrow Manglier leaves, while her feet took off towards the weather-worn house.

"No account Paul Rubidoux," Nettie fumed. "Sorry excuse for a *père*. No good ever come outta Bayou Chene, though I hear tell he weren't from there. Prob'ly runnin' from a shady past, ehn?" A sneer crept into her voice. "He had such a liquid way o' movin,' oozin' on in here, sneekin' 'round like the devil hi'self. Had him a peek at your *maman* and… Or was it your brother Georges, this time?"

"Doesn't matter." Stella paused to let Nettie catch up. "What one does, the other will do."

"*Desolèe, chère.* I'm so sorry."

Stella shrugged a shoulder. "Not goin' back there anymore anyhow. Tired o' bein' whacked like a dirty rug on the line. Had enough o' that, *moi*." She couldn't admit, even to Nettie, that the abuse had taken a turn for the incestuous. She shook in horror at the memory of Georges pawing at her as he ridiculed and demeaned her. It was by the grace of God she escaped. *Merci, Jésus.*

"Think your *père* won't come fetch ya?"

"I can run faster'n him. I done it a time or two."

"Hmph! I'd pay to watch a race between you two, long as you win." Nettie stumped up the two sagging gallery steps. "Got some *choupique* stew on the fire."

27

"My nose can sure enough tell. You do have a way with herbs and spices, Miz Nettie."

"Well now, should do, after eighty-nine years."

"Why Miz Nettie, you can't be that old!" Stella opened the door for them with her first grin in ages. She loved their little game.

"I turned eighty-nine last March, Stella Rubidoux, as well you know. Let's git on into the house and git us some stew. Got some cornbread to go with it."

Stella returned the shotgun to the corner by the small table, grateful she hadn't needed to use it. To take anyone's life would stab her to the core, but she vowed to defend herself against *Père* and Georges from this moment on, their victim no longer.

The women laughed and chattered over their comforting meal, calming Stella's uneasiness.

Nettie sobered and said, "I wish just once, you'd call me *Grand-grand-mère*, 'fore I die."

Tears sprang up. "I'd be honored... *Grand-grand-mère*."

Nettie's face glowed with pleasure. "I daresay I am your great-grandmama, *moi*, seein's how my boy René married your grandmama Charlotte, after her Édouard passed and left her with two young girls to raise on 'er own."

"That's sure 'nuff true. Miz Nettie, tell me more about *Mamère* Charlotte an' my *maman*."

The old woman's mouth flattened into a thin line. "They died, *chère*, same as we all do." Stella deflated and Nettie softened a smidge. "Your *maman* Lulu was a pretty thing. Same dark eyes an' hair as you. But you favor her sister, Celié—her spirit an' image. Anyway, Celié wrote a silly goodbye note an' took off with a lumberman we never met nor even heard of, an'…" She cleared her throat and chirped, "Well! How 'bout some blackberry jelly for this cornbread? We need us some dessert. Remind me to git some more sugar, soon."

"Yes, ma'am." Stella had hoped Nettie would tell her more, but no. *Someday, I'll find out what happened.* Her mother passed away when Stella was about three, and no one would answer her questions. Villagers swapping stories at Jacques' store said the swamp took Lulu, born Lucille Dupleix. Stella suspected it was not an accident.

Suicide? Mayhap something worse. She remembered little of her mother, but always, her *maman* cried.

The memory of her first and only year of school, however, remained intact. One blessed day in her sixth year of age, Miss Nettie confronted *Père* about it.

"Poor, motherless chile! She needs clothes, Paul Rubidoux. Ain't you got no compassion? How you can clothe your son but not your daughter be beyond me!"

"Stay outta my business, ol' biddy. It don't concern you."

"Paul, she can't go to school like that! 'Stead o' buyin' you a new *shotgun*," referring to his latest purchase, "git 'er some clothes an' shoes."

"Nunya business, ol' woman. She don't need schoo'."

"Don't you business me! 'Course she needs school. You send her on over to me and I'll put some clothes on 'er. Better'n nothin', which those rags clearly are!"

"Ain't takin' your charity."

"Tain't charity if she cleans my house for it," she said, as if to a simpleton.

"Plenty o' work to home. Leave me be."

"Won't. It's a crime to treat a chile the way you do. A whole family o' rats could hide in her hair. Send her on over, now, I mean it. I'm her godmother, after all, and sworn to take a hand in her upbringin'."

Père growled at Nettie and grabbed Stella's arm, yanking her toward the bayou below the general store where they had been shopping. Nothing bought for her, of course. *Père* wouldn't even allow her to accept a piece of candy, a *lagniappe* from Jacques LeBlanc, the store's owner.

Was it because Jacques is Nettie's nephew, or is he just hateful? Prob'ly both.

Her attention remained fixed on Miss Nettie, longing to stay with her, a much safer adult than her father, but *Père* cured the course of her gaze with an extra yank.

"You hear me, Paul Rubidoux?"

A small crowd of witnesses gathered nearby, meaning Nettie had won this round, as much a law in their village as "Thou shalt not steal." But would he admit he lost the battle? *Mais non.* Of course not. One must save face by not conceding on the spot. He snapped at Stella to walk faster. Certain he plopped her into the *pirogue* facing away from Miss Nettie on purpose, she didn't dare glance back. But she fought the urge something fierce.

Next day, to the victor went the spoils, and *Père* sent her over to Miss Nettie's. Sure as sunrise, however, he told her to be back in time to fix his midday meal.

"I better not have to come fin' you. I got work to do."

Plenty scared, she nodded as if with a tremor, grasping his implied threat perfectly. Stella scatted on over to the healer's cottage down the bayou, not wasting a thin second, fearing his hand or his boot on her back.

His demands denied me the right to lunch and playtime with classmates and all the afternoon classes once school started. Had to work extra hard to keep up, but after that one school year, Nettie tutored me herself, in reading, writing, arithmetic, healing and life.

I learned so much by watching Nettie. She wrote recipes, studied her notes, calculated doses, and taught me to do the same. I fetched whatever supplies she needed, and putting foot to floor helped me recall the use of each herb or tool or ingredient. I gloried in producing the exact item Nettie needed before she even asked for it.

I didn't atall mind the work at Nettie's—cooking, cleaning, feeding chickens, foraging and studying, because of the love and praise she gave me. No such things came from Georges and Père.

At home, she cooked, cleaned and dodged swinging fists, her nerves on high alert. Whether or not those fists connected with their intended target, she found comfort at day's end in the beauty of night wonders such as stars or blinking fireflies. She had no window in her little cabin corner, but she could glimpse them between the boards. Bayou concerts of bullfrogs, owls, crickets, beetles and cicadas lulled her to sleep, soothing the pain of the day.

It suited me no end when Père lit out on extended hunts. Took my own blissful trips of escape into the magical world of books. Enchanting stories of elsewhere and else *when* distracted her from the frightening *now*. Reading helped dispel the dread of her father's arrival, but back when she was twelve, she learned the hard way to hide her books.

That day, her younger self wept in Nettie's lap at the loss of another treasure. Books were too dear to be launched into the bayou, but launch them he did.

"*Il est couillon, oui*! A prime fool," Nettie said as she comforted Stella. "Books do gall him somethin' awful, *n'est-ce pas*? Prob'ly 'cause he has no idea what's in one. Thinks each one is a secret plot against 'im. Best not take any more books home, *chère*. Around here, a book is too precious to lose."

Stella agreed and wiped away her tears, determined to keep all books away from him. *Nettie's right—Père has no more schooling than do the chickens.*

Jacques, down at the general store, aided and abetted her appetite for reading. He never announced in *Père's* presence that another book had arrived but used their secret system. If he drummed his fingers on the counter, she would glance at him and get a wink. She would sneak back alone to fetch the newest book. *I always wondered who paid for those books, Nettie or Jacques.*

Nettie's door burst open with a bang, bringing Stella back to the present. She leaped up, pulse pounding, ready to fight or run. The man she feared most appeared in all his raging glory. "Git on home, girl!"

"Ain't doin' it."

With deliberate calm, Nettie rose, too. "You git outta my house, Paul Rubidoux. You ain't fit to darken my door."

"Shut up, woman. She my girl and I'm takin' 'er home." He started forward, his intent unmistakable.

So fast it made Stella jump, Nettie snatched up her shotgun and took a bead on *Père's* chest. "Let her alone, Paul. She's taken enough wallops from you."

He halted, watchful. "Stupid ol' biddy. Ain't dat gullible, *moi*. A healer don't kill people."

Nettie pulled back the hammer slowly. "Don't know as I'd bet on that, Paul. I kills any snake crossin' my path and I been itchin' to pull a trigger on you, ever since what happened to Celié and Lulu." His eyes widened then narrowed, twitching. "You're wonderin' how much I know, I 'spect. Let me give you a hint," she spit out with venom. "I know you are a shaved hair away from a watery grave yourself 'cause o' what you done."

He backed up a step. "You don't know nuthin'," he countered, his bland bravado lacking the spice of conviction.

"*Non?* Lulu was mighty chatty the day before she *drowned.*"

Retreating in earnest, now, *Père* banged his heel on the door jamb.

"You git on outta here, Paul Rubidoux, an' don't let me catch your twisted self in my house again. Otherwise, I be scrubbin' your guts off o' my walls."

The scathing glare her father flashed at both women before he disappeared skittered down Stella's spine. Sinking into her chair, she prayed, *"Jésus, Joseph et Marie,* may I never see that man again for all my remaining days.*"*

"Amen to that!" Miss Nettie said with gusto and kept her gun at the ready as she checked out the door before slamming it closed. She stepped backwards to her chair, still on her guard, gun a bit closer this time. "Never turn your back on a pestilent snake, *chère.*"

As if begging for a lifeline, Stella said, "Tell me what happened to *Maman* and *Tante* Celié. Please!"

"It's an ugly tale, child, too terrible for your ears."

"If you ain't here when he comes back, I'll need it for protection. Besides, I turned seventeen a week ago. I'm old enough to git married, an' I'm old enough to know the truth, *n'est-ce pas?*"

"Hm. Reckon that's for true, *certainement.*" Nettie drew a strained breath. "Lulu been crying all mornin' when I went for a visit, so I fetched her home with me for a little chat. Lo and behold, he'd been steppin' out on her on those long hunts o' his, comin' back with nothin' but excuses. A friend of hers spied Paul with another woman out to Assumption parish. Didn't announce it to ever'one, just Lulu, but maybe she shoulda done, ehn?"

Nettie checked out the window, using the gun barrel to part the curtains a smidge before resuming her tale. "Lulu flew home to fix his supper, but next day she was dead. Paul claimed she drowned. Oh, she was all soaked through, all right, *oui,* but I suspect she confronted him, and he put her in that water on purpose. Good thing her friend was just passin' through, or he woulda kilt her, too, ehn? Celié herself come back, not long after. 'Member that?"

Stella shook her head. "*Mais non.* Don't recollect *Tante* Celié atall."

"Well, now that I think on it, 'tis unlikely your *père* took you over there," Nettie said. "She weren't here for long an' your *maman* had just died. Charlotte told me Celié turned up, all thin an' sickly, leadin' her skinny young'un by a rope of all things. Stayed with Charlotte, who was alone after my boy René passed. No more'n a couple weeks later, your *Tante* Celié drowned, too."

"That's terrible."

"*Vraiment.* Tsk. Poor Charlotte. Lost both her girls sudden-like, an' it weren't too long before she gave up the ghost herself. Celié's boy landed on a shrimp boat, workin' at a man's job. It's God's own wonder he didn't die on that boat."

"How do you know?" Stella asked.

"Mm… Heard tell. But no, I don't know for true what happen' to Charlotte's girls, but when I threw it up to him, your *père* showed his guilty-as-sin face, *n'est-ce pas?*"

"*Mais oui,* he did kill 'er. I'm sure of it. You think he kilt *Tante* Celié, too?"

"God alone knows, but after his reaction, I'd bet on it." Nettie glanced sharply at the window, sending a spurt of fear through Stella, but no one appeared.

"Then he could kill me, too," she said, willing herself to calm down.

"He'd kill us both without a speck o' remorse, *certainement*."

***

Stella awoke to an eerie stillness. *No. No!*

Rising in panic from the trundle bed, she found Nettie lying in eternal repose. "Oh, *Grand-grand-mère* Nettie," she said, weeping. "How will I manage without you?"

She gave her tears free rein, remembering all she'd been given of this dear woman. When spent, she reached across the old tick stuffed with Spanish moss to stroke the cherished lady's thin, white hair. "You made life bearable and at times even joyful. *Merci. Merci.*"

Disappointment mingled with Stella's grief as she hurried down the bayou to fetch Jacques. Antoinette LeBlanc left this world with a firm grip on the rest of the family secrets. The door to possible further enlightenment closed with a bang.

~CHAPTER 4~

Strange Portents

*"And it shall come to pass afterward, that I will pour
out my spirit upon all flesh; and your sons and your
daughters shall prophesy, your old men shall dream
dreams, and your young men shall see visions…"*
Joel 2:28, *The Holy Bible*

2048, Orem, Utah

On his way home from his dad's place, Oliver
mourned the downward spiral of what used to be a
thriving city. *Empty buildings and trash everywhere. So
many businesses gone. The latest pandemic killed more
than just people. I'm starving. I'd give my last dollar for
a bacon cheeseburger and onion rings. And a cookie
dough shake. Nothing comes close, anymore.*

Oliver's mouth watered. *I wish there was still a
burger joint around here. I heard there was one up in
Salt Lake City, but it has bars on the window and a very
long line. I could do sushi, I guess. Blah. I'd rather have
a sandwich at home, if there's any bread, that is. I think
I'm out.* "I guess it's sushi again, today."

As inconvenient as some aspects of life were,
Oliver considered himself blessed to have a job and a
couple of internet businesses, but rumors flew around the
water cooler and tension mounted at work. He could *act*
unconcerned. Plays and musicals in theaters throughout
two counties filled his resume, so *acting* chill wasn't an
issue. Actually achieving peace? Not so much.

Ignoring the nearest police drone while he sat at a stoplight, Oliver frowned at the clutter on the floor of his ancient two-door, including a program from the last play at his parents' theater, the Crescent.

I should clean out my car. That was four years ago. The economy tanked and audiences dwindled, forcing smaller theaters like the Crescent to close. *Mom and Dad were bummed, but it didn't hurt my feelings. I couldn't scare up any motivation to continue that career, not after Cami.*

Oliver Michael Talbot and Cami Shalise Trent, two attractive people who starred in many shows together, tied the knot in a lovely temple wedding.

It was supposed to be the start of a Celestial marriage. Ha. More like an eternity of hell. I'd heard of people who changed into unrecognizable fiends after the wedding, but I would never have imagined that of Cami. It took me months to stop denying the evidence that piled up like the dirty laundry she never bothered to take care of. It always fell on me to do it.

At first Cami insisted on having her way over the tiniest things, and in his efforts to be flexible and do his part to keep her happy, he gave in. The whining and pouting increased, the manipulative requests morphed into demands, and before long he served a tyrant in full throttle. *She wouldn't even pretend to play her part as a loving newlywed. It was that pro basketball game that convinced me to give up trying.*

They had attended the game with his parents, during which she said little for a change, except when she was sighing or complaining about something, obviously bored.

"I did say you didn't have to come," he reminded her. "But you insisted." *Besides, I could have used a break from your abuse.*

"Oh, but, Olly," she said, dripping with insincerity, "I don't want you to go anywhere without me."

Yeah, more like you don't trust me out of your sight, you little control freak.

Afterwards, in the press of the crowd, he and his dad excused themselves to visit the restroom. Cami shoved open the men's restroom door which slammed into the wall behind it, making all the vulnerable guys around the corner jump. She bellowed, "OLIVER! I did NOT say you could leave! Get out here RIGHT NOW!"

Charming girl. Dad offered to help me find a good lawyer, but it was my mess, so I found my own lawyer. Ugly marriage, ugly divorce. She took the car and everything else of value, even the dog. I miss that dog. God help her next victim.

He had to find another apartment, another car, another life. Nix on finding another wife, however. Anytime someone not in the know asked about his new bride, he replied, "I'm assuming she's fine, since she won everything in the divorce."

He might have avoided the whole fiasco had he reviewed his patriarchal blessing before committing his gravest error to date. It indicated that it would be ages before he found his eternal partner. Maybe not even in this life.

At least I could adopt another dog. Bless Yatzy. She's such a good companion—undemanding, calm and happy to greet me when I come home. Nothing like Cami.

His phone rang, ending his reverie. He hit the button on his Bluetooth. He didn't own the latest technology, but it worked. "Hey, Boss, what's up?"

"Talbot!" Karl Winters, hands down the best supervisor Oliver ever had, never wasted words. "You finish that paperwork for the BVC?"

"Yep. I'll send it to you as soon as I get home."

"Good. Their CEO is breathing down my neck. Where are you?"

"Went to visit my dad. Be home in a minute."

"Come into the office tomorrow. Time for reviews."

"Already? Seems like just last year we had to do those."

"Ha ha. So, yeah. Ten o'clock. Don't be late."

Oliver worked from home for an ad agency, going into the office maybe twice a month, which suited him and his situation well. He could be home with Yatzy, tend his online businesses, work on family history and church assignments, attend the temple and in the down time play his favorite video game, *Dark Hordes XII*. He, his twin brothers and their friends hosted rousing online tournaments. *We have to keep up our zombie-stomping skills, after all, in case of any random apocalypse.*

Sundays, he attended a Young Single Adult ward, where he served as second counselor. He and the other members of the bishopric spent the whole day each week in visits and interviews. Monday nights, they always supported the ward's Family Home Evening activities, and other nights, they visited apartments to assess the members' needs.

At 29, he had settled into the routine of avoiding remarriage. *Well, until the Holy Ghost directs otherwise. Not going through another nightmare marriage if I can help it.* Many in his YSA ward had also survived abusive marriages, which helped to assuage his pain in a sort of we're-in-the-same-boat kind of way. *Some people who have third-degree emotional burns find it difficult to attempt Act II, and I'm one of them.*

His parents sold their theater in 2044 and sent his twin brothers on their missions, both in Guatemala. They accepted their own call to a stay-at-home family history mission for their Church. *They loved it so much, they hoped to go to a more exotic mission, next time. But you know what they say: If you want to make God laugh, tell Him your plans. Mom did travel farther away, if you count going beyond the veil.*

The diagnosis of pancreatic cancer brought with it heavy rounds of chemo, but she suffered through it and died anyway, becoming the angel Oliver always knew she was inside. Her barely audible last words to the family were, "Remember our motto: Trust in the Lord…"

Her children finished it for her. "…with all thine heart, and lean not unto thine own understanding."

"Yes… Keep the faith… Follow the Spirit. I'll be watching over you."

She was so weak, all she could do after that was whisper, "I love you." I tried not to cry while Dad held

41

her until the end, but we all did. That was so hard. She was my first and best friend.

David and Drew, the twins, had returned home from Guatemala two months before her death. *Dad wheeled her into Sacrament Meeting when they gave their homecoming talks. Who knew it would be her last Sunday at church?* Once her funeral ended, the twins plodded through their respective lives on autopilot, refusing to reveal their inner workings to anyone but each other. Oliver's sister Brooklyn, Brooke for short, married with two toddlers, had been the hardest hit, at least in discernable ways.

Yeah, men may handle their emotions better in public but inside is a war zone. Dad had it rough too, of course, but he's pretty much his old self, with his own singles ward issues. He said he only goes there because his bishop called him to do it and that he isn't interested in inviting another woman into his life. I'm okay with that. No one can take Mom's place.

⚬ ⚬

At 9:58 the next morning, Oliver and his colleagues gathered around the big conference table. He caught a whiff of impending change. The calm he felt didn't warrant "impending doom" status. Something would happen that would change his life. Not good, not bad, just different.

Blowing into the room like a category five hurricane, his boss hovered at the head of the table without bothering to pull out a chair. Oliver knew a pivotal moment when he saw one.

Karl wasted no time. "Guys, this is a tough day in a tough year, but the bottom line is, the economy's folding, and so is the company. We're *all* out of a job." Expressions of shock and dismay erupted throughout the room. "God help us. I'm sorry, believe me. Clean out your desks and turn in all company property. Doors will be permanently locked by five. And if you need a reference from me, you got it. Let me know."

Avoiding eye contact, Karl whisked back out of the room, leaving Oliver shocked and confused. He stared through the glass partition at nothing. *I need to call Dad.*

By the time he climbed into his car twenty minutes later with his small box of supplies, Dad beat him to it. "Oll, I know you were just here yesterday, but can you come back over? I had a troubling dream or… vision, maybe. I don't know what to call it. Anyway, I'd like to talk about it, and not over the phone."

"You bet, Dad. I'm free from all obligations. Be there in a few."

On the way over, surprised, somehow, that his dad had a revelatory incident, Oliver contemplated his own dreams and visions. One recurring dream haunted him. In it, he directed hundreds of cars into parking spaces, close together, destined for disuse. One driver rolled down his window and said, "I have to go home and bring more stuff. Where can I unload?" Across a field, surrounded by mountain peaks, people scurried to set up large tents before a storm descended. There, the dream ended, the last haunting image one of tall grass waving in the blustering breeze.

Another night vision consisted of a bleak landscape suffocated by dirty air. Rocks rolled and bounced in an earthquake. People writhed in pain. He ached with helplessness. Intensely vivid, the earthquake jarred his body, and he choked on the dust. His mom appeared beside him, saying, "Olly, don't give up. Don't you dare give up. You have the power."

Were those dreams symbolic, prophetic, or a mixture of both? I've pondered and prayed about them and I still don't know.

Arriving at his childhood home, he caught a whiff of change. *What's different?* He couldn't pinpoint it until he reached for the doorbell—the front door had been painted a lighter version of the old moss green. *Odd. It wasn't that way yesterday. Looks nice, but who bothers with paint, these days?*

The door chime hadn't finished ringing before Rick opened the door. "Come in, come in," he said. "There are cold drinks in the fridge and some cookies a neighbor brought over." They headed for the kitchen.

"The neighbor that keeps trying to get your attention?"

"Yeah, but she's not my type. Good cookies, though. Here, try one."

Oliver reached for a chewy square and took a bite. *Mmm, coconut. Where does she buy coconut? On the black market? She must be desperate to impress Dad. Come to think of it, he's probably quite the sensation in his "oldies" singles ward. No pot belly, a touch of gray hair on the sides of a nice face. Of course she likes him!* "She the one who painted the front door?"

Rick opened the fridge. "What do you want to drink, Diet Coke or Pepsi?"

"Got any milk?" Oliver said around a mouthful of chewy goodness. "Cookies are better with milk, Dad." *Ha! He's avoiding the question. Must be a yes. Too funny. Painting the door **and** baking cookies. This woman is serious! Does she bring meals over, too?*

"Oh, yeah, yeah… here. It's nine bucks a gallon, now, can you believe it? Too many cows died in that last epidemic of bovine flu." He poured half a glass for each of them and plopped down at the table, exhaling as if he'd been carrying a big load. "You like the cookies? Have another one."

"Dad, forget the cookies. You're avoiding."

"Yeah, well… it's weird. I was in the recliner watching the news on my phone and fell asleep, I suppose, but it was so real." He paused, a far-off look on his face while he chewed his lip.

Oliver crossed his arms and leaned back, figuring he would have to let his dad go at his own pace. Steady, dependable Rick gave the unusual impression of being a bit shell-shocked. *Well, that makes two of us. I have no job. Am I in shock or at peace? Guess I won't know until some time has passed. Time. Hmph. I have a lot of that now. I'll have to concentrate my efforts on app sales.*

"Have you noticed, Oll, that General Conference talks tend to focus on strengthening us for future trials? Even a lot of the hymns are about the Second Coming."

"I've been thinking the same thing for years. It's all about being ready to meet Christ."

Rick perked up. "I'm not sure we've ever had a conversation on this topic, before."

"We're having it now, Dad. I've had visions and significant dreams, too, if that helps."

"Wow... Okay. So, in this one, I was driving down a wide road in an industrial park, watching buildings crumble all around me. The road collapsed in front of my car and fell away, like a great canyon. I had no trouble stopping in time, so I didn't go over the edge, but lots of cars did. I yelled at them to stop, but more and more drove right off, like a waterfall. So many people in terrible distress. The noise of cars crunching... the screams, the crying..."

Rick paused so long in freeze-frame that Oliver jumped in. "I'll ask you what I've been asking myself, Dad. Was it symbolic, prophetic or both?"

"I've been thinking it's prophetic, but now that you ask, it could be symbolic. Our world is crumbling in several ways, isn't it? Morally, spiritually, and economically, too, with more and more businesses folding. And people are going over the edge. Thousands, at least in Utah, have left the Church. That could be it."

"And you're *not* going over the edge. You stopped in time. Stopped...?"

"Stopped... buying into the world's ideologies, maybe? Stopped caring what people in the 'great and spacious building' think. Stopped swearing, too, by the way."

Oliver laughed. "Reminds me of the swear jar. None of my friends charged their dads for swearing. Their parents charged *them*." Rick chuckled, embarrassed. "So, yeah. I think we're onto something. Now help me decide what my visions mean."

An engrossing discussion followed that stimulated both faith and determination to better prepare for future possibilities, spiritual and temporal. About two hours and three sandwiches later the doorbell rang, and Rick excused himself to answer it. Oliver heard his dad say "Hi," and a woman's pleasant voice say, "Hello. Am I interrupting anything?"

"No, I think we're done. Let's go sit in the living room. Oliver! Come join us."

Rounding the corner, Oliver pulled up short, sensing another pivotal moment.

~CHAPTER 5~

Regroup and Retrench

"...ye have not as yet understood how great blessings the Father hath in His own hands and prepared for you: ...nevertheless, be of good cheer, for I will lead you along..." Doctrine and Covenants 78:17-18

2048, Orem, Utah

"JoAnne Gephardt." Oliver had the presence of mind to find his way to a chair, sit down and act normal, but his spidey senses tingled.

"Hello, Oliver."

JoAnne had performed in several shows with the Talbots, so he knew her as a talented actress, much older than Rick.

"Been in any plays since the Crescent shut down?" he asked, attempting to ignore his alarm and make small talk.

"No," she said, "I felt that chapter of my life needed to end. My husband died from Parkinson's, and by the time I felt ready to reengage in life, my focus had changed."

Clarity hit him. "Your husband died. What a surprise," Oliver said with a dash of sarcasm. "Sorry to hear that," he hurried to add with more sincerity.

"Thank you," she responded, her expression one of disappointment. He avoided eye contact with both of them. *I hope this is just my imagination, 'cause otherwise, it's totally cracked.*

After JoAnne left, Oliver asked, "So, Dad. What's the deal with Jo Gephardt? You do realize she's no different from the cookie lady and every other single female on your trail, except for one minor detail."

"Which detail is that?"

Incredible. "Dad. She's too old."

"Hm." Rick sat back on the sofa, acting as if that had not occurred to him. "I ran into her at the Home Depot the other day, and the Spirit told me that she would play an important role in our lives."

"But marriage? Dad, come on. The Spirit could have meant something else."

"Like what?"

"I don't know, but she's crazy too old for you! The cookie lady isn't your type, but Jo Gephardt is? Didn't she play your mother-in-law in a show, once?"

"Let me ask you a question, Oliver. Would you rather I married someone young and sexy that outshines your mom physically?"

"What? No! You don't have to marry anyone."

"The Lord has made it clear that I do."

The front door opened to admit Drew, one of the twins. "Hey? Anybody home?"

"Come in!" Rick called while Oliver collected himself. *What's happening? This isn't like Dad. Has grief for Mom short-circuited his brain?*

"Hi, guys! Who's that old lady? She looks familiar."

Oliver raised his eyebrows at his dad.

"All right," said his father, "You may as well know. That's JoAnne Gephardt and I'm going to marry her."

"What the heck, Dad?" Drew protested. "She's as old as Grandma."

"It's the right thing to do," said his dad, watching out the window as her car pulled away from the curb.

Drew guffawed. "Huh? What's that mean? You got her pregnant?"

"Shut up, jerkwad," Oliver ground out, more in frustration with his father than his younger brother.

"So you're okay with this? You can't be serious. It's only been two years since Mom died."

"Thanks, both of you," Rick said dryly, "but let me make something clear. I will marry JoAnne. Even if you don't agree with my choice, I expect you to be civil to her and respect my decision. It's not up for discussion. Am I clear?"

"Yeah," said Oliver with resignation born of helplessness in the face of his dad's apparent loss of reason. This added the bitter cherry on top of his whole day—remembering Cami, losing his job, and discussing strange dreams.

Drew shook his head and walked into the kitchen. "Sure, Dad, if you say so. Is there any food?"

"I think I'll be heading out," Oliver said. "Thanks for lunch and all." He moved to the front door and opened it. "Oh, and good luck breaking the news to Brooke. That'll be fun." He just missed slamming the freshly-painted door on his snarky remark, pulling back at the last second. *I'm not a child anymore. It's his life.*

He can do what he wants. Once inside his dingy little apartment, he cuddled Yatzy the rest of the evening, dwelling on the implications of his dad's irrational announcement and his own job loss.

⚬ஃ❀ஃ⚬

As Rick made the twenty-minute drive to Brooklyn's townhouse, the next day, he contemplated her metamorphosis from a well-adjusted child to a manipulative, often-offended, entitled woman of strong opinions. She had gone from "I know this church is true" to "Your church is so off base," ever since she stopped reading the scriptures and listened more to the disenchanted than the stalwart.

Rick lingered in the car in front of her house, tempted to bail. *Maybe we should elope. Or maybe Brooke will surprise me. I won't find out if I don't get out of the car and ring the doorbell.* He strengthened his resolve and pushed forward.

Brooke invited him in. "It's too bad my partner's out with the kids. "They should be back soon, though. Have a seat."

"It's okay," he said, as he appropriated a chair with no toys in it. "I wanted to talk to you alone, anyway."

"Sounds serious," she said, dumping toys out of another chair to use.

Rick rested his elbows on his thighs, ignoring his nagging dread. "Long story short, I'm getting married, and it would mean a lot if you could be happy for me."

Her mouth dropped open at the 'M' word. "You have to be kidding, Dad. And it's not funny."

"I wish you'd be more positive about it."

"You can't be serious. How could you *do* this to me?"

"It's not about you, Brooke." Experiencing a searing insight into her inner being, as a dying man sees his own life rush past, he sorrowed for her soul.

"Ripples in a pond, Dad. This will ruin my life!"

"I don't understand how."

"How can you not? You're replacing our mother and you don't think this will hurt us? Are you blind?"

"I'm not replacing her. I'm moving forward while I wait to be reunited with her."

"Hot take," she said as she launched herself from the chair and left the room. "I'm not putting up with this. I don't think you ever loved Mom."

"Brooklyn!"

She pivoted to face him with deadly fire. "Here's another hot take: You will never see your grandkids again if you go through with this insanity. She is not their grandma!" His daughter, the one he swore he would protect like a papa bear, stormed up the stairs as she finished her short and spiky tirade. "You know where the front door is," she hurled back down. A door slammed upstairs with a finality that stabbed him.

He hated upsetting his daughter. If he hadn't received a message straight from God that this marriage was the correct choice, he wouldn't have gone through with it. *But **why** is it correct?*

Brooke's family pulled into the driveway as Rick emerged from the house. He savored their happy babbling and enjoyed sweet hugs from each of the children. He didn't warn his son-in-law about the drama, preferring a stress-free, loving moment with them, in case it never happened again.

⁂

Brooke watched from an upper-story window, certain that this tender little moment with her children would set her dad straight and remind him of what he would miss should he not comply with her demand.

Her world crashed and burned with her mother's death; now she sought security by controlling everything and everyone around her. It made sense to her to take over the reins from an uncaring, incompetent or non-existent God, and do things her own way.

Confident in the outcome, she resumed composing her rant on social media with a satisfied smirk.

⁂

JoAnne's children, overall, accepted the situation better, being older and more mature, but she did have to field their questions and doubts. Three weeks before the tentative wedding date, three of her four children, Sarah, Emmalee and Austin, visited her in an intervention of sorts. Austin carried a laptop computer, so that his brother, Raynor, away on a business trip in Bangkok, could weigh in by satellite.

Jo sat in the easy chair, *un*easy about this gathering. They settled in on the couch opposite her chair, while she prayed within. She received an impression to allow this meeting to unfold without her emotional involvement. Tamping down her irritation, she pasted a pleasant smile on her face.

As soon as Austin had Raynor onscreen, Emmalee, the youngest and most opinionated, began. She expressed their collective doubts and fears, while the other three nodded. Before wrapping up, they encouraged her to set up her assets in a trust, handing her a lawyer's card.

"Thank you for your concern. I promise to make an appointment." *That's about all I can manage without exploding. And I hope this will be the end of it.*

After some deliberation, she consulted with Rick.

"Do you think a trust is the best way to handle this? It bothers me what they're implying," she said, irritated.

"You mean they think I'll clean out your bank account," Rick said with humor.

"That's exactly what I mean. Part of me wants to tell them to take a hike, but what they're asking is a relatively small thing to do, so, I guess I'll play along."

"Because you love them."

"Of course, but I resent their thinking that they can run my life," she answered with some bite.

"I believe," said Rick, as he put an arm around her, "it's because they care about you. Do any of them seem greedy for money? No? Then yes, I think you should comply with their wishes."

"Fine. But I'm naming Raynor as the trustee and primary beneficiary. It'll be his responsibility to divvy up my assets when it's time. He's the oldest, the least volatile, and the one most adept at smoothing ruffled feathers. That way, they can never drag you into this."

"Sounds like the perfect solution," Rick said.

JoAnne met with her attorney—not the one on the card her offspring gave her, who arranged everything to her complete satisfaction. She took Raynor a duplicate hardcopy of the paperwork as soon as he returned to the states.

"I hope you're okay about our meeting, Mom," said Raynor in a worried tone. "We just want you to be safe and happy." He had always been the most sensitive one of the children, even more so than her girls.

She hugged him and said, "I am happy. And now all of my assets, except for my little allowance, are your problem."

"Mom, what did you do?"

"It's all in the paperwork. I'll let you know when the wedding will be. That is, if we don't elope," she said with a mischievous grin. She kissed his wife and the only grandchild still living at home and waved goodbye.

I told Raynor that I'm happy. That may be more optimism than truth, but I do have peace about it.

JoAnne and Rick sat on his couch, deliberating their options for the wedding. These included whether or not to have a guest list and who should be on it; getting married down at the courthouse versus at the church; and what kind of honeymoon trip to take, if any.

Conflicted, Jo stared at their clasped hands, the peace she enjoyed earlier having vanished. Part of her questioned her own sanity, as well as the Lord's wisdom, heaven help her. *Forgive me, Father, for doubting. I recognize that it's Thy will that I marry this man, and I will comply. But why is Rick willing to marry me? He's so kind and funny and wise. We'll get along fine, I'm sure, but—*

"I think a quiet ceremony down at the church, with the bishop and a few of our supportive friends and family members would be best," Rick said.

"I agree," she answered. "I'll ask about using our ward building." *I'm sitting next to a terrific man, yet I'm still so alone... Oh, how I miss James! I can't say that to Rick. The Lord is directing this marriage, and it will be good, eventually. I hope.*

"Let's reserve my ward building, instead," Rick continued. "It's newer. And the Relief Society would provide some simple refreshments, I'm sure."

"All right." *It will be all right. Have faith. Trust in the Lord. I can. I will.* She kept up the internal dialogue all the way back to her condo. *He kissed me goodnight with no passion to speak of. Not surprising, of course.* "I'm too old for him," she moaned.

That evening before retiring for the night, she felt prompted to open the Book of Mormon to First Nephi, chapter one and read it, receptive to guidance. Verses fourteen through sixteen told of future horrors shown to Lehi in a vision, yet he "rejoiced and praised God." In verse six, he "quaked and trembled," but his whole attitude changed by the end.

Why? Because he focused on the positive—the majesty, power and salvation from God, and the gift of receiving heavenly direction. Have I been doing that? No. I'm stuck on "quake and tremble." Maybe it's time to rejoice and praise God that He has directed me to someone good and wise.

"Thy ways are beyond my comprehension, Lord. Forgive me for being fearful."

⚜

"I'm not going to the ceremony," Brooke insisted.

"You should go," her husband said. "It's never good to burn bridges. I can stay home with the girls, since they're still sick. They'll be too cranky for a wedding. We wouldn't want them to ruin it."

"Ha! That might just be what we do want."

"Brooke."

"Yeah, yeah, I hear you."

To please him, she dressed up, took the invitation with her, and without his knowledge, drove to a friend's house to borrow a car that wouldn't be recognized.

I'll just sit here in the dark at the back of the church parking lot. No one will even notice. She watched that despised building ingest and regurgitate people all evening, till her brothers, the "happy couple" and all their remaining well-wishers chatted a while in the weak lamplight before driving away.

When the last of the clean-up committee took off, quiet reigned, except in the mind of the missing daughter. The streetlights blurred and blended through her tears.

*I can't believe he threw my kids away for her. And my brothers played along. Traitors, all of them. I hate them. I hate her. I **hate** her.*

Seething with powerlessness, resentment and pain, Brooke grabbed the steering wheel with both hands and screamed in frustration. A dog in the yard behind her kicked up a fuss and a couple of porch lights came on. She laid her head down on her fists and sobbed, desperately missing her mother.

Wallowing in memories, she relived mani-pedi parties, cozy chats, movie nights, bake sales for charity, shopping for her prom dresses and her wedding dress and many other treasured moments with her mom, frozen in time.

Spent, she blew her nose, grabbed the invitation off the front passenger seat, and with great satisfaction tore it into tiny pieces.

                                        ❦

"Dad, sorry to bother you, but I need to confess something," Oliver said in a voice text to his dad about two weeks after the wedding. *I hate to interrupt the honeymoon, but I need Dad. Do old people have a honeymoon? Never mind. TMI. I don't want to know. Ick.* "Call me."

Four whole seconds passed before the phone rang. "What's up, Oll?"

"I can't find another job. I've searched every network available, but there's nothing. One cringy interview—that's all I've had. My web sales are down. I have some savings and investments, too, but the interest rates are zilch."

"Whoa, back up. What happened to your job at the ad agency?"

"The company folded that day you announced you were going to marry JoAnne. My lease is up for renewal, and, well… that's not happening."

"Sorry to hear that. Tell you what. Move out of your place. I'm moving into Jo's condo, so you could hold down the fort here. You'd be doing me a favor. How about it?"

"Aw, Dad. It's like giving up."

"These are the Last Days, son. We have to hunker down and prepare for the storm. I suspect things will worsen before the end comes."

"It's not like you to be so fatalistic. Where's my wild and crazy dad?"

"The signs are there, and I'm getting more nudges from the Spirit. Not kidding. I'll help you move. Let me know when."

Rick, Jo and the twins showed up to help on moving day, so counting the cleaning, the whole operation lasted less than two full days. *Good thing I haven't collected much since the divorce. Simplifies a lot.*

Wound up from all the commotion of packing, Yatzy latched onto Jo when she arrived. The new human gave lots of belly rubs, treats, walks and sweet talk, while the men loaded the moving truck. Oliver shook his head at the slobbering puppy love, but having his fur baby out from underfoot reduced a lot of stress.

As Oliver unpacked and settled into his childhood home, he found more things he could discard—things that no longer served him. He picked up a copy of the Book of Mormon in French, a souvenir from his mission, and started to add it to the boxes going to the local thrift store, but the Holy Ghost stopped him. He stared at the book. *Why should I keep it?* His pulse sped up. *What the..?*

~Study it.~

But why? Scriptures are on my phone.

No answer.

~CHAPTER 6~

Gators and Grit

"Nevertheless, I did look unto my god, and I did praise him all the day long; and I did not murmur against the Lord because of mine afflictions."
1 Nephi 18:16, *The Book of Mormon*

July 1879, Sainte Jeanne, Louisiana

Stella took over as the healer for her village and at first, carried Nettie's stubby shotgun without fail. As more time passed, she didn't hold it every minute but kept it in Nettie's skiff on trips away from the house, just in case. *Never know what poisonous critters might be lurkin'. But could I pull the trigger on my own kin, rotten as they are?*

Thank heaven she hadn't needed to face that particular Goliath. In the five years since Nettie had passed, *Père* had not shown his face around the settlement, and Stella had not been called upon to treat him *or* plug him with shot.

Her good-for-nothing brother, Georges, did light into her as she left the general store one summer day soon after *Père* disappeared.

"He packed up all his guns an' tools an' lit out, 'cause o' you." Georges said, every word dripping with blame. The skin on her arms prickled. "Said he was gonna fin' another woman somewhere else. He left for good, an' ain't comin' back."

63

"Ain't you man enough to live without 'im?" she asked in disgust.

He stepped toward her with menace. She backed up and wished for a weapon. *Shouldn't 'a left the gun in the skiff. But Jacques would hear me scream, oui?*

"I'm more than man enough," he said between clenched teeth. He sneered at her, let his gaze slide down her dress, and laughed without humor as he sauntered away.

Stella rarely caught a glimpse of Georges after that, for which she thanked the Virgin Mary. He must have spoken against her when he *was* around, since some locals called on a treater in the next settlement over instead of asking her for help. *That's fine by me. If they've a mind to listen to him, then they'd probably deal with me the same nasty way he does.*

The remaining residents often extended their greetings and gratitude, though never thanking or paying her at the time of service. That would undo the prayer she offered on their behalf. "God's the Healer," as Nettie had often said. "I'm the helper."

Someone from the family, though, would come around in the next day or two, and leave an offering of eggs, a chicken, a meat pie, some venison or fish as a "gift," not payment. But whether they fed her or not, she couldn't starve in this rich delta land bursting with wildlife and nourishing vegetation.

One miserable, sweltering day in July, identical to every other day when residents of Louisiana resembled boiled crawfish, the screen door on Jacques LeBlanc's general store banged. He jerked from his snooze at a precarious angle over the Mississippi Times and righted himself.

"Hm? Oh. Ah. How ya'll doin,' Stella Rubidoux?" Jacques sidestepped the custom of asking about her family; she had none left worth mentioning. He rubbed his face, folded up the paper and stashed it under the board over two barrels he used as a counter. "Come on in here an' set a spell." He pointed to the same barrel she always perched on.

He reveled in being the centerpiece of this tiny town of Sainte Jeanne. All the citizens, sooner or later, entered the store to trade, buy, or stir the muggy air with their *flux de bouche,* swapping tales of any height, short or tall. And if any disputing parties called for arbitration, he had the legal authority to act as constable or judge. It gave him great satisfaction.

"Set right cheer, and gitcha half a swaller o' this lemonade," he said, pouring her a mug of sweet and sour goodness. "Cool and refreshin' on a hot day like today. Hoo, *oui!* If it ain't a fryin' pan!" He slapped at a mosquito with gusto. "Dang *moustiques!* I'm thinkin' they wait on the screen door just bidin' time till a body opens it. At least it keeps *most* critters outta here." He had seen the newfangled door in a catalog and had to have it. First one in Sainte Jeanne.

As much as he loved that door, Stella owned a greater portion of his heart. He once hoped to marry her *maman* and considered the sweet girl the daughter he should have had.

Georges, on the other hand, reminded him too much of Paul, whom he deeply resented for ruining his chances with Lulu. Jacques seized any opportunity to go behind either Georges' or Paul's back and befriend their targets. Years before, he mailed Lulu's letters to her absent sister on the sly, since Paul forbade personal correspondence. When Lulu died, Jacques returned Celié's last letter, writing on the back of it, sending news of her sister's demise.

Maybe I shouldn't 'a done that. She come back to the village soon after and died, too. Much too suspicious, that, but I couldn't prove a thing.

"You been keepin' yo'self all right?" he asked.

"Finer than frog's hair, Jacques." Settling on the squatty barrel, she slapped at another mosquito. "Lemonade sounds mighty appealin', though, *certainement*. What's this? *Parfum*?" She picked up one of the pretty little bottles set off to the side and examined it.

"Those came yestidee. Give it a sniff." He pushed the mug closer to her before adjusting himself on his own barrel, drink in hand.

Stella explored the fragrance before replacing the stopper. "Mmm. I like that. *Eau de Jasmin*," she said, reading the label. "What is it?"

"A flower, baby girl. That *parfum* comes all the way from Massachusett'."

"I wish it grew 'round here."

"That'd be right nice, *n'est-ce pas?* Maybe it will, someday. You seen Hélène Boudreaux, lately? She come in here last week, lookin' pretty peaked. Ain't been well since she lost that last baby, ehn? How many she lose? Two? Three? You suppose she needs your he'p?"

"Wish I knew, *mon ami*," Stella said between swigs. "Ever since she married Henri, she's been scarcer than snow 'round here. I tried to visit her a couple months back when the last baby died, but Henri's got her scared of havin' company, an' now she won't even open the door."

"That right? Even to you?"

"*Oui*, an' it grieves me. We was close at one time, but now…Tsk." She shook her head and sipped some more lemonade.

As a child, Stella had little time to play with friends, but he had witnessed many exchanges of tiny treasures and shy smiles with Hélène. *Those two had a bond.*

"I know you was, an' it's a cryin' shame he don't git 'er the care she needs." He craned his neck toward the screen door long enough to identify the owner of a passing skiff, another reason to love that door. *Easy to tell who's going which-a-way on the bayou. Yep. Mighty useful.* "You ain't been orderin' so many books anymore, ehn?"

"Not much time for readin,' Jacques. Busy, busy. Here's my list o' supplies I be needin'." She laid the small piece of paper on the counter but kept her hand on it. "You wouldn't know how I could git me some new shoes? Mine are plumb wore out."

"Well, now, I might have some you'd like to try on. Feller come in here a while back, wantin' to trade. Makes these boots his own self, he does."

"Boots?" That girl lit up like a falling star, then faded just as fast. "Aww, they prob'ly wouldn't fit me."

"They might." He half-stood and stretched to root around in some boxes a moment. "Here they is," he said before plopping back down. He pulled the drawstring of a black cloth bag and removed a pair of fawn-colored feminine footwear crafted from alligator belly.

"*Très belles,*" she cooed, touching the leather with the tip of one finger as if afraid to ruin it. "So beautiful. Ain't seen boots like these, not on anyone."

"Try 'em on, *chère.*"

"Oh, no, Jacques, I can't pay for such fine things."

"Ya could if folks gave more a than hunk o' meat for your prayers an' remedies. Why you think I didn't wanna be a treater? Try 'em on!" She stroked one heel with a reverence that melted any doubt in his mind. *Those boots were made for her.* "If you don't try on them boots, I'm gonna pitch 'em inna bayou, I swear."

She grabbed the boots in a protective hug and cried, "No you don't, you mean ol' man! I'm tryin' 'em on."

He grinned wide enough to suck air through the gap between his teeth. "'Bout blamed time."

She shed her ratty old shoes that should have sunk to the bottom of the bayou months ago and reached for the first boot. She had to give it a firm tug, but it fit.

Her eyes widened, and she donned the other boot *tout d'suite.*

He swelled up fit to strain a muscle. "They's fiiiine. I reckon ya gotcha some new boots, *n'est-ce pas?*"

She blinked. "How much?" Fear fought with joy in her face.

"Not a thang, baby girl. Them boots is yores."

"It can't be, Jacques."

"It shorely is. You gotta take 'em, 'cause I ain't takin' 'em back. Puttin' yo' filthy socks in 'em," he grumbled as he wiped off the counter, finding himself in dire need of some busy work. "Who'd try 'em on, now?"

"I never had me anythin' so *magnifique, moi,*" she said, her voice quavering. "Won't know what to do with myself. You gotta let me give you somethin' in return."

"No, I don't. Them boots was meant for you." He grabbed her list of supplies and hopped up to fill the order with a sniff. It hurt to watch her cry, even with happiness.

New boots tapping on the well-worn floor, Stella skirted the counter and came up behind him. She wrapped her arms around his generous middle, her head on his back. "*Merci,* Jacques. *Merci.* You an' *Grand-grand-mère* Nettie are my only true family, and she's gone."

He patted her hand and gave it a squeeze in reply, not trusting his voice.

"At least let me bring you some herbs an' such for your shelves," she insisted, her voice still trembling. "Made an extra batch o' *caïman* oil, too. Could be some

69

powerful need will come up. Best be prepared, *n'est-ce pas?*"

"Oh, all right," he groused, clearing his throat. "Yo' a bigger pest than them *moustiques*." He took out his hanky and blew his nose, jostling her head.

Stella gave him another squeeze before taking the bag of supplies he passed to her, thanked him one more time and slipped out the screen door.

"*Pas de quoi*, baby girl," he whispered. "It weren't no trouble atall."

⁂

Mere days after her visit with Jacques, Henri Boudreaux shocked Stella by bringing Hélène to her. She directed him to place her in the chair, hiding her astonishment and attempting to regain her poise.

Focusing all her attention on her sweet friend, she could tell at once that poor Hélène hovered near the end of her mortal fight. As Stella finished her fervent pre-treatment prayer, Hélène sighed with her last breath.

"Oh, Hélène…" she said with a sniff as she pushed aside a strand of her friend's raven hair. *Wish I coulda done somethin' for her.* "She in the arms of *Jésus*, now."

Henri raged at her, making her jump and cringe. "Arms o' *Jésus*? Arms o' *Jésus*? She should be heah, alive, in my arms! 'Stead of prayin' an' carryin' on like a priest at high mass, ya shoulda been doin' somethin' to help. You ain't no friend o' hers. I'll teach you a lesson for this," he hissed through his teeth, and picked up his wife's body. He stalked off, cursing at Hélène for having the temerity to pass on to greener pastures and kinder companions.

He blames me for his own doin's! I can't fathom how he persuaded Hélène to marry him. That snake would not hesitate to kill me no matter who is on my side. Even Jacques, both as a friend and the local law, bless him, cannot protect me from Henri's malice.

"I hafta leave, an' Lord, I hope he don't follow."

As soon as Henri digs a hole on his property and covers up poor Hélène's body, I wager he'll tell his version of the truth to anyone he can find, just to color me evil. Some folks would believe it, and he'll hunt me down, justified in his sick, sick mind.

His knife, whistling between the trees as she gathered herbs, would catch no one's attention but hers. She'd age a century from the suspense of expecting it. Stella raced to pack up some necessities, including herbs, dried fish, jerky, fruit and medical supplies, her thoughts keeping pace.

A man like that musta had some powerful pain in his past, to be spreadin' it around like mud on his boots. Reminds me of Père and Georges. I been mighty comfortable with the lack of abuse these last five years. Too bad it's over. Best move on down the bayou.

Stella started out the door as if a demon were on her trail. *And so he will be, sooner than soon.* "Aaiee! Almost forgot the gator oil. Can't afford to be *moustiques* feed. Ain't no pleasure being covered in itchy welts." She grabbed what remained from having given Jacques the greater portion. She checked the

71

tightness of the cork in the small, earthen jug, nestled it into her pack, slipped out the door and around back.

Taking a less-traveled back path through the underbrush to her father's shanty, she moved low and fast. Stella wanted one of his hand-carved *pirogues*, the best way to navigate the narrow, shallow backways of the swamp.

She prayed as she neared the old cabin that Georges was elsewhere and had left a *pirogue* behind. "Shoulda had my own, I know, Lord, but I been busy…" Carving a canoe out of a log herself would have taken way too much time and strength from her healing work.

Stella peeked around a tree at her childhood cabin, its broken door gaping wide. *All will be lost if my brother catches me. He might very well help Henri torture me. Two peas in a pod, they are.* She shivered in horror at the prospect of being on the receiving end of Henri's special talent, that of skinning a live 'possum in under ten seconds.

Nothin' movin'. Good sign. She eased her burdens down behind a bush, crept onto the short gallery porch, then slinked around the doorpost like a cat. *Humph. Père ain't the only one who kin ooze.* She scanned the unholy mess that had grown like mold in the five years she'd been living elsewhere. *Sacre bleu, I really did do everything for those varmints.*

Then, certain he must be out on the trap line or perhaps down to the store listening to Henri spin his wild tale of injustice, she gathered all she could carry from here, too, while keeping a sharp lookout. Her conscience pricked her for only half a second. *Ain't stealin'. He owes me for undue vexation my whole life.*

Stella spied Georges' gator pick, as he called the eight-inch, razor-sharp knife. She slipped it into her boot, sheath and all. No matter the reason he had left it behind, she considered it a blessing.

Merci, Lord. Could come in handy, for certain true, though I daresay Georges will pitch a fit at losin' it. "Aw, let 'im foam at the mouth. I won't be here, God willin'."

She edged out of the shanty and out to the bank of the bayou, using vegetation as cover. Two anchored *pirogues* bobbed in the water. Relief! Stella scurried back to the tree for her other stuff, then padded down the short, steep path to the water's edge, keeping her eyes peeled like an owl's and trying not to grunt from the weight.

One bag at a time, she pitched her gear into the cleanest *pirogue,* pulled up the grapple hook and pointed her vessel toward the swamp. Thinking that Georges preferred to head west or southwest to hunt, and Henri living dead south, she steered east towards Houma, away from them both and anyone else she knew.

Or so she assumed. Coming around a massive cypress, she backpaddled to duck behind it. Georges occupied his skiff up ahead, concentrating on his trap line.

"He was lookin' the other way. *Merci, Lord,*" she whispered. "I didn't know he'd be out here."

She scanned the area for somewhere to lie low and spotted the last house's dock. *It'd be a tight fit, and heaven alone knows what creeping critters call it home, but nestled in some bushes as it is, it's a good hidey-hole. Better than going clear around the island. That'd be the best way to put myself in Henri's path.*

Stella maneuvered the *pirogue* backwards into place, bumping her head on the underside of the rickety pier. Keeping low, she hoped to avoid repeating that mistake. She pulled the oars in close to her sides, ready to go as soon as she deemed it safe. *Got a good view in both directions through the branches, hidden in the shadows, here. Best settle in for the duration.*

A tickle on her neck made her jump and swat at it. An eon passed before Georges slid by. *More neighbors coming, too. Better wait a mite longer. They could give me away to Henri whether they mean to or not. Can't risk it.*

The minute her back cramped from hunching over, bayou activity ceased. She re-launched, rowed all evening and far into the night, anxious for a good head start. Well before sun-up, fatigue overtook her.

My shoulders and arms are fixin' to turn to jelly. Best pull out and make camp.

Next day, Stella steered clear of the town of Houma, and turned north towards Thibodaux, keeping away from major waterways when possible. She pushed on across the swamplands, careful to avoid snakes, people and alligators. The latter floated on the water's surface, but they also liked to settle down on the bottom, with bubbles on the surface a fleeting clue to their presence.

There were times when she had to backtrack, having chosen a bayou thread that did not pan out, due to a fallen tree, a dam or a lack of water. For the most part, though, she continued north until she reached a wide bayou.

Stella hugged the bank, traveling under the cover of shore vegetation when possible, hunting for a short and less exposed spot to cross. Expecting Henri to overtake her at any moment crippled her confidence. In a low voice, she prayed, "*Jésus*, I need Your assurance that it's safe to cross this bayou. No one in sight…"

Here, she opened one eye and checked her surroundings before settling back into the attitude of humility. "Never can tell who or what might be hidin' nearby."

"Well, I ain't the Lord, but I can tell ya it's pretty durn safe 'round heah."

Stella took off across the waterway as if shot from a gun. A cackle of laughter and a "Fare thee well!" followed her.

A calming peace enveloped her, slowing her pulse. She continued rowing to the other side without further incident and paddled up the bayou.

An opening into another water thread appeared between some trees and she considered that sign enough. "*Merci*, Lord. An' I'm shorely grateful that old man or woman (couldn't rightly tell) meant me no harm." Around a few turns and bends, she pulled out and made camp.

In the early morning, Stella packed her kit into the *pirogue* and took a good gander around for intruders before reaching out to unhook the grapple anchor from one of the handy boscoyo.

Better check for caïman.

Keeping her left hand on top of that same protrusion from a cypress tree root, she bent down to scout for bubbles to her right. An alligator launched from the duckweed-covered water behind the *pirogue* to her left and latched onto her bent arm, snapping the lower bones, her elbow almost centered in the gator's mouth.

Stella yelled in surprise and blinding pain. The river monster jerked her into the water, past the boscoyo, which she grabbed with the other hand without thinking or even seeing and wrapped her legs around it. That quick action kept the six-footer from dragging her underwater, although he did loosen her arm in its socket. His cold stare bore into her. Why he didn't take her arm right off she did not have half a second to contemplate.

She inched her right hand down the boscoyo and into the water to her boot, easing the gator pick out.

Can't slip. Won't be another chance. Pushing through the agony, resisting the beast's efforts to dislodge her, Stella concentrated on not dropping the knife as she positioned it and jammed it up into his throat. She let go of her perch and stood up in the water, shoving the knife upwards with a vengeance, and pushing him backwards to the far side of the cypress.

Water's getting deeper. "Let go, you devil!"

Enraged, he opened his jaws, hissed and scrambled through the air. Her crippled arm fell, while she kept his 170 pounds or so at arm's length with her knife. Due to a life of arduous work and plenty of meat, she was no weakling, but his weight overwhelmed her in seconds.

Stella guided his fall to her right, but he ripped her scalp open with a sharp claw as he struggled. She whipped the knife out of his throat. Reversing it, she shoved the blade under the back of his skull with a determined and masterful back-jab.

Kilt my share of caïman, before, but this one almost kilt me first.

Blood-filled eye closed, she shook from the searing pain in her head and left arm and inexpressible exhaustion. Stella's knees threatened to buckle and sink her into the water beside the gator's lifeless carcass. Fresh blood does an astounding job of calling to the carnivore through air or water and this time, the bait dripped from Stella's arm and face.

Gotta get out of the water, moi. Another one could be here tout d'suite. With her last ounce of strength, she flipped one leg into the *pirogue* and slid her gator pick into that soggy boot. Cradling her broken arm, she rolled into her skittish vehicle, her skirts hanging over the edge.

Jésus, Joseph et Marie, help me.

~CHAPTER 7~

Heeding the Call

"Depart ye, depart ye, go ye out from thence,
touch no unclean thing... For ye shall not
go out with haste, nor go by flight."
Isaiah 52:11-12, *The Holy Bible*

2048, Orem, Utah

Oliver moved his things into his parents' old bedroom and hung his clothes in his mom's empty closet.

A year ago, her things were still here. He had been visiting his dad and had run up the half-flight of steps to use the bathroom. As he finished, he headed to his parents' room.

Maybe I shouldn't, but I want to. He listened for signs that he might be interrupted before opening her closet, touching her clothes and drinking in her fragrance. Overwhelmed by raw longing, he slammed the door closed and stared at it. When she died, his heart had been clawed out of his chest and had gone skidding down a rough road, leaving him empty and bleeding, doomed to somehow survive without it.

Reliving his memories of Mom, he stood as if in a trance: her laughter, her silly jokes, the way she connected eye-to-eye, how she'd belt out Broadway tunes no matter who was around, making up dances on the fly... All the fun and endearing things about her swarmed around him.

Oliver asked her, once, why she hadn't become a singer. She possessed a superb voice.

"I'm a singer all the time, Olly. I sing at church, at the theater and at home."

"That's not what I mean, Mom. I mean professionally."

"I am professional. You mean why don't I sing for a record company?"

"Yeah. Or even go to Broadway."

"I'd rather sing for you and the locals. Besides, nothing's better than being a mom."

That day, he had gathered all those tender memories into a bouquet and trudged back downstairs, holding it close.

Today, after not finding any of her things, he concluded that he didn't need to. He would never stop missing her, but had healed enough to move forward in peace. The rawness had scabbed over and wouldn't bleed anymore, as long as he didn't pick at it. And now, it comforted him to put his things where hers had been.

His dad's closet held a bunch of stuff for camping out: dutch oven, propane stove, tent, solar lights and many things he couldn't identify without removing them from their boxes. He asked Dad about it at the next family dinner.

"It might be needed for a long-term bug-out situation," Rick said. "I have a feeling that scenario may play out in the not-too-distant future. Pass the gravy, please. Thanks… When our society does crumble, we'll lose our savings, anyway, so we may as well use it now."

"Wow, Dad. That's pretty extreme. What about retirement?"

"Doesn't matter, as long as I'm following the Spirit."

"A few years ago," Oliver said, "I would have called that being a doomsday nut, but now it actually makes sense."

"I'm surprised," JoAnne said, "that the bank didn't flag your purchases and freeze your account. They frown on spending sprees."

"I guess even the mighty banks are powerless before the Lord," Rick said with a wink.

⁂

A month later, Oliver woke up on a jumping bed. *What the heck?* Pictures, artwork and mirrors shimmied off the shaking walls. Horrendous crashes occurred somewhere in the vicinity of the kitchen.

Oliver ducked straight into his closet from the bed for protection the moment before his bedroom window shattered. As soon as the shaking ended, he jammed his sockless feet into his Nikes before exiting his safe place.

Gotta call my family... Shoot. No service. Hallway's clear, but holy crapola, downstairs defines the word "chaos." My shoes'll pick up a bunch of glass shards and hafta be thrown out.

Windows, knickknacks and lamps had joined the wall decor and the bookshelves in a free-for-all on the floor. The kitchen, though, shocked him. *Wow, what a mess. All these glasses and dishes must have flown out of the cabinets.* The pantry door stood open, broken jars oozing jam, peanut butter, oil, syrup and condiments.

I'll be cleaning this up for days. Maybe weeks. So much for running around barefoot. I'm buying paper plates and cups from now on.

Despite the trials, he found tender mercies. *At least the structural integrity of the house is still fairly intact. Could've been way worse.* Down at the hardware store, Oliver heard that this was the strongest earthquake in recorded Utah history—a 7.1 on the Richter Scale. When online service resumed, he learned that at least two hundred thirty-eight people had been killed, and hundreds more were homeless.

It took a week to make an *appointment* to place an order for windows, a top priority. Demand far exceeded supply, and delivery dates were not guaranteed. Insurance and disaster crews were overloaded and impossible to contact.

It's gonna be a pain to round up enough stuff to cover all the openings till the windows arrive. Corrugated cardboard blocks light, but it would keep out pests. Maybe I should board up some of them. Hey, isn't there mosquito netting in the preps closet? That'll work great for the upstairs windows. Good thing there are plenty of staples in my desk. Let's hope the new windows get here before winter, or before looters hit the neighborhood.

In the rubble, he found his copy of *Le Livre de Mormon* and dusted it off. The prompting to study it hit him with considerable force. *Guess I'd better get back to reading this. Don't know why, but "Trust in the Lord"*

and all that. And who knows when we can no longer use
our phones to study?

⚜

"Unshakable!"

Utah's new rallying cry showed up
everywhere—on billboards, bumper stickers and T-
shirts. Rick ran his thumb over this new motto on his
breakfast mug. He liked to think of the slogan as not only
physical resilience, but spiritual, too, sorely needed in
these troubling times.

*Glad things aren't as bad in Utah, yet, but with
so many chapels being vandalized, I'm sure we're not far
from the breaking point.*

JoAnne opened the front door of the condo, keys
jangling and grocery bags rustling. She didn't wait to put
everything down before she asked him, "Did you hear
the news?"

"Oh, no, now what's happened?" Rick asked,
only half joking.

"There's a special adult meeting on Sunday, after
church. Have you heard anything about it?"

"I haven't."

"No one admits to knowing what it's about, but I
suspect it's for safety reasons."

"Spiritual or physical?"

"Both, maybe."

"Guess we'd better be there."

In the meeting, they learned that the prophet
invited God-fearing people in any denomination on this
continent to gather to camps similar to pioneer trek

83

reenactments. These would be held at local, church-owned and donated campsites all over the United States and Canada.

Rick leaned close to JoAnne and whispered, "The bishop is pushing this big time. I don't think it's an optional activity."

"I agree," JoAnne whispered back. "It's too important to brush off."

As soon as they reached the condo, Rick called Oliver to let him know that he and Jo would be coming to retrieve their gear and pack up.

His son met them at the door of the house with an ethereal light in his eyes. "It's happening," he said.

Rick grinned. "It really is. So, maybe it's a good thing that you aren't tied to a job, right now?"

"I think you're right. And get this—they called me to go up early, to help direct cars to the parking areas. I'm heading up there, tonight."

"Wow, son. Just like your dream."

"Exactly like the dream."

Oliver helped him load the trailer, the truck and two cars, since all three of them would drive.

Rick hugged his son goodbye and said, "Did you leave your house key, phone and cards?"

"Over on the console."

"Make sure your phone's plugged in."

Oliver had balked at discarding all that, but Rick insisted. "It's the Lord's money, after all, and He can distribute it as He sees fit. Phones and cards might soon be useless, anyway."

"Then why leave them plugged in?"

"I don't know. It doesn't matter, as long as we're following the Spirit."

"Hey, that reminds me." Oliver ran upstairs and returned with his missionary copy of the Book of Mormon. "Without my phone, I need a hard copy."

"Good plan," said his dad cocking his head to see the book front better. "That's different. Is it..?"

"French, yeah. I can't get enough of it, these days. *C'est magnifique*." Oliver scratched Yatzy behind the ears as Jo held her. "Thanks, Jo, for... well, everything."

She beamed at him and said, "Of course. I'll love having her with me, and she can join you tomorrow."

"Okay, see you up there."

Rick's phone rang almost the minute Oliver left.

"Dad," David said. "I had kind of a spooky dream before I woke up this morning that all the cars were disabled. Everything stopped, and people were back to walking or riding bikes. I tend to ignore dreams, but this one won't let me. What do you think it means?"

"I think it means you should pack up all your necessities and come with us to camp. We're leaving tomorrow morning by eight."

"Aw, Dad. I'm not sure that's the answer."

"Your dream will be fulfilled, David. Trust me on this one. It'll be safer where we're going."

"Is this a bug-out?"

"We don't know for sure, but it feels that way to us."

"Who's 'us'?"

"Joanne and me. And a few friends, too."

"You're leaving everything? I can't do that. What about my car payments? You're retired, but I have a job and an apartment lease. And what about my savings?"

"Use your savings to pay off the car and don't worry about anything else."

"I don't know. This is major."

"Pray about it, son. Then get over here. Don't wait for an answer. God won't steer a parked car."

"Yeah, okay. Thanks, Dad. I'll think about it."

"Don't think too long. There's room for you and some more stuff. Try to talk your twin into it, too. He hasn't given me an answer either way."

Rick and Jo called their remaining children and grandchildren to encourage them to come or to say goodbye. They mourned having to leave their family members behind who were not committed to Christ or following the prophet. Brooke wouldn't answer the phone, so Rick called her husband, who let him chat with the two grandkids. Afterwards, a few tears fell while JoAnne held him.

"Thanks, Jo. You're a rock of strength… Jo?"

He caught her as she collapsed.

"Jo! What is it?" She answered with a moan. He laid her on the couch and prayed. Positive that the Lord had plans for JoAnne other than death, and that they could ill afford to squander their time in the emergency room or the hospital, he unpacked his consecrated oil and gave her a priesthood blessing.

In it, he commanded her to be healed. *Gutsy, but it feels right.* He also counseled her to remember that their children are God's children.

"… only Jesus can and will save them. Keep praying for them and never give up hope. There is always hope in Christ." He felt the Spirit directing that reminder to them both. It brought him peace with his own children's future trials and misery.

When finished, he asked, "You okay, now?"

"Much better, thank you."

"Do you know what it is?"

"My heart. Pretty sure the Hulk had a grip on it."

"Sound's pretty serious. Are you sure you're okay?"

"My lungs are working better, and the pain is disappearing."

"Good. I'll check on you in a few minutes after I finish loading up."

"I should be helping."

"Don't even think about it."

She lay on the couch with Yatzy, recovering, while church-appointed deputies with a truck arrived to collect their food storage. It took the quiet, efficient crew about fifteen minutes to load it all. Rick thanked the Lord for the prompting to organize it in time.

Bright and early Monday morning, Rick emerged from the house following one last inspection. To his surprise, Drew showed up in time to add his gear to the loaded truck without a word.

"Good morning, Drew! Glad you came," Jo said. He nodded to her as she climbed into the driver's seat of her older but trusty SUV.

Rick grabbed his youngest by two minutes in a big bear hug. "You're here! Great! You can ride with me. Park your car in the driveway and leave your keys, phone and bankcards on the console."

"Are you kidding?"

"I know it doesn't make sense, but that's what the Spirit is telling me. I've got goosebumps."

Drew stared past his dad, jangling his keychain while he waited for the Holy Spirit's confirming witness. "Wow. You're right. I don't understand why, but there it is."

Rick gripped Drew's shoulder in a one-handed, reassuring squeeze and signaled to JoAnne that they were almost ready. He hopped in the truck and switched on the engine, while his son disappeared into the house.

⁂

Drew emptied his pockets onto the console in the family room, just as his dad's phone rang. Recognizing the caller, he sighed. *Will it always hurt like this?* He carried the phone outside and climbed into the truck, saying, "Surprise."

"Did David call you?"

"Nope, he called you."

"Is he coming?"

"I don't think so." *The gut doesn't lie when it comes to my twin.*

Dad opened the screen and returned the call while Drew battled grief at leaving his wombmate. He and David had seldom been far apart. Even their missions had been in the same small country, where they connected at zone conferences and by phone. He questioned the wisdom of his decision to come, but deep inside, he knew he had to.

Call it "twin-tuition," but I'm thinking we'll be apart for a lot longer than a week. Am I gonna have this ache the whole time we're separated?

"Dad?"

A stab of pain hit him at hearing his brother's voice, this time on speaker.

"You called," Rick said. "What's up?"

"I had another dream."

"Talk to me."

"Is JoAnne there?"

"No, she's driving her car. Tweedle's here, though. That all right?"

"Yeah. Of course. Hey, Dee."

"Hey, Dum. You should be here." The ache in his chest made it so easy to continue last night's argument.

"Yeah, about that..." The silence dragged on. Drew glanced at his dad. Rick killed the engine.

"It was a super-specific dream," David finally said. "I think it means I'm supposed to stay here and help rescue people. Some pretty bad things are gonna be happening, and the Lord needs me."

Drew watched out the window, fighting his emotions.

"Sounds like a whale of a calling, son," Dad said, sounding a bit strangled. *He's probably trying not to cry. That makes two of us.* "Have courage and keep the faith. All those supplies we talked about? Make sure you're ready."

"I will. Thanks, Dad. Love you."

"Love you, too, David. Always. Be safe."

David cleared his throat and said, "You, too, Twerp."

"Same here, Dweeb. Don't die or I'll know."

"Yeah. Pretty sure we'll meet again in this life."

"If not, I'll miss your ugly face."

"*Mi cara es tu cara, sí?*"

Drew grunted. "Yeah, I got it."

"Okay, bro'. Signing off," David said. "Bye."

They echoed him before falling silent and still.

JoAnne appeared at the window. Rick opened the door as she asked, "You okay?"

"Yes. Well, sort of. David called. He's convinced he's supposed to stay behind and rescue people. It's, you know, hard…"

She touched his shoulder and said, "I know."

Drew tried to ignore their interaction, not wanting to add to his pain by missing his mother, but pain happens. *Please make it go away, Heavenly Father. Isn't missing Tweedle enough to deal with, right now?*

"But I'm trying to trust the Lord," Rick said. "Your heart okay?"

"It's fine," said JoAnne. "The great Healer worked on it. You helped, too, as I recall."

That stirred Drew's curiosity, but he wasn't willing to ask. *Why doesn't anyone ask if I'm okay?*

"That's a relief," said his dad. "I'll put the phone back in the house and we'll go."

Drew watched in the side mirror as JoAnne returned to her car. He saw a golden head pop up in the passenger seat. *Yatzy.* "Why does she have Oliver's dog?" he asked as his dad climbed back in.

"*She* has a name."

"Okayyy. Why does Mrs. Gephardt have Oliver's dog?"

"It's Mrs. Talbot, and she has Yatzy because Oll went up yesterday to work at the camp and couldn't take her." Dad restarted the truck, backed out of the driveway and waited in the road for his new wife to back into it and turn around.

Dad's new wife. So bizarre. I saw them get married and it's still strange. She's okay, I guess, but…I miss Mom. I miss Tweedle. This is harder than going on a mission. He hunched close to the door and leaned his head on the window. *I left a decent job, too. And what about Sophia? We had one whole date, but we hit it off. She's gonna think I ghosted her. I should have texted, but what would I say? "I'm going away indefinitely. Not your fault." Like saying, "It's not you, it's me." Or what about, "How would you like to go camping with me for the rest of your life? We don't know each other, but trials are a great way to bond." Riiight.*

Neither one of them spoke the whole trip across the county and up the twisting canyon road until the turn-off to the campsite came into view. Snow still haunted spots here and there, being the month of June at about 7,000 feet in elevation. Drew saw a sign a while back that said 7,300, but they dropped into a high valley after reaching the summit, so he was estimating.

"Here it is," said Dad. "Potgut Pass. Sorry I haven't been good company. My thoughts have been on friends and family we left behind."

"Mine, too, Dad," he said. Up on the right, Drew glimpsed several men directing cars. Only one looked familiar. "Isn't that Oll's green baseball cap?"

Oliver waved. Dad rolled down the window and stuck his head out.

"Where to, son?"

~CHAPTER 8~

Tents and Trials

"... I will be on your right hand and on your left,
and my Spirit shall be in your hearts, and mine
angels round about you, to bear you up."
Doctrine and Covenants 84:88

June 2049, the mountains of central Utah, America

"Are you sure? I don't mind sharing a tent. It's big enough for two."

Drew reconsidered the possibility but ended up turning down Oliver's offer a second time. "Naw, dude, thanks. I'll set up my own. I'm sensitive to dog dander."

"Since when?"

"I don't know. Since I need to be alone."

"Being alone will make missing Tweedle worse, bro. Tell you what," Oliver said, "You be alone at night if you want, but help me out during the day, 'k? I've been called to ride herd on the teenage boys, and they are seriously missing their electronics."

"What are you planning to do with them?"

"Anything that isn't illegal or immoral," Oliver said with a laugh. "Games, fishing, target practice, stuff like that. Help me out?"

"Okay, sure. I could teach them how to hunt with a wrist rocket," Drew offered. "And we could invite Dad to go ice fishing with us in winter."

"Spectacular," Oliver said. "Let's do that."

Kids weren't the only ones missing their electronics. Drew itched to battle virtual zombies. Game nights, therefore, soon became his favorite nights, with active sports in good weather and table games anytime.

With camp schedules established for everything from meals to meetings to bedtime, Drew soon settled into a comforting routine.

The leaders divided the camp into companies of fifty or less with a captain for each section, three sections to a ward. The captains were, in effect, the bishop's counselors, though not all were Latter-Day Saints. Camp buzz indicated that the policy of handing out assignments regardless of denomination helped everyone feel included and represented.

On Friday, Drew heard the announcement that this camp would be the place to ride out the worst of the Last Days' destruction. They were expected to stay here until the Lord directed otherwise.

I was right about that, but I wish I wasn't. Father in Heaven, I pray I will see my twin again, soon.

Some campers panicked at the announcement and fled back home, citing jobs and other responsibilities, but most accepted the call.

Good thing more didn't defect. There's plenty to do. We're practically pioneers, here, working in sub-standard conditions and we need everybody. Drew volunteered his time and effort to whatever need he saw, and that included helping his one remaining brother.

He gained new respect for Oliver, watching him spend a great deal of his time in this assignment to lead the twelve-to-fourteen-year-old boys. Though not his job, it gave Drew pleasure to assist Oliver and fewer opportunities to mope. He had a lot of fun with them all through summer and fall. And as winter set in, he and Oliver both shared some of their heavy-duty cold weather gear with the less-prepared, so that the boys could all go ice-fishing together instead of in shifts.

Yatzy made a great little mascot, joining in whenever allowed. The ice burned her paw pads, so JoAnne made booties for the pooch. Yatzy's high-stepping efforts to shed them provided a riot of amusement for the humans. She eventually resigned herself to the new feet protection, since no one agreed to remove them outside of Oliver's tent.

Drew's tolerance for JoAnne grew and developed into a grudging acceptance. *She's okay, I guess. She tries to be helpful. But still, Dad's remarriage feels disloyal to Mom.*

Rick admired JoAnne's ability to adapt and create. Her hands were rarely idle; she crafted winter scarves, mittens, and hats for the children, providing warmth and comfort as the cold weather set in. She also crocheted booties for her beloved grand-puppy, ensuring the little dog could join in the fun without discomfort.

JoAnne's talents extended beyond clothing. She took pleasure in making quilts and baking bread alongside the Relief Society sisters. These efforts contributed to the well-being of everyone at camp and fostered a sense of community and togetherness.

But whenever Rick observed his wife doing too much, he did his best to protect and stick up for her. He informed the squad captain that Jo couldn't work outside in the fields as much as they expected her to, which earned him her fervent gratitude.

Rick received more thanks the evening he smashed a rat under the tent with the back of a shovel. JoAnne shuddered and struggled to suppress her moans and screams, as he wreaked havoc in the tent his exuberant efforts to corner his prey.

"Got him!" he exclaimed as he beat the hump under the tent floor to the point of creating a red-black stain on the floor. "Oops. Guess I whacked him too hard. I'll go fish him out. What can I use?"

"How about the snow broom?" She referred to an inglorious but helpful tool crafted out of a long car window-scraper with bristles down one side, duct-taped to a broom handle. They used it to knock snow off the tent roof.

A laugh escaped at her pained expression when he presented his prize at the open tent door with satisfaction. "It has been an honor to slay the hairy little dragon for you. You may call me Sir Knight." Rick bowed with a most dramatic flourish, the rat tail still between the fingers of one hand and the scraper in the other.

She laid a rag rug over the spot left behind and responded with a meek "Thank you, Sir Knight. I'll try not to be such a princess. Make sure you sanitize that scraper, please. And for heaven's sake toss the rat."

"Admit it, Jo, this is high adventure."

"Oh, yes," she said. "Exciting on so many levels. But I prefer more sedate activities like temple work and quilting."

"If I had to choose," Rick said, "I think temple work is my favorite."

"And you love mentoring kids who want to write and act in plays."

"Yeah, those kids are fun. And highly creative. I'll go deal with the rat."

"Good plan," she said with a wink. "It's getting late. Almost time for scriptures."

Rick tossed his hard-won rodent far out into the woods, washed his hands and the ice scraper while pondering on life, here. *We have the beginnings of a genuine Zion society. It's great how we all pull together to solve problems and keep the camp running smoothly.*

He entered their tent and prepared for bed. They used the last half-hour of each day to read scriptures by lantern-light, if necessary, then have their "couple's prayer" before turning in. They slid into their sleeping bags on cots and held hands across the narrow divide between them, talking of many things before slipping off to sleep.

This evening as they lay in the darkness, Rick told JoAnne about a comforting dream he had recently about Allison, and asked about James, her first husband. "How did you find each other?"

"We were both attending BYU," JoAnne said. "He had returned from his mission to Canada, and I was a freshman in my first semester. We dated, but I dated other guys, too.

"One day in December, he said, 'I'd like to get to know you better. I think I want to marry you.' I said, 'That's sweet, but I'm on a quest for an education, first. If you're still around after that, we'll talk.' He didn't much like that plan."

"I'll bet."

She shifted a bit in her sleeping bag. "The Spirit whispered, 'Don't throw this away.' That caught me off-guard. My stepmother and my mother had both given me the talk about not getting engaged that first year, but the Lord gave me the opposite message."

"What happened?"

"He eventually proposed and I accepted out of obedience, as if in an arranged marriage. I begged the Lord for confirmation that this was the right thing to do, but it was slow in coming. Maybe three weeks later, we sat across from each other at a library table. Our knees touched, and… fireworks. I fell in love." She chuckled. "God is good."

"He is." Rick squeezed her hand. "When the Spirit told me to marry you, I felt the same way, like this was an arranged marriage. I hope you're not offended."

"I figured as much. I couldn't think of any other reason why you would marry a much older woman."

"'Love looks not with the eyes, but with the mind, and therefore is wingéd Cupid painted blind,'" Rick quoted.

"Twelfth Night?"

"A Midsummer Night's Dream."

"Ah, that's right. It's been decades since—"

"Jo, listen to me. I have always admired you. Your laugh lines are adorable; you light up a room with your smile. I could see that for myself without the Spirit's help."

"Thanks, Rick. You have been a great blessing to me."

"Goes both ways... And Jo?"

"Hm?"

He tugged on her hand. "I do love you."

No response for a few moments, which puzzled him, until he detected quiet weeping.

"Jo?"

She sniffed and returned the sentiment in a whisper.

⁕

JoAnne woke in the middle of a deep winter's night for one of her usual latrine visits.

Rick's cot is empty. He didn't say he would be gone. His guard shift this week is the eight-to-ten-pm block, and it has to be later than that. Much later. The fire in the stove has died down. Is he out for a potty-break, too?

Hauling herself out of her sleeping bag, JoAnne donned her snow gear, jammed another log into the woodstove and left the tent. Her trek across camp dragged on as her worry mounted.

Where could he be? She used a pair of tethered scissors to cut a piece of cloth from the rags designated for a toilet paper substitute. They had run out of the manufactured variety early on.

Positive that sleep would elude her until she had solved this mystery, she took a roundabout route on her return to the tent. *At least, I **hope** it's nothing to worry over. I've already lost one husband, Lord. Please let me keep this one a while longer.*

As JoAnne reached the farthest row of tents, she found him standing guard and sighed with relief.

"You have a bad dream?" Rick asked as she gave him an intense hug.

"No, just glad to find you," she admitted, flooded with gratitude for his safety. "Why are you out so late?"

"I traded with someone else. You were sawing logs, so I let you sleep. Were you worried?"

"A little."

"No need. I'm fine. Well, I'm stinkin' cold, but I'm okay. Hope you can get some more sleep before dawn."

JoAnne tramped her way back to the tent, kicking herself for being foolish. *I'm a silly old woman, but I am grateful he's alive. Thank You, Father. Please keep him warm.* She lifted her gaze upward, admiring the canopy of twinkling stars overhead. It settled over the camp like a protective blanket. Even in this dreary time of year, great beauty abounded, if one paused to appreciate it. *I'm very blessed.*

"Why aren't you out on your usual guard duty, Rick?" JoAnne asked. "Did you do another shift exchange?"

"An angel relieved me of duty."

"How kind." *Must be someone who doesn't mind extra time out in the bitter cold, though I can't think who that might be, right off.*

She started to ask, but Oliver called out, "Knock knock."

Rick let him in and offered him a five-gallon bucket "stool."

Oliver commenced his news mid-air before landing on it, holding his hands close to the stove. "Do you know angels guard the camp, now? Boyd Cramer saw them. No more guard duty!"

"Real angels?" Jo asked, as she sank into her camp chair.

"I told you about it," said Rick.

"You meant a *heavenly* angel?"

"You know?" Oliver chimed in.

Her husband sat down before answering. "That's why I'm not out there, right now. I've been relieved. We all have."

Oliver grinned. "Spectacular!"

"Yep. I'm delighted to stay in my sleeping bag at night."

"I am, too," her stepson agreed.

"If you don't mind," Jo said, "I'd like to say our evening prayer, tonight. Would you like to join us, Oliver?"

"Sure."

※

After the "amen," Oliver walked back to his tent in the twilight, hoping to glimpse something special.

Too many people must have the same idea. I've never seen so much foot-traffic this time of night, and no angels anywhere. Maybe I'll see them some other time. The Holy Ghost testified to him, though, that they were on the job and would continue in that capacity as long as peace and harmony reigned.

Yatzy barked a short greeting as he entered his tent.

"Good girl."

He changed into heavy-duty thermals before snuggling down into his sleeping bag. His pooch jumped up onto her usual spot beside his feet.

I thank Thee for my blessings, Father, and for angels to guard and protect us. And with the peace that comes to the faithful, he drifted off to sleep.

※

Without saying much, Oliver and his brother walked back to their quarters from a tense ball game with a bunch of men and older boys. Severe squabbles were rare, but the camp currently boiled over with hard feelings. A hunting party had returned two days ago without one of its members, who had fallen behind, the rest of the hunters unaware. Blame and fear reared their ugly heads, and a fight broke out at today's game.

He and Drew both participated in search parties sent out to scour the countryside for the missing man. No sign of him surfaced, so another attempt was scheduled for later this afternoon.

This has everyone on edge, with accusations flying anytime two people converse. Guilt clawed at Oliver for participating in some of those conversations, and he repented for it. Once he regained the companionship of the Holy Ghost, he believed angels no longer guarded the camp.

⁂

Oliver stared at the tent wall as he lay on his side in the dark. He couldn't tell if the woman's scream that woke him was part of a dream or not. He rolled over and caught a glimpse of an indefinable black shape disappearing through a hole in the tent.

"What the…?" *What was that? Where's Yatzy?* He jumped up and called for her. Crushing silence answered him. "Yatzy?"

Trembling in fear, he bundled up and scurried out to search for her, running into his brother.

"I heard Yatzy scream," Drew said in a rush. "What happened?" Other faces peeked out of their tents.

"I don't know. I was asleep. Are you sure it was Yatzy? I thought… Never mind, I can't find her. Maybe that animal snatched her. There's a huge hole in the tent."

"Let's get Dad to help search."

The sun rode high in the sky when they found the dog's remains. Oliver didn't have to dig much of a hole to bury her.

The violent loss of his sweet canine companion added to and compounded many previous losses: his mom's death, leaving a comfortable home, the absence of a convenient megastore or delivery service, the constant need for diligence to survive, the physical and spiritual welfare his absent siblings, his failed marriage and loss of the dog he had back then, as well as the friends he had to leave behind—all weighed on his soul.

Oliver trudged back to his tent and collapsed onto his cot in a stupor of sorrow and self-pity. *Yatzy gave her life for me. I'm sure of it. She was probably trying to protect me. Why didn't I wake up in time? She didn't deserve to suffer.*

A minute later, Jo called out, "Oliver?"

Grief constricted his throat. *Maybe she doesn't know I'm here. Besides, I want to be alone.*

"I'm so sorry about Yatzy. I want you to know that your dad and I are mourning with you. She was such a loving little thing. We will all miss her, but I'm sure it will be hardest for you."

Oliver could not stop the tears from flowing at the tenderness in Jo's voice, but neither could he answer or unzip the door. *She's a good person and loved Yatzy, I know, but I'm not ready to be vulnerable with her. I don't know that I ever could.* Her slow, diminishing footsteps crunching the snow magnified his guilt and heartache.

Of course, his crew of boys also mourned Yatzy. She had been the best of companions for all of them. They arrived with Drew to express their sympathy. This time, more in control of his voice, Oliver poked his head out of his tent and said, "Thanks, guys. That means a lot." He declined their invitation to join them and did not invite them into his ravaged tent, despite a few teary faces.

Drew asked the boys to give them a minute alone, and they trudged away with lowered heads and hunched shoulders. "Bro, I'm sorry. I'm here for you, if, you know…"

"I know. Thanks."

His brother gave a thumbs-up and hurried to catch up with the young men.

As Oliver repaired the damage to his tent, he pondered on the need to also mend a certain relationship, one he had not spent enough time nurturing. He sewed the rip in the canvas with upholstery thread and reinforced it with extra canvas and cement glue. Confident it would hold, he opened his French Book of Mormon and spent the rest of the day searching for comfort and direction. *Maybe I need to rethink being vulnerable.*

The next day, he headed to his dad's tent. Rick welcomed him and offered a five-gallon bucket seat.

"Where's JoAnne?" Oliver asked.

"She's on bread-making duty, today. She'll be here soon. Why?"

"I need to make something right."

~CHAPTER 9~

A Balm in Gilead

*"And also upon the servants and upon the handmaids
in those days will I pour out my spirit."*
Joel 2:29, *The Holy Bible*

August 1879, north of Bayou Lafourche, Louisiana

I'm a soggy, bloody mess. Must have passed out.

Stella pulled herself upright, careful not to jostle her broken arm. Her skirts wicked up the bayou water as they hung over the edge. She dragged the skirts into her craft, one waterlogged handful at a time, doing what little she could with one hand to wring them out, a fruitless effort. Blood dripped from her arm and head onto her dress.

This won't do. Gotta dry out. And scrounge up some dry rags to stop the blood and bind my head. And set these bones. Too many "gottas" to shake a stick at. Where do I start?

Glancing around at the new congregation of intrigued reptiles, she prayed. *Holy Mother of God, You know I wouldn't survive another go-'round with a caiman. Please send a few angels for protection. Even so, I'll keep the gator pick close to hand. Not going down without a fight, moi.*

Shaking, but determined, she washed and bound up her wounds one-handed. *Now I need a splint.* She considered the paddles. *That'll do. Can't use both, now, anyways.* Gasping and moaning with the effort, she popped the bones into place and wrapped cotton strips around her arm and a paddle.

Didn't think I'd use 'em for such a need as this.

Exhausted, one eye on the alligators, Stella gingerly climbed onto the bank and up an easy tree, spreading her skirts out to dry. *Can't stay on the ground. Them caiman would love a go at me, and could surely climb out of the water. Jésus, help me stay awake. I thank You for Your mercy in sparing my life. I'd surely hate to waste that blessing by falling out of this tree.*

By the time the skirts had dried to a manageable dampness, Stella's stiff body ached all over, and she carefully dropped out of the tree, determined to resume her journey. Having acquired a good deal more caution, she cast off and began paddling, moaning, wincing and crying out at times from the pounding pain. *Unlikely as it is that Henri could be within earshot, I'd best be ever so quiet, now.*

She climbed out onto land only twice more that day to relieve herself, since her greatest urgency lay in escape. Not bothering to make camp, she slept in the *pirogue.*

Stella's last thought that night centered on the idea that she could have lost her eye and her arm. "*Merci, Jésus,* for miracles," she whispered. "Please keep this *pirogue* movin' on up the bayou." As a baby rocked in a cradle, she eased toward sleep.

Awakening the next morning to a blue sky in a world of pounding pain, Stella moaned, "*Mon Dieu,* forgive my trespasses, an' have mercy on me." Not expecting a direct answer, since that would be a first, it surprised her when a Man's voice filled her mind.

~*Danger. Hide.*~

Pushing past the pain in the crucial need of the moment, Stella hauled herself up to a sitting position and brought her remaining paddle down into the water. She jabbed awkwardly away from the bank, guarding against the tendency to paddle in circles. Heading for a dense buttonbush to the right, she slid under the overhanging branches.

I thank You, Jésus. Weren't no wadin' birds lurkin' here to squawk and give me away.

The foliage camouflaged a notch in the bayou, leading to another branch of it. She made slow, quiet progress with one oar, sliding deeper into the thicket. This bayou thread curved until it lay parallel to the last one, though dense vegetation blocked her view of both it and the sun. Stilling the paddle, all nerves at attention, she shivered. *It must be Henri.* Her left arm throbbed.

A wonderful warmth stole over her, as if angel arms encircled her. She wept in silent relief, bowing her head in gratitude. *Merci, Lord. Merci.* Paddle splashes from the other vessel snagged her attention, but she focused on the peaceful warmth, and the sounds faded.

Traveling on, Stella's tiny bayou thread increased in size, till it crossed a small freshwater river. *Best pull out and make camp. I'm needing that clean water to bathe myself and redress these wounds.* Her upper and lower arm sported teeth holes, but no rips. She explored the gator's handiwork on her face and scalp, but all she could do about the long slice was to wrap her head with one good hand and hold it lightly with the left arm. It made the paddle stick up in the air but gave her a chance to tuck the ends of the strips under to secure them.

This'll make a big, fat scar, unless I can find someone to sew it up. I'd do it myself, if I could see what I'm doin'. Need a traiteur.

Stella napped for awhile to regain some strength, and upon awakening, studied the waterway.

I've had me a good rest and still have no strength to paddle upriver, and downriver is the wrong way. She groaned with the effort of standing. *I do hate to ditch the pirogue, moi.*

~*Go downriver.*~

Stella blinked. "*Mais non.* That can't be right," she said. "My imagination's playin' tricks on me."

~*Go downriver.*~

This she considered from all angles. *Maybe it ain't that my mind is sick. Could be Jésus is sure enough speaking to me. Or one o' His angels, mayhap. Either way, it's a wonder and a blessing. But what if I'm off in the head? Well... can't let it hold me back.* She hefted her packs one-handed into her vessel. *If I'm crazy, so be it. I am all done in.*

Stella climbed in with great caution and followed the river half a day, before coming up to another bayou going northeast.

"This it, Lord?" A warmth washed over her once more, so she awkwardly guided her vessel into the bayou and navigated that for the rest of the day. Spent from using one arm and battling pain, she pulled out and made a simple camp.

Back in the *pirogue* again the next day, Stella passed a freshwater stream. Urged to abandon her vessel by her unseen guide, she followed this new waterway, walking inside the tree line for cover. She stumbled a few times under the load of her pain and packs.

No stopping, no stopping, no stopping. The continuous self-talk in her head turned into a mindless chant echoing all around her, until she staggered into a settlement, murmuring, *"Traiteur",* and collapsed.

Unclear on how long she had been there, her eyelids opened as slits upon two Creole women in calico. *"Traiteur,"* Stella moaned. One woman took her good arm; the other carried the packs. The trio made slow progress down the grass-tufted, muddy road to a tidy cabin near an herb garden.

"Barnabè! Barnabè!" The first woman's free hand banged on the door as she hollered.

Stella's head hung low, and she saw little of the man who opened the door.

"Whatcha need?"

"We found this woman on the road. Can you he'p? She's Cajun."

"Bring 'er in, then." The women laid her on the bench covered by a woven rug and asked if he wanted them to stay and help. *"Non, merci,* though I be beholden if you'd fetch Odette. I believe she's down to the henhouse."

They left, and in true healer fashion he began with prayer. Stella's whole body relaxed into the swirl of familiar and comforting words. Barnabè removed the bandage and cleaned her head wound. "What's yo' name?" he asked.

"St…" *Aaiee! I nearly gave myself away. Not far enough away from home, yet. Think of something that starts like Stella.* "S-Steele. Ruby Steele." *Kinda my name backwards. Am I thinking straight? Not certain sure.*

Someone arrived through the back of the house, saying, "Odette had an egg deliv'ry, so I'll he'p you, *cher*. Who's this?"

"Ruby," he responded. "He'p me hoist 'er onto the table." Stella pried her heavy eyelids open to find a motherly woman's caramel-colored face hovering above her own. A cheerful kerchief covered her hair.

"You got yo'self in a bit of a state, now din't you? Don't you worry none. We'll fix you up right quick." She laid out a worn blanket on the table, then she and Barnabè heaved her up.

"Now he kin work on you without tearin' up his back."

Stella murmured, "*Merci*," her mind a nest of cotton. The feather-soft voice of the sweet woman coaxed her toward unconsciousness.

"Why 'tain't no trouble atall. You rest easy, an' I'll hang onto you, in case you git jumpy with the pain."

Stella whispered, "Bless you."

⁂

The Cajun girl fainted. *All the better.*

Barnabè's wife, Marie, echoed his thought. "Well, that'll make it easier on all of us, now won't it?"

she said as she wrapped the unconscious girl in a firm but kind embrace. "I'll still hold her, just in case. Who is she, for true? Ruby ain't no Cajun name."

"I know it," he said, unconcerned. "But that be what she said, an' we'll let it pass."

"Well, all right, then. *Pauvre ti bête.*" She shook her head and clicked her tongue. "Po' little thing. She's a mess."

Barnabè unwrapped Ruby's raggedy arm bandage, sniffing the poultice. "Hm. She do know herbs," he admitted and set aside the spent wad of cloth.

"What happen', do you suppose?"

"Cocodrie attack, I 'spect. See heah? The way these holes line up, her arm be bent when he chomp' down. Bite this size? Mercy, Lord, that gator musta been pushin' two hunnerd pounds. How she kept her arm be beyond me."

"The good Lord be watchin' out for this one, for certain true," Marie stated with conviction. "Least we can do be to he'p Him out."

"She did a good job splintin' and dressin' it one-handed, I give 'er that. One bone gotta be reset, though," Barnabè said as he explored it with his sure fingers, "or it be healin' crooked. Ain't stitchin' it, bein' tooth holes an' all, but I'll clean it good, an' make her a special amulet. Should keep the poison away."

He cut her hair short along the gaping wound and sliced a sliver of scalp off both sides of it. It had started healing and wouldn't close up well unless the cut was fresh.

This might git the poison, too. Can't risk it. Starting at her eyebrow, he stuck the needle in for the first stitch. If the two sides of scalp did not quite match up as he ended, at least it would at some point be camouflaged by her hair.

Odette, their daughter, appeared in the back door and came closer for a better look. "Who's the patient?"

"Ruby," Barnabè said without glancing up from his grisly, tedious work. His audience watched as he tied off the catgut on Ruby's scalp.

He stretched and rubbed his neck to relieve the tightness. "Fetch me supplies for a cast, daughter."

When Odette returned, her *maman* asked, "You finish yo' egg deliveries?"

"No ma'am. I'm gittin' outta the sun for a spell. Ever'body's talkin' 'bout a wild Cajun woman with a paddle strapped to her arm, an' I was itchin' to see for myself. Be back in no time," she said as she headed out again.

"All right, then." Marie repositioned her arms around the patient. Barnabè bound up the broken arm for stability before rebreaking it with a mallet covered in padding. The girl stirred and moaned but did not wake.

He splinted and covered the arm in plaster-soaked cotton strips from wrist to elbow, while Marie cleaned up the surgery implements and wrapped Ruby's head, leaving the unscathed eye bare.

◦◦◦

Ruby roused a scant twenty minutes later, moaning in misery.

"Heah, now, you drink this tisane," Marie said, putting the cup of sedative to Ruby's mouth. The patient, though semi-conscious, drank quite a bit.

"Now fo' the soup." But her charge did not swallow much before falling asleep.

Mother and daughter took turns watching over her through the night, since the patient had to be kept still and steady while the slow-drying plaster hardened.

When the Cajun girl woke the next morning, Marie deemed the cast tough enough. Her husband had done his work and left the rest to the women. "We'll he'p you bathe an' git a nightie on, Miss Ruby."

The *cocodrie* victim gave a start, confirming Marie's suspicion that "Ruby" had given a false name. "Mmm-hm. Gots to be careful. Cain't git no water on that cast."

"Merci, Madame…"

"Now, you kin call me Miz Marie. You need a bit of recuperatin' before you kin git to where you was goin', so you rest up an' git better."

"Merci, Miz Marie."

Marie called Odette to bring in something else for Ruby to wear. Her daughter laid a muslin nightgown and a light-blue calico dress on the bed, both of which Odette had helped sew. The patient balked, but the women dismissed her protests. Removing her boots first, Marie found a knife in a sheath. "You keep this knife in yo' boot?" she asked.

"Yes'm. That knife saved my life," the girl answered. "Cain't give it up no ways."

"That be all right, then. We'll leave it be."

Marie and her daughter removed the rest of the girl's clothes and washed her with care, cooing and clicking their tongues at her injuries and the state of her blood-caked hair.

"You's all shiny, now, Miss Ruby. Let's git you dried off... Bring that nightie over heah, Odette."

"*Oui, Maman.*"

"This ol' nightie be so soft and clean and ever so much better than this muddy brown thing," Marie said, with a dismissive toss of the blood-stained, ripped dress onto the floor.

"These sleeves'll go right over yo' new cast," added Odette.

By the time Marie and Odette finished with her, Ruby slipped toward unconsciousness once more. They tucked her into the bed and covered her with the worn, patchwork quilt.

"You suppose you might need this dirty ol' dress, Miss Ruby?" Marie asked doubtfully.

Her daughter snatched it up and said, "I'll wash it, *Maman.*"

"*Merci, chère.* There's a good girl. Don't know as you'll git the blood out, but you kin try. Good thing it be brown. Wash the socks, too, ehn?"

"Yes'm."

"Miz Marie?" Stella murmured.

"*Oui*, Miss Ruby?"

"Where am I?"

"You in Belle Rose, North Assumption Parish. Where you headed?"

"Dudn't matter. Just tryin' to git away from him."

"Him who? The *cocodrie?*"

"Henri. Thinks I kilt his wife… But I… loved her." And with that, the girl that survived an alligator attack drifted off to sleep, incapable of besting a flea.

◦᾿ᐟ◦

Henri Boudreaux reached the Mississippi River and crossed it on a ferry. He haunted docks and "business districts," searching for a certain brunette up and down the east side where most of the ports lay. He clung to this vendetta as a hungry dog would a bone and found no other purpose to living but to take her life in exchange for Hélène's.

Each night, in any town he came to, he found the doggeries or saloons and inspected all the prostitutes for that one familiar face.

Where the hell is that Rubidoux woman? No one can trust her as a healer; selling herself must be the only way she can eat. Positive in his logic, he did not bother to widen his search. Disappointed at each day's end, he drank away his discouragement and grief. Or tried to. The pain fell asleep when he nodded off in some back alley and woke again a moment after he did.

Henri kept his nose out for any wind of his quarry but soon felt the pinch of poverty. The most logical solution lay in working on a steamboat. *Boats are boats, oui? I know shrimp boats. Is a riverboat so different? Bigger, o' course. I could ride to the next port while earning beer and bread. Where else would she be but at a port? But which one?*

117

One evening, he glimpsed a familiar face at the far table in yet another pub and moved closer, the raucous company cloaking his approach. Hovering over his target, he waited until the laughter died. "Lefroy?"

The man glanced at Henri, eyes widening. "Boudreaux?" Popping out of his chair in surprise, he grabbed Henri's head in a feint of a wrestle, then clapped him on the back. "Why you old mudfish, you! *Assieds-toi*. Have a chair." In English, he called out, "Bring the likker for my old shipmate, here, barkeep!"

"An' who'll be payin' fer it, I'm askin'?" the Irish proprietor called out without a break in the rhythm of his work drying washed mugs.

"Aww, McNairy, this a special occasion!"

"Not to me i' 'tain't."

"A'right, boys! Pitch in a bit for my friend, heah, will ya?" Good-natured grumbling accompanied the ante-ups, and soon a pint sat in front of him. First, Lefroy translated all that had transpired in the last thirty seconds. "Now, Boudreaux," he said in French, "what you doin' heah? You was always itchin' to be back inna bayou, *non*? And heah you is in Greenville, Miss'sippi."

"Steamboats stop heah. What's the main payload?"

"Cotton, o' course. This boomin' town be a cotton-tradin' hub."

"Cotton," Henri said in disgust.

"Don't be snubbin' King Cotton, *mon ami*. Smell' better than shrimp, ehn?" Lefroy said something in English, presumably about the fragrance of sea creatures, which prompted healthy laughter. "Now, I ask you again. What brings you to this muddy town on a great muddy river?"

"Business."

"*Mais oui*, o' course it's business, but what kind o' business?"

"Revenge business." Henri took a swig of the fragrant brew, while Lefroy translated for his fellows, who sobered, studying him. "She kilt my wife, an' I won't rest before I send her to hell."

"You needin' some assistance on that hunt?" Lefroy wanted to know.

"*Mais oui*, if you're offerin'," returned Henri. "But right now, I'm needin' work. Couldn't 'a bought likker on my own, that's how empty my pockets be."

After Lefroy enlightened his friends, a man named Teasdale asked, "What work you looking for?"

Lefroy put the question to him in Cajun French.

"I know shrimp boats," Henri answered, "though I ain't hungry enough to go back to that, yet. I can skin a mule in one minute flat, *moi*. Smaller animals in less."

"Nasty work, that," Lefroy replied. "Not much call for that 'round heah." He explained to his tablemates Henri's special talent.

McKee said in an undertone, "Tell him there be other things a strappin' fellow like himself can do, though 'tisn't the place to mention it." He gave Henri a pointed glance as he placed a stubby forefinger to the side of his nose.

"*Oui*," agreed Lefroy with a wicked gleam in his eye. "It's the place to be spendin' the proceeds." He glanced over at a working girl and the others laughed.

Henri's eyes narrowed with speculation, first, and keen interest as soon as Lefroy filled him in.

⁂

Stella idled many days at the treater's home, hoping to regain her strength without unnecessary delay. She helped out the family as soon as she could, having no other gift to offer the *traiteur*. As tenacious as a leech, she worked at small, odd jobs, despite the pain of her wounds and Marie's fussing.

Early each evening, exhausted, she fell asleep to Creole music played out in the lanes under the stars. Guitars, banjos and disturbing lyrics lulled her into unconsciousness, infiltrating and twisting her dreams.

As Stella recovered, she worked more and more for Barnabè's family, allowing for her weakened condition and skills, and learned to answer to "Ruby" with natural ease. By the end of the third week, however, she admitted to restlessness.

Ever the mother hen, Marie counseled her, "Stay on with us, Ruby. I could use the he'p, and you could use some more time to heal."

"This ain't far enough away from Henri Boudreaux." Determined to leave, she balanced work and rest a few more days, before shedding the head bandage and resuming her journey.

As Stella prepared to set out, Marie handed her a sunbonnet and said, "Cain't let the sun burn yore tender spot. An' don't you be gettin' that cast wet, Miss Ruby."

"Yes, ma'am." The motherliness oozing from the *traiteur's* wife delighted Stella. She missed that first and foremost from the absence of her own mother, and now from the void of Nettie's passing.

"You take care o' yo'self, ya hear? Keep a-goin' that-a-way, an' you be comin' to the great Mississipp'. An' don't you be takin' on no more cocodrie, ehn?"

Stella turned back around with a big grin and waved to the kind woman. "I won't! *Merci beaucoup* to you an' Odette and Barnabè! *Adieu!*"

"*Adieu,* you crazy girl," called Marie as she waved an arm. "God go with you!"

~CHAPTER 10~

Faith in Every Footstep

"Trust in the Lord and do good; so shalt thou dwell in the land, and verily thou shalt be fed."
Psalm 37:3, *The Holy Bible*

Spring, 2053, the mountains of central Utah

Rick had consoled JoAnne the best he could as she wept on her cot the night before, though she refused to confess the cause. Now, with his son asking for her, the clues weren't difficult to assemble.

"Ah," Rick said. "She cried."

Oliver offered a quiet "I'm sorry," and stared at the tent floor.

Rick waited for inspiration before speaking. "It was difficult, at first, to accept direction from the Spirit to marry JoAnne. It would have been hard to marry anyone. No one can compare with your mother."

His voice broke. It took another moment to gain control. "But as JoAnne likes to say, comparisons always hurt somebody. So, here it is: she's not better or worse than Allison. Just different. And I have learned... well, I'm still learning that love is not divided by how many people we let in. It's multiplied. It grows, filling us and changing us into people more like our Savior."

Oliver nodded, not looking up from the floor until the tent door unzipped and JoAnne slipped in.

"I'm wearing the aroma of fresh bread," she said as she zipped it back up, "so it might make your stomach growl." Noticing their visitor, she said with kind civility if not warmth, "Hello, Oliver," and sat in her camp chair next to Rick. "I hope I'm not interrupting, but I need to sit down."

"No problem," Rick said. "We were waiting for you."

"Oh?" Disheveled from slaving over bread dough, she batted away stray wisps of fine, gray hair, exhaling her fatigue. Streaks of flour decorated her clothes.

Rick's concern intensified. *She's looking her age, today. She works too hard.*

"Um, JoAnne," Oliver said, "I was in my tent when you came by the other night."

She shrugged a shoulder and picked at the dough under her nails. "I know. I saw you go in."

"Sorry. I couldn't answer—too choked up, and… I'm sorry I didn't let you in… I've never been able to let you in." Her head lifted. "I would like to, but it feels disloyal to my mom. I know you loved Yatzy and I know you love Dad. Thank you for that."

He rose, picked up the bucket and set it closer to Jo before plopping back down on it. He took her gnarled and workworn hand in one of his own roughened ones, a first for him. "Please forgive me, and… I…"

"I love your mother, too," Jo said. "She was, and still is, I'm sure, a fantastic woman. I loved being around her at the theater and I love her children. But so far, they haven't accepted it."

He inhaled as if gearing up and said, "I'll do my best."

"Thank you," she said. "I don't understand why your mom had to leave, and why I had to be here. But as with any trial, we have to make the best of it."

"Sure."

"I believe with all my heart that Allison's mission hasn't changed regarding her children, either. She's still working hard to protect, guide and bless you."

Rick approved of both the way Jo handled it and his son's efforts to be humble and accepting. *My boys may not ever be comfortable around their stepmother and trust her, but I detect some progress.*

That eased some of the pain from his daughter's rejection. Brooke appeared to him a dream months ago, saying, "I'm sorry." No information was imparted in that abbreviated visit. Could it have been revelation? Did her spirit come to him? Was she still in mortality? More questions emerged than answers, but he knew enough to leave it in God's hands. *And Allison's hands.*

⁂

"JoAnne!"

She could hear Rick yelling for her, but she couldn't answer with much volume. The earthquake that hit the camp bounced her around under the clothesline at the edge of camp, bruising her all over, especially her shoulder. Panting with pain, she waited for him to move close enough to hear her before calling out again. *At least I'm not lying in the snow, just a little spring mud.*

"There you are!" Rick rushed past the laundry on the line to her side. "Are you okay?"

"It's my shoulder. I think I'm going to need a blessing."

"You bet. Let's get you into the tent, first."

Rick carried her into the tent and recruited the camp doctor to reposition her dislocated shoulder, nearly causing her to pass out. Finally, his dear voice penetrated her mind-fog as he invoked the power of God. Afterward, he and the doctor conferred outside the tent. She could hear little of what they said in quiet tones. He re-entered and announced, "All right, milady, you are hereby banned from any work whatsoever."

"But people are depending on me," she protested. "And you gave me a blessing. I'll be fine."

"You're not fine, yet, so until you are, you have to rest and recuperate. Doctor's orders."

"Oh, all right. But surely I'm able to do some needlework. Knitting, maybe, or quilting?"

"We'll see," Rick said with reservation.

JoAnne had to ease into handwork slowly, since even that affected the sore shoulder, but three weeks later, she had made decent progress to the point where she could once again help sew.

I'm grateful, Lord, and so blessed. I thank Thee. Summer crept into camp while I recuperated, and now this green valley surrounded by mountains capped in white is exquisite. She and the quilt club labored on their latest project under a canopy, leaving them open to the fresh breeze and a view of camp activities.

The bell reserved for mandatory meetings clanged late that morning. JoAnne left her needle in a safe place and gathered with Rick, his boys and their ward in the designated area. It took a while for the whole group to settle down on their chairs and blankets.

Their bishop, up on a low platform, raised his hands in a signal that he would begin. They and the other wards holding similar meetings in the distance quieted. Low winds rustling through the spring leaves brought the scent of new adventures.

"You've been called, today, for a special announcement," Bishop Albert began. "Some have their marching orders, and some will receive theirs later today. The time has come to leave our camp." He waited, arms raised, for the ensuing clamor to die back, before lowering them as if patting down the noise level.

I'm surprised. We're doing so well here.

"Elder Jorgenson let us know that our General Authorities are pleased with our progress, and now it's our privilege to move on. God bless us in our new endeavors. Go eat lunch first, then report to your captains."

JoAnne enjoyed the rumble of excitement during lunch. She kept her concerns to herself during the mealtime conversation. When she and her squad gathered with their captain, the campers acted too keyed up to compose themselves. Children ran around and adults chatted. A few tried the shrill whistle technique, which hurt her ears, but it did the job.

"Take what you need and can carry in a backpack. Don't overload yourselves," said Brother Preston, their current captain. "It will be an arduous journey, so keep that in mind. And though it makes sense to take a wheeled cart to carry things, the terrain is extra rough out there due to earthquakes, so it may be more trouble than it's worth. You decide, then pray about it before moving forward. You'll have the rest of today to pack and say goodbye to friends, then take off early tomorrow morning."

Brother Calhoun piped up. "Why have we been slaving in the fields if we're leaving? We should have been told. It would have saved a lot of work." Others added their grumbles of agreement.

Brother Preston shook his head, and said, "Others will use this valley, too. Our labor has not been solely for ourselves. In fact, some will be assigned to stay behind and help with the next wave of campers."

"And hopefully, someone else will have prepared the place where *you're* going," said Rick. "Trust in Heavenly Father's plan." Jo linked arms with her wise husband, who had grown into a giant in her estimation.

"Thank you, Brother Talbot." Brother Preston addressed the congregation. "Don't worry about all that you have to leave behind, it will be taken care of." He paused, an expression of love and concern on his face. "We have not been bothered by enemy troops here, but there is the definite possibility that you will encounter them on your treks."

Alarm burst out all around Jo in a flood of exclamations. *I didn't know that the country had been invaded.* From the group's chatter, they didn't know, either, but Rick's face told a different story. "How did you know?" she whispered.

"I'll tell you later."

Their squad captain said, "Depend on your Heavenly Father for inspiration, always, and *do not be afraid*." His emphasis confirmed that fear would be as much of an enemy as soldiers. "Have confidence in the Lord. He has promised protection to the faithful. We have reports that there has been a lot of destruction out there from war, fires, plagues and earthquakes. Most of the LDS temples are okay. They were built on holy ground and designed to withstand the worst."

The crowd settled down more with the mention of temples, and Brother Preston continued. "Some chapels of other denominations made it through, as well. That being said, all religious buildings not used for aid stations and emergency housing were closed for the war and heavily guarded to repel vandalism and hostile takeovers, since there's been a lot of that."

Another wave of chatter rose and fell.

"Those of you assigned to gather at a temple will find a guard there consisting of four sets of couple missionaries strengthened by angels. All houses of the Lord will open as soon as large bodies of willing hands gather around them and everything's in order. Work hard to build up a strong community with physical and spiritual fortifications. Listen, folks, while I read your assignments."

Anticipation quieted the group, except for the occasional child's noise or an outburst of surprise.

The four Talbots and six other men and women were directed to trek southwest to the Diamond Fork Campground on a rescue mission.

As they walked arm in arm back to their tent, Jo asked Rick, "So, how did you know?"

"I attended the meeting with Elder Jorgenson when he arrived last week, before his address to the whole camp. And he instructed us not to tell anyone, yet, the logic being that it would cause unnecessary alarm."

"The Spirit was so strong when he spoke, I'm sure the Lord's with him. He's a new apostle, so one of the other ones must have died, right?"

"Yes."

"Do you know who?"

"Several of them, I understand," he said.

"How sad. Everything is so different, now." *What a day for revelations.*

As she collected gear for the trek, her mind turned to her physical inadequacies. *I hope I can do this. How far are we going?* "I haven't been to Diamond Fork," she said. "Have you?"

"Allison and I took the kids there a few times, so we kind of know the lay of the land, but there have been earthquakes, and plus, we're coming at it from a different direction. It'll be an ordeal. I hope you're up to it."

"So do I," she said, unsuccessful at keeping the concern out of her voice.

~Don't worry; I will help you. ~

The Spirit of peace enveloped JoAnne, and she relaxed. *I thank Thee, Lord, for all the help I receive. I will do my best to fight off fear.*

Their band of ten tramped over fractured mountains on the way to Diamond Fork, striving to follow the guidance of the Holy Ghost, and never crossing paths with another soul. The course of rivers and streams had been either altered or obliterated, leaving the campers to find a few muddy waterways and one small, clear pond. They filtered the water through cloth; then using the power of the priesthood, cleansed and increased the water as needed.

Fire-charred areas yielded no game for food, but in the healthy spots, the occasional rabbit or a bird appeared as they walked. Drew, having his slingshot handy, would provide a meal for them. JoAnne took that opportunity and any others she could spot to compliment her stepson and thank him.

Strengthened to keep up a grueling pace, she pushed on despite blisters, thirst and fatigue. Gratitude flooded her, too, that they did not encounter any enemy troops, though they were spotted off in the distance twice.

I suspect that we will cross paths with them. I pray that we'll be safe, Father.

❦

Rick woke before the sun did, alone. *What a strange dream, but so clear. It must have been a vision. If it was, then we'll be called to missions across the globe. And strangest of all—my body will be translated to help me better fulfill those missions. Where's Jo? I want to tell her.*

He spotted his wife leaning against a tree standing, if one could call it that, at a forty-five-degree angle. No one else had left their sleeping bags. He sat up.

In one word, he expressed his greeting and concern for her wellbeing: "Jo?"

She wiped her tears and faced him but said nothing.

"What's wrong, sweetie? You okay?" He easily hopped out of his sleeping bag. "That's different. Nothing hurts. I'm always stiff and sore in the morning." He stopped, wide-eyed. "It's happened. I've been translated! I just had a dream that promised it would happen, and it already has."

"That's fantastic," she said, eyes shining with love and tears. "I'm happy for you."

"Ah. You were hoping..."

"Yes, but it's apparently not time for me to receive that blessing. I'm glad you did, but... the thing is, the pain is relentless." She tugged on a branch of the tree supporting her. "And I'm so tired. Sleep eludes me much of every night... I'm sorry, Rick. I don't mean to whine. There must be something else I need to learn from all of this before it'll improve."

"Or something you need to teach," he replied, indicating his snoozing sons.

"Perhaps. I did receive a message that we will..." She grimaced. "Never mind. It's not important. At least, not right now." She stretched her back with a small groan and brushed off her hands. "Let's start breakfast, since we're up." She chuckled. "Can translated beings cook?"

In an instant, he appeared next to her, having transformed to match her in age. He grinned at her double-take and spoke in a low voice. "All I did was pray, and *voilà*."

She laughed and threw her arms around this wonderful gift, her temporary husband. "You're crazy." She ruffled his suddenly thinner, whiter hair.

"Yeah, but you love it."

"I do," she said, and they kissed with uncharacteristic passion.

He whispered, "You and I will what?"

Matching his tone, she said, "We will go to Africa on a special mission and be teachers there."

He brightened. "I received the same message."

"You did?"

"That's right. So, hang on, and the change will come for you, too. I think I've been changed now because we're in for some pretty hairball situations, soon, and we'll need an ace in the hole."

"Makes sense. Who would suspect a little old man of having such great power?" she teased.

"Exactly."

"Thanks, Rick."

"For what?"

"Thank you for your pure heart full of charity, and for being so devoted to God that He would trust you with this gift of translation. I think we have an honorary member of Enoch's Zion, right here."

He grinned, gave her another hug and a kiss, and helped her gather up some food that he could multiply for the little band of travelers. Their company soon woke to find a new yet old Rick. He refused to answer any of their surprised questions, so they dropped the subject—with him, anyway, and whispered between themselves.

His brother shrugged it off, acting unconcerned, but all that day Oliver studied JoAnne and his visibly older dad. They laughed a lot and walked close together, holding hands, talking in undertones. He didn't grasp what had happened any more than anyone else did, but suspected, after much consideration, that this change was on purpose, somehow, and done out of love.

God moves in more mysterious ways than I ever imagined.

David Talbot, the twin chosen to stay behind, led a small band of two men and several women and children—escapees from the horrors of unchecked disease, gang violence and foreign occupation. He performed his duty with exactness and honor, treating his flock as the Savior Himself would have, with compassion and patience.

Impressed through the Holy Spirit to take this little band of survivors over the broken mountains to the east, David led them on an exhausting route over and around rough crags and boulders. *Diamond Fork campground has to be around here somewhere, but the earthquakes have rearranged things, and these people are exhausted.*

"Looks like a good place up ahead to make camp, guys," he said. "It's greener than any area we've found so far." *Too many fires and earthquakes have wrecked these magnificent mountains. Thank the Lord there are no cremation piles here. I could go a long time without seeing another one of those.* "Let's move these rocks and dig a latrine."

Equipment and food were scarce, but gratitude flowed from everyone for their escape from the current dystopia.

After about a month of barest survival, the campers spotted a small number of hikers on the hill across a shallow ravine and warned their leader.

David shaded his eyes and watched the new arrivals before running forward, heedless of the rough terrain. "No danger!" he cried, "It's my family!"

The other Talbots hurried to close the gap. Drew reached him first, and a greater bear hug never happened in the whole history of mankind.

"I missed your face, Dee!"

"What, the earthquake break all the mirrors, Dum?" The twins laughed without breaking their grip, spinning around in place, identical sandy beards to the sky, stumbling in their exuberance.

Rick, arriving with JoAnne and the others, cleared his throat, and said, "If you two Tweedles are finished, I'd like a hug, too."

"Dad? Is that you? You look a lot older! Life beating you up, old man?"

⁂

Rick enjoyed watching his sons work together as a solid team. He suspected that they would not willingly separate again and prayed for direction.

~Their separation became necessary for their progression. They must now continue as one to fulfill their calling and to bring to pass much righteousness. I will guide them.~

The twins announced one evening that they had been prompted to take their Diamond Fork band back to the church camp to continue their growth and learning, as well as to have better shelter in the vacated tents.

At that announcement, Rick discerned that the time had come to move on.

"Where to?" asked JoAnne.

"We're going to help build New Jerusalem in Missouri."

~CHAPTER 11~

Earth and Hell

"...Our God, whom we serve is able to deliver us!"
Daniel 3:17, *The Holy Bible*

April 2053, Eastern Utah

The spiritual gifts Rick experienced as a translated being included acute awareness of the thoughts and feelings of others. He waited while JoAnne struggled to haul herself out of fear-mode.

"That's kinda far away," she said with an air of panic. "Couldn't we work at one of the local temple sites? Zion is everywhere the saints are gathered."

"I'll help you, Jo." It astounded him how much he had come to love this woman. And he would do anything within his power for her, but ignoring heavenly direction was not in him.

Jo wilted, resigned.

Some of David's people were inspired to go with them to Missouri, and some of Rick's people elected to stay, having skills that would bolster this small company's chances for survival. In all, twelve people commenced the trek east, including Oliver.

None of the mothers with children opted for a trek to Missouri. *That's best. They'll be safer in camp, of course. And so will my boys.* Rick found it difficult to bid the twins goodbye, but not debilitating. He trusted in Heavenly Father's magnanimous nature and had faith that they would all meet in His good time. And in their goodwill, off the charts at this point, the twins let JoAnne hug them. That lifted his spirits, and he moved forward with greater peace.

On the evening of that first day of traveling, Rick, as leader of this expedition, instituted a new routine of assigning someone to read a scripture and lead the group in singing a hymn. He chose Oliver to begin.

Facing these determined and steadfast saints, Oliver recited from memory one of his favorite verses.

"This one is Doctrine and Covenants six thirty-four. 'Therefore, fear not, little flock; do good; let earth and hell combine against you, for if ye are built upon my rock, they cannot prevail.' I have a strong suspicion," he continued, "that though we will receive angelic protection on this trip, earth and hell *will* combine against us, and the only way to fight them is with faith."

Dad said, "Absolutely. Thank you, Oliver. Let's keep in mind, people, that though evil forces may hurt us, they cannot win, so remember to look up. God is on our side, because we are on His."

"Amen!" the entire pack chorused.

Oliver said, "Let's sing 'Press Forward, Saints'." He led out with the strong baritone voice which he had used throughout his musical career.

"JoAnne, will you offer a prayer, this evening?" Rick asked, "then choose someone to do it tomorrow night. You, too, Oliver. I propose this format for each evening. All in favor?"

"Aye!"

Over the course of their journey, the "Zion or Bust" crew crossed paths with other small bands of people. They often traded for what they needed and shared what they had when they had it. Rick multiplied their food through the holy priesthood when they didn't have much. His flock also ministered to other trekkers according to manifested needs, whether emotional, spiritual or physical. On occasion, a few joined their party going east.

Oliver's respect for his dad grew, watching him follow the guidance of the Holy Spirit. Fires burned all around, but Rick never faltered and never led them into danger—from fires, at least.

Early on in their journey, they rounded the bottom of a bluff north of Vernal and found themselves in a camp of foreign troops. Watchful, Oliver's heartbeat jumped and tumbled, reminding him to send up a silent prayer. Immediate reassurance eased his disquiet.

~All these things shall give thee experience and are necessary for thy growth. Be at peace.~

Oliver practiced peace and complete trust in the Lord, but it did not come easily. "Cooperate and pray for them," his Dad's motto for dealing with ungodly forces, marched through his mind.

"Take them and search them." These few but well-armed foreign troops were thorough in their stoic inspection of clothing and backpacks. They roughed him up as well as some of his trek-mates, questioned them as to their purpose in the area, but released them about an hour later with orders to keep moving.

The next enemy encounter proved more difficult. Rick had led them out of Utah east of Flaming Gorge and north of Dinosaur National Monument to enter the northwest corner of Colorado, where they experienced more earthquakes and dodged more fires, then into Wyoming, following its approximate southern border.

"Why couldn't we have gone east from Vernal?" asked Oliver.

"I don't know," said his dad. "The Spirit didn't fill me in. Maybe there are fewer obstacles, this way."

"Speaking of obstacles… Look." A distant circle menacing troops were closing in. Their fellow trekkers stopped and huddled close.

"I know. But it will not result in death."

"You sure about that?"

"Yep. The Lord will save us."

He didn't, though, not for many days. The trekkers were captured and kept as slaves, doing all the dirty work the troops couldn't sully their hands with at a compound that might have been a resort in another life. *This place gives me the creeps. There's a bad spirit, here, but Dad doesn't act too concerned. He says it'll be over, soon.*

On his way back from the latrine to resume chopping wood, Oliver walked under a window of the neighboring building. He overheard the soldiers discussing their struggles in maintaining control over this country. The angry movement of the earth, an attempt, perhaps, to shake humanity from its surface, discouraged them. This battalion, cut off from their command post in every way, wavered between staying in place or retreating.

Ha! So they're not as invincible as they like to pretend. Good to know. "Dad," Oliver whispered as soon as he found him. "I overheard the soldiers—"

Gunfire split a tree branch close by, and he ducked.

"Get down!" Rick yelled at those too shell-shocked to take cover on their own. The prisoners nearby dropped. The guards fled their posts and joined their comrades inside the three largest buildings, leaving the captives to fend for themselves. All the enemy troops stayed hidden while returning continuous fire.

His dad grabbed him and said, "It's American guerillas. This should keep our captors busy for a while. Round up everyone on that side of the compound and head north. I'll look on this side and meet you at the base of that hill over there."

"Got it." He crawled on the ground between the northernmost buildings of the compound. Slaves were not allowed in any building but the latrine, so they were already segregated.

"We're leaving," Oliver said to each person he found, whether an original member of his group or not. Crawling behind and past bushes on the side of the compound away from the gunfire, he gathered a total of eight people. *I hope Dad found JoAnne. I didn't see her anywhere.*

A thought occurred to him. "Anyone in the latrine?" he asked.

"I'll check," said an older teen named Joni, who crawled back to the last building and around the corner amid more gunfire. *That's a brave girl.*

In about half a minute, Joni reappeared with JoAnne crawling behind her, bullets bouncing off nearby buildings.

"Thank you, Lord," he whispered. "I almost left her. Let's go, guys," he said a little louder. "This is our chance to make a break for it. These bozos don't need our help to battle it out."

"What about the others?" one wanted to know.

"They'll meet us out there."

⁕

Oliver happened to be walking next to JoAnne soon after their escape and admitted his frustration. "Dad always says we shouldn't fight enemies unless the Lord directs us to. Drives me crazy not to put up some kind of defense. It's definitely an exercise in self-control."

"And trust in the Lord," JoAnne said. "But I've pondered a lot about why the scriptures say that Zion will be 'terrible as an army with banners.' Does that mean we'll eventually be able to either disable or turn their weapons against them?"

"I like that," Oliver agreed. "Maybe we already have that power and haven't tapped into it."

"That could be. But I know for a fact that your father is led by the Lord, so we have to respect his counsel, and not fight back unless he directs us to."

Oliver enjoyed their conversations and walked with JoAnne more often, supporting her whenever he could. The more time they spent together, the more she shared her inner workings. One day, she told him how she employed the pioneer method of persevering.

"I aim for a rock or some other object far ahead, and say to myself, 'I can make it that far, and that's all. I can't go any farther.' Then, when I get there, I'll pick out something else to shoot for. It helps."

After that, Oliver suggested landmarks for her and coached her to reach them. He began calling her "Mama Jo" with affection.

"Thank you, Oliver. That means more than you know," JoAnne said. "I acquired a new stepmother at sixteen and struggled to accept her. Oh, I never meant to be bratty, but it took years to warm up to her. Having your kindness and care, I assure you, is a rare gift."

⁂

"I pray that my brothers back at camp have the angel protection we do," Oliver said to JoAnne on one of their walk-and-talks, somewhere in Nebraska, he suspected.

"We're so blessed, for sure," she said. "Oh. Look at your dad."

Leading the column of trekkers, Rick pivoted to face the group, holding out his arms as if to embrace them.

"You know what that means," Oliver said.

This brave body of believers gathered in a large circle, linking arms. The angels accompanying them hid them from the sight of a passing gang, as they had done a few other times, too. And it always inspired in Oliver a euphoric gratitude for such miracles. *Way better than being picked on.*

Trekking across miles and miles of incinerated prairies, they stayed between sandhills and rivers, or what remained of them, avoiding cities as much as possible. This interminable leg of their march, continuing into what may have been northern Kansas, tried Oliver's patience the most.

Day after day he and his fellow saints and their acquired ex-slave friends experienced a depressing parade of blackened or burning fields, homes, and piles of incinerated bodies. *If this isn't hell, it comes close. So creepy. It straight up reeks.*

The stench both horrified and discouraged talking and singing, but he and the others pushed on with the hope of a glorious new beginning once they reached New Jerusalem.

One dingy morning, the sun a mere lightening of the murky sky, they woke to find themselves surrounded by a fierce gang, sootier than they themselves and with a far worse aroma.

"Get up, toads. We have a ways to travel before we kill you."

The hulking spokesman kicked some of the slow risers having a difficult time separating themselves from the unforgiving ground, JoAnne among them.

In the past, Oliver would have retaliated, but after catching his dad's eye, he gathered meekly with the others. He knew the routine: Watch, pray, and leave at the first opportunity.

Rick studied the whole evil crew as he prayed. He watched for weaknesses and quirks and listened for God's direction.

"Notice all those piles of burnt bones?" The sizeable man employed his entire body to appear intimidating. "We did that. Breakfast, lunch and dinner. And you're next."

Maniacal laughter erupted from the others, a motley assortment of men, women and everything in between.

"Yeah, yeah, so you better do what Fletch tells you, kiddies," said a tall, skinny, gender-neutral human wearing chains.

Another person of non-descript features called out, "Hey, Fletch, could I have this one?" referring to Joni, who paled. "I'm hella hungry."

"We're all hungry," the big guy retorted. "We'll see what's in their backpacks, first. Maybe we won't have to eat 'em. Today." He strode ahead, leaving the others to round up the prisoners. "What I'd give for a pig to roast."

Their captors bound them and forced them to walk three-plus miles to a burned-out brick building, which served as headquarters. They roughed up their victims for sport, then searched them for food, beating them again if they found nothing. The gleeful quasi-demons called it "tenderizing the meat" and walked away laughing.

"Huddle up, guys, and let's pray," Rick called quietly.

They prayed in whispers and wept in silence. One of those devils returned later to slit Joni's throat, leaving her to bleed out while his cohorts started a large fire. Outraged, the captives protested, except for Rick, who resigned himself to the Lord's purposes of this trial.

Fletch growled to two of his minions, "Shut 'em up." More abuse descended on them for their futile protests. Some wept, some dry-heaved, but all prayed for deliverance.

Sorrow for this demonstration of evil washed over Rick. JoAnne stared at him, silently pleading, but he shook his head and mouthed the message to wait. The Lord through His Spirit affirmed that this, as well as all other trials, would transform into blessings and seal righteous judgments upon the wicked.

In their excited anticipation of dinner, the gang's rowdiness built to a frenzy, culminating in a huge fight.

Rick led his group in another whispered prayer, reminding them of the strength of the Lord they served, and to "count it all joy."

~Now.~

He broke the ropes that bound him before breaking everyone else's and took Joni's hand. "In the name of Jesus Christ," he said in a low and powerful voice, "Rise up and be healed."

The others sucked in a collective breath as Joni obeyed without surprise or comment, as if she knew exactly what had happened. Perhaps she did. Women pulled her into their arms, tears streaming, while she beamed with residual peace from beyond death's gate.

Veiled by the Spirit, Rick's group followed him out of camp. A safe distance from the cannibals, he led the group in another quiet prayer of gratitude and praise.

That ghastly-turned-miraculous experience took its toll on JoAnne. On a cool morning soon after, Rick insisted that the others proceed on their journey without him and Jo. He didn't want witnesses to his intended purpose. She had not recovered from the beatings, though she kept up surprisingly well considering her limitations.

This day, however, her fruitless struggle to move filled Rick with compassion. She resembled a corpse in her grayness, staring up at the smoke-hazed sky.

"Jo?"

"Rick," she whispered between labored breaths. "I don't... think... I can..."

"I'll give you a blessing," he said firmly. In that blessing, he assured her that she would be fine. He ended with, "Shake off despair. It hinders your progression. Rise and move forward to New Jerusalem. We'll be catching up with our companions without any trouble. Amen."

"I'm... to be healed, then?" she asked, still fighting for air.

"Do you have the faith to be healed?"

"Yes, but..." she whispered.

"No buts. Do you, or don't you?"

She relaxed and acknowledged his "tough love" with a slight smile. "I do."

Transcendent, pure peace settled on him as he and a host of sentinel angels watched her change from a wisp of her aged self to a more vibrant and radiant version.

Her eyes opened wide. "Rick?"

He chuckled. "We're both translated, now. And you look ten years younger."

"Don't joke, Rick."

"Not a joke, sweetie. Hop up and put your new-and-improved self in motion."

She rose with no difficulty, surprised. "I feel great! Wait. Who are all these shiny people?"

"Our angel helpers. They weren't allowed to appear to us often. But they've been with us all along."

"Miraculous."

"With God, nothing is impossible," Rick said.

"Thank you all for your loving attendance," JoAnne spoke to the flock of heavenly guardians.

As they acknowledged her gratitude with radiant joy and love, Rick said, "I haven't yet tested the warp capabilities of this upgraded body, so we'll take a test drive to catch up to our cohorts. I'm sure our angel escort can keep up."

"That'll be quite an adventure, but let's offer a prayer of thanks, first. I have a lot to be grateful for."

"Good thinking."

⁂

Oliver admired his dad for his superb leadership. JoAnne surprised him, too. She had fully recovered and functioned like a decades-younger woman, helping and comforting wherever needed. And most needed it, considering the horrors they had encountered.

Dad's priesthood power is phenomenal. First Joni, and now JoAnne. The Lord is really with him. I wanna be like him when I grow up, ha.

As they neared New Jerusalem in what had been known as Independence, Missouri, Rick's band of saints encountered fewer evildoers and absorbed more clusters of humble people. By the time they stumbled and limped into the Lord's central city of Zion, the New Jerusalem, this little army of God had expanded to fifty-one members. It took three and a half demanding months of travel to reach their goal in August of 2053.

"So many people are already here," Oliver said. "How many, do you think?"

"Not sure," Rick answered, "Maybe around eight thousand?"

"Could be. And it sure smells better, too. No nasty cremation fires."

"Not only is the air cleaner," JoAnne added, "it hums with vitality."

Oliver found great joy in following the example of the Zion-dwellers by helping in different capacities, including participation as a construction crew member. The buildings, somewhat primitive in contrast to big city structures, used more natural materials, such as adobe and stone. Many of the buildings incorporated objects gleaned elsewhere, including used bricks, glass bottles and scrap metal in unique shapes from sometimes indistinguishable origins.

After having worked in this new city for a mere three weeks, Oliver accepted the call to travel farther East to the state of West Virginia and escort people back to New Jerusalem, picking up as many as would join them along the way. It was not a cushy assignment, but Oliver accepted the challenge, dismissing his disappointment at not remaining in the freshest, cleanest and happiest place he had experienced since leaving home. *I've learned a lot from Dad about wise leadership and dependence on God. I'll do my best.*

Oliver and his assigned companion, Kenyon Pratt, a new arrival from Indiana, hit it off immediately. *He's awesome. We'll work well together, I'm sure.* They each bid their families and friends goodbye, before setting off for the east on foot.

"Shades of the early days of the Church," Kenyon said. "I just got here and have to go right back through my home territory on the way to West Virginia."

"I have to go in the opposite direction from home," Oliver said.

"Where's home?"

"Utah."

"Either way, it won't be easy," Kenyon said, "but with the Lord's help…"

"We can do all things which are expedient."

"Amen, brother."

⁂

As forewarned, Rick and JoAnne were called to serve in Africa and arrived using the time/space portal tucked into a private room in the office building where Elder Theodore Wilson worked.

Their assignment: to escort a coalition of saints through the center of the continent to the Zion community surrounding the Kinshasa Temple on the far western side of the Democratic Republic of Congo. In the recent war there, the natives divided their land into three new countries, one of which had reverted to the DRC's former name of Zaire. Each of these new divisions followed their own "laws," which included killing anyone from a neighboring state.

The Talbots' fellow travelers, whom they attended and nurtured on this trek, still had a few more days to go, at this point, before reaching their shining goal.

Being translated, Rick and Jo could appear as dark as the natives to whom they were assigned, or any other human form that they deemed necessary. All they had to do was pray, ask and receive.

"So, when this is over, I could appear to be your age, couldn't I?" Jo asked Rick one night in private.

He grinned. "Using it for vanity is not allowed."

"Vain? I?" she said with a smile, not in the least offended or deterred.

~CHAPTER 12~

Steam and Steele

*"Having been visited by the Spirit of God; having
conversed with angels, and having been spoken unto by
the voice of the Lord; and having... the gift of speaking
with tongues, ... and the gift of translation..."*
Alma 9:21, *The Book of Mormon*

Late August, 1879, the wilds of Louisiana

Stella tramped her way north through wood, bog
and bayou, eating herbs, wild berries and the fish she
caught, though those were few and far between,
struggling as she did to keep her cast dry. *The durn things
are mighty slippery. Wasn't a challenge when I had two
good hands.*

Still, what she could gather supplied her need,
and after six days, she neared the west bank of the mighty
Mississippi River, concealing herself in the thicket of a
shoreline plantation.

Grateful for the cover, she took in all the
steamboats, lorries and rafts strewn across this mother of
all rivers. She could have watched for hours. *Those tall
tales are sure enough true. All true.*

Shaking herself from her reverie, she cleaned
herself and her scuffed and muddy boots in the murky
water as best she could, mourning their sad state. *What
would Jacques think of these boots, now?* She returned
the sheathed knife to her right boot and donned Odette's
blue calico dress, ripping the sleeve slightly while

pushing her cast through it. *It'll have to do. Time to mosey on down the road, come what may.*

Stella dogged the riverbank, ducking behind trees and outbuildings to avoid rough characters until reaching Donaldsonville at the head of Bayou Lafourche. Asking around, she found no work and no healer there. Restless, she resumed her journey upriver.

Coming to the town of Plaquemine, she couldn't find a *traiteur* but did locate a doctor. She liked the graying, middle-aged gentleman at first sight, despite her people's reluctance to trust *les américains*—non-Cajuns.

More confident than the last time she had given a false name, she said, "*Je m'appelle* Ruby Steele. I read your sign out front, *Docteur* Grant (she pronounced it Grahn'), an' I could help you out here, if you would remove my cast when it's time."

Doctor Grant demonstrated that he knew some rudimentary French, so she and her new employer managed to communicate without too much difficulty, adding smiles and gestures.

He situated her in the back room, where he sometimes stayed overnight, he explained, but it would be hers for the duration.

She spotted a small mirror over the wash basin and used it to examine her scalp. The trauma had caused the hair around the scar to grow in white. She stroked the short, blanched fringe in surprise. "I heard tell of such a thing but never seen it."

"It happened to my mother," the doctor said. "She lost my father on the voyage to this country, and I suppose the shock of feeding his body to the sea creatures overcame her. She turned white-haired at thirty-four." This required a bit of pantomiming, but Stella soon absorbed the gist of it.

"*Ta mère?*"

"*Oui.* Let me check whether the stitches are dissolving properly… Hm. You had a skilled surgeon."

"*Chirurgien? Non, traiteur.*"

"A *traiteur* did this?"

"*Oui.*"

"It's well done. Fairly small stitches. How were you injured?"

"*Caïman.*"

"Good God!"

"*Mai Oui.* My god is very good," she replied, brimming with gratitude.

❧

That evening, Mrs. Grant's husband surprised her by bringing home a rather primitive young girl to their dinner table, though it in no way displeased her. In fact, Sophronia Grant welcomed this opportunity to practice her schoolgirl French on someone besides her husband. She chattered the evening away while feeding her exotic guest just shy of explosion. Or so said the guest.

"Now, Miss Steele, I insist that you move into our guest room," Sophronia said as the conversation wound down. "It will please me immensely." *Never mind that my well-to-do neighbors would have the vapors at such an idea. They would not allow this bayou beauty anywhere in their homes but the servants quarters, if at all. I, however, will do exactly as I please, and that includes placing her under my personal supervision. I find it suspicious that her name is not French. Is this swamp girl who she claims to be?*

"*Merci beaucoup* for the offer, *Madame* Grant," said Ruby, "but I have an enemy, an' must not be out on the street, if I can help it. Best to roost at the office, if it's all the same to you."

Sophronia and her husband both protested.

"You see," the young girl reasoned, "*le docteur* could sleep in his own bed from now on, barrin' emergencies, while I watch over anyone needin' overnight care."

She does have a worthwhile point. "Well, young miss," Sophronia said, "I have to admit that having my husband home more often would be a great blessing."

And a blessing it proved to be. The girl made herself useful in this regard many times, which eased her suspicions.

Mrs. Grant visited the office daily, although she had neither the temperament nor the stomach for nursing. She simply offered support or food, including tantalizing baked goods. Or, when patients overran the clinic, she placated fears and cheered up children as a mother hen would.

Her physician-husband did not raise an eyebrow at her unusual attendance. She suspected he knew her motivation and if he resented it, he never said so. Partners in a decades-old marriage tend to comprehend each other with minimal discussion.

Ruby never failed to welcome her, thank her and ask after her health, which made a good impression and further relieved Sophronia's misgivings. *I love my husband, and I desire to trust him, but any man in an intimate situation with a nubile young girl can be tested.*

"Oh, I'm about as well as can be, *merci*," Sophronia always responded. "A doctor's family has to wait for everyone else to be served, so it's a good thing I'm healthy, *n'est-ce pas?*"

Doctor Grant formed an excellent working partnership with his new assistant, as they learned each other's strengths, weaknesses and languages. He applauded the gusto with which she tackled any job within her scope, scarcely allowing that cast to hold her back. She managed some light housekeeping in addition to brewing up tisanes and applying first aid. Her contributions relieved a portion of his load, inspiring his gratitude.

He even valued the fact that she knew more than he did about certain methods of healing. Yet, a different aspect of her expertise caused him grave concern.

One evening at dinner, Sophronia asked, "How did things progress at the office, today? I regret that my ladies club took all my attention and kept me away."

"Better than it used to before Ruby arrived, my dear. She is quite helpful and even exceptional in some ways."

"How so?"

"She is knowledgeable in handling simple wounds and sprained limbs. She is well-versed in what to apply to reduce healing time. I would like to learn more about herbal preparations, myself, but do not have the time to gather such plants nor prepare them."

"Are they remedies that could be ordered from the general store?"

"Perhaps. Wouldn't hurt to ask, but *she* acquires them by sneaking outside the town boundaries to gather them herself."

"She did say she needed to avoid a dangerous individual."

"Yes," he said, still pensive.

"But something else troubles you, does it not?"

He plonked his fork down on the fine china dinner plate with a force that caused his wife to wince. "She also wants to apply the most ridiculous 'cures' that I cannot condone, and I don't know how best to discourage that without crushing her spirit. Are you aware that she once recommended a tisane of dog scat?"

Her own fork clattered alarmingly. "Good heavens!"

"Precisely. Her folk medicine can be troubling at times. Yet, she appears to be of sound mind and very bright. I'm considering teaching her a bit of surgery. Stitching up wounds, that sort of thing. What are your thoughts, m'dear?"

"First, make sure her hands are clean, but I suppose she would do well at whatever she attempted. Dog scat! Saints preserve us."

After spending another few days weighing the matter, he found opportunities to teach Ruby some minor surgery, minus any fanfare. In return, he learned more about herbs, despite the fact that most doctors he knew were moving away from natural remedies and embracing the use of chemicals, which in many cases were derived from natural sources. But he believed in anything that worked, and that included his young assistant.

He also learned that she refused to treat anyone without praying first, reciting her *grand-grand-mère's* philosophy often: "God's the healer, I'm the helper. It's only fittin' to ask Him to lend a hand, and to thank Him for the blessin'."

He possessed no religious leanings, himself; nevertheless, he would not begrudge her the right to her faith, apparently every bit as effective as the girl herself.

When the time came to remove her cast, he asked her to continue to work with him. "You're gifted, Ruby Steele, and I think you're an asset to my practice. I'd like you to stay on, with a raise in salary."

"Don't know as I should, *Docteur*. There's a vicious man on my tail. Thinks I kilt his wife, though he wouldn't let her have any treatment till it was too late to save her. Now his guilty conscience is salved by revenge. I've changed my name, but he would still recognize me."

"Do I understand you properly? You changed your name?" At her assent, he replied, "That may be wise, but 'tisn't likely he'd ever find you here."

"This ain't far enough away from Sainte Jeanne, *Docteur* Grant. Henri's a bloodhound, an' he's got my scent."

"Stay here, Ruby. You're well protected. I'll tell anyone who asks that you're my daughter. Clara left home when we lived in Boston and has not come to see us. No one would know the difference, except Sophronia, who would be honored, I'm sure. And if Clara did visit us, she'd find out she has a sister she hasn't met, yet," he said with understated humor.

Stella agreed with thanks, which pleased him. He had never employed a better assistant.

⁂

2054, New Jerusalem, America

Rick and JoAnne responded to Elder Wilson's summons to report on their mission. "Tell me all that you accomplished, and how you felt about it."

They took turns expounding on their time in the countries in central Africa.

"It may have been our most challenging assignment to date, yet the most rewarding," Jo said, "at least for me. The people there, those that follow Christ, have true power that comes of faith. Nine of them were translated on our way to the temple."

"They are the most remarkable people I've ever known," said Rick. "They glowed with perceptible light."

"I loved being with them. Elder Talbot did, too." Jo beamed at Rick with her own noticeable light.

One side of Elder Wilson's mouth quirked up. "You're still in mission mode, Sister Talbot. You can call him Frederick, now."

"Frederick?!" The two Talbots spoke as one, but Rick didn't stop there. "I've never gone by Frederick, and I have no intention of starting now."

"I think I've only heard it at the wedding," said JoAnne.

"This assignment requires more formality, so you'll go by Frederick and JoAnne, dress like the locals, and utilize your thespian expertise, in a way."

"Well, don't keep us in suspense, Elder Wilson," Jo said with a mischievous smirk. "*Frederick* loves acting."

Rick nudged her with his elbow. "So do you," he shot back under his breath, and she snickered. "You should have seen her bamboozling a gang of thugs in Africa," he said to Elder Wilson. "She had them believing we were cannibals instead of pilgrims."

"Our harsh encounter with genuine cannibals on our first trek here provided the idea," Jo said. "I told our dear brothers and sisters to face the intruders as if guarding me, so they wouldn't observe my transformation back into an old white woman near death. I asked Rick to tie me up and gag me, too."

"I enjoyed that part," Rick teased.

"I'm sure you did," she answered with a nearly straight face. "Anyway, he coached our group to hold their knives and other weapons up and act menacing. When the men approached, our brave little flock informed them that they were not willing to share, and threatened to eat them, too." She grinned. "The rovers didn't argue. Maybe they decided I didn't look all that tasty, anyway."

"Ingenious."

Rick put his arm around JoAnne's shoulders with a squeeze of approval.

"Now for the specifics of your new assignment," said Elder Wilson. "You'll be facilitators, again, this time for a trip to the year 1879. JoAnne, you'll be taking Winnie Crane with you as an extra pair of hands. She knows her way around that time period and will be a valuable resource. And the Lord Jesus Christ Himself will oversee this project."

Struck by the immensity of such a sacred calling, Rick reached for Jo's hand.

"Your son, Oliver, will also go with you. He, too, has just returned from his last assignment, so we're moving forward. This mission includes meeting his future wife."

"A future wife... in 1879? Sounds like a past wife."

The counselor chortled. "Funny, Rick."

"Intriguing," Jo said.

"Yes, but also fraught with danger. Not for you, being translated—for Oliver and his intended. She's a Louisiana-born girl named Estelle, nicknamed Stella. She used the name 'Ruby' to protect herself, though it proved ineffective in the end, and she died young. The Master wants these two to spend some time together in mortality, so you'll chaperone and teach her."

"Teach her the Gospel?"

"Teach her many things. She is, or was, a healer, but some of the methods she used were crude and superstitious. You will teach her good hygiene, better first aid methods, comportment, elocution, anything and everything you feel moved upon to address. I know she sounds primitive, but she is, in fact, intelligent, literate, humble and courageous. In short, she's a woman of integrity."

"She must be a wonderful girl," JoAnne said.

"Absolutely."

"That's a relief, after what his first wife put him through," Rick said.

"Rest assured that Stella is Oliver's eternal companion. Your task is to polish, refine and protect her. One caveat: you are not to use your power to heal her in *any way*. That is for Oliver to learn for himself. Later, he, too, will be in grave danger, and you must not heal him either. Let it play out as it will. Our Lord Jesus Christ will guide you."

Rick and Jo communicated silently before responding to Elder Wilson.

"When do we start?"

"Today, but first we must convince Oliver. Oh, and JoAnne? Now would be a good time to appear younger. Perhaps in your fifties. You, too, Rick."

"Ha!" Jo said with a triumphant grin.

Sunday, October 28, 1879, Plaquemine, Louisiana

Tree leaves turned gold and red, and the Mississippi River beckoned to Stella in insistent whispers.

I'm itching to move north as far as my boots or a steamboat can take me. Tomorrow's a good day to drag myself down to the shipyard. Best keep an eye out for Henri whilst I watch for promising transport. She practiced what she would say in English to convince a clerk or captain to give her a ticket and now felt prepared.

The Grants, bless them, did their best to discourage her from leaving, but she possessed the determination of an alligator. After checking on the boats for four days and toting her meager belongings each trip to the docks, she spotted the *SS Daybreak*.

A promising prospect. Oui, I think it will do.

With more gumption than money, she located the ship's clerk in the melee of passengers and cargo coming off and on.

"*Monsieur*, you are the clerk, *oui*?"

He glared at her, eyebrows touching.

"I am a healer," she said in halting English, "lookin' to trade my remedies for a ticket to ride this boat."

His lip curled up in a sneer, and he motioned to two deckhands. "Be off, girl. We need none of your voodoo witchcraft, here."

Seized by rough, leering men, she wondered why she had left a perfectly good job, and would the *docteur* take her back?

A women's voice she did not recognize said, "One moment, please."

~CHAPTER 13~

The Worth of Souls

"Whosoever therefore shall humble himself
as this little child, the same is greatest
in the kingdom of heaven."
Matthew 18:10, *The Holy Bible*

Thursday, November 1, 1879, the Mississippi River

JoAnne Talbot stepped forward with Rick and spoke to the surly clerk of the *Daybreak*. "We overheard your conversation with this young woman and would gladly purchase her ticket." She sent a deliberate glance to the deckhands detaining Stella, then rested a cool gaze on the clerk himself.

"As charitable as your offer may be, ma'am, we don't encourage the riffraff," he replied. "Soon we'll be overflowing with such baggage."

"What's this, Mr. Dodds?" The clipped tones of the newest person to join the circle emanated from none other than the captain himself, who flung a scathing glance at Stella.

"This little witch thought to beggar a ride, Cap'n. And these people are offering to buy her ticket," the clerk said with distaste.

"I see. Are you paying passengers?" The captain's cool gaze brooked no shenanigans, well-acquainted as he must have been with charlatans and schemers.

"We are. We are the Talbots," said Rick in his equally no-nonsense voice as the clerk checked his passenger list, "and are willing and able to purchase this young woman's fare."

"Hmph! I must agree with my clerk, Mr. Talbot. Please allow us the privilege of deciding who may board."

"Are you a gambling man, Captain?" Jo asked.

He scowled at them both as if angry that her husband did not keep a tighter rein on his wife. "Why do you ask, madam?"

"We are willing to wager this young woman will be no bother. Should she prove otherwise, we will not protest at being removed from this ship at your earliest convenience."

He met her firm gaze with his own speculative one, glanced at Rick and flicked his head at his deck hands. They slowly released their prisoner with impudent smirks and lingering hands.

"Thank you, Captain," JoAnne said. "I anticipate a pleasant excursion on your lovely ship."

He dipped his head the barest minimum courtesy demanded. "Welcome aboard, Mr. and Mrs. Talbot," he said without warmth. "Please excuse me. I have much to do before we can be underway."

"Of course, Captain," she said, indulging in a satisfied smile, which she directed to Stella.

Rick handled the transaction with the clerk. Jo guided Stella to stand off to the side while chatting in perfect French. Being translated did have its perks.

"*Je m'appelle* JoAnne Talbot. My husband and I are missionaries. We believe in bringing God into the lives of people the world over and educating them, when appropriate. Knowledge, especially such knowledge as you possess, generates the power to help ourselves and others. Do join us. We can benefit each other."

Jo reached for Stella's arm on the impulse to take it but restrained herself to a mere light touch. She yearned to embrace her and celebrate her return from the dead, if one could call it that. In more accurate terms, it was a heavenly pre-emption of death. *Heavenly, indeed. The last time I saw Stella, she lay dead in a casket.*

"You convinced *le capitaine* to allow me to ride, *merci*, but… I'm now in your debt, *moi*."

"Then you can redeem yourself by sharing your expertise," Jo said. "Didn't we hear you tell the clerk that you are a healer and want to trade your services for a ticket? Now you can."

"*Oui*, I'd be happy to do that, *merci*," Stella said with obvious relief. "*Je m'appelle* Ruby Steele."

⊷⊰⊱⊶

Monsieur Talbot joined them, saying, "We are so grateful to have found you. I believe you can be of great help in our work."

"I will do my best, *merci*." It amazed Stella to discover that these kind, first-class people desired to associate with her and even pay her way. A gift from heaven, and in light of her treatment by the captain and his men, a true balm for her soul. *Merci, Lord. I pray they are trustworthy. I am in Your lovin' hands.*

167

Madame Talbot and a handsome woman in a plain dress accompanied Stella to her stateroom, which held a small bed, a washstand and a simple wooden chair. Each end of the room held an access door. The one leading to the main deck consisted of shutters, which provided both privacy and air; the other, a solid door topped by a transom window led to the "Main Cabin," as *Madame* Talbot called the large common area in the center of the boat where the passengers dined.

"I never been on such a large riverboat, *moi*," said Stella, fascinated by the lovely accommodations and the Main Cabin with its decorative ceiling two decks high, festooned with chandeliers and heavy molding.

Carved details embellished all the whitewashed wood trim, and the elegant furnishings far outshone anything she had ever beheld. She stroked the coverlet on the bed with awe and tested the firmness of the mattress, finding it altogether satisfactory.

Delighted by the idea of so much space in which to sleep, Stella said, "I've only ridden on a little packet steamer. A dirty ol' bunk in a room with heaps of people was a luxury, *certainement*."

"You will enjoy it, I'm sure," *Madame* Talbot said. "And this is Winnie, who will be our lady's maid. She will help you with whatever you need."

Winnie said, "Let me take your bonnet, Miss Ruby."

As Stella complied, JoAnne said, "I must say I admire your white streak. It's quite distinguished and gives you an air of mystery."

Unimpressed, Stella worried more about the scar that traveled from the top of her head to the middle of her left eyebrow. Stepping to the frameless mirror on the wall to examine it, she dug into her pack for her chamomile balm. "I'd better put some more salve on this, so it will keep on healin'."

"I believe it's healing very well. I'd like the recipe for that salve."

"Of course," Stella said, pleased.

"Let me help you wash up, Miss," said Winnie.

"*Mais oui*, I'd love to, but I'd have to crawl back into this dirty dress, or a worn-out brown calico. They're all I have. Didn't have much use for dressin' up in my last place of employment, and no bathtub."

"We've brought extra clothes, Miss, as well as underthings that will do for you, I'm sure," Winnie said.

Uncomfortable with charity, Stella struggled to be a gracious recipient. "I suppose… I can't be lookin' like a mess o' duckweed," she admitted.

"It's true," *Madame* Talbot said. "You're a healer and a teacher. You must fit the part. Besides, a good first impression is vital."

With the clerk's treatment of her and the captain's contempt fresh in her mind, Stella had to admit the truth of that, but protested when Winnie produced two pairs of shoes. "You mustn't allow this, *Madame* Talbot. Shoes, they are too *chères* to be passin' out to all the beggarwomen."

"They're yours. And please, call me JoAnne."

"*Merci,* JoAnne," she murmured as she held the proffered shoes in her arms, marveling at her blessings, yet her walls of defense remained firm. She feared there may be a pitfall to all this generosity.

"You are most welcome," said JoAnne. "I suspect you are worried that we will exact some sort of payment?"

Startled at the question's accuracy, Stella held her peace.

"Let me assure you that our intent is to help, and in turn, learn from you. Although… we do have a handsome son you may like to meet."

Stella stiffened in three parts surprise and one part alarm, but the kind lady redirected the conversation, so rebuffing her offer proved unnecessary.

"I'll let Winnie assist you in washing up while I find my husband and get settled into our own stateroom." JoAnne moved to leave, yet hesitated. "I hope you don't mind—I have no wish to offend, but your speech patterns could use a bit of polishing. I'd be happy to help. That way, you will command greater respect from those with whom you must interact."

Stella's gaze strayed over JoAnne's shoulder to where the captain stood a few strides away, beyond the open cabin door. He glanced in her direction with contempt as he spoke with one of his officers.

Stella grasped the import of this offer and had to agree. *I have no desire to embarrass the Talbots. Fine feathers do not a peacock make, I know, but a bit of spit and polish on a pair of old boots does give a man or a bayou girl more confidence. If I learn to walk, talk and dress with greater care, my prospects would surely improve. It might also make me less recognizable.*

"*Merci,* JoAnne. I'd love to learn."

She did, with gratitude. Pleased to share her knowledge with the Talbots, she in turn absorbed all they taught her, including plainer speech and better word forms. During her transformation into a shinier version of herself, she caught the attention of shipmates and the crew and carefully avoided the latter.

Even the captain refrained from casting glares in her direction, though he never condescended to speak to her.

⁂

"If that woman's on the river, we'll be findin' 'er," Lefroy promised, watching Boudreaux's jaw twitch. Lefroy and his cohorts, McKee and Teasdale, had had woven a fine little web of compatriots and former shipmates as spies, one in almost every riverport south of Illinois. *Power such as this should be used for more than manhunts, but one thing at a time.*

"It would help to have a likeness," Teasdale said. "Like a circular."

"True," added McKee. "There's many a dark-haired lass with big brown eyes in these parts. You draw, Boudreaux?" He slung a sheaf of paper toward Boudreaux and Lefroy translated before signaling the other two to join him at another desk.

Henri scratched away, shoulders hunched, muttering now and then, using several sheets of paper, ripping up his first few tries. Lefroy kept an eye on him while he and the others talked strategy. *Man's like a*

171

thundercloud—always rumbling, fixin' to break open on our heads.

Their scheming halted mid-sentence as Henri rose abruptly. He flicked the finished product to Lefroy, plainly disgusted with having to look at her for so long. "It be a fair likeness," he said, his voice flat.

"*C'est bon.*" Lefroy held the portrait up to a sunbeam piercing the rain-spattered window. A fine young girl stared back at him. "Quite the artist, you is. We'll print this up and pass it to our new league. Let 'em know who they're watchin' for."

Teasdale studied the portrait. "Resembles you, ol' man," he remarked to Henri.

Lefroy translated, and the thunderhead burst.

"*Mais non*, she ain't nothin' like me! You find her, and I'll work your 'odd jobs' without pay for a month, *moi*."

Boudreaux huffed out of the linty, stifling room in a warehouse that served as their "office." The largest cotton company employed them to sabotage the competition by arson, burglary, or whatever mischievous means came to hand—enough to cause losses without raising any serious suspicions.

Lefroy eyed Henri's exit. *He gets riled mighty easy, certainement.*

"She could be a relative," McKee said. "You don't suppose…"

"Nah," Lefroy answered. "Boudreaux never had no fam'ly. All Cajuns have dark hair an' eyes, as do I."

McKee snorted. "You look nothin' like him."

⁓⚬⚶⚬⁓

Stella's days aboard ship with the Talbots included English and elocution lessons as well as expounding on herbal remedies, which sometimes led to discussions of medical theories.

During one fascinating exchange, *Monsieur* Talbot said, "Doctors tend to base their treatment decisions on empirical evidence, having scant knowledge of human physiology and the causes of disease. They are more concerned about *what* works, rather than *why* it works."

"*Mais oui*," Stella agreed. "We know what works, because it works in most cases, but why? Why does fat rendered from a *caïman* repel *les moustiques*, for instance? Or why does a tisane of lemon balm relieve anxiousness? Or why do two nodes of ergot make a woman expel the baby without causin' gangrene, as it will do in higher doses?"

JoAnne blinked at her, glanced at her husband and said, "Yes, we want to know *why* these things work. Our quest for answers is ongoing. And of course, we also hope to educate. We're often sent on missions to relieve the suffering of the poor and educate the ignorant."

They've been educating and relieving **me**, *certainement, for which I'm grateful. But why did she seem confused for a moment?* She decided to ask.

"Ergot is dangerous, as you have mentioned," *Monsieur* Talbot answered, "so we're surprised you use it at all."

"Ah, but I am so careful, *Monsieur* Talbot, an' it can save a weary woman many hours of labor."

173

"I see."

"It's good, Ruby, that you are cautious," JoAnne said. "On another topic, you are doing so well with your language lessons. I'm very pleased."

"*Merci*, JoAnne."

"Furthermore, perhaps it's time for you to call *Monsieur* Talbot 'Frederick'."

Stella caught the laughing glance JoAnne sent her husband, and the grimace he returned. "I do not understand," she said, a question in her tone.

JoAnne used a mock conspiratorial whisper. "He hates his name. I call him 'Rick.'"

"Reek? I should call him *Monsieur* Reek?"

Laughter erupted from the other two.

"Yes, that's perfect," JoAnne said.

"It's better than 'Frederick'," agreed the grinning *Monsieur* Reek.

⁓⚜⁓

On the one Sunday spent aboard the *Daybreak*, a congregation of Christians gathered to hear the word of the Lord and sing hymns. Unfamiliar with the songs, Stella didn't catch many of the English lyrics, but she enjoyed the Holy Spirit settling upon them like downy feathers. Even though she could plainly discern that they were not Catholic, she supposed that the Holy Spirit could land on others as well as it could light upon her.

That evening, she broached a question to JoAnne and *Monsieur* Rick. "The Protestants in the meetin', today, prayed to God without askin' any angels to attend. In my home village, it is not done. We believe that saints an' angels are ready an' willin' to move on our behalf an' attend to our prayers."

"They may indeed move on our behalf and attend to our prayers," JoAnne said, "but we believe that our Father in Heaven is the one to direct them, assigning them to whatever needs doing."

"But He is too busy to direct angels! That is the province of *Sainte Marie*."

"He is never too busy for you," said *Monsieur* Rick. "It is no hardship for Him to hear and answer your prayers."

"But I am no one," Stella said.

"You will discover your worth someday, my dear," JoAnne promised, "and you, too, will become a queen in heaven, as Mary is."

"*Mais non*! Forgive me, but that is blasphemy. She is the Holy Mother of God. I could never aspire to a place near her."

"You are humble, Ruby," *Monsieur* Rick said. "You love the Lord, you obey Him, you are virtuous and you serve others. Other than giving birth to the Son of God, that is all that Mary did. Her Son died for us, not just to save us from Hell, but to change us into heavenly beings, bright and pure enough to live with Him as equals."

Shocked, Stella decided not to argue. But as *Marie*, the Holy Mother of *Jésus* herself had done, she kept all these things in her heart.

Stella never tired of the sights, sounds and fragrances of riding this enormous river. All too soon, the Talbot party disembarked at Memphis, Tennessee, and secured rooms at the Chambers Hotel.

As they rested, Stella answered JoAnne's questions regarding her childhood and why she traveled. By now, she trusted her latest mentor enough to unfold the drama back home. She ended by saying,

"If I had it to do over, I would insist on attendin' Hélène in spite of Henri and provide the cures she needed. She was a good woman and didn't deserve her *crotte* of a husband." She sighed her regrets and gazed out the hotel room window to the south, where the river flowed into the far horizon toward home. "Ah, well, no use wishin' to reverse time. Can't mend the past."

"We will board a special boat, soon," JoAnne said, "that will allow you to do that very thing."

"Hmph! Impossible," she replied with an impatient toss of her head. *These people have such strange ideas. Reversing time? Bah!*

~CHAPTER 14~

Only Believe

*"And straightway the father of the child
cried out, and said with tears, Lord,
I believe; help thou mine unbelief."*
Mark 9:24, *The Holy Bible*

Early November, 1879, Memphis, Tennessee

Stella lingered in her regrets and memories, until the clink of two trunk buckles and the rustling of fabric caught her attention. Winnie removed exquisite ladies' apparel from the largest trunk, their quality surpassing the clothes she grew up in by a Mississippi mile.

"*Magnifique!*" she exclaimed, moving to investigate.

"They're yours," replied JoAnne. "This entire wardrobe was made to your measurements and preferences. You used to own these clothes. In fact, the ones we gave you on the last boat belonged to you."

"How can that be?" She sniffed one of the dresses, which conjured up strange sensations as she recognized her own scent mingled with traces of a rich floral *parfum* that reminded her of the little bottles at Jacques' store. *Eau de Jasmin. Jasmine.*

"Well, darling girl," said JoAnne, closing the empty trunk and perching atop it. "We've met before."

"Before that last boat, you mean? *Mais non*, I think not. I would have remembered that."

177

"Of course, you don't remember. You have experienced it only once, but for us, it has happened twice. I realize this is difficult to believe, but I hope your knowledge of my character allows you to at least consider the possibility that I am speaking the truth."

Stella's brow furrowed while she pondered this, then conceded with the tiniest of nods.

"You were almost a member of our family, before the man hunting you found and killed you."

At this pronouncement, Stella sank onto the edge of the bed. "Henri Boudreaux."

"Indeed. We traveled back in time to prevent it from happening. But here we are in Memphis, where Henri committed the crime. And he is still at large. It isn't safe yet to be out alone, nor to use your real name."

Her world ground to a stop. "My… real name?" All nerves stood at attention.

"*Oui*," JoAnne said. "Stella Rubidoux is a lovely name, but you must not use it for the time being. Going by 'Ruby' is indeed best."

Frozen, she stared at her tutor. She knew without question that she had not revealed that information. This revelation, together with the telltale signs of her ownership of the clothes, battered her wall of disbelief. She scurried to discover a loophole in the overwhelming evidence.

"Tell me how we met. If you didn't buy my ticket that other time, how did I manage the boat fare? You saw them preparin' to toss me off."

"You returned to your job of working with Doctor Grant in Plaquemine to earn enough for the fare."

Her mind reeled. *I never told her about Doctor Grant. Sacre bleu.*

"That's where Oliver became acquainted with you," JoAnne continued, "before inviting you to join us on our steamship. Now, let's pack up all these things. We have that same ship to catch—an extraordinary one, and very exclusive. It is the device we used to save you from being murdered."

Stella remained still. "I may be more like a lady, now, but I have no money, and I don't want you and *Monsieur* Reek to pay my fare, again. I kept my ears on and learned that ridin' with the animals and cargo near the boiler costs four dollars, so I know you must have paid near twice that for my room."

"There will be no fare, this time, and the shipmaster already knows you are coming. He's the one who sent us to retrieve you."

"The shipmaster knows me?"

"*Mais oui*, he knows you well and expects to renew his acquaintance with you, soon."

"What's his name?"

"He will introduce himself. We address him as Captain. The shipmaster, the pilot and the captain are normally three different people, but in this case, they are one and the same, though he does employ helpers."

"Someone who knows me well. Someone I met in my forgotten other past, I suppose. I'll have to be patient and wait until I can meet him… again," she said.

"That's the spirit," said JoAnne.

"You mentioned that I almost joined your family. Do you mean…"

"Marriage to our son, Oliver." Stella remained quiet. "Would you like to know more about him?"

"Not keen on marriage, *moi.*"

"Then, perhaps it's best if you wait until you meet him."

The mention of Oliver did pique her curiosity. On top of the announcement of time travel, however, doubts and fears clawed at her. She helped Winnie finish packing while she pondered this new development, caressing each item she folded, sometimes sniffing it for reassurance before laying it in the trunk.

"Winnie, I detect *Eau de Jasmin* on these dresses."

"That's right, miss. You favored jasmine above any other fragrance."

"I like it very much. Might we purchase a bottle of it, if it ain't—isn't too costly?"

"No need, miss. It's packed away among your toiletries in the smaller case. I'll set it out for you on the next ship."

"It's already mine? Of course, it is. Why else would it be on these… my… clothes." *Astonishing. All of it. What other surprises are waiting for me? Mayhap I'd better not ask. Could be too much for me.*

Watching the porters carry their trunks out the hotel door and onto the waiting wagon, Stella continued to weigh JoAnne's assertions. The temptation to slip away from these people and return to a solo journey crossed her mind. *All this talk about time travel and a life I cannot remember is too fantastic to believe.* It took great self-mastery to play along and step from the dock across the stage of the *SS Infinite* toward an unknown fate.

As she did so, peace dissolved the fear. Order and respect replaced the racket of the last boat. No one leered or grabbed her. Absent were the shouted curses of the crew at the deck hands, longshoremen and roustabouts, and gone were their bawdy songs. Instead, they sang rousing spirituals praising the Lord.

Stella relaxed. *Everything will be all right.*

The ship's two towering smokestacks topped with brass fluting reminiscent of great, gold crowns caught her attention, adding to the awe of this experience. This ship, with distinct though understated luxury, rode the water with the dignity of a king's palace.

JoAnne, Stella and Winnie settled into their shared stateroom, an even bigger room than on the last steamship.

"I could dance a jig in all this space." Stella explored behind a lacy screen shielding a generous corner of the room. "What is this big ol' thing? A place to wash clothes?"

"A place to wash ourselves. A bathtub," Winnie said.

"A bathtub? We could use it for a boat!"

Winnie demonstrated how to use the faucet, which produced hot water in a few moments.

"Never seen such a wonder, *moi*," Stella said. "How can this be?"

"Quite simple," Winnie said. "Water is pumped through pipes from the boiler."

"Like heatin' it on the stove, but easier."

"Precisely."

The remainder of the room contained three narrow beds covered in sumptuous gold satin quilts, an armoire, a vanity and a highboy. A Persian carpet of blue, red and gold graced the wooden floor. *Such comfort and elegance are fit for a queen, not for a bayou girl.* That thought reminded her of JoAnne's comment about becoming a queen in heaven. *Can't fathom that atall.*

JoAnne interrupted her reverie. "Rick and Oliver will join us later in the voyage. They have a different assignment from ours."

"We have an assignment?"

"Charitable service is the fare expected of these passengers. We will, among other things, return you to your home to help your friend."

I dare not believe it. Poor Hélène's moldering in the grave.

"Now, then," JoAnne continued, "It's a warm day for early November. Let's go out onto the deck and relax in the sunshine while we chat about tomorrow's work. Wear a cape. The breeze is still chilly. We'll leave Winnie to unpack and stow our belongings."

"Of course, *Madame* Talbot," her helper responded.

The two women, tutor and student, strolled around the deck and settled into comfy loungers. Deck chairs on other boats did not allow a person to recline. These, though still wooden, were curvy, slatted and sloped, covered in thin but comfortable cushions.

"So," Stella said as she settled back, "what assignment do the men have?"

"All I may tell you is this—they have gone to witness Henri's fate. Now, let's discuss tomorrow's errand."

⚜

Late February 1880, Memphis, Tennessee

Oliver's mental anguish gripped his entire body. *I did not sign up for this.* He and his dad, two out of the three men most invested in this trial, waited in the muggy courtroom heated by a tiny woodstove and an excess of spectators.

At first, he studied Henri in repulsed fascination. As the trial progressed, sickened by him and most of the proceedings, Oliver ignored all of it, except when called to testify. The dreary rain splattering the windows provided a movie screen, whereon precious scenes of Stella replayed themselves repeatedly, punctuated by his vision of pre-mortality.

When the jury spokesman read the one-word verdict, Oliver again watched Henri.

The bailiff translated the announcement into French for the condemned man, whose countenance darkened. "*Coupable.*"

"I hereby sentence you to be hanged by the neck until dead," the judge intoned, before pounding the gavel. "Court adjourned." The courtroom's occupants voiced their agreement as they rose to exit.

"Let's go," Rick said.

Near their hotel, the crowd thinned enough to give Oliver the privacy to speak his mind. "We should

183

have brought an umbrella… Why did we have to be at the trial? It was more depressing than this freezing rain."

"We needed to be there to add our witness."

"There were other witnesses."

"Ours carried more weight," Rick said. "I've been mulling it over, myself, and I suspect that when Henri originally killed her, before our involvement, he must have escaped the consequences somehow. Since I wasn't there the first time to capture him, maybe he escaped with the men we heard him call out for. I don't know. But what has helped me is to review First Corinthians chapter thirteen, concerning charity. You might try it. It may sustain you through Henri's execution."

Dread clutched him. "We have to stick around for that?" He ducked under the dripping awning to enter the dank hotel and sprang up the stairs ahead of his dad, eager to change into dry clothes.

"We've been assigned to follow this scenario to its final conclusion, which includes Henri's burial," his father said as he joined him at the top.

"Joy." Oliver found the key and opened the door of their shared room.

His dad gave a little snort of humor. "Maybe not," he said, "but when all this is over, we'll have a much more pleasant assignment, I promise."

"Oh, why? This has been *so* much fun."

Sarcasm notwithstanding, Oliver desired peace and clarity as well as faith in the future, so after exchanging his damp clothes for fresh ones, he studied scriptures, pondered and prayed.

Three days after the trial closed, construction on the gallows complete, Oliver and his father sat inside the jailhouse with little to view besides two wooden cell doors. After a swift glance, he ignored the women's cell altogether, despite their suggestive invitations and pleadings.

The time-travelers had received permission from the sheriff to visit Henri, hoping to impart a last message of Christ's redemption. *I doubt we could make much difference in Henri's salvation, now that he refuses to listen. We've spent an hour warming wooden seats, with nothing to do but read scriptures. Well, Talbot, there are worse ways to spend time. I just wish we could do more. Or leave. What good does it do to stick around?*

"Visitors for Boudreaux!"

Henri kicked and pushed cellmates aside and gave the two new arrivals a cursory glance through the small, barred window. He growled and returned to his corner, recognizing them as Stella's inept protectors and witnesses at the trial.

I have nothing to say to them. They should not have been fooled by the Rubidoux girl, but I care not. I care for nothing and no one but Hélène. He had buried his wife along with the only tears he ever shed as an adult. Childhood tears ended early on, for they did him no good. After his mother lost her mind, no one cared a

185

whit about him, not even the shadowy figure of his *père*, faint in his memory.

The prostitutes in the other cell attempted to engage the visitors, but the catcalls soon petered out, and he assumed the women were unsuccessful. *I wonder if any of them will be hanged. Some women deserve to die. They can be as cruel as men.*

Stella's death, however justified it may have been, did not alleviate his pain in losing Hélène. No balm for him, no peace, only death and dark satisfaction in his victory.

Henri kept his back to the door and the other inmates. The strain of dread caused sweat to trickle down his temples, marring his cloak of apathy. Now that construction of the gallows had ceased, the silence chilled him, bringing up the memory of the brief letter he received last night. The note had fallen through the high, barred window after Lefroy called to him from the rain-soaked darkness. His hopes of rescue fizzled as he read:

So sorry to have left you alone in your hour of triumph, but to shout or even speak our names for all to hear is betrayal, mon ami. But we wish you well. Put in a good word for us on the other side, won't you?

Bon Voyage, etc, etc.

No signature, of course. Bon voyage, yourselves. To the devil.

A clanging bell jarred and unnerved him. Two deputies opened the cell door, fought off his feisty cellmates attempting to escape and bound his and another man's hands without a word.

More men joined his escort, including Henri's visitors. He swept a cold glance past them as the lawmen led him out the door. *Why are they here? Rubbin' it in? Wishin' they could end me themselves? Hopin' to see weakness?* Defiance steeled him.

The cluster of men, Henri at its center, moved as one to the gallows, the bell still ringing. He spared no glance for the instrument of his death, keeping his attention on the ground and his defenses intact. His façade might slip should he face the death mechanism squarely.

A bare pine step appeared before him and a sharp nudge to his back compelled him to climb. *I'll never breathe the sea air again. All that's left to my nostrils now is this new wood, dust and my own sweat. I should never have trusted Lefroy or his friends. That accursed bell finally stopped. Oh, Hélène! I wish I had made you happy.*

Henri stumbled as the deputies maneuvered him into position. The lawmen hauled the other prisoner up and set him into place under another noose. Henri glanced at the second man set to be hanged, and a sudden camaraderie flared like a match before sputtering out. Loneliness squeezed him, the future a yawning abyss. He lifted his glance to the cloudless sky, the storm having blown over, but a black hood soon cut off all sight. The noose around the mouth of the hood against his neck weighed heavily.

What I would give for a knife to cut myself free. Henri twisted his wrists in futile defiance, close to suffocation.

He stilled, heart thumping, at an unintelligible announcement, expecting immediate execution. The voice then intoned a Bible verse in French. "'Blessed be the God and Father of our Lord Jesus Christ, which according to his abundant mercy hath begotten us again unto a lively hope by the resurrection of Jesus Christ from the dead.' Reach for *Jésus*, Henri. And may He have mercy on your soul. Amen."

A mechanism clicked. Falling, he cried, *"Jèsus!"*

⁓⁓⁓

Oliver scanned the crowd around the gallows for his father without success, until the pastor reading a Bible verse snagged his attention. *What the heck? Is that Dad in the role of preacher?* He barely registered what his dad said, until he heard the same verse read in French, and the words "Reach for *Jésus*..." sank in. *He did it. Dad accomplished what the shipmaster assigned us to do.* He echoed Rick's "Amen."

The deputy pulled the lever of the trap door, and Oliver closed his eyes at the sickening sight. His gut knotted at Henri's cry for divine help, the squawking crows an eerie backdrop. The other criminal made no sound.

Yes, Henri. Jesus saves us all. Even you. Even me. Save me now, Jesus, I beg of Thee. I've seen too much death. Please grant me some hope.

❦

November, 1879, the Mississippi River

I love this work. I'm happier than I have ever been.

Stella relished her charitable activities with JoAnne, providing food, clothing, fuel and blankets to the unfortunates living a hair's breadth from starvation. They sought out those poor souls in towns and cities along the mighty Mississippi. Winnie accompanied them, lending a hand with all the supplies the shipmaster had authorized for distribution.

With Henri ever on her mind, Stella asked about the dangers to unaccompanied women in the seamier parts of towns they visited.

"We have protection you cannot see," JoAnne said, "but you mustn't go out alone."

The women also provided medical assistance and received many words of gratitude, though never payment. *This is how it should be.*

Some days, the three women set up a place for donations in business districts or visited company owners to solicit funds and encourage philanthropy.

Stella spent all of November and part of December engaged in fulfilling charity work. Soon, the day arrived for her first assignment to go back in time.

"It will be a simple yet important opportunity," JoAnne explained, "designed to accustom you to time travel as well as to serve."

Stella kept silent, preferring to reserve judgment and cooperate with prudent caution.

JoAnne escorted Stella and Winnie into the Portal Room, all three wearing white pinafores over plain, modest, full-skirted dresses, not pulled back into the current bustled style. A large ring, tall enough for a good-sized man to walk through, dominated the small blue room. Indeed, no other object existed there.

This three-inch-thick, nine-inch-wide band-like ring composed of thin layers of different metals fascinated Stella. The outermost layer consisted of a white, opal-like substance. Its delicate colors shifted and sparkled, pulsating as if to music. Nothing stabilized the bottom of the large ring where it met the wooden floor, yet it gave no impression of falling.

Stella reached out a curious hand to the ring, but JoAnne pulled her back. "Not safe," she warned. "The shock would harm you. You must simply walk through it. The 'lightning' will surround and move with you. I'll go first, and you follow. Winnie will go behind in case you need a push." Winnie chortled behind her. "Have courage, and don't pause inside the ring."

The snapping and crackling "lightning" outlined the older woman's form as she stepped through the portal, then died back as she passed and disappeared. *Lord, give me strength.*

She glanced back at Winnie, who sent her silent encouragement. *Into Your hands I commend my soul, Lord.* As she took her turn, her scalp prickled and the hair rose on her arms and neck, but she experienced no adverse effects.

The three women emerged onto a battleground at dusk in time to witness survivors from both sides vacating the scene, leaving bodies strewn everywhere. Anxious, weeping women trickled in to search for their lost ones.

Stella offered open arms and loving support for the grieving, sometimes screaming, women. She, JoAnne and Winnie helped load the bodies of the dead onto wagon, litter, skiff, or travois. She mourned with and comforted the bereaved as best she could.

"Which side are ya on, North or South?" one of the mourners asked Winnie.

Ah, this is the War Between the States, some fifteen years ago. It ended when I was seven, but it still isn't over, even now. Her community and state possessed divided loyalties, which pitted neighbors and even family members against each other.

Winnie's firm voice said, "We are on the Lord's side."

After working alongside her companions the entire night, Stella balanced on shaky legs to watch the sunrise. It mimicked the bloodbath of the previous day with its own sanguine splendor, dyeing the sky and the river or bayou to the south shades of scarlet and persimmon, matching her stained pinafore. *The coming storm will wash the blood from this field, but not the horror. Jésus, Joseph et Marie, forgive them.*

"We must return to the ship," JoAnne said. "This way."

Stella tore her gaze from the horizon to stumble with exhaustion behind the other two women into the woods at the edge of the battlefield. The promise of a long and blissful sleep beckoned.

191

Magically, blue walls surrounded her, and the women descended the ship's stairs to their quarters, saying little. Thoroughly spent, Stella declined the evening meal and crawled into bed, not moving till morning.

~CHAPTER 15~

The Fluidity of Time

"And be ye kind one to another, tenderhearted,
forgiving one another, even as God for
Christ's sake hath forgiven you."
Ephesians 4:32, *The Holy Bible*

December 17, 1879, the Mississippi River

JoAnne roused Stella from a fitful sleep to give her the opportunity to have breakfast. "How are you, today? You missed supper, so I thought you might not want to miss breakfast."

"So tired." The young woman yawned and stretched, still prone. "But at least I got some sleep. Those widows and mothers had none atall last night, *certainement.*" She yawned again. "I wish I could have done more." And with that, she drifted off once more.

JoAnne let her doze until the midday meal, though Stella ate little of that. Afterwards, they took a leisurely turn about the ship. They passed other passengers, a collection of carriages used while in port and a few crates of assorted necessities. This vessel carried no payload; instead, its cargo consisted of supplies to distribute to the poor. Absent, too, from the premises were spittoons for the gentlemen. *Thank heaven those on board this ship do not indulge in that revolting habit.*

Stella sighed when they reached the deck chairs and settled into the first one. She situated herself, repeated that sigh and asked, "Where's Winnie?"

"She is off on errands of her own."

"How is it that you and Winnie are not as fatigued as I am?"

"We have done it many times and are used to it. It changes the body, so that one is able to do more before needing rest. In my day, before any cross-time missions, I would have needed at least two weeks to recover from our mission last night."

"Your day? You aren't from this time?"

"I haven't been allowed to tell you until now, but yes, this is not my time, nor is it my husband's. We came here for you."

"When is your time?"

"I was born over one hundred years after you were, in 1977. I may appear older, but in a way, I'm much younger than you. Let's just say I'm newer."

"You are..? I am...?"

"You were born more than a century before I was," JoAnne said.

"Unbelievable... *Mais non*, I suppose it isn't, after what I now know... This has been quite educational. The shipmaster sent you to me?"

"Indeed."

Another few days of recuperation passed before Stella voiced her uppermost question. "When will I meet the shipmaster, JoAnne? I have *beaucoup* questions, and you said that he wanted to renew our acquaintance."

"All in good time," she answered, enjoying her own joke. "You must be fit and thoroughly rested for our next task."

"And that is…?"

"Tomorrow."

⚜

Tomorrow came, as it tends to do.

"Good morning! Feeling better, today?" JoAnne asked.

"I am, *merci*. And hungrier, too." Stella stretched as she sat up in bed, the gold satin coverlet falling to the side.

"Excellent! I have some good news. The shipmaster has requested your presence as soon as you have your breakfast and wash up."

"Oh!" She scrambled out of bed. "I must dress at once. Winnie!"

"Over here, Miss." Winnie stood at the armoire holding up two dresses. "Choose one and I'll help you dress."

As a rule, Stella found the art of this *à la mode* dressing style tedious, but cooperated in full today, desiring to look her best for her interview.

"I don't suppose I need to add my gator pick to this fancy boot, today."

"Good heavens, child. Don't tell me you've been concealing that thing in your boot all this time."

"Comes in handy for a lot of things, *vraiment*."

"I'm sure that's true, but you are correct. You'll have no need of it for your interview with the captain."

After breakfast, she hurried up two flights of stairs past the hurricane to the texas deck and found the door labeled "Captain," adjacent to the portal room.

"Come," he said, as soon as she knocked.

Stella twisted the knob and pushed the heavy oak door. A fine figure of a man in a plain, white uniform, gazed out the window. Rather distinguished, he had medium brown hair that cradled the nape of his neck, an aquiline nose, and a close-cropped beard. *I hope he's more pleasant than the captain on the last ship.*

"You asked for me, *Capitaine*?"

He moved away from the window and approached, hand outstretched.

"Welcome, Stella. Close the door and have a seat."

She complied, her mind unsettled. *Why would JoAnne have given away my secret?*

"Don't blame JoAnne," he said as he strode over to the desk and sat behind it. "I have always known you."

His eyes were a surprising mixture of brown and flecks of turquoise, and his direct gaze penetrated her soul, striking a familiar chord. *Where could I have met him before?* "Why don't I remember you?" she asked.

"Because that is how it should be." Mystified, she did not respond, and he continued. "I believe that you are ready to step into a greater challenge. I've given directions to JoAnne, so she will instruct you. All I will tell you is this: You must forgive anyone who has hurt you, or will hurt you, completely and without reservation. Can you do this?"

"Even Henri?" He dipped his head. "Even *Père* and Georges?" Another nod, his direct gaze sharpening. She swallowed hard. *How can he be so sure they are the least bit forgivable?* "They do not deserve it."

"Perhaps not, but you must grant them grace before you can receive it for yourself and heal."

Stella studied her hands a few moments and raised her chin with a new determination. "*Mais oui*, I understand. *Jésus* commanded us to do that, and if He commands us, then there must be a way to do it, *n'est-ce-pas?*"

Le Capitaine brightened. "*Oui.*"

"Then, *oui,* I can do it. 'I can do all things in Christ which strengtheneth me'."

"Yes, you can, and yes, He does. I promise. However, you must rest a few more days before departing." With a small wave of the hand, he indicated the door. "You may go."

She rose with reluctance. "But I have many questions, *moi.*"

He stood and stepped to the side of his desk, laying his hand on a stack of books. The title of the topmost one stood out: *The Life and Works of Josephus.* "Stella, the answers you seek must come through experience. They will mean more and stay with you longer."

"I see," she said but made no move to leave. *I've met few men like this one—kind, warm, wise. Like Jacques, but stronger, somehow. I wish I could stay. Or come more often.* He gestured to the door with a slight tilt of the head.

Disappointed, she said, "*Merci,*" and slipped out of the office.

⚜

This trip to the Portal Room, Stella wore her mended blue calico and carried a small rucksack that she and her companions had packed. It contained food, water, medical supplies, extra clothing and various sundries. Last of all, she slipped the sheathed gator pick into an alligator boot. *Since this isn't a fashionable call, knife and boots may serve me well.*

JoAnne said, "I'll be with you on this trip, yet invisible, so you must trust that I will be nearby. The captain has consented to let you do this with supervision, but in essence, you will be on your own. One more thing—when in doubt, forge straight ahead. You will receive the help you need."

The first thing Stella observed after passing through the portal was the deep, heavy green of a Louisiana back-country. Spanish moss hung from large, stately trees in a canopy over her in every direction. That and the temperature indicated mid-to-late Spring, a pleasant change from the cold December weather she experienced this morning.

The third thing to come to her attention was the absence of her guide.

"JoAnne?"

"Don't worry," floated a whisper on the heavy air. "I am with you."

Stella remembered the earlier directive—*When in doubt, forge straight ahead,* and began moving forward through the trees, a lazy bayou behind her. She did not recognize the lay of the land, nor the littered property she glimpsed between the trees to her right, farther back from the bayou than most. She moved to pass it by but sensed that this residence was her first destination and swerved toward it.

As she neared the house, skirts swishing through the tall grass, a foul stench rose to greet her. She lifted the hem of her dress and looped around to the left to circumvent the garbage and feces, the odor intensifying. Coming around behind the house, she found an undernourished, dark-haired young boy. He was tied by a leg to a post twice his height between two outbuildings, no food or water anywhere.

The dirt-encrusted, insect-ravaged child, who couldn't have been more than four years old, sat up like a shot and cried out, as if he witnessed an apparition or worse.

Whoever did this to the boy might be around. Best stay out of sight of the main cabin.

Crouching behind a tiny building, which must have been an outhouse by the stink of it, she kept her voice soft and soothing. "*Pauvre ti bête.* You poor little thing. How long you been tethered?"

Fear on his face, he didn't answer.

"It's all right. I won't hurt you," she assured him.

"*Maman?*"

Taken aback, she said, "I am not your *Maman.*"

"*Tante* Lulu?"

Maman's pet name. Coincidence? She shook her head. "*Non.* What's your name?"

"Henri." In his immaturity, it sounded more like "ahn-WEE."

Thunderstruck, Stella asked, "Henri Boudreaux?" He nodded. "And your *maman's* name?"

"Celié."

As soon as her mouth dropped open, she snapped it shut. *My cousin!* Her mind whirled. *Henri was the one who did not die on the shrimp boats. My cousin is the one who killed me, but he could not have known. Nettie alone knew. I'm sure of it.*

This adventure promised to give Stella the key to a whole closet full of family skeletons, where Nettie had shown her one or two. "Anyone else here?"

He started to shake his head, glanced at the house in fear and back at her with beseeching brown eyes.

"Your *maman?*" she asked. He lowered his head, sheepish. "How long since you've had food?"

"You got some?" he asked with a flicker of hope.

"Some," she said, clutched by an urgency to flee. "*Désolée*, there's no time, right now." He drooped, the picture of hopelessness, and remorse seized her. "We'll eat later, I promise. I'm gonna to get you out of here, first." She snatched the gator pick out of her boot and set to work on the rope.

"Her won't like dat," he said in a dull tone.

"Who won't? *Ta mère?*" He nodded. "She tie you up?"

"*Oui.*"

"Does your *maman* not love you?" She spent her fury on the rope. *How could any mother...?* She fumed.

Was *Tante* Celié so completely different from her own *mère*?

"What is love?" he asked in a bleak little voice.

She groaned. *Jésus help me. Help me love him. I want to. Give me the strength to love him as You would, Lord.* "You have a *père,* Henri?"

"He comes sometimes. He hurts me."

Not surprised. The rope dissolved in the energy of her fury and disgust, releasing Henri's ankle and her tears. She shoved the knife back into her boot and grabbed the urchin in a fierce hug, filthy clothes and all.

"You listen to me, Henri Boudreaux," she declared, her voice catching. "*Jésus* loves you. I've been sent to help you. We're going to a place where you will have food and clean clothes and people who are kind to you. That is love. Do you believe me?"

He nodded against her shoulder. She pushed up from the ground with him still in her arms, grabbing a handful of skirts, and scurried off, toting her pack of provisions as well as Henri.

A bullet whizzed past her head. and Henri yelped during the immediate report.

"Thief!"

"*Mon Dieu,*" Stella whispered. "Not a sound, Henri. Hang on tight." She sprinted awkwardly, dodging behind trees to keep them between her and the shooter.

"Thief! *Mon pullet!*" Another shot. "MY chicken!"

First the man, now the mother. Do I have a target on my back? Jésus save us both! Henri clung to her with arms and legs as she wove a winding though hurried path through the trees. The hazy memory of what Nettie had revealed before she died flitted through her mind. Perhaps more details would come back to her when she was a teeny bit less occupied with survival.

Two more shots punched the stillness, farther away, this time. *She isn't pursuing—just firing into the woods.*

The two fugitives emerged into a clearing without a familiar landmark. "Which way, JoAnne?" she asked through her ragged breaths. No answer, but her original instructions came to mind, and she jogged straight ahead, across a clearing and into another wooded area.

Not ten seconds later, another shot sounded, fainter still. She carried the child at a walk another thirty yards, before putting him down. She examined the wound on his forehead and determined that it could wait.

"Think you can walk?" she gasped, her breaths coming hard.

"*Oui.*"

"Think you can run?"

"*Oui,*" he said, but being so malnourished, he weakened in about thirty yards and crumpled.

Stella pulled off her pack and sat with Henri at the base of a sycamore tree. After washing his hands and hers, she shared her jerky, water and some dried fruit. *This child is one meal away from starvation. He's hardly chewing it.*

"Slow down, Henri. There'll be more later."

After a good rest, during which Stella kept a careful watch, the two pushed on, crossing bayou threads twice. The first crossing they made on a fallen tree, then walked through cane fields; the second time, they caught a ride with an old fisherman who asked no questions.

As soon as the Good Samaritan let them out of his skiff, Stella opted to make camp before dark set in. She chose a fine spot a few yards away, nestled in a thicket near the water.

She led Henri to the thicket. "Sit here, *petit*. I want to clean you up and examine your injuries." She knelt in front of him and cleaned his face, using water from her flask before dressing his wound. It hadn't bled much, being a mere nick. He stared at her during the process, fascinated with the scar over her eyebrow.

"*Caïman*," Stella said. His sharp intake of air and wide eyes revealed his awe. "You have *caïman* bites?" she asked.

"*Non*," he said in horror.

"Shall I show you mine?"

"You got bites?" he squeaked.

"*Oui*. I fought the nasty *caïman*. Tell you what. You let me bathe the rest of you and wash your clothes and I will show you the bites." He took a moment, but he agreed. "Very well, Henri. Are you afraid of the water?"

He shook his head, not with courage, but out of fear. "*Caïman!*" he whispered.

"All right, *petit*. I will bring the water to you." Rummaging in her pack, she brought out a small, wooden bowl and a rag, and used them to scrub him with bayou water. "No sense in usin' drinkin' water for anythin' besides your face and hands. We do not have enough to wash the whole body."

After drying him off, Stella scouted around for catmint, cut a bunch of it with her knife, and handed a stem of it to him. "Rub this all over you," she instructed, then rubbed some leaves on her own exposed flesh as he watched.

"*Pour quoi?* I don't like da smell," he said, wrinkling his still babyish nose.

"Neither do the chiggers and *moustiques.* You already have plenty of bites and don't need any more, *oui?*" That convinced him. He wore out the leaves on his legs, then grabbed more for his face and arms. She applied salve to his bruises, cuts and rashes, and put him in a flannel nightshirt she had been prompted to pack. *Merci for that blessing.*

Stella rolled up her left sleeve to show Henri the scars, which he duly admired.

While she scrubbed and hung up his clothes on branches, Stella reminisced on her flight away from home. A suspicion that she would end up back in her village took root.

They bedded down for the night close together in the cool grass, dead leaves, and flowers, encircled by the remaining catmint. Stella picked the remnants of the latter from his hair, before pulling him into her arms to stave off any night chill, her gator pick close to hand.

Henri fell asleep first, his thin, innocent face the picture of contentment.

~CHAPTER 16~

The Healer's Touch

"And the King shall answer and say unto them,
Verily I say unto you, inasmuch as ye have
done it unto one of the least of these…
ye have done it unto me."
Matthew 25:40, *The Holy Bible*

Early May 1857, Southern Louisiana

First aware of her little cousin's soft breathing as he slept snuggled up to her, Stella opened one reluctant eyelid and peeped at an out-of-focus, molasses-brown head. The sun's infant rays frolicked in Henri's messy hair, creating an angelic halo.

Would that he always stayed so innocent and sweet. A far-off boat whistle wormed its way into her awareness. She jumped up in a rush, convinced that they must catch that vessel. "Henri, wake up!"

Reaching the clothes-adorned tree, she snatched the garments in a rush that calmed in short order, her shoulders sagging in disappointment. *I calculate we're too far from where that steamer docked. Won't be catchin' it today, now, will we? Best not waste a moment, howsomever.*

"*Tout d'suite*, Henri," she called. He sat up halfway, supporting a thin, tired torso with one arm on his grassy bed, the other hand rubbing an eyeball.

Checking his clothes for signs of dampness, Stella concluded that sometime during the night, a

205

certain someone must have worked on them. Besides being dry as they hung around on various branches, they were also mended and pressed, with buttons replaced. Even her beloved but worn alligator boots appeared new.

"*Sacre bleu,*" she whispered with reverence. "Miracles, they happen every day, and still, I am in awe, *moi. Merci,* JoAnne. *Merci, Jésus.*"

They broke their fast with the same dried food as yesterday. Henri inhaled his before changing clothes while Stella packed.

"Whut's yo' name?" he asked as he straightened his shirt.

She paused, her mind racing to form a plan. "Henri," she said, "would you call me *Maman*? It will help us." She spied a flicker of a smile on his face as he finished dressing. *I'll wager that's the first one in a long time. Maybe years.*

"Let's go, *cher,*" she said, taking his hand. The duo turned their backs to the water they crossed the night before and tramped off. Half an hour later, they encountered another bayou, much, much wider this time. Checking up and down the course of it, she spotted a dock sticking out into the waterway, some forty yards from their position. They followed the path that hugged the bank till they arrived at a trading post.

"*Excusez moi, madame.* Where are we?" she asked the somewhat familiar, plump young woman yanking dried clothes from a line.

"You ain't from around here, is ya?" the woman responded without pausing. "This here's the general store. My mister and I run it."

"It's charmin'," said Stella. Henri gripped her hand tighter, perhaps needing reassurance.

"Best spot on Bayou Lafourche!"

"I believe it. *Mon petit* and I are hopin' to catch a steamboat home. Will a boat be stoppin' by here?"

"Ain't no boats going to Thibodaux today. You can catch one tomorrow, though."

"But… the whistle."

"Yes ma'am. That was the paddle steamer going up the bayou, and it's already left. It'll come back down to Labadieville after it docks awhile in Napoleonville."

"Ah," said Stella. *Labadieville on Lafourche, not as far up the bayou as Napoleonville, and Thibodaux is down the bayou. Now I've got my bearings.* "Perhaps I could trade my services for a skiff or a *pirogue*?" she asked, eager for the two of them to be on their way.

The woman removed the last article of clothing, picked up the reed basket and straightened, gawking at Stella. "What happened to yo' face, if you don't mind my askin'?"

At this, Henri brightened and squeaked, "*Caïman!*"

"Fo' true? A gator got yo' *maman*? If that don't beat all! Well, now, I think you might enjoy visitin' with my little girl, *petit*. Why don't we go inside, and I'll fix you up proper with some biscuits and milk."

Henri's trembling hands tightened on hers in a silent plea. Stella returned the pressure and led him forward. "*Merci, madame*," she said. "You are too kind."

"Not atall! Call me Patrice. We're glad for the comp'ny." The woman trudged up the plank walk with the clothes basket on her hip. "Don't hardly see a soul, these days. Ever'body's got the *maladie,* and ain't no *traiteur* around for miles an' miles. Used to be one up in Napoleonville, but he passed."

Patrice opened the wooden door, which rang the little bell hung from the ceiling, and held on long enough for Stella to catch it before bustling up the stairs to the left. The store full of merchandise occupied the greater portion of the ground floor. It brought back sweet memories of Jacques.

"Ya'll come on up! My girl's name's Marcelle. What's yo' name, *petit*?"

Glancing at Stella for reassurance, he said in a puny voice, "Ahn-WEE."

"*Bonjour,* Henri." They followed Patrice up and into a cozy, cheerful space with a fireplace, two closed doors, and a small kitchen.

"Now, you two set right down at the table, and I'll fetch those biscuits. Marcelle!" Her visitors jumped at the unexpected shout. A tiny brunette, a year younger, perhaps, than Henri and dressed in a dainty floral shift, appeared at one of the two remaining doors. "Come on in here and meet our comp'ny!" Marcelle sidled in. "This here's Henri and his *maman*, uh... What's yo' name, *chère*?"

Lord, help me say the right thing. "Miz Patrice, may I tell you a bit of our story? Then you'll understand my hesitation."

"Why shore!" Eyes bright with curiosity, the cheerful woman deposited the plate of sweet biscuits in the center of the table built for four and smoothed out her cheerful red apron. "Sit yo'self, Marcy. Now, *chère*, what's your predicament?"

"We're escapin' from an abusive situation. Henri's *père* may find us before we can return to the safety of my childhood home; therefore, I fear to give you my name. I know you wouldn't betray me on purpose; nonetheless, one slip…"

"Say no mo'. I savvy yo' dilemma," Patrice said as she poured four mugs of fresh milk. "But we can call you *somethin,'* cain't we?"

Stella glanced at Henri, whose expectancy reminded her that she had not given him any name to call her except *Maman*.

"Call me Ruby. Please."

Since that satisfied the two concerned parties, she relaxed and enjoyed the small repast while Patrice filled the space with her *flux de bouche*. Stella did ask one question as soon as her hostess wound down.

"How much are tickets on the paddle steamer to Thibodaux?"

"They cost 'bout three dollars, and children maybe half that."

"The price varies?"

"*Mais oui*, dependin' on which clerk on which boat."

"Ah," Stella responded, deflated.

"And I kin see by yo' face ya ain't got close to half that much, Miz Ruby."

"You are a most perceptive woman, Miz Patrice. Yet, the afflicted need a healer, and since I am one," pausing to accommodate the other woman's surprise, "perhaps I can be of assistance. Do you suppose we might collect enough 'gifts' by tomorrow to pay for the boat if we visited everyone in the area who needs me?"

"Prob'ly so, though they may not bring hard cash. They'll bring what they have. But I'm sure you know that." The little bell jingled downstairs. "Ah!" she said. "Customers. *'Scusez moi.*" She barreled down the stairs, leaving the three of them alone.

"Marcy!" she hollered on her way down. "Mind yo' manners!"

As the good woman hit the bottom step, those left at the top let out a collective sigh. *That woman is a hurricane,* Stella decided. Marcelle's demeanor echoed that sentiment.

As Patrice attended to her customer, those remaining upstairs had a chance for some quiet conversation, yet no desire for it. Stella savored the delicious silence along with the baked treats. No more than ten minutes later, though, she braced for impact when the wind changed, and the hurricane blew back upstairs.

"That was Miz Etienne," Patrice said before she hit the top step. "She needed medicine for the baby's colic. Good thing he don't have the *maladie*. We're out of ever'thin' for that."

"Do you have much Mamou growin' 'round here, Miz Patrice? And perhaps some Prickly Ash and Calumba root?"

"Could do, Ruby. I recall a thicket of Calumba out back a ways an' to the south. Whut you thinkin'?"

"We'll need it to battle the *maladie*, plus more prayers than a passel of priests. Henri and I will scout around outside. You have a large sack I can borrow?"

The two seekers investigated the woods and boggy places for medicinal plants, shrubs and trees they could use. Stella instructed Henri on many things that morning. He surprised her by repeating and remembering what she said.

Might Henri replace me someday as a healer in Sainte Jeanne, since my service there ended so soon? Or... will rescuing Henri change everything?

By the time they returned to the store, Patrice's husband, Sebastien, had arrived. He agreed to tend Marcelle while his wife escorted Stella and Henri by skiff all around her community's islands. She stayed in the boat and knitted, so as not to bring home the disease to her family.

"I don't know why we ain't been infected, considerin' we are the hub of our settlement," she explained, "but best not tempt the Good Lord."

"We'll stay in this end of the skiff as we travel around," responded Stella, "and we'll wash outside before enterin' your home. And Miz Patrice, we haven't discussed lodgin'. Do you know of a place for us to sleep tonight? I don't suppose there's an inn anywhere close by?"

"What a good idea, Ruby! We been huntin' for another way to bring in some money, and an inn would be just the thing. There is one up in Napoleonville, but as for yo' present need, we have some empty attic space not doin' a blessed thing but settin' there."

They visited all the homes in need that day, with Patrice sharing bits of information that might help her navigate each family's situation. Stella sometimes found the herbs she needed for a particular home between bayou and front porch. Herbal medicine was familiar to everyone; however, most of the residents she visited had not stored up much for the present crisis, nor were they healthy enough to go traipsing around to find and prepare it themselves.

Many prayers ascended to heaven that day from the healer on behalf of the sufferers. Stella witnessed a few prayers from the patients, too, in gratitude for the blessing of relief. And everyone wanted to know from whence she hailed.

"Merely passin' through, stayin' with Miz Patrice and *Monsieur* Sebastien for another day," she answered, informing them indirectly to be prompt with their thank-offerings and where to leave them.

Henri, fascinated by the entire process, hovered too close to the afflicted on occasion, but other than that, made himself as useful as a four-year-old can. He would listen to the prayer, watch Stella prepare a remedy, then tidy up here and there or fetch something on demand from the larder or henhouse, for which he received thanks from both the healer and her clients.

For the most part, though, he watched and learned as "Ruby" explained concepts such as washing hands well with soap after cleaning up diarrhea, and general handwashing at all times, even during health. She enjoyed having a bright pupil.

The last family attended to, Stella leaned back in the skiff with the tiniest of moans, exhausted from the day's labors. Henri cuddled up in the crook of her arm with his own sigh.

Patrice put down her handwork and took up the oars.

"You've made quite a bit of progress on your knittin', Miz Patrice," Stella remarked.

"I did. A good day's work for you and me, both."

"Indeed it was," said Stella with a squeeze of the boy's shoulders. "Indeed it was. You're a good helper, Henri." He brightened right before her eyes. *All he needs is kindness. As God is my witness, he shall have it.*

After a simple supper, Stella said, "*Merci beaucoup*, Patrice and Sebastien, for takin' in a couple of strays, and sharin' your meal with us. I hope I'm not bein' rude by sayin' I must find a place to lay my head, soon, or I will join *mon petit* an' sleep on my plate."

She gathered Henri in her arms before his drooping head absorbed much meat sauce, and the master of the house and store excused himself to sit by the fire and enjoy his pipe.

His wife led Stella to the empty attic space, with pallets of quilts already on the floor.

"I hope this will do for you and the boy," said Patrice in hushed tones. "I'm afraid it's all we have."

Stella brushed off her apologies. "This is a king's palace compared to sleepin' under trees. *Merci.*"

"*Pas de quoi.* You're welcome, o' course. But maybe by the next time you visit, we'll have that inn, Miz Ruby, with proper beds."

The following morning, Stella made herself useful by sweeping and dusting the store merchandise and any other odd jobs Patrice and Sebastien could rustle up, while Henri and Marcy played outside. Soon, villagers trickled in, some recognizing her.

Gifts piled up on the wooden plank porch, so the children were recruited to gather them and bring them inside. Sebastien set up baskets on a table to collect the offerings, though not much accumulated in the way of cash.

"Tsk. Now, didn't I say that might be the way of it?" Patrice commented when she examined the gifts. "Tell you what. We'll figger this out after supper." She glanced at her close-mouthed husband, but of course Patrice filled any undisturbed air with ease. "I'm certain we can get you those boat tickets."

"*Merci*, Patrice, Sebastien," Stella replied. "This might work."

"It might at that." The kind woman beamed. "And thank *Jésus*, while you're at it. He shorely has a way of helpin' us out, now don't He?"

"He surely does, dear lady."

It took a fair bit of deliberation, that evening, to select what food gifts should go with them on the paddle boat, and what should stay and be exchanged for the ticket or extra cash. Though convinced she should leave the chickens and the eggs behind, it pained her to give up the fish and venison.

"If only there were time to dry all this. What a fine thing to take on the trip!"

"We have some jerky we could exchange for the chickens an' all, if you like, Ruby," Patrice offered. "And some of the eggs could be boiled."

"Oh, now that would be grand. If we can trade with you for the price of tomorrow's boat, the remainder must go to purchase a *pirogue* for the last leg of our journey." They both deferred to Sebastien, whose dour face daunted them a bit; however, in the end, Stella garnered enough for their needs and a little extra—some more jerky thrown into the bargain.

"Well!" she exclaimed. "That's a generous *lagniappe*. More than I ever expected. *Merci beaucoup.*"

The next morning, before the sun burned off the mists, Stella and Henri waited down by the dock for the steamer to come, their food for the journey knotted into two large kerchiefs. Patrice, keeping watch over Marcy, handed Stella a green calico bonnet, another generous *lagniappe*.

A paddle steamer sounded its whistle and rounded the bend a hundred yards or so up the bayou.

"Ruby, *chère,* it's purely been a pleasure." Her plump arms enveloped Stella in a warm embrace. "I do wish you could stay and be our very own *traiteuse.*"

"*Merci*, Miss Patrice," she replied. "I wish I could." A field across the bayou visible through the trees snared Stella's attention. *Is that…? Oui. Sacre bleu.*

"You ain't comin' down with the *maladie*, now is ya?" Patrice asked.

"*Non.*" Stella, transfixed by the vista before her, relived memories of assisting war widows one terrible night in the future. "I see a devastatin' battle in that field 'cross the bayou not many years from now."

She dragged her teary gaze from the battlefield to Patrice. "But take courage. I'll be back to help you that night." She now understood why the first sight of her hostess sparked a phantom of recognition. Night-veiled images of a mortally wounded, nearly unrecognizable Sebastien and his soon-to-be widow from Stella's first cross-time mission flashed in her mind, stunning her and filling her with pity.

⁂

Patrice, struck dumb for once, gaped at Ruby. The boat met the dock, and her unusual guests boarded it without another word. She watched the back of the steamer chugging down the bayou while her daughter waved. Henri waved back. His *maman*, who stared at the field across the water at least as long as the boat stayed in sight, did not.

Is she a traiteuse? A prophetess? Or a witch? Troubled, Patrice took Marcy by the hand and returned home.

~CHAPTER 17~

Through a Glass Darkly

"O the depth of the… wisdom and knowledge
of God! how unsearchable are his judgments,
and his ways past finding out!"
Romans 11:33, *The Holy Bible*

May 1857, Bayou Lafourche, Louisiana

Stella, Henri and most of the other passengers sat on rocks or grassy areas, fanning boredom and impatience away more than the late spring heat. They had little to do besides watch the boat crew labor to free their grounded vessel, a common issue when the water level dropped.

Fussing with Henri's hair's a symptom of my frustration, certainement. Poor child. He's handed from one crazy mother to another. Why couldn't I be taken back through the portal? Or given a pirogue? I could have paddled straight home to Bayou Black without wasting time going down to Thibodaux, first.

An enlightening thought interrupted her agonizing. She shook her head at her own foolishness.

"Henri," she said. He raised his head to study her. "I'm too spoiled, *moi*, receivin' so many miracles."

It must have been God's timing for me to be in Labadieville to help all those people, to do what I do best. Why is trust in God so difficult for us mortals? We do not have His vision. We desire the pilot's job, not to languish in the back end of the boat, or in our case, the shore. Her epiphany brought relief. *Thy will be done, Lord. Just promise to show me someday why we are stuck here going nowhere. Of what possible use is it?*

That night, as they lay in their narrow bunk (and lucky to have it), Stella waited for Henri to sleep, before whispering into the dark over his head, "JoAnne? What is it that I cannot comprehend? Why is this taking so long?"

"Shh, dear girl." Her mentor's voice came as soft as mist. "Impatience hinders peace. You will soon have your answer. Let this journey unfold as a slow bayou with all its twists and turns."

Mais oui, of course. And with that assurance, Stella could relax and drift off to sleep.

⁂

Early the next morning, the captain announced that all were permitted to stay aboard while the crew labored to free the boat, confident their journey would resume in short order.

Another sternwheeler approached, whistle blasting, heading up the bayou. Stella ignored it until Henri suppressed a cry of fright and hid behind her, burying his face in her dress.

"*Père!*" he whispered in terror. Peering across the fifty feet of copper water between the boats, she caught sight of her father in silhouette, elbows on the rail at the far end of his steamer. She gasped and jerked her head down, shielding her face.

As she peeked around the brim of the bonnet Patrice gave her, horror crawled over her skin. *Père.* It was the man knew as Paul Rubidoux. Her chest constricted with a dull ache. "I thought your *père* was a Boudreaux."

"*Mais oui,*" said Henri. "Phillipe Boodwoh. *Maman* says his name *beaucoup*. She hates 'im. She fwoze t'ings."

The door she assumed forever shut sprang open, spewing answers right and left, shouting in her mind.

Sacre bleu, il est mon frère! My own brother! Maman's friend who saw Père with another woman recognized Tante Celié. Maman knew and told Nettie. That's why he killed her!

The boats just passed each other when Stella risked one more peek. She locked eyes for an eternal second with that brutal man and jerked back around, shaking with fright.

~Fear not.~

That bracing admonition of spirit and verse enveloped her mind, quieting her nerves as she wrapped her arms around Henri.

~It is all unfolding as it should.~

Stella's anxiety eased. *Mais oui, of course. This needed to happen. He'll get off that boat at the next stop and come after us. We may have two days' head start, or perhaps even three, if his boat hits a snag.*

Her insight deepened. *What if we hadn't crossed paths? He would have stopped in Labadieville, gone to Celié's place, and when he came home, he would know that I am an imposter. If the boat had not been grounded and behind schedule, we might have met him in Thibodaux or even closer to home. Merci, Lord. Thy wisdom is beyond my comprehension.*

Their paddle boat broke free of the duckweed and mud and resumed their eastward journey amid riotous cheers, a fitting backdrop to her own enlightenment.

Relief perked up even the grumpiest passengers. In a matter of an hour and a half, the paddle steamer reached Thibodaux and pulled up to the wharfboat to unload.

With her newfound faith in the Lord's care, Stella walked with more confidence. She and Henri crossed the stage from the paddle boat, commenting on both the fascinating and mundane merchandise stacked inside the wharfboat awaiting retrieval. When Henri's attentiveness waned, she led him across the gangplank and surveyed the dock.

"Needin' transportation, are ya, little miss?" A nearby cabbie twitched a loop of reins, while his horse pawed the ground, itching to move.

"I could use a *pirogue*. Would you know how I could come by one?"

"A *pirogue*, you say? I happen to have an old one I won off a Houma man. Ain't pretty. You int'rested?"

"*Mais oui*, though… I can't pay much."

"Ain't asking much. Be good to get the ugly thing off my hands. What would *I* be needin' with it, ehn? Cain't put my horse and dray in it!"

Crude in form, this *pirogue* had not been carved by the artist Stella's father was. On the other hand, it functioned well. She stationed her newly-discovered brother in the front, while she paddled in back. *Ahh. It's invigorating to take the oars of a pirogue with both arms in fine shape this time. Bless Barnabè.*

Henri exclaimed over the fine view, other boats and the critters he spied in the water and in trees, appearing more excited than frightened to glimpse alligators here and there. Skinny arms wide, he threw his head back and joyously crowed.

He's had such a troubled life, but he's so happy, now. Merci, Lord. May it do him good.

The trip home via bayou from Thibodaux to Sainte Jeanne took much less time than it did going the other direction as she ran away from home; however, even at a straight shot on the main channels, they couldn't do it in what remained of the day. Stella pulled out at a promising spot and made camp.

Being late Spring, dark took its sweet time coming; however, the *moustiques* did not. *Those bloodsuckers love dusk.* Henri slapped at them while gathering more catmint, rubbed it all over and donned his nightshirt, this time by himself. Stella delighted in the progress he had made in such a short time.

By the time the two wayfarers found Nettie's place the next day, it drew on towards early evening. Stella hardly recognized the property. *The house is whitewashed and the trees are smaller. That's right. We're here sometime before my birth, but how long before?*

221

She strolled towards the little house, holding onto Henri's hand, savoring the air of home. It *was* her home, much more than the shabby shanty she shared with her father and Georges. And at that moment, a younger and more robust Nettie emerged from the cabin's lone door with an egg basket.

"Nettie!" she cried.

Nettie dropped her basket, exclaiming, "Oh!" "Celié? You're back! When d'you git here?"

Sadness washed over Stella. She would not be able to tell her cherished godmother and *grand-grand-mère* her true identity. That took the joy down a few ticks. "You remember me?" she asked.

"Remember?" Nettie stooped to pick up the basket, then straightened and moved closer. "Of course I know you, chil'. I'm not senile, *moi*. And this must be your son," she said, cocking her head in his direction.

"This is Henri Boudreaux," Stella said.

"*Bonsoir*, Henri. *Moi,* I'm Nettie LeBlanc. Come with me to fetch some eggs, then we'll have supper. You must be starved!" Nettie led them into the henhouse, as Stella drank in the surroundings, stink and all. *I love chickens. This used to be one of my favorite chores.*

And she loved Nettie, who chatted the entire time while gathering eggs.

"Lulu said you was out Assumption way. How long did it take to git here? You been to see your *maman*, yet?" she asked, not waiting for an answer as she led her visitors back to the small house and up the steps. "She's been poorly ever since my boy René passed. Ya'll come on in. Got some catfish gumbo on the stove, some cornbread hot out the oven…"

Lulu said? Is Maman alive, now? And my Mamère Charlotte, too? Stella didn't register all of Nettie's chatter, distracted by this skin-tingling sensation. *Could I perhaps be near them? Touch them? Is it all a dream from which I must wake? Will it all fade in the morning? This is too sweet and rare to lose again.*

She teetered between not wanting to arouse Nettie's suspicion or even concern, and the desire to soak it all up and bask in the joy. One tear escaped before she could stop it.

"Celié, you all right?" Nettie's worried face brought her back to the task at hand.

"I don't know where to start, *moi*."

"Well, you might start by pullin' up a chair and havin' a seat. No hurry. Whatever is on your mind can wait a blessed minute while you eat."

Nettie plopped down bowls of soup and a pan of cornbread as Stella and Henri eased onto their homemade chairs—the same chairs Stella remembered.

Seating herself on a milk can topped with a cushion Nettie asked, "Shall I pray?"

Stella, overcome by emotions, stared at Nettie, forgetting to bow her head. *If this is a dream, may I sleep forever.*

"Virgin Mary, Holy Mother of God, we are thankful for our bounteous blessin's, an' for this food we have before us. May it do us the good we're in need of. We thank you that Celié and Henri are here an' safe, an' we pray that we may reckon-ize the hand of God ever' day in our lives. In the name of the Father, the Son an' the Holy Ghost. Amen."

Nettie crossed herself and twisted around on her milk can to grab a bowl of butter to add to the little table. After buttering the cornbread and passing it around, Nettie put down her knife and said, "Now. You gonna tell me what happen' to your face?"

Henri spoke for the first time since their arrival, delighted that the conversation hit upon his favorite topic. "*Caïman.*"

"*Sacre bleu,* Celié! Do tell!"

Her altercation with the gator brought Stella no pleasure but describing it surely did. Her spell-bound audience gave her a dash of appreciation for her tangle with the bayou beast.

Henri sighed with obvious satisfaction and admiration for his rescuer. Stella stifled a laugh.

In the back of her mind, though, she prayed to be given what to say on the more important subject that must be dealt with. She also desired heaven's help to keep to the truth as much as possible, and that this would all play out according to God's will and timing.

After downing another two bites of gumbo, enjoying the exclamations from Nettie on her intense ordeal, Stella laid down her spoon and cleared her throat. "Miz Nettie... I have reason to believe that Henri's *père* and Lulu's husband are the same man." Nettie froze with her spoon suspended, dripping elastic gumbo broth. "He is going by the name of Phillipe Boudreaux. He only comes to us on occasion, and when he does, he is cruel."

Her glance strayed to Henri, who kept his head down, spoon in hand.

"Caught a paddle steamer out of Labadieville, two days ago," Stella continued, "and passed him going up Bayou Lafourche on our way down to Thibodaux. He saw us, so he will surely be here, *tout d'suite*. In two, three days, mayhap. The water level is low, and the duckweed thick. In any case, we need your help and protection."

Nettie banged her spoon back into the bowl, making Henri jump. "That man! I never liked him, *moi*! He's horrible to Lucille and leers at all the girls, grabbin' at 'em at dances or whenever he can sneak a pinch. I would give a *lot* to... Wait. Hold on. Hold on just a chigger-bitty minute." Her eyes met Stella's with a new light. "I has me an idea, *moi*."

⚬◦❊◦⚬

Babette LaCour, the designated bait in the trap set for Paul Rubidoux, kept vigil at the general store, confident in her power to snare any man within the radius of her smile. *Père's near to having a fit that I'm doing this, but he admitted it's needful. Paul's a dangerous man. He's gotta be stopped.*

When the varmint at last appeared, she bid Jacques *adieu* and the storekeeper bid her *bonne chance*. With his "Good luck" to shore up her courage, she made sure the screen door slammed behind her to catch her prey's attention.

Paul searched all over for Celié and Henri, frustrated that since he wasn't supposed to be acquainted with them, he couldn't ask outright regarding their whereabouts. His agitation intensified. *Where could they be?*

As he approached the general store, the screen door banged. *Babette. Such a tasty morsel.* His imaginings intensified as he watched her saunter down the boardwalk to join him on the path.

"*Bonjour,* Paul," she cooed. "May I walk with you?"

"O' course, darlin'. Anybody at the store 'sides LeBlanc?"

"*Non.* You lookin' for somebody?"

He shrugged a shoulder. "*Non,* jus' curious. You wanna tell me what's got ever'one so all-fired happy, today?"

"It's a dance, tonight!" Her high color gave her extra sparkle. "I hope you'll be there, Paul."

His attention dropped to her lips. *M-mmm. She is a fine fille.* If the father, Jean LaCour, knew what he wanted to do to the daughter, he would have a fight on his hands, *certainement.*

"Save me a jig." He winked at her and whistled as she veered off down the path to her home.

"*Mais oui!*" she called, sending him one last eye-flutter before disappearing through the trees.

Hungry and a mite peeved at not finding Celié, Paul's spirits buoyed at the promise in Babette's manner. He hopped over the bank to his tethered *pirogue.*

Lulu better have dinner ready. I'll wager she won't be at the fête tonight, bein' eight months pregnant an' all. She'll stay home with Georges. He's too young to care, anyway. Now that she's a mother, she ain't so much fun as she used to be.

Tonight, though, he would be free to hold a pretty girl—Babette, of course, and perhaps her younger sister, too, who would doubtless develop into another beauty. She had a promising start. He chuckled. *Gettin' in a habit of collectin' sisters, moi!*

He reveled in his prowess with the ladies. With his comeliness and charm, he could keep a woman in every parish in Louisiana. Besides Celié in Assumption, he maintained a wife over in Saint Charles and another in East Terrebonne, so he was well on his way.

I'd have to invent more names for myself, but why not? I am clever, n'est-ce pas? How about Louie Broussard? That be a fine name. He had picked it up somewhere and tucked it away, awaiting a chance to take it out and polish it up.

Nagging questions about Celié and Henri dimmed his eagerness. *Did they stay in Thibodaux, or come here to Sainte Jeanne? No sign of them anywhere.* Two people matching their descriptions, though, were seen leaving the paddle steamer and hiring a driver. He had taken the time to make inquiries, but when the trail grew cold, he pulled his *pirogue* out of its hiding place and started for home. Well… this home.

He found it empty with no lamp burning. *Strange. Where else would Lulu be in her condition? Prob'ly Nettie's. Irritatin' woman, that traiteuse.*

Always stickin' her nose where it don't belong. And Lulu loves her. That fact alone sticks in my craw.

He scrounged for something to eat, irked on top of irritated that food had not been prepared.

She shoulda been here. Her hands aren't pregnant, just her belly, so there is no excuse.

I'll make her sorry.

~CHAPTER 18~

Law and Love

*"But behold, ye cannot hide your crimes from
God; and except ye repent they will stand as
a testimony against you at the last day."*
Alma 39:8, *The Book of Mormon*

May 7, 1857, Sainte Jeanne, Louisiana

Foot-stomping tunes and enticing aromas wafted through the air from the schoolhouse that did triple duty as the dance hall and chapel, as well. Paul threw out the anchor of his *pirogue* and climbed over the bank, other vessels blocking access to the dock. He inhaled with relish. *Mmm. I could do with some more food.*

"Quite the *fais-do-do!*" he said aloud. " 'Afore I left, I never heard tell of no fête." *It's not Saturday night. Must be a last-minute celebration. But what?* He strutted up the path in anticipation, smoothed down those errant black curls women could not resist and stepped through the door. The delicious aromas and the volume of the music increased.

Babette appeared, her eyes aglow and welcoming. "You came," she purred and captured his arm.

"Just for you, darlin'," he said as his glance raked her curvy figure for the second time that day. Her maroon dress enhanced her natural beauty and set his body tingling. "Let's have us a jig."

229

"*Bienvenue*, Paul!" Jacques LeBlanc gripped the other arm and propelled him forward. "Come join the party!" The crowd parted for them, and the music stopped. His pulse quickened as two women across the room pivoted in his direction.

Babette released his arm and the crowd absorbed her in a protective motion.

His mind reeled. *Celié and Lulu! Is this a trap?*

"Now, Paul," LeBlanc said, "or is it Phillipe? Court is now in session. *Assieds-toi*. Have a seat."

A chair appeared before him, and Paul attempted a desperate dash for the door. Several hands grabbed him and forced him down, two of which belonged to Jean LaCour, Babette's *père,* who gave him an extra shove.

"This the best seat inna house," Jacques announced. "All polish' up niiiice."

The men brought another chair for Jacques, but he waved it away. "*Non*, we gonna finish this up *tout d'suite.*"

Sweat beaded up at Paul's hairline. The village's shopkeeper, constable and judge all rolled into one commanding personality, on the other hand, appeared as cool as a stiff winter breeze.

Jacques raised his head and his voice. "We has us a little problem, but nuthin' we cain't handle on our own. We don't call in the Fed'ral law 'round here, no sirree! We deals with our own problems ourselves, ain't that right?"

"That's right!" chorused the townsfolk.

"And you is a problem," he added to Paul. "These women both claim that you is their husband. Hoo, *oui,*

Paul! Or is it Phillipe? Phillipe Boudreaux? That right?"
Paul swallowed hard. LeBlanc's lip curled up in a sneer.
"I think it's impor'ant that we put the right name on the
gravestone, don't you?"

"Phillipe" found it difficult to inhale. *He wants
Lulu, certainement. He's thinkin' he'll get my wife and
revenge on me at the same time!*

"Now, Miz Boudreaux," Jacques began, "you say
that he married you first, *n'est-ce pas?*"

"*Oui,*" said Celié.

"This that very man?"

"*Oui,* Your Honor."

"Fiiine."

"Don't be listenin' to her! She crazy!" Paul half-
rose from his chair, but firm hands pushed him down.
Celié's eyes got big. At least the one did. Her hair hung
over the other one.

"I'll be the judge o' that," Jacques snarled.

Baby Georges, sitting on Nettie's lap, whined in
her arms. She pulled him closer.

*I do hate that woman. 'Course, I hate ever'one
here. Them LeBlancs especially.*

"Now, Miz Boudreaux," Jacques said, "how was
you treated by the defendant?"

"He treated me like the mud on his shoes and hurt
me *beaucoup.* Hurt us both."

"You an' who else?"

"Henri, his son." The boy peeked out from
behind Celié's skirt, then pulled it into shields around his
face. Georges stared at Paul as if waiting for another
explosion.

"Fiiine. And when did you find out he married somebiddy else?"

"For certain sure? Not till I showed up two days ago."

"And when did you discover that other woman is your sister?"

"After we made it home, and I could talk to 'er. But I suspected long before."

"How so?"

"When I met Phillipe at the timber camp, before we was married, I told him about my family—*Maman, Père* René and o' course, my pretty little sister. He acted more int'rested than he should be. And then, the way Lulu described him in her letters, that suspicion kept growin'."

"Fiiine. Now, Miz Rubidoux, did you know your husband married your sister?"

"*Non*, your Honor. Not till Celié came home and we talked it over. She ran off with him without bringin' 'im home and called him Phillipe in her letters."

Paul's helpless ire compounded. *Lulu defied me. She been writin' to her sister.*

"An' how does he treat you and your boy?"

"He hits us an' says hateful things," Lulu said with a shaky voice. "I wanna be free o' him."

Stupid woman. I hardly ever hit 'er.

"Fiiine." LeBlanc cleared his throat with gusto. "By the power vested in me by the state of Loozianna, I declare you, Celié Dupleix Boudreaux, and you, Lucille Dupleix Rubidoux, free women. Divorced. *Finis.* Bring on the paperwork." He winked at the crowd. "I finished drawin' up the papers today," he said, as if it were the master stroke of the evening.

LeBlanc is enjoying this. At my expense! "You cain't do that! I won't stand for it! We were married before God by a priest!"

"Hmph. You'll stand for it, all right," Jacques said. "You'll stand before God to account for marryin' more than one woman."

The silence in the room pulsated. Paul's face burned with anger, his sight a mouse hole in a red mist.

"If you think God gives you the right to marry an' abuse women an' children, Boudreaux, or whoever you is, I'm inclined ta disagree, an' you will lose that fight."

Jacques' assistant brought over the papers for Paul to sign and handed him the pen. Shaken and angry, he snatched it, spraying ink across the papers and his clothes.

"Now, don't forget which name to sign to which paper, Paul-Phillipe!" yelled a man hidden in the crowd, triggering a rumble of laughter.

He gripped the pen, irresolute, his vision still hampered by searing anger and growing fear. Staring without comprehension at the two papers side by side on the lap desk, he considered defying them all and escaping. Weighing his chances, he found them less than promising. He inscribed a shaky "X" on each line provided. *Time to get this nightmare over and done with.*

"Hoo, man, that the best you kin do? You kin make up names, but you cain't write 'em?" Paul's impotent rage deepened into hellfire as the crowd chortled at LeBlanc's jab. "Well, that's all right. Won't make a bit o' difference in the end. And the end is near!"

The clerk whisked the lap desk over to his wives. *LeBlanc took my wives away from me.* Paul sweated and stewed while the women signed where the clerk indicated. *Good thing I has me a couple more he don't know 'bout. And when I come back here, in body or spirit, he gonna die inna bayou.*

"As for you, *monsieur*," announced his enemy. "I will jus' say this: Now would be an excellent time for you to become a prayin' man. That would be an improo'ment, ehn?"

The crowd laughed and answered, "*Oui,*" and "Amen!"

"If you have any more wives, you better blow 'em a kiss *adieu* from here. It's time to meet your fate. Take 'im away!"

The townsfolk cheered as Jacques motioned to his cronies. Nettie stood in triumph and Georges ran to his mother. Celié and Lulu held each other, the last scene Paul beheld before the men dragged him out the door and down the path to the bayou.

He groped around in his thunderstruck mind, attempting to straighten out the mess of his up-ended world. The music and laughter resumed. Music? They were celebrating his demise? People he'd known for years? Well, four years. Or was it three? This couldn't be the end of him! *My tools! My guns! And the food.*

"Aww," Paul groaned. The feast tantalized and mocked his hunger, and his loss of women and children

ignited a slow burn till the canker of bitterness consumed his soul.

La musique had begun but the dancing had not. Stella basked in the warm community love surrounding her. The villagers chattered and congratulated each other on a ruse well-executed. *"Il y a pas d'quoi!* It was nothing!"

After all, Nettie and Jacques cooked up this scheme. Besides Babette's heavy eyelash fluttering, all anyone else had to do was show up with food. The whole shebang went down slicker than okra.

And Stella, so delighted with Jacques' stunning coup that she wanted to throw her arms around him, happily settled for hugging her mother instead. The "sisters" held each other in relief as the children held onto them, while the merry fiddlers spun out a snappy reel.

The townsfolk expressed their support before joining in another dance. Nettie and the tiny fatherless families sat in a corner for the rest of the evening, venturing out only for food and drink.

"He won't hurt us anymo'?" Henri asked over the din, as Stella handed him a small plate of goodies.

"Never again," she assured him.

The village men tied Paul into the skiff and took him down the bayou east, before heading south into

Bayou Black. *Where they takin' me?* At one point, many miles from Sainte Jeanne, the suspense overcame him, and he dared to ask.

One grunted and said, "Such a pity to feed healthy flesh to the *caiman,* and so we will trade you for some *boudin* an' rum."

The men laughed. "And bread!"

"And sauce!"

"We will feast!"

Jean LaCour, the father of Babette, snorted. "I do not mind feedin' the *caiman,"* he said, his needle-sharp glares piercing Paul in the low light of the skiff lantern. "It would save us much time and work, *n'est-ce pas?"*

I chose the wrong girl to hanker for. That man would kill me if he got the chance. I best be on my guard, moi.

True to their word, when the skiff arrived at Bayou Dularge after dawn, the villagers put him on a boat destined for Dulac on the way to the bay, with strict instructions that he must never be let loose in this country. The men received a bag of coins in exchange for him, laughing as they rowed away. All except LaCour, his face set in stone.

Hauled down into the hold and shaking from hunger, fear and fury, Paul took advantage of the moment his new guards freed him from the rope tied around his wrists. He made a valiant effort to escape, but pain exploded in his head.

He awoke with an agonizing headache and found himself trussed and chained to a ring on a beam below deck of an American merchant ship, dried blood down his face and all over his shirt. He raged, fidgeted and swore while her crew finished rounding up criminals and unsuspecting drunks for what turned out to be an endless stretch of service on the saltwater road to Shanghai.

⸙

Quite unsettling to be in two places at once. Here I am, two feet on solid floor, whilst my infant self is cradled in Maman's womb, a whole new childhood ahead.

Eerie as it was to glance at her mother's round belly and contemplate her own beginning, Stella preferred to focus on ensuring that Henri enjoyed a better life from now on.

Receiving no counter-instructions from JoAnne, she stayed on in Sainte Jeanne long enough to lay a sure foundation for his well-being. She observed her *mère* growing to love Henri and figured if *Maman* could not accept him as her husband's other son, she *could* accept her sister's son and welcome.

Stella also visited her *Mamère* Charlotte, a treat and a blessing, since she couldn't remember her mother's mother well. She kept her hair parted on the right and hanging over half her face to hide her scar and white streak, not only for her grandmama's sake, but also in case she met villagers.

She feared, at first, that *Mamère* Charlotte would see through the ruse, but she needn't have worried. *Love is a powerful thing, certainement.* "I think her joy in havin' Celié clouds her vision, *oui*?" She asked aloud, traveling by footpath back to Nettie's.

237

"Oui," JoAnne whispered. "But I helped."

Stella laughed. "Good thing I'm alone in the woods, *oui*, JoAnne? Some might think I'm as crazy as Celié."

"Oui, my darling girl."

The four of them—Stella, Henri, Lulu and Georges—spent so much time at Nettie's avoiding Paul's cheerless shanty, that the community, led by Jacques, proposed another plan. They voted to add another room onto Nettie's house to accommodate the extra bodies, with one more soon to come. Their generosity and kindness touched Stella deeply. *All three of us children will have a better life with Nettie and Maman taking care of us together.*

Her hope in this new childhood for Henri blossomed into a surety that he would take her place as a healer when Nettie passed on. He had a good start on that, absorbing all she and Nettie taught him.

I've been here for twenty days, now, and it's two days before my birthday. I must be leaving. Stella wrestled with how to stage her exit. *I could strew my alligator boots and perhaps a basket or some such thing at the bank and let them assume I lost another fight with a caïman. No, I refuse to fool the people I love into broken hearts.*

In the end, JoAnne whispered that she must say goodbye, and to Henri alone.

He sniffed and clung to her as she knelt before him in a little clearing in the woods.

"I will miss you, Henri," Stella said with tenderness, "but we will meet again."

"When?" he questioned with a pitiful wail.

"In heaven, *cher*. In heaven." Her own tears threatened to overflow.

"Are you a' angel, Wooby?"

"In a way, *oui*. Angels do the work God has sent them to do. I rescued you, *n'est-ce pas?* That is God's work. But now I must go, and you must stay and be happy." She tousled his hair. "*Adieu, mon petit*. You mind *Grand-Grand-mère* Nettie and *Tante* Lulu and grow up to be a kind man." *One that doesn't throw knives at people, I hope.*

Henri bowed his head and a tear slipped down. She embraced him one last time, whispered a little secret in his ear and cradled his face with love. JoAnne's urgency intruded and Stella sighed, wishing she could spend more time with Nettie, Jacques, *Mamère* Charlotte and most of all, *Maman*.

Leaving the tenderest love I've ever known is harder than fighting that caiman, but the sweet outweighs the bitter. I thank You, Lord Jésus, for the time I did have with these dearest of people and two little boys who just might grow up into fine men, after all.

Stella moved into the nearby line of trees and submitted to JoAnne's nudges guiding her through the invisible portal.

⁂

Henri ran after his angel to the first tree trunk in his path and clung to it for support as she vanished. Her tracks through the soft soil caught his attention. He followed them, but soon, they simply stopped. *Her really did go back to heaven.* He searched the sky and surrounding treetops for any sign of her. If a leaf rustled or bird fluttered, he jerked toward it expectantly.

Every minute he waited drained him of hope in her return. *Her not comin' back.* He returned with heavy feet and drooping head to his new home. He loved it there, but without Ruby, his pretend *Maman*, angel, protector and friend, the house would forever have an empty space where she should have been.

⚜

"Where's Celié, Henri?" asked Lulu at supper. She had to sit farther from the table to accommodate her swollen belly. The baby kicked if she bumped into anything hard. *Sainte Marie, may I be delivered of this infant, soon.*

His lip trembled as he whispered, "She gone."

"Gone? Where?"

"Back to heaven." He mashed his fingers into his closed eyes, mouth twisting in sorrow.

Nettie sat up straight. "She died?"

"*Non*, her jus' floated away," he said from behind his hands.

"Floated away on the bayou?" Lulu asked.

"*Non.* To Heaven."

"Henri," Nettie said, "What are you sayin'? Celié is kind, but she's no angel."

"Her weren't Celié. Her was Wooby. Wooby, my angel." He sobbed, head over his plate, face streaked with tears and dirt, his fingers inadequate to stop the gushing.

"Ruby?" Lulu asked, glancing at Nettie.

"*Oui*! Woobeeee!" he wailed.

She left her chair, eased her heavy body down to kneel beside him and moved his head to her shoulder while he sobbed. Georges' face crumpled in sympathy, lower lip quivering and tears welling up. She mentally rolled her eyes at such woe from both boys at once but treated them with tenderness.

When Henri calmed down, Lulu spoke to Nettie. "I suspicioned she changed so much 'cause of the way Paul treated her. She acted less like Celié ever' day. Still, she *looked* like her, even with the scar and the white streak. Her voice, too, for that matter."

Nettie agreed. "Her spirit 'n' image." She handed a wet rag to Lulu, who cleaned Henri's face and hands while they took turns asking more questions to draw him out.

From his answers, they pieced together a wild tale—how his real *mère* had gone crazy, treating him like a chicken in need of a tether, withholding food, water and shelter; that wondrous day when Ruby freed him; how his *mère* shot at them ("See dis? It bleeded!"); their adventure in the woods and in Labadieville; and last, spotting his *père* on the bayou.

"Lord 'a mercy," said Nettie, crossing herself. "Stranger things I never heard tell of."

"We have to find her and bring her back here," Lulu said.

Henri hiccupped. "I tol' you. Wooby's gone to heaven."

Lulu stifled a laugh. "Not Ruby, *cher*. Celié. My sister."

He shook his head. "Her will shoot you!"

"I'll find someone to help me. It'll be all right. She needs us, and we can help her get better."

His brow furrowed as he put his little hands on both sides of her face. "You won't let 'er hurt me?"

"Never." She pulled his hands from her face and kissed them.

He relaxed, comforted, and returned to his dinner. Nettie boosted her up from the floor and guided her into a chair.

Mid-bite, Henri stopped, swallowed and asked, "What's wrong, *Tante* Lulu?"

Lulu winced and rubbed her sore knees, tiny moans escaping.

"Her body's achin' to shed that infant she's carryin'," Nettie said.

"I forgot to tell you!" Henri cried. "Wooby tol' me a secret. Her did! Her said *Tante* Lulu's baby is a girl, and her name is Stella!"

~CHAPTER 19~

Second Chances

*"Trust in the Lord with all thine heart; and lean not
unto thine own understanding. In all thy ways
acknowledge him, and he shall direct thy paths."*
Proverbs 3:5-6, *The Holy Bible*

December 18, 1879, the Mississippi River

Stella and JoAnne reported to the shipmaster in his elegant oak office on the texas deck below the pilot house. He situated himself behind his desk and directed the women to other chairs. "How did this mission go?" he asked JoAnne.

"Very well, Captain. I think she will handle many more assignments with aplomb, were she called upon to do so."

"Excellent. And you, Stella? How would you rate your efforts?"

She weighed her response, desiring to pour out her feelings. Instead, she answered, "I did my best."

"Good. And what did you learn?"

After a moment, she answered, "That *everythin'* we do or say will make a difference, for good or ill. I learned, too, to trust in *Jésus* and not my own wisdom." She paused, a little embarrassed. "I cannot see as far as He can."

"Understandable."

"*Merci, Capitaine*, for lettin' me go back. I needed it as much as they did."

He radiated approval. "That is right. You are learning important lessons."

"*Merci*."

Stella tried to relax with JoAnne on the hurricane deck, the next day, but the questions she wrestled with refused to allow it.

"What ails you, Stella?"

"So many things confuse me," she answered. "How is it you could be with me and not be seen?"

JoAnne gazed into the distance. "Remember my saying that going through the portal numerous times changes you? My body has been changed to a translated state."

"Translated? Language is translated, so that people can understand one another, but how can bodies...?"

"That is an excellent way to think of it. My body has changed to a higher state of being. It now *understands* a holier way to exist."

"Is my body changing, too?"

"In small steps, yes."

JoAnne's explanation satisfied her for the present, and she turned her attention to her family.

"Now that Henri will grow up safe and loved, why would I have left Sainte Jeanne if he wasn't tryin' to kill me? I can't comprehend it."

"Things have a way of working out for the best, no matter what. If you had not left the bayou, we would have found you anyway. We were sent for you."

"Why?"

"For Oliver."

"Ah, *oui*... But JoAnne, how will it change the future? Will there be backwash?"

Stella detected sorrow in JoAnne's answer. "There will be repercussions, yes. But if the shipmaster assigns us to rescue a person from someone else's poor choices, I promise you it is wise to do so, no matter the consequences. Did you know? Henri was hanged for killing you."

Stella clutched her neck in horror.

JoAnne patted her arm. "But he will have freedom to choose a better path, now."

"What if he doesn't? Then all our efforts will be wasted." Despair threatened to take over at the thought. She had invested herself fully in Henri's well-being.

"Are you certain? Didn't aiding Henri foster your ability to forgive him? And didn't you touch his heart? He loves his angel. Dear girl, Jesus died for all of us, whether or not we cherish Him for it. It was His *joy* to do so. Didn't it bring you joy to help Henri?"

Her tenderness for the innocent child flooded her, and her shoulders relaxed. "*Oui.*"

"And don't you think he will be happier and healthier, in mind and body?"

"Oh, I hope so."

"And didn't you want to rescue Hélène? I believe she will benefit from this new Henri."

245

Her mind eased and her eyebrows separated. "Of course."

"Well, then, mission accomplished, no matter what the future holds."

Full of gratitude, Stella realized her evening prayers would be quite different from what she could possibly have supposed ten minutes ago.

⚜

Between all the humanitarian work and her time-traveling exploits, Stella found this a marvelous and satisfying way to live. "I would love to go on doin' this work forever," Stella remarked, three days before Christmas Eve.

"Oh, you may," returned JoAnne, "for as long as you wish."

Astonishing. "This is beyond anythin' I've ever wished for, JoAnne."

"Oh, Stella," said JoAnne. "It gets better. Tonight is the Christmas gala—a very special evening. *Monsieur* Rick is coming, and you'll once again meet Oliver. Wear your finest dress."

"*Mais oui*, I must wear the dress you gave me, JoAnne." The deep magenta taffeta, an appropriate color for Christmas, enhanced her olive skin. She had held it up in the mirror to gauge its effect and couldn't wait for an occasion that deserved such finery. *That dress makes the tedious art of dressing worth it.*

"I'm so pleased you like it," JoAnne responded. "Winnie has a marvelous idea of how to style your hair for tonight. She's gifted that way. Let's go back to our stateroom and begin our preparations."

Having bathed and powdered, Stella sat at the vanity while Winnie arranged her hair. Incorporating locks from both sides of the scar, the sweet lady's maid covered the short white fringe with a braid, which she worked into a woven chignon on top.

"Winnie, you've created a masterpiece," JoAnne said.

"*Vraiment,* Winnie. It's miraculous," Stella agreed. She examined her new hairstyle in the mirror. Only a dollop of white graced the top of her forehead like an angel's kiss. "I love it. *Merci.*" She removed her dressing gown and reached for the jewel-toned dress.

"Let me help you, Miss."

Stella welcomed the assistance and let her mind wander far from these proceedings to the endless labor of her childhood. *How lovely to have the freedom to be still, on occasion, though I wouldn't care for a life of pure idleness.*

Winnie finished the ensemble by fastening a simple set of jet beads around the girl's neck and adding the matching earrings.

"*Merci*, Winnie." Stella beamed with excitement and pleasure. "And thank *you*, JoAnne, for this exquisite dress."

An unfamiliar princess stared back at her from the mirror. From the top of her coiffure to the pretty black dancing slippers on her feet, she appeared to be a pampered woman of leisure, but oh, how she loved doing the Lord's work!

"You're so welcome, Stella. You are the picture of perfection," pronounced JoAnne. "Thank you, Winnie."

"*Oui, merci beaucoup,* Winnie." Stella glanced once more into the mirror. "Hope I don't need my gator pick, tonight. No place to hide it in this costume."

"Indeed not," JoAnne said. "No one here would harm you. Thank you again, Winnie. Join us, soon, won't you?"

Surprised, Stella cried, "Your maid?" then sent Winnie a silent expression of apology.

"She is not a servant as you understand the word," explained JoAnne. "She, too, is on the ship's roster and loves to help. We are grateful to have her, and she is welcome to enjoy the delights of the evening as well as we are. Will you come, Winnie? I could help you dress."

"Thank you, Mrs. Talbot, but I can enjoy the music in here, and I have a book to savor, which suits me fine. It wasn't available in my time, so it's a priceless treasure, and I can't wait to read it."

Surprised by this double revelation, Stella stared. *Winnie can read. She, too, comes from another time. Is this true of everyone on this boat but me?*

"Very well, then. We'll be off," said JoAnne.

Stella, coming out of her shock, hesitated, tugging at her black, opera-length gloves. "JoAnne, these gloves are long enough to tie up a hound, but they don't quite cover my scars." She normally depended on sleeves to disguise the marks of the gator's teeth and didn't trust mere gloves to stay up.

"One little tooth mark wants to peek out, but no one will notice," Winnie said. "They will only admire your beauty."

Appeased, Stella let the matter drop and thanked Winnie with a hug.

Stella entered the Main Cabin transformed like the cinder girl in "The Little Glass Slipper" by Charles Perrault, her favorite childhood book. *I'll meet my own prince tonight, if JoAnne is correct.* Though the gala had not yet begun, the room buzzed with anticipation, increasing her own.

As she followed in JoAnne's wake, Stella took in the sparkling room that should have taken days to decorate, though at the noon meal all appeared as usual. This room had been transformed, garnished with flowers, garlands, ribbons, candles and crystal. Chandeliers chock full of candles blazed with increased brilliance. Tables in the corners covered with white cloths were laden with delectable treats designed to both tempt and refresh.

"Frederick," cried JoAnne, "there you are!" She rushed into *Monsieur* Rick's arms while Stella watched with affection and happiness.

After their brief hug and a gentle kiss, he addressed Stella. "My dear girl, it's good to see you," he said. "Allow me to introduce our son, Oliver. He has anxiously awaited this moment."

A tall, blond man stepped out from behind *Monsieur* Rick. His attractive face had love written all over it. She didn't know this person, whom she gauged to be in his thirties, yet an unusual commotion stirred inside her.

"May I have the honor of this dance?" Stella's possible prince held out a hand, and she who had fought an alligator and dodged bullets mustered all her courage to take it. His gentle and steady support, though, eased her hesitation.

As they closed the gap between them, the small string orchestra began to play, and her partner gently guided her. Unfamiliar with the steps, she stumbled. Village dances included the waltz, but she never had much use for them. *Well, I never had much use for being grabbed and pawed at. These men are different. More respectful.*

"Oh," Oliver said, stopping. "Forgive me. I forgot that you didn't know the waltz before I taught it to you. And now, well, we're starting over, aren't we?"

"I suppose so, though I don't remember the first time."

"Of course not," he said. "None of that has happened for you. Let's practice, shall we?" His unhurried, patient manner helped to calm her jumpy nerves.

⁂

Though his rapid heartbeat threatened to dictate the tempo of this reacquaintance, Oliver knew not to rush her. But... *I'm holding her! She's living and breathing and real.* It mesmerized him into near incoherence.

This afternoon, he had returned to the ship with his dad, who informed him that the Christmas gala was slated for this evening.

"I can't, Dad. Please don't expect me to go. It would rip my guts out to be there without her."

"Your choice, of course, son, but you'll be missing out on a grand reunion."

"The only reunion I want is with Ruby. I mean Stella."

His dad only grinned.

Curious, Oliver said, "What?"

"This is December twenty-first, 1879. She's still among the living. Let's make sure she stays that way."

This unexpected announcement, coming less than two hours after his prayer for comfort at Henri's execution and immediate burial, left him so shaky, his knees buckled. He wept and laughed with joy as he hurried to change into formal clothes.

At this moment, holding her as firmly as he dared, he functioned in high gear, praying for help to do and say the right things. Despite his anxious energy, he somehow managed to conduct a believable dance lesson. *At least, I **hope** it's not too obvious that I'm jumping up and down on the inside. This is an incredible blessing beyond my wildest imagination. Dad was right. With God, all things really are possible.*

Once Stella achieved some confidence with the basic steps, he led her out amid the dancing couples. After a few minutes of nervous chuckles and gradual proficiency, the two young people relaxed a bit and began a tentative conversation.

"You're a good teacher." So awestruck by this whole situation, Stella had taken forever to come up with that one conversational offering. *Heaven help me through this.*

"Thank you," he responded. "You learn quickly." The waltz ended and he bowed.

She glanced at the other women curtsying to their partners and dropped a quick one.

Oliver offered her his hand once more. "Shall we stay for another?" She consented and off they twirled. "I can't believe I'm holding you again," he admitted. "And you're alive and well. And, might I add, even lovelier? That color was invented for you."

Stella, her cheeks growing warm, turned her attention to the lights, her dress, the dance steps, the dancers—anything but the uncomfortable closeness of a very masculine partner.

Oliver spoke in a low tone that she could scarcely discern over the music. "I've made you uncomfortable. Forgive me. It's been pure torture for me ever since you died in my arms. But here you are alive and…" He broke off as Stella faltered in her steps. "Are you all right?"

"I need a chair."

He led her to some seats not far from his parents. "Why don't you stay here, and I'll bring us something to drink?"

"Mama Jo. Ruby… um… Stella needs you."

"Of course," JoAnne responded and sought out her would-be daughter-in-law. She prayed for discernment, listening for the quiet whisper of the Holy Spirit.

~*Just listen. Just love her.* ~

She sat next to Stella and laid a light hand on her arm. "Tell me."

"I hardly know. I feel…"

JoAnne waited. And waited a little longer.

"I'm so tired," Stella said. "May we go back to our room?"

"Yes, of course." They rose and wove their way through the press of people to the door of their room. JoAnne spotted Oliver coming with two cups of punch and gave a tiny shake of her head. He followed behind them at a discreet distance.

"Perhaps you would like to go out onto the main deck for a bit of cool air?" she said, raising her voice enough to reach him.

"Very well," Stella said without enthusiasm.

As they moved through their room and the door leading to the main deck, Winnie glanced up from her book, eyebrows raised. JoAnne answered the unspoken question with a grimace before grabbing two capes and closing the outer door behind them.

⚜

The nippy air on her face and neck helped calm Stella's disquiet, though her hands tensed around the railing. Watching the river by the ship's deck lights for long moments, she asked, "I died in Oliver's arms?"

"Yes, darling," said JoAnne. "You two were betrothed, this very night, in fact, and were out shopping for rings the day you were killed. Rick and I followed behind you, close enough to join in should you need us, though far enough away to afford you some privacy. You stopped and embraced a moment and then…"

"How did Henri find me?"

"I gather his spies were stationed up and down the river. One of them must have identified you from Henri's description and alerted him. He slipped through the crowd in front of us and threw the knife. Rick seized him the next moment, but… too late."

"Henri went to a lot of trouble to find me. I know he is—was, a dangerous man, but to go to such lengths!"

The minutes ticked by in silence while Stella examined her feelings, grateful JoAnne did not push.

"I think Oliver is… kind," Stella said at last. "Handsome, too, but I don't know him. It feels… it feels like an arranged marriage, as if your friendship and all we've been doing together was one big scheme."

"In one respect, that's true. The shipmaster sent us to find you. But 'arranged' doesn't have to exclude love. Both of my marriages were arranged by the Lord, and both have been wonderful."

"Truly?"

"Oh, yes. He may not be familiar to you, but I can assure you Oliver loves you very much."

"But… what if…?"

"What if you don't feel the same? It's your choice, of course. But if our Father in Heaven knows that you two would be happy, and I believe He does, then I think a little trust is in order, don't you?"

Stella's brow furrowed. "I suppose so. Still, I would like to know for myself that I will be happy and safe with him."

"Safe?"

"Wasn't I killed as he held me?"

"Ah. It makes you nervous to be placed in the same position."

"*Oui.*"

"You may have a witness through the Holy Spirit, if you will ask."

"I will." Stella studied the stars for a few moments. "I'm still desolate from leavin' *Maman* and Nettie and Henri, even knowin' what he did to me. And now, this." She lowered her head, spent.

"You're overwhelmed and tired from your trip back home, I'm sure. Take one day, one moment, at a time. Would you rather skip the party?"

Stella had a lot in common with a worn-out scrubbing rag, at this point. "*Oui, merci.*" They reentered their state room and proceeded to undo all of Winnie's skilled artistry. Sleep proved elusive with the music in the next room, yet she couldn't face Oliver again.

Not tonight.

⁂

Oliver exited through the main cabin's principal entrance and located the women just as JoAnne explained the murder scene. He hung back in the shadows, gripping the crystal cups, until the women finished their conversation and slipped into their cabin.

The gala music behind him faded out of his awareness. *I want to be the one to comfort her. Why did it have to be someone else? Her natural distrust of men, sure, but...*

Oliver wandered to the opposite side of the ship, head low. Just because Dad and Jo had been given this assignment by the shipmaster to change the ending, to prevent her from going to the world of spirits too soon, it did not guarantee success. *But I need her!*

No one promised, however, that *she* would need *him*.

He leaned his forearms on the railing and hunched over it, twirling the cups by the handles around his fingers, the contents dumped into the Mississippi. His thoughts, too, spun around and around. To discover that she lived! He ached to wrap his arms around her and never let go, but her reluctance held him in check. *What if she doesn't discover, this time, that she loves me?*

The prospects of their relationship being the same as before her death were quashed. His chest constricted with a deepening ache.

Breathe, he told himself, struggling to do so. *Remember the family motto: "Trust in the Lord with all thine heart, and lean not unto thine own understanding." I assumed I trusted the Lord, but maybe I don't.*

He would have to hang on until he did.

And breathe.

~CHAPTER 20~

Christmas Surprises

*"And the angel said unto them, Fear not, for behold, I
bring you good tidings of great joy…"*
Luke 2:10, *The Holy Bible*

December 22, 1879

Oliver found the woman he had lost and found
once more on the main deck, the following day, and
welcomed the chance to do a little more persuading.

"Would you stroll around the deck with me?" he
asked her, offering his elbow.

"Very well."

As they settled into a slow amble, Oliver
ventured to ask, "Would you like to hear about how we
first met?"

"*Oui,* I believe I would."

*Spectacular! All right, Talbot. Don't screw this
up. Humor might go over better than a tsunami of
emotion.* Sending up a prayer, he launched into it.

"Late October, I arrived on this ship from my
time. Since it was docked at Plaquemine, I thought I'd
pick up a few supplies from the general store that we
don't have in my time. Like razors. They're different
here."

"How so?"

"Well, they're long, here, with only one blade. I
usually buy the kind that are short with as many as five
blades." *Or use my electric shaver, but we'd better not*

257

go there. "I had paid for my purchases when I noticed a commotion about a block away from the store, so I wandered down there to investigate. Arriving at Doctor Grant's office, I discovered that a particular gentleman, and I use that title with great reservation, had strong objections to a certain young healer's use of prayer before turning her complete attention to his broken finger."

"Ah."

"He complained first to her, then to the doctor, who escorted the man from the premises due to a severe case of impatience with complainers."

Amusement softened her expression.

Encouraged, Oliver added, "On a side note, you told me you felt safe there, tucked away in one of the treatment rooms. And neither the doctor nor his wife, who often showed up to assist, caused you any concern."

"*Oui*," she concurred. "They are lovely people."

"You were safe with me, too, Ruby. I would never hurt you. Anyway, the doctor squawked at the man to be off, and you insisted that he come back inside, so that you could set his finger. But he kept complaining to the gathering crowd about your 'rudimentary and superstitious methods of treatment.' His words. But bless that crotchety man, for had he not called attention to himself, I would not have found you so quickly."

She lowered her eyelashes. "I see."

Sensing a crack in the walls of Jericho, Oliver gambled again. "I was impressed by your mastery of the situation amid all the chaos. Relieved, too, to find that my new heroine and the young woman I was sent for were one and the same. I fished around for some ailment or other that I could make use of, to draw your attention. But alas, my traitor flesh and bones stood firm and hale; therefore, another method had to be discovered or invented."

Here, Ruby let a little giggle escape, casting him a sidelong glance. "And what did you discover or invent?"

"Oh, I'm very resourceful," Oliver answered. "I just happened to be at the docks, the next day, of course, since I lived on this boat. When a swinging crate split open a roustabout's head, I volunteered to help the poor man to the surgeon, out of pure benevolence, of course."

"*Mais oui*. How convenient. And such delightful nonsense. Is this for certain true, or has it been embellished?"

He halted, straightened his shoulders and laid a palm on his breast. "It's as true as the North Star." He slid a little peek in her direction. *Sweet! It's working.* His mock drama brought a true grin to her face, which she squelched, but couldn't quite erase.

"I watched while you stitched him up," Oliver continued, "admiring your skill and mesmerized by the way you speak, the way you handled people and the white streak through your hair, like moonlight on the Mississippi."

Her amusement faded. "And my scar?"

He stopped and caressed it with a glance. "I wanted to kiss it."

She blushed and pulled away.

"Ruby, please give me a chance."

"Stella."

"Hm?"

"My name is Stella. You called me Ruby. Twice."

"Oh. Sorry, it's a habit. It wasn't safe to call you Stella, then, and it's only been a little over a week ago, for me, that you died." A shadow passed over his mind as the memory of the danger and her death rushed in. She put her arm through his once more. A mixture of relief and hope welled up inside him as they resumed their stroll.

Oliver dared to place his hand over hers where it nestled in the crook of his arm. "I've missed you more than I can tell you. I've missed your inquisitive eyes, your touch and even your scars, but mostly your love and your *joie de vivre*. I'm so grateful we can start over. I wish…" Caution stifled further speech.

"You wish I could remember?" Stella asked. "So do I."

He squeezed her hand. "It's hard to have to start over, but it's better than losing you forever."

"Tell me more about our beginnin'," she said.

"I visited you every day for about two weeks, returning to the ship to sleep. We took short walks, since you hated to be gone from the office and feared for your safety. Plaquemine turned out to be safer than Memphis. My invitation to take you on a tour of the SS *Infinite* softened your resistance. That day, you wouldn't promise to come, but the next morning, you did, which surprised me. You insisted, however, that I give you a few more days to prepare. It was early November, by that time, and cold—just like today," he said as he shivered. "I discovered later that you were embarrassed by your dresses, which couldn't keep a flea warm, and needed time to have another one made. A cape, too. It was the blue one with black trim."

"Is this for certain true?"

"Every word."

"I guess I couldn't resist a free ride on a steamer."

"*I* guess you couldn't resist my charm and good looks."

She burst into laughter as his parents approached.

"This is a good sign," said JoAnne.

"At least she finds him amusing," said his dad.

"It's a start," he replied as he glanced sideways at his enchanting companion. "It's a start."

❦

December 23, 1879, the Mississippi River

Stella descended the stairs to the main deck the next morning wearing her violet suit, a long black cape and a small, fur-lined bonnet. She whisked between clusters of passengers.

Do these people time-travel? It's none of my business, yet I would love to compare notes. The nippy breeze tickled her airways. *Tomorrow is Christmas Eve. Will this ship provide Mass for the Catholics or am I the only one?*

She caught a glimpse of Oliver lounging on the deck, reading, and approached. Watching him, she examined her inner self for signs of love or even

261

attraction. What she found was expansiveness, an unfolding of her soul after being crumpled.

"*Bonjour*," she said, a few feet from his chair.

"Good morning," he responded with what might have been surprise and... what? Hope, perhaps? Whatever it was, he brightened in her presence.

Do I do the same? Is that love? She couldn't deny that a little tingle flared inside her when he met her gaze.

"Rest well?" he asked as he rose from the lounger.

"I did, *merci*." She shied away from spending too much time immersed in his eyes and turned her attention to the bedraggled book in his hand. "What are you readin'?"

He adjusted his neck scarf against the cold and closed the tattered book on his finger to hold his place. "*Le Livre de Mormon*. The Book of Mormon. It's a history of the people who lived on this continent in ancient times. Jesus visited them and taught them everything he taught the Jews, and then some. I'd like you to read it."

"*N-non, merci*. I'll pass." *Jésus couldn't have visited others besides the Jews, could He? Better to steer clear of that topic for the present.* "I'm goin' ashore with JoAnne to distribute food to the poor. Would you care to come with us?"

He dropped his gaze to the book he held in his lap. "I'm sorry to miss that. I'm supposed to go with my father on an errand for the shipmaster." He met her eyes, again. "Will I see you at dinner tonight?"

She strove for nonchalance. "Perhaps."

"You know… you should read this book."

She raised her one perfect eyebrow. *"Pour quoi?"*

"Because it will change your life," he stated with conviction.

"My life has changed already beyond what I ever could have dreamed of. It's amazin'."

"So… you can't accept any more amazingness?"

"Is that a word: amazin'ness?"

"It is now," he said, a grin blossoming.

Stella couldn't help but hold his gaze this time, enjoying his playfulness. *He is pleasant and gentle. I do hope to cross paths with him again. But is this love?*

She couldn't give a definitive *"oui,"* yet, but perhaps soon.

Winnie, under protest, dressed her in the magenta gown and jet jewelry once more.

"You have other lovely dresses, miss."

"This one wasn't worn long, and I like it best." Her hands fussed with the gloves barely covering her scars, while her attention wandered elsewhere. *Will I catch something special in Oliver's expression, tonight? If I do, will it affect me?*

She mingled with other passengers before dinner, that evening, listening for clues as to whether any of them time-traveled, but she couldn't follow the rapid English very well. No one but the Talbot party spoke French to her. *I ought to practice my very poor English.*

Seated at dinner next to JoAnne to her left and Winnie to her right, Stella admired the festive boxes wrapped in shiny red paper and topped with white bows, surrounding a lighted candle on a heavy candlestick and set on a white tablecloth. Each round dining table held a similar arrangement.

"What charming *cadeaux*, and what a lot of work!" she said.

"I enjoyed it," said Winnie.

"You did this?"

"I helped with some of the other tables, not this one, so these gifts will be a surprise."

"My apologies for being late," Oliver said, sliding into the seat beside Winnie. "My cravat staged an open rebellion." He froze at the sight of her, his expression one of deep admiration. Glancing at Winnie, he started to speak but stopped and returned his attention to Stella.

Severing their silent exchange, Stella asked of no one in particular, "Will the ship provide Mass this evenin'?"

"I don't believe so, no," said *Monsieur* Rick, "And since we haven't docked, we must forgo that privilege."

"Though we are not Catholic," said Oliver, "we have attended Midnight Mass with friends. I enjoyed it very much, the singing most of all."

"You sing, Oliver?"

"Yes."

She met his gaze and lingered there—for how long, she couldn't have said. She returned to admiring the gifts, her face growing warm and her skin prickling. *So, he does affect me.* The bows sparkled and the paper reflected the chandeliers, but all she could think of were the lights in a certain pair of blue eyes.

JoAnne distracted her. "I think you'll enjoy the program, this evening. It's about the birth of Jesus. Perhaps that will compensate somewhat for the lack of church services?"

Except for the absence of the Eucharist, it did. Folding doors across an entire adjoining room opened. Helpers slid massive screens out of the room and propped them on either side of the opening. More screens lined the inner walls of the room and softened its corners. It made a charming stage depicting a nighttime scene in far-off Judea. Attendees maneuvered into better viewing positions before the lights dimmed.

"That room is reserved for this express purpose," JoAnne whispered to her.

"It's *parfait.*"

"Perfect, indeed."

The back of the stage lay in darkness. A soothing male voice narrated the story of the angels' visit to the shepherds. Actors demonstrated the ancient, joyous events. Stella lost herself in the story as awareness of all else fled.

When the angels sang, Stella shared their joy. The interior of the stage lightened, and a star appeared over the Holy Family, nestled between manger and stall. The shepherds hurried to kneel before them.

Stella desired with all her heart to join them.

From his vantage point between Winnie and his dad, the circular table facilitated Oliver's enjoyment of two shows: the birth of the Lord Jesus Christ and Stella's delight in it. *I almost asked Winnie to trade seats with me. Good thing I didn't.*

Urgency to push her into accepting him swelled up, but he had acquired some measure of temperance and patience from his treks to New Jerusalem, losing Stella and forgiving Henri. *Trust in the Lord's timing, Talbot, and chill.*

As the lights returned to their usual brilliancy, she blinked as if waking from pleasant dreams. His dream consisted of waking up to that face each and every morning, scar and all. Forever.

The narrator's voice interrupted his reverie. "Please select a package from the center of your table. These gifts represent the treasures of the Magi and the gift of God's Only Begotten Son."

A tubular, tooled leather case and a card lay in the box that Oliver chose. The card read,

To the man who had the vision to see beyond the horizon. Best wishes for a wonderful future.

He opened the case to find a six-inch, filigreed brass telescope appropriate for a captain of the sea in this century. *Wow. This is some craftsmanship.* He extended the telescope as far as possible and peered through it before returning it to its case.

"Fantastic. Thanks, Dad," he said, leaning in for privacy. "But you know how hard it was to see past my nose that day."

"The gifts didn't come from us, son."

"Then who?"

"I'm sure the shipmaster provided them," said his dad, who stroked the cover of a slim, leather-bound volume entitled, "The Book of Lehi."

"Is that what the author *thinks* is in the Book of Lehi, or…?"

Rick checked the title page. "Nope. It *is* the lost one hundred sixteen pages, including the first few chapters of Mosiah the Book of Mormon is missing."

"Dad, that's incredible. I hadn't heard it was found. How did the shipmaster get it? He must be somebody pretty high up to have access to it."

"I'm sure you're right. Look. It's inscribed to me."

"But how did he know where we would sit?"

"We always sit here, Oll." Rick was already into the new volume, so Oliver let him be, despite his desire to read it himself.

Winnie opened a gift. This, too, contained a book. Oliver and the women spoke at once.

"What is it, Winnie?"

She answered in a daze. "The Diary of Eleanor Talbot, Secret Queen of England. I've always been curious about her and wanted to know more."

"Then, it's *parfait* for you, *oui*?"

"*Oui*, Miss Stella."

"Talbot? Any relation?" asked Oliver.

"I don't know," Winnie answered. "You'll have to check your family history. I didn't think my curiosity about her had anything to do with my being here. But, now... Perhaps they *are* connected."

"They say there are no coincidences."

"I can't wait to find out."

JoAnne reached for a flat package and removed what appeared to be a thick letter. She read very little of it before returning it to the envelope.

"Mama Jo?"

JoAnne shook her head, and said, "Not now. Stella, I believe the remaining box is yours. Read the card aloud, won't you?"

Stella complied. "Forever in my heart."

Removing the wrappings and opening the small box, she stared into it, quite still. Oliver asked, "What is it?"

JoAnne, sitting next to her, peeked in. "It's a remarkable likeness. What a special gift!"

In slow motion, Stella reached into the box and removed a three-inch painting. "A portrait miniature. How is this possible?" She stared at it, frozen.

"Who is it?" Oliver asked.

"*Maman.*"

Stella set the dear little portrait on the small table next to her bed before kneeling in a prayer of praise and gratitude. Certain she would not sleep for the wonders of this night, she nevertheless climbed into bed.

And though Winnie's reading lamp still burned, Stella drifted off into a dream of a joyful, mother-filled childhood. She saw herself and Georges out in the yard entertaining two young siblings she didn't recognize. *Maman* hung laundry on the line.

"Where's Ahn-wee?" one of the little ones asked.

"I'll find him," Stella answered.

"Don't wake the baby!" called *Maman* as Stella headed into the house and followed the pungent aroma of oil paints.

"What are you workin' on, now?" she asked. She came up behind her brother and peered over his shoulder as he touched up a tiny painting. He appeared to be around twelve years old.

"Can you tell?" he asked, tilting it toward her.

"Oh, it's *Maman*!"

"Shh. Not so loud. It's a surprise."

"All right." She reached for it but knew not to touch the paint. "It's so pretty."

"Good, then it's finished. Keep it a secret, *bien*?"

"I'm nine. I'm old enough not to tell, *mon frère*. But will it dry before her birthday fête?"

"*Oui*, I believe so. I used less oil and more turpentine. Do you think it's good enough?"

"Oh, Henri, it's *parfait*."

* * *

Rick paused his exploration of this fascinating gift book, sensing a significant moment. His wife, who had moved into his room now that he had returned to the ship, radiated deep emotion. "Jo?"

She looked up from reading the letter she had received at the program earlier this evening. He leaned over the arm of his wing chair, read the name "Annie-Jo" written on the envelope and raised an eyebrow.

"I don't know that I can tell you without crying, Rick." She folded the letter and laid it in her lap.

"I thought translated beings don't cry."

"We sorrow for the sins of the world, don't we? And weep for joy. *God* weeps for *us*."

"Okay. I'm here when you're ready."

She sent him a grateful look. "Thank you."

"One question: Who called you Annie-Jo?"

"James."

"The letter is from James? When did he write it?"

She exhaled and rested her head on the high chairback, appearing to address the ceiling. "That's three questions. You're over your limit."

He chuckled.

She didn't. "Parkinson's disease took his ability to write or use a computer or even speak," she said, "so he must have dictated it quite some time before he died, but to whom?"

"Did you ask those who came to visit him?"

"Yes, but I may have missed someone. And his speech was nearly incoherent by the time he said something about it, so I could have misheard. I ransacked the house, anyway, looking for it, but no luck. Even after his death, when I moved into the condo, it never surfaced. And now..." She waved in a helpless gesture.

"It shows up here," he said.

"Yes."

"Did the Captain explain?"

"No." Jo picked up the card and handed it to him.

Aloud, he read, "It pleases me to grant your deepest desire."

"Jesus is the only one who could possibly have known about this or located it." She sniffed. "It's truly a miracle."

Rick took her other hand and squeezed. "He's phenomenal, isn't He?"

~☙❦❧~

~Chapter 21~

Consequences

*"...and the blood of the innocent shall stand as a
witness against them, yea, and cry mightily
against them at the last day."*
Alma 14:11, *The Book of Mormon*

December 31, 1879, the Mississippi River

Christmas week gained added significance for
Oliver as the Talbots, Winnie and the bayou girl
delivered gifts and assistance to those in need.

Even though they had no "Christmas vacation"
from their mission, he walked with a lighter step and a
more joyful heart for two reasons. One, he served the
Lord and his fellowman, and two…

*She is here, alive. Every day, I can be with her
and love her, though she doesn't completely accept it.
But she's softening. There's hope.*

At each day's end, the loving quintet of
missionaries gathered for dinner. As pleasant as it was,
Oliver wanted to push for more. It frustrated him to never
be alone with her.

Tonight, he promised himself, as he and his dad
finished some house repairs for a destitute family. He
wished to be with her every moment, but handled it
calmly, quietly making plans. *At midnight, it'll be a new
year and a new beginning.*

"Would you care to go into town with me?" he
asked her late that afternoon after washing off the day's

273

grime and changing clothes. Only one more hour remained before dusk. "We could have dinner out, instead of here on the—"

"I would. I want you to show me where I died. JoAnne wouldn't do it while we were in town, today."

His gut reacted as if lunch didn't agree with him. "Stella. No. Please. It's dangerous."

"*Mais non.* It can't be. Henri is not a threat."

"It's dangerous for my heart," he said. "Please don't ask it of me." He couldn't say why the idea appalled him, but his whole being balked at the thought.

"Very well, I shall go there myself. JoAnne mentioned somethin' about a department store on Main Street. Shouldn't be too hard to find, *oui*?" She strode with purpose toward the steps leading to the main deck. Ladylike mincing didn't suit her.

"No, Stella, please don't. There's an excellent restaurant over on Second Avenue. We used to—"

"I'm goin', Oliver, with or without you," she called out in a pleasant tone as she descended the steps.

Oliver grappled with the dread of going and the opposing reluctance to allow her to go alone, before bounding down to join her.

Once inside the carriage, neither spoke, but watched out separate windows as the vehicle moved across the ship's stage, up the riverfront road that morphed into Beale Street up on top of the city plateau. They passed a large expanse of unoccupied property and some warehouses, before turning onto Main.

Troubled, he prayed. *Father, what happened to that great feeling that this would be our new beginning?*

Should I be firm with her and insist we not go? Or should I give in and go along with her?

~Be at peace, my son.~

He relaxed and sent up a silent thank-you. In two blocks, the driver pulled into a free space. She reached for the door on her side.

"Stella. Wait. Let me go first and hand you down."

"I'm not helpless, Oliver. And I am not afraid. There's no danger."

Her answer stabbed him on two levels. One with the way she always said his name, yet she did not say it with love, and again because she rebuffed his efforts to protect her. "That may be true, but let me do this much, at least."

"Very well," came the stiff concession.

Irked, he stepped down and reached a hand up for her. She did not hesitate to take it but pulled away at the first moment politeness allowed.

When he offered his arm, she declined.

"Stella. This is a busy street with no apparent traffic rules and it's not safe. Allow me. Please. I am not the enemy."

She hesitated so long that he raised his eyebrows and his elbow a little more. She took it with more formality than warmth. *Maybe she likes me, but she's not acting like it right now. What's come over her?*

They crossed the street and strolled along the crowded sidewalk, saying little. Oliver stopped in front of the jeweler's shop. "This is where we shopped for wedding rings. Would you care to see which ones you favored? I hoped you would choose one with rubies—"

"*Non, merci.* I'm not ready for a ring. Is this where it happened?" She would not be distracted.

At least, not distracted by me, but she's always had difficulty resisting window displays. I'll bet that softens her up.

He indicated Goldman's department store two doors down. She perused the contents of the windows they passed without lingering. *She's not stopping. That's unusual.*

"This is where it happened," he said when they reached the department store. His aversion to the place intensified. She glanced around the busy street. With no indication of spotting anyone suspicious, she stepped to the closest window in a sweep of skirts.

Her regal movement brought back Oliver's wrenching loss in a wave of emotion. Same woman, same location, same wares displayed in the windows, precisely as they were on that horrible day.

"Ooo, porcelain. And crystal," she cooed. For a moment, humor eased his stress as he remembered her delight the last time they occupied this spot.

I'm an idiot. Nothing will happen. It's over. She's safe.

He approached the window to her left and studied her reflection in it as before. She exuded vibrancy and self-possession, and her whole demeanor softened in the lure of pretty things to behold. Her small derby hat with its beaded netting camouflaged her scar and white streak.

In his era, she would have made the perfect model for a steampunk novel.

Oliver's eyes slid from watching her in the glass to a reflected movement behind him. The setting sun glinted off a metal object in the hand of a scruffy man. Already on high alert, he assumed that danger threatened his beloved once again.

He grabbed her upper left arm, spinning her to face him and pulling her between him and the glass. A clap of thunder exploded in his chest and a scream in his ear.

Utter silence enveloped him. Oliver spun around to discover that a man had fallen on top of Stella, pinning her to the sidewalk. The man's top hat had rolled off his head, leaving a hat line in his dark blond hair. A puddle of blood on the back of the man's suit expanded at an alarming rate. The disheveled, middle-aged man pointed a small revolver at Stella.

And Oliver could do nothing to stop him.

Stella's scream abruptly ended when Oliver landed on top of her, cutting off her air. High commotion from the crowd replaced her cry of fright.

"Didn't think I'd be back, did ya, Celié? Twenty-two years I've waited for revenge!"

Dazed, pinned under Oliver's lifeless body, Stella located the gunman's hate-twisted, purple face, much older now.

Père.

He shifted the gun to aim at her head.

277

In an eerie echo of Stella's death scene, Rick disarmed and restrained Paul Rubidoux, a.k.a. Phillipe Boudreaux. Jo skirted them and ran for the two lying on the sidewalk.

The police arrived, questioned every eyewitness, commandeered the gun and the perpetrator. As soon as the doctor confirmed the cause of death, an officer offered to send a messenger to fetch the undertaker. Rick, again under strict orders not to heal anyone, struggled to suppress the desire to save his son. It was, for him, the hardest commandment of all to obey.

Even as a translated being, he could be tempted, as Christ was, to use his great power for selfishness. *I want my son to live, but I know that's not the plan. Father, forgive me for desiring what must not be.*

~Peace, my son. Temptation does not equal sin.~

Stella, swaying with the moving carriage, occupied the seat between Oliver's parents in the dusk-darkened carriage wending its way back to the docks.

"It's my fault. I insisted on coming here." Her restrained tears heightened the pitch of her voice. She had learned to suppress her emotions due to childhood abuse, but the violence, the sight of her enraged father, the loss of Oliver and searing regret at her own foolishness shattered her confidence and fractured her nerves.

She recalled his unintended prophecy that this outing would hurt his heart. Why hadn't she listened? What did she hope to gain by revisiting the scene of her death? *Mon Dieu, forgive me. Forgive me.*

Less troublesome than her mental anguish was the pain of the wound where the bullet passed through his body and cracked her sternum. It left a corsage of mingled blood, his and hers, on the front of her shirtwaist. *I wish the bullet had taken me, too, for that would have put an end to this terrible ache.*

"No doubt he insisted on coming with you," said Rick in a heavy voice.

"*Trés désoleé.* I'm so very sorry." Her hand went to the hanky she had stuffed under her blouse to staunch the bleeding. *The blood's nearly dried. I don't think Winnie can save this shirtwaist. I must discard it as I discarded Oliver.* She crumpled.

"Stop blaming yourself," said JoAnne. "It isn't over yet."

"When the villagers took *Père* away, I thought they killed him." Her agitation increased. "Jacques kept hinting at it."

"Stop." JoAnne put her arms around Stella's shoulders and spoke in a low tone. "It's not over. Jesus is in charge, and He will set it right… eventually. Reach for His peace and trust Him."

Tears crawled down Stella's cheeks as the carriage rolled to a stop. JoAnne removed one arm to hand her another handkerchief before holding her again. *Monsieur* Rick's arms encircled them both. Their tenderness with her after what she and her father had done destroyed her last shred of composure and she sobbed without restraint.

The driver opened the door for them.

"Give us a moment, please," JoAnne told him.

"Of course, ma'am," he replied, and closed the door.

When she calmed down, the three of them exited the carriage and climbed the stairs to the hurricane deck, intent on reaching their rooms.

Monsieur Rick asked if she would like a blessing.

"You're a healer?" she asked in a cheerless voice.

"Not like you, but yes."

He invited her to come with him and JoAnne to their room.

"Sit down, dear," Joanne said, removing Stella's hat for her. "Rick will lay his hands on your head to pronounce a blessing."

JoAnne seated herself nearby and took Stella's hand. Only a moment passed before *Monsieur* Rick's hands came from behind to rest softly on her head.

His blessing promised healing, comfort and assurance. Warm peace infused her whole being.

"You *are* a healer," she said when he finished, "but you use different words."

"I hope it helps."

"It already has, *merci*."

"Tomorrow we will have Oliver's funeral. I want you to be there."

"*Mais oui,*" she said in a small voice. "I will."

On the first day of 1880, the icy wind nipped at Stella as she fought the temptation to fall into Oliver's grave with him out of sheer guilt. *I can't imagine what his parents are feeling. It pains me to think on it. My wound doesn't hurt nearly as much. Only when I breathe, but I care not. It'll leave a scar, but it'll heal. Will I? Will they?*

Afterwards, Stella moved as if underwater. She cringed at food, spoke and thought as little as possible, for when she allowed her mind to wander, recriminations ganged up on her. Even the fight with the alligator had not left her so fragile. She kept reminding herself of the marvelous blessing she received from *Monsieur* Rick and the attendant peace, but now, that peace eluded her.

She and the Talbots performed small errands and tasks for seven more days. Stella then received a new assignment from the shipmaster, despite her reluctance and the fact that her wound hadn't healed.

The captain handed her this new commission with the directive of "Do your best," without asking how she felt about it. *I prefer to stay, but living and working with those I've hurt may strain our friendship, so I suppose it's best to leave.*

Oliver's parents came with her to the portal room to say goodbye and offer encouragement. "You can do this. We'll meet again someday."

How can such people exist? Near as I can tell, they've forgiven me. More than that, they treat me as the Good Shepherd Himself would, if He were here. They're so composed, even in their loss, and can look me in the eye. That feat alone amazed her, since she found it so difficult to return the gesture, but their peace and pure love granted her some measure of reassurance.

Gathering her courage, her faith and her backpack of medical supplies and necessities, she stepped through the portal alone.

CHAPTER 22

The Fellowship

*"That I may know Him, and the power of His
resurrection, and the fellowship of His sufferings..."*
Philippians 3:10, *The Holy Bible*

Mid-January, 2054, Southeast Illinois

As she passed through the mysterious ring, Stella yearned to see Oliver again, whole and hopeful, blue eyes shining with love. She regretted not embracing that love with her whole being and even rebuffing him right before he died. In an instant, she remembered the shipmaster's last words, "You will be there."

"Where?" she asked.

"Wherever you desire. Desire, itself, is powerful; therefore, use it wisely."

Adjusting to the murkiness of wherever she had landed took some moments. She found it difficult to breathe the thick, dirty but cool air, and put down her pack to tie her kerchief around her face and her shawl around her shoulders. She hoisted her heavy pack and, as usual, forged straight ahead.

Soon, Stella could discern the shapes of rocks and unidentifiable debris. She bent down, careful with the heavy load on her back and tapped her fingernail on what appeared to be a scratched, broken glass box.

Odd. It doesn't ring like glass. Where am I?
~Where you wanted to be.~

283

"I wanted to be here?" *Incredible.* A woman screamed. Stella jerked, heart thumping. She felt both isolated and vulnerable to attack in this broken and bleak landscape.

~Fear not; I will help you.~

"*Merci*, Lord. I will do my best." The same voice that screamed cried out again off to her left, this time in a weaker voice. "Someone needs my help."

Instant illumination filled Stella's mind, not in words, but more as a network of knowledge, which could have taken pages to explain, but in essence meant:

~Let your light so shine, that many may see your good works, and have hope in me. Remember that you must forgive. Prepare to accept the truths that will be shown you. I am the same yesterday, today and forever. I speak, and those who have ears to hear will hear. Encourage others to use the power they have. Learn from them. Feed my sheep until I come. Behold, I come quickly.~

"Amen. Even so come, Lord *Jésus*." Picking her way through the debris and rocks, she imagined a kinship with her town's patron saint, Jeanne D'Arc, who heard the voices of saints and angels, and had the courage to obey. Buoyed by that connection, she made good progress despite visibility of around fifteen feet.

The woman cried out again, weaker this time.

Stella followed the moaning while managing the obstacle course of rocks and man-made junk, until a space clear of rocks and rubbish appeared. A bedraggled dozen and a half people of various skin colors occupied the clearing, most either lying or sitting on the ground.

Strange masks covered their noses and mouths, though a few had kerchiefs, so she wasn't alone in that.

As she wandered through the group, she found a lone person on his feet—a tall, drooping man with a scraggly ponytail of unwashed hair and a long beard with glints of red in it. He watched her approach, weariness and curiosity in the clear blue eyes above his black mask.

Stella cried, "Oliver!?" Surprise and joy increased her volume. "You're alive! *Merci, Jésus!* I have found him!" Elated, she started toward him.

He stepped back. His wariness stopped her cold.

"*Désolé*. Sorry," he said. "Do I know you?"

Her rapture crumbled into piles like the rocks all around her.

"Do you have any medical supplies?" Oliver asked. "We're in dire need, here." His French was rusty, but she understood him.

Hurt and confused, she swung the rucksack off her back to the ground and opened it. "I have salves, disinfectant, a few bandages, and many herbs to make poultices."

"Disinfectant?" His hand reached out like a thirsty man in the desert.

"Yes, alcohol." She rummaged in the bag and pulled out a large flask.

"Isopropyl?? Where did you buy this? On the black market?" He grabbed it without a trace of politeness, attesting to the deep need of the moment.

"I'm not familiar with that name, nor a black market. It's one-hundred-fifty-proof rum, distilled from sugar cane. Not for drinkin'—for washin'. I have two flasks of it."

His eyes widened, then he let out a breathy laugh. "Well," he said, "that works." He was still chuckling as he walked off, twisting the large cork. Pausing, he asked, "Did you say you have bandages?"

"*Oui*, but not many, and if the need is great…"

"It is great, sister."

Sister? As she attempted to comprehend why he would call her such a thing, his gaze dropped to her butter-yellow calico dress and took it in with a hungry look. Embarrassed, she stepped back.

"Oh. Forgive me," he said. "I'm not after your body; I'm coveting your skirt. That's a lot of fabric, and to my knowledge, there are no more sources. Anywhere. That dress would make a lot of bandages. It's *clean*, even. Where did you find it?"

He wants me to give up my dress to make bandages? To avoid both the spoken and unspoken questions he posed, she did what she was born to do and squatted down beside a wounded woman. At least, she assumed it was a woman from the timbre of the moaning behind the cloth mask. The dull, shapeless clothes and the chopped red hair offered no clues. Curled into a ball on her side, the woman lay on her side, one foot thrust out.

With a groan, the victim opened her eyes a fraction. "Help me."

"I will," replied Stella, "but you must be as brave as you can. Where are you hurt?"

"Everywhere," she said, and closed her eyes.

"Her foot is broken," said Oliver. "She's badly bruised and may have internal bleeding. She fell into a crevice opened by that last earthquake. We had a hard time getting her out. Most of these women, in fact, have injuries from falling."

Stella stood up and adjusted her kerchief higher over her nose. "Earthquake? How long ago?"

His eyebrows shot up. "Who knows, since there aren't any clocks around here, but I'm sure you couldn't have missed it."

"*Mais oui*, I did miss it. I have just arrived." She dug into her rucksack and pulled out an embroidered case housing a pair of pointed scissors with a twinge of regret for her dress. "Where are we?"

⁓❖⁓

Oliver couldn't help it. The new arrival fascinated him. *She's pretty and scarred and strange and smart and clueless—the whole spectrum. Those scissors remind me of the ones stylists would cut my hair with years ago. Too long ago. A very fine woman drops out of the sky, and I have to look like this. Bummer. I stink like a cave man, too.*

The young woman began cutting off her skirt a few inches below her waist, leaving a sort of ruffle that covered the top of her white gathered skirt underneath, while he answered her question.

"I think we're in northern Kentucky, or maybe southern Illinois. Not sure. And I'm positive it's January something, but the climate has changed so much that it's

287

almost warm. Very strange. Pros and cons to that, but I'm sure you know."

She straightened up and handed him the scissors, having already cut the yellow dress as far as she could reach.

"Here, finish," she said. "Try not to nick my petticoat."

Surprised but game, he took them and continued to cut the cheerful fabric in back, careful to end where she started.

It is clean. She's clean. And pretty, even with her facial scar. And she knows my name. She missed the earthquake. Seriously? How is that even possible?

He finished cutting, and handed her the scissors, while she stepped out of the dress. *And who wears a skirt under a dress? Reminds me of costumes from plays I was in long ago, in another life.*

One possibility occurred to him. *Heavenly Father? Did you send her?* A spirit of peace answered him, which lightened his load. His posture straightened with renewed hope. *I thank Thee.*

The newcomer sat on a convenient rock, bundling the skirt into her lap. She proceeded to make small cuts all around the waist edge, then handed the scissors back to him.

"Cut off the ruffle to make rags," she said. "The rest of this can be bandages. Wait. Use the first one you cut to wipe your hands with a little of the rum."

He followed orders, impressed with her efficiency and calm demeanor. "Whew! That stuff is potent." He winced at that and the sting on his abrasions.

"Any cold stream nearby? It will help with the swelling," she said, while ripping the skirt into strips of varying widths.

"It would," he said, "but no, we have to stay away from the river. Gangs guard and hoard the water. We do have a few containers, though, in case we find another source, and one filter. Should still be good."

"*Filtre?* Something that removes particles?"

"Yes, but if they're large particles, we'll have to use one of your pretty rags, first."

Her head came up, and he smiled at her behind his mask. An olive branch, of sorts, after not sharing her excitement when she arrived.

"It will last longer that way," he explained.

"I brought water, too."

All those nearest her perked up, and the news spread quickly. "She has water!"

The mobile ones lined up with their cups. She entrusted new volunteers to serve the water and resumed her task of creating bandages.

"Thank you for the water," Oliver said between swigs. "God knows we need it. And thank you for sacrificing your skirt," he continued, admiring her hands as she ripped and rolled the strips and removed pesky loose threads. *Everyone has broken, stubby nails but her. Those hands are not only clean, but the nails are intact.*

"*Pas d'quoi.* It was no trouble," she said for the twentieth time that day. "I was sent here to help in any way I can. And to wait."

"For what?"

"For Lord *Jèsus.*"

His longing to meet his Savior intensified. "Same here. It's what keeps us going."

"Of course. Is there someone who can help roll bandages? That's the slowest part of this operation, and I need to take care of that broken foot. How long has it been damaged?"

She's avoiding the subject of the earthquake. "I don't know. Maybe half an hour. Why does it matter?"

"Treatment changes with time. What's her name?"

"Yvonne." He considered which of these brave and battered women might be up to helping, then took off to locate her. He spoke in undertones to Sam, a brunette in her late-thirties, who followed him back to the strange, new woman.

"This is Sam. Samantha."

"*Bonjour*, Samantha. I am Stella."

Nice name. It fits her.

"Hold out your hands, please, Samantha," she said. "This may sting, if you have any scrapes."

Sam glanced at Oliver, who nodded his encouragement, and allowed Stella to wipe her hands. The telltale hiss of air between Sam's teeth prompted her to say, "*Désolée,* Samantha, but your hands will heal faster, and we can use the help."

"No problem. But please call me Sam."

"Very well, Sam. *Merci* for your help. Remove the loose threads from the strips, then start rollin'."

⁂

Stella understood a little better, now, Oliver's anxiousness to reunite after her death. Her whole being ached to return to their former rapport, tentative though it was. She glanced at him now and again as he offered sympathy and reassurance to all. The irony of their reversed roles weighed on her. This time he didn't know, and she did.

Now I must wait for you to learn that you love me. And though she didn't care much for his shaggy hair and ratty clothes, she would rather have him unkempt than not at all. *Yet, I do not have him in the least! He is not mine.* She forced her disappointment aside and focused on her tasks, receiving thanks for water at short intervals. "It was nothing," she repeated again and again. "*Il y a pas d'quoi.*"

In between their declarations of gratitude, Stella puzzled over things that confused her: the women's whacked-off hair, for one, while Oliver's hair was quite long; Sam's shortened, masculine version of her feminine name; their raggedy, strange clothes, including all different lengths of breeches and not one skirt among them; and, strangest of all, the dark women were not separated from the white ones, nor did they act as servants any more than the others did. They were treated as equals in every way she could discern.

The only thing she dared to ask was whether these people were believers in Christ. Having determined that they were, her prayers on their behalf grew more confident and powerful.

As they finished making piles of rags and bandages, Stella stood up with care, using the front of her petticoat to hold them all. She asked Sam for somewhere clean to dump them, but her own rucksack was the only solution.

Grabbing a wide bandage roll, Stella returned to Yvonne and knelt again, praying, "*Marie*, Queen of Heaven, have pity on this helpless band of believers who suffer, havin' gone through a mighty shakin' of the earth. Will you send down your angels to carry God's tender mercies to these believers and heal them. This woman, in particular, needs your help. Shine your light on Yvonne, in this dark and dreary land, I pray, in the name of the Father, Son and Holy Spirit, Amen."

She crossed herself quickly and proceeded to mix and wrap a poultice around Yvonne's swelling ankle. Once that was made secure, and her patient situated more comfortably, Stella checked on everyone else, Sam by her side.

After examining everyone, tending wounds, stitching up a few and praying over them, Stella asked Sam, "Why is there only one man and one child here?"

Tears welled up in Sam's eyes. "We lost many men to the war, though we did have another man with us for a while—Kenyon Pratt. He lost his life rescuing my son. Many people, including children, succumbed to plagues. And some were taken by the government, before it collapsed, and afterwards by foreign troops."

"Taken! But why?"

Sam's head wobbled in a hopeless gesture of horror.

"Mon Dieu," whispered Stella, and continued her prayer in silence, while Sam gained control over her

emotions. *Please comfort the children, if they are still living, and comfort the families who lost them. This bayou girl has a soft spot for wounded children.*

"I had four kids," Sam said. "One was stolen on the short way home from a friend's house. We never found her. Another was a boy, led by school counselors to transition into a girl. He committed suicide. My other girl got into drugs and left or… I don't know. We couldn't find her, either. I lost my husband when the invaders rounded up the men in our town and shot them. Benjamin is all I have left. He's so traumatized, now."

Overcome with empathy, Stella put her arms around Sam, who undoubtedly belonged to the Fellowship of the Suffering of Christ.

"Everyone here has a hard story to tell," Sam added over Stella's shoulder. "I'm not special. But Jesus is our hope, and we know we'll see our lost ones again."

"Mom?"

Stella released Sam, who bent over and flung her arms around her anxious son. Holding on, she stood up, lifting him to her level.

"I'm here Benj. I'm here."

~CHAPTER 23~

Press Forward, Saints!

"...Has the end come yet? Behold I say unto you, Nay;
and God has not ceased to be a God of miracles".
Mormon 9:15, *The Book of Mormon*

January 2054, Southeast Illinois

That evening after Stella had tended to everyone in need, most wore at least one yellow bandage, as if to show solidarity with their select fellowship. More cheerful, now, the pilgrims gathered and sang a hymn unfamiliar to her. A tall, regal, dark woman introduced herself as Ember and started the song in her rich contralto voice. The others joined in, muffled by their masks.

A pale, older woman, the hardships of life etched into her face, stood in stark contrast to Ember. Perhaps Ember had not suffered less, but her youth, health, and grace hid it better.

"I'm Fiona, for our generous newcomer," she announced in her high-pitched, Southern accent. "Bless her heart, she prob'ly can't remember everyone's name, yet." Stella sent her a short wave of acknowledgement. "I want to read a passage from Zechariah which I think applies to us, tonight." A third woman brought a lighted stick of some kind, holding it for her to read by.

"'And it shall come to pass, that in all the land, saith the Lord, two parts therein shall be cut off and die; but the third shall be left therein. And I will bring the third part through the fire, and will refine them as silver is refined, and will try them as gold is tried: they shall call on my name, and I will hear them, and I will say, it is my people: and they shall say, the LORD is my God.' Amen."

"Amen," echoed the others, and Stella joined in.

Day after arduous day, her new "fellowship" made what progress they could across the difficult terrain with their injuries. They kept the Ohio River in sight and avoided gangs when they could, submitting when they couldn't. Night after night, as long as they weren't forbidden by bullies, hymns were sung, scriptures read, many unfamiliar to Stella. She never questioned them until…

"I, Nephi, having been born of goodly parents, therefore having been taught somewhat in all the learning of my father; and having seen many afflictions in the course of my days, nevertheless, having been highly favored of the Lord in all my days; yea, having had a great knowledge of the goodness and the mysteries of God, therefore I make a record of my proceedings in my days."

Hallie, the young sister who shared the verse, continued, "And as we should liken the scriptures to ourselves, it helps to remember that we can be, and are, 'highly favored of the Lord' even during deep afflictions. We *have* been blessed. We have a way to breathe in the dust and smoke. We drink through miraculous means. We have been guided to avoid gangs, or in our little Benjamin's case, kidnap him right back."

The crowd gave a low-key cheer, and Sam squeezed her son's shoulders.

"And food, though scarce, does come every day. I'm so grateful." Hallie paused to wipe her tears and her nose. "I'll say the prayer…"

They all bowed their heads.

"Dear Heavenly Father, we thank Thee for Thy tender mercies and for our blessings. We thank Thee for food and water when we need them, and for sending Stella to us, to heal and bless us. We thank Thee for Ember, who watches over us, and Oliver, who helps protect us and who holds the Holy Priesthood. Please continue to send the Holy Ghost to guide and comfort us, as He has been doing. We will never stop asking for…"

Here, Hallie's voice broke. "…for our Savior to come. Please send Him soon. We desire to sing the songs of Zion with Him and to rejoice for the end of wickedness. In the name of Jesus Christ, Amen."

Stella forgot to say Amen, this time, curious about these new concepts. She asked the older woman sitting next to her, "I've never heard of… Nephi, was it? Where is that readin' found?'

"In the Book of Mormon," said Noelle, a woman in her fifties, perhaps, with short, still-dark hair.

"I am not familiar with that book. Is it in the Old Testament?"

"No, but it was written about the same time. Nephi's family escaped from Jerusalem, about ten years before Babylon wiped out the city, then they sailed to this land in a ship they built themselves. They kept a record of their dealings with the Lord, and long story short," she glanced with humor at the attentive eavesdroppers before refocusing on Stella, "we have a copy of that record."

"The Book of Mormon, you say?"

"Yes," said Noelle. "It's another testament of Jesus Christ. It's filled with His teachings."

"Besides the Bible? That has all the words of *Jésus*. There can't be any more."

"So, you think He hasn't spoken to anyone except ancient Jews?"

Stella admitted, "He speaks to me."

"I'm not surprised. So, then you must feel that no one is allowed to testify of Christ, except those people who lived in Israel?"

Stella let out a rather unladylike snort. "*Mais non.* I testify of Him all the time."

"You do, and it's wonderful. So, if it's all right to testify of Him, and since He still speaks, it makes sense to me that people would write about what He has said to them and pass down that sacred record from generation to generation. Those descendants would then add whatever else they receive from Him."

Teri, Noelle's sibling, added, "Jesus said, 'And other sheep I have, which are not of this fold: them also I must bring, and they shall hear my voice; and there shall be one fold, and one shepherd.' This," she said as she indicated the open book in Noelle's hand, "is a record of some of those other sheep He spoke of and visited with after His resurrection. We only have two copies left, now, so it is even more precious to us."

Stella pondered this for a moment, praying for truth. *Is this of You, Lord Jésus?* The answer came as swiftly as a hawk on the hunt.

~Find out for yourself.~

"May I read this book?" she asked.

"Here, you can read mine," said Oliver, and handed her the very book he had tried to give her long ago, a bare couple of weeks to her. "It's not as big and heavy as hers. Plus, mine is in French," he added with a wink.

Her heart skipped a beat, and so did her brain, but she recovered enough to ask, "Why is hers so large?"

"This one," answered Noelle, "has the Bible in it, too. And a couple of other books of revelation."

"Ah," she said as she took Oliver's copy and pressed it between her palms. "This is the same book you tried to hand me before, Oliver, though it isn't as worn out as it was then. I'm sorry I wouldn't listen last time, but I'll read it now."

At his puzzlement, she flipped through the pages, without registering any content. "*Mais oui.* You don't remember." *So sad that he has no memory of me, as if nothing on that boat happened atall. But it did.*

"I'm confused," said Ember. "Why would she want it in French?"

"Okay, I'm *mega* confused," said Oliver. "She speaks French. She *always* speaks French."

The clamor over that one threatened their safety.

"No, she doesn't!"

"Oliver, are you crazy?"

"She speaks English just fine."

Ember shushed them and said, "Stella, do you speak French?"

"*Mais oui.*"

"Do you speak English?"

"*Un peu*, a little, but not very well."

"Well, sistahs, I believe what we have here is the gift o' tongues."

"As it says in the Holy Bible?" asked Stella.

"*Oui*," said Oliver. "Reminds me of that verse in the Doctrine and Covenants, section 88, maybe? It says, 'For in that day every man shall hear the fulness of the gospel in his own tongue and his own language.' Stella is hearing it in French no matter which language we use."

"I found it. It's section 90, verse eleven," Noelle said. "And you remembered it pretty well."

"Thanks for finding it, Noelle." He raised his voice to speak to the whole group. "I think this calls for a prayer of praise and thanksgiving. Ember, will you lead us?"

Following the prayer, Stella settled in next to a boulder to read, until the firelight shrank to a pulsating glow. Subsequent evenings, they gathered to study the Book of Mormon, answering Stella's questions and engaging in gospel discussions as they walked during the day. One burning question could not be contained. "Why do you call each other 'sister'? You aren't nuns."

They laughed. "Because we are all God's children, brothers and sisters."

Simple enough.

One evening, they lounged around once they had their miraculously adequate meal.

Stella asked her companions, "What is this priesthood you say that Oliver holds?"

"It is the power of God on earth," came the simple answer, "to multiply our food, to perform saving ordinances, to heal the sick, to bless the emblems of the Lord's flesh an'—"

"Oliver," Stella demanded, "you have the power of God to heal people? *Sacre bleu.* Why haven't you been usin' it? Is it not real?"

"Oh, it's real. But I'm almost out of consecrated oil, and well, we lost Kenyon Pratt, our other priesthood holder. We need two, in order to do it right."

"What!?"

"Actually, that's procedure, not doctrine," said Teri. "We have enough faith to make it work. Having two priesthood holders is ideal, of course, but these are not ideal conditions. You can do it, Oliver."

Murmurs of assent scattered around her as understanding dawned. "That's what *Jésus* meant. He desires you to use the power you've been given, and me to learn from you." Her gaze swept over the trekkers. "All o' you, I surmise. And another thing," she added, refocusing on Oliver. "If you have this power of God, then you can do what Elijah did to the widow's cruse of oil. You do it for our food; you can do it for your sacred oil. No more excuses."

Ember chimed in. "Now, that's what I've been sayin' all along. Besides, sistahs, we've been endowed in the temple with power in the priesthood. We can pool our resources."

"You have great faith, Stella," said Oliver. "All of you sisters have outshone me in spiritual strength. And yes, Ember. I should have listened to you. You've been a great strength to me, after losing Kenyon."

"We're all learnin,' Oliver," Ember conceded.

"You mustn't compare your spiritual strength to that of others, Oliver," Stella said. "Comparisons always make somebody feel small. JoAnne taught me that."

"JoAnne? My stepmother?"

"*Oui.* What happened to Kenyon?"

"He tried to protect me," Benjamin said, "But they killed him."

"*Desolèe*, I'm so sorry. Ah, *oui.* He was the man your *maman* spoke of."

One of the women called out, "Hey, Stella, you've never told us how you got that scar."

"*Caïman.*"

"You tangled with an alligator?"

Everyone chattered at once. Stella, confused by the animosity of a pretty blonde named Ivie, overheard her say, "Oh, poor little princess."

The others clamored for the story of her bayou showdown, so she complied with a condensed version, remembering Nettie and Henri's wonderment the last time she recounted her fight for life.

"You're a powerhouse, Stella Rubidoux," Fiona said. "You're like a ride at Disney World. We can hardly keep up with you, and our heads are spinnin'."

Titters bubbled up from the women like a fountain. Stella asked, "And what, pray tell, is Disney

World?" That cut off the laughter, and astonished murmurs erupted.

"It's a magical place of fun and adventure," Teri volunteered. "The happiest place on Earth. Or was, until the war."

"Where are you from, Stella, that you've never heard of Disney World?" asked Ivie with contempt.

"Well, it's gotta be down where gators are, yeah?" Benjamin pointed out.

"*Mais oui, petit.* That is right. I'm from a tiny village near Bayou Black, called Sainte Jeanne, in Terrebonne parish, South Looziana."

"Oh." The women quieted, pity on all faces except Ivie's.

"What? You all have upset stomachs?"

"Forgive us, Stella," said Sam. "We're just sorry for the loss of your home."

"My home is lost?"

"It was covered by the ocean in '46. Didn't you know?"

"Which '46 we talkin' about?"

Noelle said, "Two thousand forty-six. Stella, for real, where are you from?"

"From… a long time ago." *I'm just now beginning to understand **how** long ago.*

"You talkin' time travel?"

Someone else let out a guffaw.

Oliver cut the conversation short. "Never mind. Grab your implements of destruction, Sister Rubidoux. Time for a trim."

303

Stella watched his retreating back, then asked Noelle for clarification. "Does he mean my knife?"

"Scissors, I'll bet."

"Ah." She yanked the case out of her pack and followed him.

He called back to the others, "I saw some berry bushes on my recon earlier, about two hundred yards in that direction. Go scrape what you can off 'em. We need something to take for the Sacrament, tomorrow."

⚜

Ivie watched until Oliver and Stella disappeared behind an outcropping of rock, her soul constricted with envy. The remaining women closed in for a juicy chat.

"Do you suppose he did know her at one time, but doesn't remember?"

"You know how she called out his name when she first showed up?"

"Uh-huh."

"I think she's crushin' on him, and I think he used to like her, too, but for whatever reason, he can't remember."

"Maybe it has something to do with time-travel."

"Shoot."

"Get real."

"Whatevs."

"Okayyy, maybe a rock hit him on the head in an earthquake. But the way he looks at her?"

"Yeah, something's there."

Ivie's hopes crashed. *It's not fair! We're all a mess. We've been through hell and back, and she just waltzes in here all fresh as whipped cream. I used to outshine her by far. Once I'm cleaned up with a manicure, a haircut and decent clothes, he'll discover what he's missing.* "Yeah? And maybe he's never seen her before," Ivie spat out with resentment. "Maybe she's a stalker."

Ember huffed. "Y'all don't know what you're talkin' about. She knows his stepmama. Besides," she added with that famous look mothers everywhere give a naughty child, "this is what we call gossip. Let's go hunt up those bushes, sistahs. I have a powerful need for somethin' sweet."

"As long as we save some for the Sacrament," Hallie reminded them.

Their attention now redirected, they followed Ember out of the clearing, away from the two behind the boulders.

But it didn't stop Ivie from wondering, nor did it quell the fiery darts stabbing her heart and poisoning her mind.

~CHAPTER 24~

Refiner's Fire

*"...and he that is faithful shall be made strong in
every place; and I the Lord, will go with you. Lay
your hands upon the sick, and they shall recover..."*
Doctrine and Covenants 66:8-9

February 2054, Southwestern Illinois

Oliver sat on a convenient stone and took off the elastic hair tie that kept his ponytail contained. Stella arrived not far behind, carrying both her scissors case and her gator pick.

She held them up, saying, "Which do you need?"

"I need a haircut, so I think I'll go with the scissors."

"Ah. This is what you meant by a trim?" Stella lifted the ruffle of her petticoat a smidge and returned the knife to its usual place. *"Bien."*

"You always keep a knife in your boot?" he asked.

"Comes in mighty handy at times, but maybe not for a haircut."

"I agree. Look, I know this isn't going to be a pleasant job. I haven't had a shampoo in months, and I lost my comb a while back, so you'll just have to do your best."

She picked up the unfamiliar hair holder he left on the boulder beside him and pulled on it in childlike fascination, testing its elasticity. "I suppose you won't be needing this thing?"

"Not anymore. You can use it if you want, since your hair's so long."

Stella attempted to gather her hair into the little circle. Oliver showed her how to do it, then handed it back to her and made sure she succeeded.

"There you go. That will help keep it out of your eyes."

"And show my scar, more."

"Yes, but that scar's a hard-won trophy, *n'est-ce pas?*" He grinned. "You should wear it with confidence. And I should've asked if you know how to cut hair. I just figured we needed some time alone, to clarify some things. So spill it."

"Pardon?"

"Tell me how you know me. How and where did we meet?"

"Which time?"

"Start at the beginning."

"That is the dilemma, *Brother Talbot*. We've had three beginnin's thus far."

"Okayyy, just... start somewhere."

As she whacked at his hair, trying not to cringe at its smelly, grubby state, she told him her version, the one she remembered. She then related his version, the one he told her—the one she didn't remember having experienced. "And if you recollect, I knew your name without being told."

Snipping away in the subsequent silence, she wished she could reproduce the hairstyle he had on the steamship. *I lack the skill for this. How handsome he was, then. Oh, well. This will have to do.*

"Shall I work on your beard?" she asked, moving in front of him. He still did not respond, staring straight through her. *Strange. It's as if he's blind or perhaps having a vision.*

Deciding not to wait for his permission to tame the brown-red overgrowth, she concentrated on that. About the time his beard hovered at two inches long, she caught him staring *at* her. Stella put the scissors back into their case, which she slipped into the pocket of her petticoat and stepped away a few paces. She risked a peek back at him. He sat in the same position, staring at the space she had vacated.

Poor thing. He's purely stupefied. I do believe I took it better than that when **he** *was the one telling this story.* She declined to pick up the trimmings, deciding they would be fine for nest-building, were there any birds left. *Or not. The odor might repel the poor things.*

⁓

As she wove her unbelievable tale, Oliver asked a few pointed questions, but she knew all the answers, and her story, or rather her stories, plural, did not contradict themselves.

Too incredible. Ridiculous, yet…

He focused on her as she held his beard in her left hand, intent on her task. Awareness of her—a quiet, capable, scarred but pretty daughter of God, flooded him and fractured his defenses. A snippet of his Patriarchal blessing slipped into the tiny new fissure:

Be patient in waiting for your eternal companion, who will only appear across a great chasm of time. Cherish her, and you will be given the spirit of love and harmony in your terrestrial home...

His thoughts whirled. *A great chasm of time. She said she came from a long time ago. Maybe she did! I assumed the blessing meant I would marry later in life, like, in my eighties, but then Cami... and now... I'll bet even the patriarch didn't know what it meant.*

He registered her absence and pivoted on his rock to locate her. "Thank you for sharing your story."

"Our story."

"Yes, well... I may have a few questions for you, after processing what you've said. Stick around, okay?"

"I will stay as long as the shipmaster allows."

"Shipmaster?"

"He's the one who sent me."

"Oh, I thought..." His eyebrows met in the middle. "Where's his ship? Can I meet Him?"

"I hope so," she said, avoiding the first question. He's... I can't think of the perfect word. All I can say is he's the nearest thing to an angel I've ever known."

He watched her as she withdrew from their rocky salon. *And you're the nearest thing to an angel I've ever known, except maybe my mother. But I can't decide whether or not you're crazy, on top of being kind and capable and intriguing. Oh, and that bit about living a long time ago. Impossible... right?*

He suspected, though, that it wasn't, which left him unsettled. *If that can happen, then anything can.*

Oliver, watching the hazy sunset, pondered the mystery of her long after she disappeared.

***

Stella hiked back to their campsite, which at that moment hosted a strange band of scavengers stealing all the backpacks. She inched back out of the clearing, but her boot hit a rock, and the marauders all froze before whipping out their weapons.

"Well, looky what we got here. Hot babe in a skirt. Well, well." A great hulk of a man sauntered in her direction, leering. "That's convenient."

She spun around to run, but her head exploded with pain, and a comforting darkness swallowed her.

***

The gang leader flung his cudgel straight to the girl's head, and she fell into the dirt with a grunt and relaxed. To his crew, he said, "Vamoose. We got what we came for and then some."

He hoisted her over his shoulder with ease and followed behind the others, aware of their resentment. His gang, being women or variations thereof, maintained a firm pecking order and wouldn't tolerate a new hen in the flock. It all depended on what he planned to do with her, but he hadn't made up his mind, yet.

Tick eyed the girl's boots. He called her that because she drained him dry with her demands. He saw her reach for them and backed her off with a snarl.

"Gee, it's not like you can wear 'em," she said in a huff. The others chortled.

"Get goin'," he growled.

⁂

Ivie started back to camp before the others, having been dismissed for cramming more than her share of berries into her mouth. She ducked behind some boulders at the sight of a gang headed north and watched them till they were out of sight, the last person a large man with a familiar figure slung over his shoulder. *Dark hair, a white petticoat and a yellow top.*

A smidgen of hope coupled with a stab of guilt entered her breast. Shoving her conscience off a convenient cliff, she did not go back to report this to the women and entered their campsite alone. She blinked. *Where are the packs? Those were OUR packs those goons were carrying?*

All she found was a French Book of Mormon lying open in the dirt.

⁂

Dark. No moon, yet. Stella struggled to free her hands tied above her pounding head to a stake in the ground. A rush of fear delayed the thought to pray and listen. When she remembered, unfamiliar voices from perhaps a hundred feet away interrupted. *Scissors.* She twisted her body up around her immobile hands, until the petticoat pocket was within reach. *Gone.* Dread stabbed her gut and her heart raced.

Snippets of what a deep, slurred voice said reached her. "All o' you shtay here… have me shum fun… ruin the mood." Laughter, banter and arguing followed.

No time. She jackknifed herself on her side, heels up to her hands, and slipped a finger inside her right boot. *I can barely reach it.* She coaxed the gator pick out with the only two fingers long enough to do the job. Shaking, she returned to her original position, vulnerable, petticoat askew. The assurance she received at the beginning of this mission returned to her as clear and bright as light—His Light:

~Fear not; I will help you.~

"*Merci*," she whispered, and worked the blade down between her wrist and the rope, cutting herself in the process and releasing only one hand, the dominant one, and therefore the most useful.

A large man stumbled closer, holding a tiny but bright light. *He's the one I saw back in the clearing.* She slipped the knife behind her head and kept her hands together, pulling a strand of rope around her free wrist.

He closed in, let out a guttural laugh and in a sing-song voice said, "Little girl, little girl, we gonna have a good time." After several attempts, he managed to shove the light in his pocket, dimming it beyond usefulness.

He yanked it back out and fell over, landing a long arm's length away from her.

She caught a whiff of her medicinal rum. *No wonder he's a sorry mess. That's in my favor.*

"We gonna have a little party, you and me." He giggled, a repellent, eerie sound coming from such a creature. Reaching over to grab her petticoat, he used it to pull himself closer, ripping it a fraction in the process.

The fingers on her free hand tightened around the knife handle as she sent up a silent plea: *Lord, forgive me.* The would-be rapist pulled himself into range and lightning-fast she stabbed him in the neck, grazing his collarbone. He choked on his own blood.

"Baaad girrrl," he gurgled, thrashing around as he fought for air. The last thing she saw was his fist coming straight for her head.

• • •

Oliver reached the gang's campsite, having followed Ivie's directions. He discovered that the beacon guiding him here was a tiny flashlight lying in the dirt. With jumpy nerves, he crept closer, careful not to alert the carousing marauders down the slope.

Two bodies lay in a pool of light and blood, one in a white petticoat, and the other, a large man, had Stella's knife protruding from his neck.

He whispered, "Good job, sister." Shining the flashlight directly in the man's face, he whispered, "*Fletch?* You're a little out of your territory, aren't you, *old friend?* Pickings get a little slim out in Kansas? You had to come this far east for fresh meat? High time you were stopped," he growled. *I'd hate to be you in the Final Judgment, dude. At least you didn't eat her.*

"You all right?" he asked Stella. She neither answered nor moved. "Stella?" Turning the flashlight on her, he saw that her head lay at an unnatural angle. He felt her jugular. No pulse. His heart slammed in his chest, beating hard enough for both of them.

"Stella," he groaned. He straightened her head, but it flopped on her broken neck. *Oh, Lord, why? I thought she was the one. I really am a fool.* He held his own head in his hands and took a minute to compose himself.

Get a grip, Talbot. Move. Oliver hauled himself up and extracted the knife from its gruesome sheath. He wiped the blade on Fletch's tattered shirt and cut the cord around Stella's bound wrist with a shaking hand, worried he might cut her. *As if it matters at this point. I've got to hurry. I've wasted too much time already.*

After freeing her arm, Oliver slipped the knife into his waistband and used the flashlight to quickly search the dead man's clothes. Finding Stella's scissors and a few other useful items, he shoved them into his pockets.

The laughter of the gang members increased in volume. *Time to go. Exit stage left.* He picked her up and slipped away.

⚜

Wracked with resuscitated guilt, Ivie confessed her crime. She waited, however, for the others figured out for themselves that Stella was missing, which wasted crucial time. Oliver demanded to know which direction they had taken her and left the clearing in anger.

Ivie sat apart from the group. *I'm a horrible person. I don't deserve to be with these people. They should just leave me here.*

Ember led them in a prayer while Ivie continued to wrestle with her conscience. "…Amen."

"Amen."

"Ya'll, let's plan to head out in case the gang follows Oliver back here."

"Night marches aren't safe, Ember. You know that," said Noelle. "This ground is too uneven, and we risk more injuries."

"But the air's cleared quite a bit, and the moon should help. I think tanglin' with that gang is the greater risk," Ember answered.

When Oliver staggered into camp, his face and limp burden told the story, causing great collective sorrow.

Ivie wept most of all.

⁓⊛⁓

"Well, Stella, this be the third time you've stopped by, girl. You gonna stay this go 'round?"

Stella basked in this gathering of family and friends. A heavenly *fais-do-do* it was, with much rejoicing and angelic music. Children played, people laughed. Even animals and flowers joined in the fun in this glowing, beautiful place.

Being here washed her mind clean of earth-life and its trials. She drank in the warmth of her mother's spirit and the love emanating from the attentive crowd.

That question from *Grand-grand-mère* Delphine, though, brought it all back.

"It's a rare wonder to be here with *Maman* and you and ever'body," she responded. "I don't want to go back. This is ever so much better."

"Can't blame you none for that," said *Mamère* Charlotte, who stood with *Grand-père* Edouard. "I was glad to get outta there, myself. And we are happy yo' here."

"It's been *magnifique* visitin' with you again, *chère*," Grand-Grand-mère Nettie agreed, glowing with love and pleasure. Her son, René, stood nearby, too. *Maman* assured her that he was the best stepfather, taking good care of her and her sister.

Lucille kept her arms around her daughter. "I don't want you to go, either, *chère*. I didn't have you nearly long enough on earth, but there's more work for you to do."

"What work, *Maman*?"

"We're all waitin' for you to help us move on to the next turnin' point in our journey to *Jésus*."

A large assembly of her ancestors gathered nearer, radiating intense love and longing—for what, she did not know.

"This isn't heaven?"

"*Non, ma petite*. It is a waitin' place, and you can he'p us keep goin'."

"How do I do that?"

"Missionaries have been teachin' us that we must receive savin' ordinances, and you can help us with that.

They have to be done for us by people still in their skins. So, go back and get busy. We wanna keep goin'!"

An enthusiastic "Amen!" rippled through the crowd.

"*Mais oui.* You gotta pull through for us, *certainement*," Delphine added.

"Besides," Nettie said, "there's a certain young man callin' out for you with all his soul, and I think you oughta listen. Can't you hear 'im?"

Surprised, and with a dash of alarm, Stella experienced a deep tug pulling at her core. She had hoped to stay here, but this irresistible sensation forbade it.

"Oliver," she said, and returned at the speed of thought to a certain campsite. The trekkers knelt around her body, with Oliver at her head, radiating renewed faith and a strong intention to revive her. She also absorbed knowledge of, and increased love for, each soul in the holy circle.

Stella snapped back into her body so fast she could not describe the sensation or how it happened.

"She's back."

"You're back."

"Thank you, Jesus."

"Hallelujah."

"How do you feel, Stella?" Yvonne asked.

"Torn right in two," she said. "I saw my *Maman* and all the family worth seein' that's been gone all these years, and I longed to stay. But I'm glad to be here with the lot of you, too." She tilted her head back to locate Oliver behind her.

"Let's move over and give him a better seat, sistahs," Ember said.

Oliver's emotion-riddled face came into view to her right. He held her hand, sniffing and blinking against the tears.

Ivie approached, wordlessly asking for a better position, too, opposite him, which the nearest women granted. "Stella, I…" She stopped and dropped to her knees.

"I know," she said softly, "And I forgive you."

"You *know?*"

She wrestled with how much to share of her experience in heightened perception. "Got me some understandin', Ivie, before I joined up with my body. I know what you did and what you are sufferin'. *Jésus* knows it, too."

Ivie collapsed with her face on her knees, muffling her sobs.

Stella touched her softly on the back of her head, full of love and forgiveness.

~CHAPTER 25~

The Road to Zion

*"And they thirsted not when he led them through the
deserts; he caused the water to flow out of the rock for
them; he clave the rock also and the waters gushed out."*
Isaiah 48:21, *The Holy Bible*

February, 2054, Southwestern Illinois

Late the next morning after their night trek, Stella
woke to a hazy sun in her face on a temperate day,
exhausted but grateful to be alive.

The group rose from the ground, conducted a
short Sacrament service with the berries Ember had
pocketed, and moved on. They had little to carry, since
their backpacks had been stolen.

Near the end of the day, they approached an
eleven-foot drop off, which extended to either side as far
as both horizons.

"It's the Mississippi," said Fiona.

"Couldn't be! Where's all that water gone?" an
incredulous Stella wanted to know.

"Dried up," said Teri, standing between her sister
Noelle and Stella, "except for those nasty puddles
clogged with algae."

"For certain true? When was that?"

"Oh, about 2036 is when it started. Been slowly
getting worse every year. The headwaters dried up, and
the drought didn't help."

Sacre bleu. Incredible, yet here lies the evidence.

"We followed the Ohio river much of the way, but it's drying up, too."

"Let's find a good place to camp, sisters," said Oliver. "We all need rest."

"Not down there," said Benj. "Too many dead bodies."

Stella caught glimpses of skeletons, some with flesh still on them, in and around massive piles of debris consisting of old shipwrecks, broken furniture and trash.

"It's creepy," Noelle said. "Could be a trap. Too many places for vermin or people to hide."

"Especially people who *act* like vermin," Teri muttered.

Stella agreed.

"But we'll have to cross it sometime," Zoey reminded them.

"Yes, but… not today. Maybe we'll find a better spot, tomorrow," Ember said.

The crew did find a more hospitable spot to cross that ghostly ex-river, at a point when hunger and thirst threatened their peace and faith. Whenever they needed water, they petitioned the heavens. Rarely did they have to wait more than a day, but this time, scarcity pinched. The uneven, wasted floor of the Mississippi did nothing to encourage them as they trudged across it, avoiding the boggy spots but stumbling in their weakness. Grumbles among the women started low and intensified.

Ember called out, "Listen up, ya'll! Remember how Moses' people angered the Lord with their fearful doubt, even though He had already provided for them in miraculous ways? Let's count the ways He has provided for us. Somebody start... Hallie?

"Stella brought us water her first day with us."

"Bottles have been left behind by other groups," Teri said.

"We've had small springs of water bubble up right by our camps," Fiona added.

"Now you're talkin'," Ember encouraged. "It's true that we've been hungry and thirsty, sometimes for a long while, but help always comes. Remember that. Is the Lord with us?"

"Yes!" they answered as one.

"That's right! Does He provide for us?"

"Yes, He does!"

"Amen!"

As the other "amens" died out, Stella detected a rumbling she couldn't identify.

"Earthquake!" Zoey yelled. "Hurry!"

They scrambled up the dry western bank of the river as if dragons nipped at their heels.

"Mom!" cried Benjamin. Sam grabbed his outstretched hand and hauled him to the top. Yvonne pulled Stella up. Most either needed a boost or gave one.

The earth shuddered. Well away from the riverbank, the trekkers divided themselves into two circles, locking arms and using their bent knees as shock absorbers. Sending up desperate prayers, they stayed upright through most of the tremors.

As they collapsed, Fiona cried, "Roll! Keep rolling!" The groaning of the earth hurt their ears and pounded into their skulls as it bounced their heads around.

A loose boulder hurtled through the dusty air with no warning. It crushed the life out of Teri and landed on Ember, snuffing her life, too. The others screamed and rallied to push the boulder off. They prayed, coughing and crying.

"Sisters, I believe the Lord is with us!" Oliver shouted over the pandemonium. "Stella was given back to us. Let's ask Him for Teri and Ember."

He laid his hands on the first woman's head and cleared his throat while the others prayed in whispers. "Ember West..."

"Wait," said Hallie. "Her name is Ebunoluwa Enugu West. She goes by Ember 'cause it's easier to say."

"Thank you, Hallie. Good thing she confided in you," he said. "Let's start again... Ebugo..."

"Eh-BOO-noh-LOO-wah," Hallie prompted.

"Ebunoluwah..."

"Eh-NOO-goo..."

"Enugu West, in the name of Jesus Christ, and by the power of the Holy Melchizedek Priesthood which I hold, I pronounce you whole, and command you to reenter your body. You have much work still to do, and your leadership is needed here. Rise and go forth to enter New Jerusalem, singing praises to our Lord. Amen."

The sisters as one said, "Amen!" Many of them held hands or laid their hands all along Ember's bruised and bloodied limbs while they watched for signs of life.

Fiona started a hymn. "Come, come, ye saints, no toil nor labor fear, but with joy, wend your way. Though hard to you this journey may appear, grace shall be as your day..." The others joined in despite dirty air and scratchy throats, watching Ember and waiting. And waiting.

Stella watched them. She marveled at how their confidence in the Lord and the power He had given them had grown. It filled her with joy that she had been instrumental in bolstering that confidence.

Ember stirred amid cries of "She moved!" "Thank you, Lord!" "Welcome back!" and "Hallelujah!"

"Ya'll sound so off-key without me," the returning woman grumbled. Gentle chuckles evolved into weeping for joy.

"It's hard to sing with all this dust," Zoey said with a cough. "Our masks are with our backpacks."

"This is what you did for me," Stella said. They responded with radiant love and inclusion in this special fellowship in Christ.

"Let's work on Teri!"

A few stayed with Ember, helping her sit up, hugging and supporting her, but most moved over to Teri. They encircled her, stroking her and pouring love and faith over her.

⁓ ⚜ ⁓

As he had done for Stella and Ember, Oliver laid his hands on another head and said, "Teri Dawn Mason..." He paused, absorbing the Holy Spirit's soft assurance that Teri's mortal life was over. His throat

325

catching, Oliver said, "We commend you into the hands of our dear Savior, even the Lord Jesus Christ. Your work here is finished. Thank you for the light that you have been to us. Thank you for blessing us with your faith, and for treating me like a son. Say hi to my mom for me, will you?"

Quiet sobs of the women intensified as Noelle draped herself over her departed sibling, weeping. Oliver removed his hands, fighting his own tears, and lifted his face heavenward. "We thank Thee, Father, for allowing us to be with her, and enjoy her sweet spiritual strength. We miss her already."

Ember, still sitting in the arms of two women, started a different verse. "And should we die, before our journey's through, happy day, all is well." The others joined in, choking here and there. "We then are free from toil and sorrow, too. With the just, we shall dwell…"

"We have no tools to dig a hole for Teri," Oliver said as the song ended. "Why don't we cover her with rocks?"

As they built up a generous burial mound, each person took a turn sharing favorite memories of her, weeping and chuckling both, until they deemed the grave complete. Heads bowed and arms around each other, they encircled the mound and sang once more, sniffling all the way through. "God be with you till we meet again…"

Oliver dedicated the grave in a short but fervent prayer. "In the name of Jesus Christ, we ask Thee, Father, that this grave be protected until the morning of the First Resurrection, when Teri will rise, body and spirit forever bound, shining in glory, and we will meet her again." After the last Amen, another kind of rumble started low, at first, then crashed into their consciousness.

Water! Lots of it! It rushed like a herd of horses into a new, wide crevasse in the old riverbed near the west bank. The trekkers inched a little closer, coughing and peering through the murky air at this wondrous miracle.

"Is it safe?" several women asked.

"I think so," said Oliver. "Anybody get a different answer? No?"

They picked their way through the rocks and debris to the edge of the new waterway. Grateful for this spectacular blessing, Oliver knelt with the rest of them, reaching eager hands into the glorious, though somewhat muddy water, drinking and washing faces and arms. "Be careful not to fall in, people!" he cautioned. "It's moving too fast. We'd better lie down."

They all switched positions, and no fatalities occurred. Refreshed and renewed, they rose and sang hymns of praise with gusto. The water level lowered after its first crashing entrance and settled about fifteen feet below them.

"We made it across just in time!"

"We'll be telling *this* story for years."

"God's watchin' out for us, ya'll!"

The West Virginia saints followed the new river north many miles and several days. Today, the Holy

327

Ghost assured Oliver that danger lurked in what appeared to be a deserted town in the distance.

"We'd better avoid it, sisters," he said, shuddering at the idea of any of any of these women being raped or murdered. "It looks deserted, but… if it isn't, I don't think we can afford their tolls."

"Hmph! We'd better go around regardless," Ember said. "Bad vibes."

"Roger that. Let's head west. Anyone disagree?"

No one did.

"The Holy Spirit just witnessed to me that we're turning here," Yvonne said. Murmurs of agreement swelled.

"Good," said Oliver.

"Amen," Ember said. "Let's go."

Their new course brought them to another river flowing approximately to the east, with many bends.

"I think this river's feedin' the new Mississippi," Stella said one evening as they camped near it. This they tended to follow as they traveled or at least keep it in sight.

"Could be," Oliver said. "This might the same one Kenyon and I followed on our way to West Virginia, but if it is, it's a lot higher and wider than it used to be."

"It's about half as wide as the old Mississippi," said Noelle. "And cleaner."

"But why aren't gangs all over it? That's unusual," Zoey added.

"It's such a blessing to have a drink whenever we need it," another sister remarked.

Days later, the group started off on their daily trek before sunrise. *Please, Father, let us see a light at the end of this long tunnel,* Oliver prayed.

Hallie, out in front, exclaimed, "Look!" The others crowded around her.

"What is it?"

"A mushroom cloud from a bomb?"

"If it is, we're doomed."

"Dang, it's glowing like a five-alarm fire."

"Is the sun shining on something? It did just come up behind us."

Oliver moved around the women for a better view, astonished at what could have been taken for an apparition. He said, "No, I don't think it's a mushroom cloud or the sun, but what is it?" *Is this what I prayed for, Father? Is this the light we need?*

Wind cleared the lingering haze, increasing visibility.

"It's Mount Zion!" Yvonne yelled.

"Mount Zion? Isn't that Jerusalem?" asked Stella.

"We have a Zion, too, on this continent," said Noelle. "We call it New Jerusalem. Jesus will have two world headquarters when He comes."

"When He *finally* comes," said Zoey.

"I'm confused," Oliver said. "The city wasn't elevated last time I was here. It was all low, rolling land. I'm not sure we're in the right place."

"We are in the right place." Ember's voice held a deep reverence. "That cloud is holy." It shone with bright inner light, distinct from other clouds, fitting the new mesa like a chef's hat.

Noelle said, "She's right. Maybe one of the earthquakes elevated it."

"I guess," Oliver answered, "though most quakes have been *leveling* the mountains. Strange to have one rise up. Anyway, it'll be great to reach it, already. I'm hoping my dad is there."

"And JoAnne would be with *Monsieur* Reek, *non*?"

"That's right. You said you knew them."

"They were very kind to me. I met them before I met you... uh," her eyes spun upwards in quick calculation, "the second time."

"Oh, we *have to* hear this story," said Ember. "Be better than all the speculations flying around this crowd." She glared with good-natured chastisement.

"What do you think, Oliver? Shall we tell them?" asked Stella.

Amid a chorus of squeals and pleas, Oliver flicked his hand in her general direction and said, "It's all you. I don't remember any of it. At the very least, they'll be entertained. Let's go, sisters. She can talk as we walk."

The women cheered. Stella had not shared much information unless asked outright, but this promised to be a day of enlightenment. They hiked in close formation to catch every tidbit.

Oliver enjoyed her story much more this time than last time he heard it. The shock had dissipated, and he could enjoy it and her more fully.

When she got to the part where she learned of her death at Henri's hands, Oliver rubbed his eyes with thumb and forefinger and said, "Yeah, you gotta stop dyin' on me, girlfriend."

The women cackled like a bunch of laying hens, and even Ivie's face twisted into a wry grin.

⁂

Oliver hiked alongside Ember and Stella two days later during their usual march. *I'm grateful, Father, that these sweet women have strengthened my faith in using Thy power for good. I assumed I was not spiritually powerful enough, but now, I understand. I can do all things in Christ. All the necessary things. Please guide us again, today.*

The Holy Spirit had been leading them to small throngs of gathered saints of various denominations, all belonging to the church of the Lamb of God. They would invite the other assembly to pray, sing, multiply food or mourn with them, as needs manifested themselves.

"Evildoers have sure been scarce around these parts," Ember said. "Not that I'm complaining."

"*Oui*," Stella replied. "And we have found more and more believers."

"And Mount Zion never seems to get any closer," Oliver added. "It just hovers on the horizon."

"That's because we still have work to do," Ember said. "More people to find and more to help."

"For certain true," Stella said. "We're doing the Lord's work, and we'll get there when it's time."

"Amen, sistah," Ember agreed. "We're right where we need to be."

Past another bend of the river, Zoey, in front of the pack, spotted a crumbling old warehouse surrounded by rubble and alerted the others.

"How is it still standing through all the earthquakes?" Oliver marveled. "Well, part of it is."

He and his flock approached, confident that they were led to it, and were warmly welcomed.

"Thank the Lord!" these new people exclaimed. "We prayed you here."

"What's the problem?" Ember asked.

A middle-aged man in worn-out khakis said, "We've been hit with a mysterious plague. Come take a look at this rash. Be careful not to touch it or get close, though. It's extremely contagious. It breaks out into bloody pustules and turns septic. We've had several deaths from it. This woman started showing signs of it this morning and is now comatose. She'll likely give up the ghost by tomorrow morning. Do you know what it is, or how to fight it?"

"Have you been ordained to the Melchizedek priesthood?" asked Oliver.

"Not sure what that is."

"That's all right. Do you have clean water? Yes? Bring some over here."

"Sistahs?" Ember said. "Let's get to work."

Despite stringent protests from the man and all his coherent buddies, Oliver and his team cleaned infected bodies, laid their hands all up and down those afflicted ones, and pronounced humble but confident prayers and blessings on each one. Only two were not slated to be healed at that time and died.

During the next five days, no new infections appeared, so Oliver's West Virginia crew shared Gospel messages before resuming their journey.

❦

Ivie announced she wouldn't climb Mount Zion, yet. "It's there, when I'm ready. Don't worry," she responded to worried faces. "I'll go. Someday. But for now, this is where I'm needed."

Stella took her aside. "This isn't because of what happened with me, is it?"

Ivie shook her head. "No, but still, it's like starting fresh with these people. They seem to believe I'm a pretty good person."

Stella put her arms around Ivie and whispered, "You *are* a good person. *Jèsus* has changed you. You are not the jealous girl from before. You are a queen. Believe it." In that moment, she understood a little better what the Talbots had tried to teach her back on the *Daybreak*.

Ivie sobbed once, wiped her tears and said, "I'll try. Thank you."

The others couldn't dissuade Ivie, either. In the end, they left her with tears and waves of goodbye and headed for New Jerusalem, singing, "God be with you till we meet again…"

She watched them until their song faded out, then spoke to her new friends. "We will meet again. I'm sure of it."

CHAPTER 26

A New Home

*"...and the willing and obedient shall eat the
good of the land of Zion in these last days."
Doctrine and Covenants 64:34*

March 2054, in sight of New Jerusalem, America

Rejuvenated by the nearness of their goal, Stella pressed on. The glorious cloud by day that glowed like a pillar of fire by night drew her like a bug to the flame. Convinced that she and her fellow Zion-seekers were walking toward *Jèsus,* her exhaustion and physical complaints eased.

The river they had followed and depended on flowed from a glorious waterfall originating from the top of the mesa. Hordes of people camped all around it, creating the effect of a huge suburb of tents, makeshift homes and gardens. *I've never beheld quite so many people in one place, not even in Memphis.*

Ember asked around for directions on how to reach the top of the mesa and was guided to the guardhouse. An envoy consisting of five women and two men from the shining city met them there and led them to a room carved into the side of the mount. It resembled a large cave with doors. The guides provided a fresh change of clothes and showed them where to shower and eat.

This new dress is like wearing a sack. At least it covers me and my scars. And it's clean.

They were escorted to the rear of the cavern to what Oliver called an elevator, a first for Stella. Unsure but willing, she held his arm on the ride up.

"Why are so many people camping around the city, when they could be going up, too?" Hallie asked.

One of the guides answered, "Because they already receive what they desire."

When the elevator doors opened, it was into a large, soft-green and white room with few windows, many chairs set up in neat rows, potted plants and garden murals on the walls.

Nauseated from the elevator ride, Stella remarked to Oliver, "That was worse by far than passin' through the time portal."

"You'll get used to it," he assured her.

The guides invited this portion of the group to enjoy the murals while waiting for the rest of their fellow travelers to come up in the elevator. The paintings depicted the creation of the earth, the Garden of Eden, the Nativity and a mountain city under a bright cloud.

When the last few exited the elevator, the tallest man said, "Have a seat, everyone, please… Welcome to New Jerusalem. Our Savior is delighted with your progress. You will each have an interview with a guidance counselor, who will help you analyze your strengths and weaknesses, skills and talents, and decide how you would like to serve here. We know because of your journey here that you will let nothing stop you from giving your all to Zion's cause."

Stella relived her favorite tender moments with this "fellowship," grateful for the privilege of traveling with them. *We did give our all.*

"Listen while I read your names," the speaker continued. "These are the ones who will meet with Elder Wilson: Stella, Samantha, Benjamin, Ebunoluwa and Oliver. These are the ones who will meet with Sister Kikuchi: Zoey, Noelle, Hallie, Yvonne and Fiona. These are the ones who…"

How do they know our names?

~Because you are mine. Welcome.~

Escorted out of the building and introduced to Jenn, their new guide, Stella eagerly absorbed all she viewed as they walked. Activity abounded. Their escort led them across a grassy area and through a prosperous field of corn, emerging near a courtyard surrounded by pretty adobe houses, all creamy white with red trim.

"This is where you will live, until reassigned," said Jenn. "One of the houses is occupied, so you will move into the empty ones. Follow me, and I'll introduce you to your guidance counselors."

Stella sat in front of Elder Wilson's desk, holding her hands together to keep them still, her insides quavering. *What would he say if he knew?*

"Welcome to New Jerusalem, Stella," he said. "I'm well aware of your origins." He pointed to a file folder with her full name in bold letters on the front of it. Though it sat upside down to her, she had no trouble recognizing the name given to her at birth.

"And I believe," he continued, "that the next step for you may be spending some time with the missionaries. You already possess a good gospel foundation. We'll build on that and give you your own copy of the Book of Mormon. You'll have plenty of opportunities to read it. In French."

"*Merci,* Elder Wilson. I have much to learn."

"You are doing well, Stella, and are where you need to be," said her counselor. "Come back and visit when you are ready for baptism."

"I will. *Merci.* But... Elder Wilson, I... I killed a man. Does that keep me from...?"

"Stella, His Grace is sufficient to cleanse your sins, and you will begin your covenant path in the waters of baptism. Do you have the faith to believe this?"

She bit her lower lip. "*Oui,*" she said, less than convinced. "One more question, *s'il vous plait.* When I died, my ancestors said I must do work for them. Do you know what that is?"

"Yes. It is priesthood ordinances—saving ordinances, performed in the temple."

"The same priesthood that Oliver has?"

"Yes."

"How do I do that?" She longed to grant her angel supporters their dearest wish.

"First things first, Stella. Learn from the missionaries, then prepare for baptism."

She deflated.

"It will happen, Stella, in God's time, line upon line."

"I understand. One cannot eat the bread before it is cooked, *n'est-ce pas?*"

"Exactly."

"Where do I go, now?"

"Sister Jenn is outside in the foyer. She will show you to the Health and Wellness Center."

"But I am not ill," she argued. "Ah. I am to work there?"

"Is there anywhere else you would rather serve?" he asked.

She chuckled. *"Non, merci."*

Jenn left her at the Health and Wellness Center with an aide named Jared, who showed her around the large adobe building. The young man explained general concepts while other workers demonstrated many different protocols and techniques that this department offered, including sound therapy, aromatherapy, massage and animal therapy.

Fascinated by the musical instruments, both familiar and unknown, she lingered. Handcrafted with skill and precision, they produced healing vibrations, resonating deep within her.

Stella sensed the transformative power of their influence. "May I be allowed to witness the healing effects of this music?"

"You already have. It has helped you."

She stared at Jared as the truth of his words registered. *How did he know?*

"However," he continued, "if you would like to join this branch of the Health and Wellness Center, you will witness many formal therapy sessions and eventually facilitate them."

"I should very much like to do that," she said as she reverently stroked a silky-smooth wind instrument fashioned from a large, polished gourd, dyed a deep red brown, as lustrous as auburn hair. When blown, its soft and rich tones soothed her as nothing else ever had. "You must teach me how to play this."

Jenn returned, and Stella stifled her disappointment at having to leave so soon. Following her guide out the door, she glanced back. A part of her would wither away should she not ever return to this place. Healing was her lifeblood, and the concept of music therapy opened a whole new quadrant of her heart closed off by abuse.

⚜

Early that evening, Oliver and his fellow pilgrims trickled back to their little village and enjoyed deciding who would live where. He received his own tiny cottage, while the women and Benjamin shared five others, two to a room. Their laughter and chatter ricocheted around the courtyard. *Thank You, Father, that we have finally arrived, and that these women are happy. It's been a long road.*

After settling in and enjoying the delicious fruit left for them in baskets on their doorsteps, they met back in the center of the courtyard to continue their nightly routine, though the radiant cloud above them added a midday glow no campfire could compete with. Two more residents joined them, making twenty souls in all.

Oliver chuckled at Stella's squeal when she recognized his dad and stepmom. She hugged them both, and he joined her, embracing JoAnne first with a mixture of love and relief.

His dad's embrace, loaded with emotion, lasted the longest. "Son… I can't express how phenomenal it is to have you here. Alive."

"Glad to be here, Dad," said Oliver.

"Did Stella tell you about…?"

"She did. Kinda hard to believe, but it must be true."

"I promise it is. The pain of losing you rivaled the loss of your mom."

Oliver glanced at Stella and Jo and saw tears streaming down their faces. All doubts fled.

The four of them stood in a tight circle with arms around each other, weeping, laughing, and chatting. With the initial greetings over, Stella added to JoAnne, "You and *Monsieur* Reek look so different."

"It's good to be here. You are lovely as always," said JoAnne.

"I think this dress will take some gettin' used to," Stella replied. "but it covers my new drawers and my scars. We tore up my yellow dress for bandages."

"I helped," said Oliver, wondering what drawers were. "She showed up at the perfect time and didn't hesitate to sacrifice it."

Ember showed signs of starting the meeting, and Oliver signaled to the others.

"This is a special night," Ember announced. "We made it to Zion, ya'll!" Her jubilation ignited the crowd's whoops and hollers. "I don't know what tomorrow will bring, but it's lookin' very good!" The others laughed and clapped. The celebration quieted as they plopped on the ground. "Oliver? I think you need to say a few words, then Stella will give us a scripture."

First, he introduced his parents. "This is my dad, Rick Talbot, and my stepmom, JoAnne. They're both pretty awesome. I'm so grateful to be back with them, and grateful for all the miraculous blessings we received on our journey here. Ditto for our unseen helpers."

"Amen!"

"On another topic," Oliver continued, "I'll be joining the Zion Fine Arts Committee as an actor and a director. I invite all of you to come participate in stage productions or at least watch the shows and clap for me."

They laughed and clapped and hooted.

"Yeah. Just like that," he said with a grin and focused on Stella. "And special thanks to the bayou angel who fell from the sky after the heavens and the earth had a good shaking. It's such an unusual story, we might have to turn it into a musical." He waited till their exuberance settled down, again. "Your turn, Stella."

As she joined him, she said, "I didn't fall from the sky, Oliver. I stepped through a portal. And I am no angel, though as I explained to a certain little boy back home, angels are sent to do God's work. So, in a way, *oui*, I am."

Appreciative chatter rose and fell. "That bein' said," she continued, "I've been more blessed by all of you, doing exactly what the Holy Father needed you to do, so you are all His angels, too."

Happy murmurs skittered through the group.

"When do we get our wings?" Hallie called out.

Stella waited for the laughter to quiet down. "Soon, God willin', but not *too* soon. Before I read, I have two announcements. One, I'll be workin' at the Health and Wellness Center in the sound therapy department, so please come visit me there. I love it already and want to share it with you. And two, I will be takin' the missionary discussions, startin' tomorrow."

This time, the little crowd erupted into bona fide cheers, whistles and clapping. Stella used the celebrations to cloak her request in privacy. "Oliver, since I know I want to be baptized, would you do the honors? Elder Wilson said that you may if you're willin'."

"I'd be happy to." It thrilled him, of course, to be asked, especially by her. *Thank you, Father, for her and her sweet friendship, and for the privilege to baptize someone again. Haven't done that since I served my mission in France. And if she's the "one," would you confirm that for me?*

As the exuberance died down, quiet peace settled over them all. Stella opened the book in her hands and said, "I've found many verses from this wonderful book to treasure. Though it's hard to choose only one, I know what I must share with you, tonight. This is the last verse in the book of Enos:

"And I soon go to the place of my rest, which is with my Redeemer; for I know that in him I shall rest." Her voice broke. She wrestled her emotions into line before resuming. "And I rejoice in the day when my mortal shall put on immortality, and shall stand before him; then shall I see his face with pleasure, and he will say unto me: Come unto me, ye blessed, there is a place prepared for you in the mansions of my Father. Amen."

Her companions echoed her. "I have heard His voice," she testified, "and I know that I will behold His face, someday. I live for that privilege." Here, Oliver put an arm around her shoulders. Stella whispered, "*Merci.*" She then raised her volume. "I will pray…"

***

Stella basked in the light and love from all the people attending her baptism: Oliver, JoAnne, Monsieur Rick, Noelle, Jared from the Health and Wellness Center, Hallie, Yvonne, Sam, Benjamin and many others.

Merci, Lord, for this perfect day in the perfect spot to take the next step in my journey back to You.

Oliver baptized her in a large pond, its waters supplied by a crystal-clear spring nestled within the wooded area of the mesa. This substantial fountain not only fed the peaceful pond but also gave rise to the waterfall feeding the river that the group had followed on the way to New Jerusalem. The natural beauty of the site created a serene and reverent setting for the sacred ordinance, enhancing the sense of peace and renewal. A tent had been erected for the occasion, where she changed into and out of a simple white baptismal garment and dried off afterward.

Ivie's new "family" also arrived that morning, so the two flocks, cleaned and polished in time for the ordinance, had a joyful reunion and celebration of new beginnings.

"Ivie," Stella said, throwing her arms around her former enemy. "I hear you've become quite the missionary, *certainement.* As you said, they needed you."

"I needed them more," Ivie said, dabbing at her eyes after embracing Stella. "And it was a privilege to continue our gospel discussions with them. I think some are really interested in learning more. Congratulations on your baptism. I'm so happy for you. Are you and Oliver…?"

Stella glanced over at Oliver having a chat with Ember. "I believe so, although we still don't have an understandin'. A turtle can move faster than that man, and I refuse to push him."

Ivie laughed. "It'll happen, I'm sure." She held out her hand to a dark-haired man. "I want you to meet someone. We found each other on the way, here, and… I don't know. Something just happened."

"I think they call it 'love at first sight'," her young man teased.

"Is that still a thing?" asked Ivie.

"It is for me," he replied. "Of course, the Holy Ghost helped."

Ivie will be all right. Their tenderness and respect for each other shine. Jésus is watching out for her. Stella spied a familiar figure through clusters of attendees and excused herself to head in that direction, accepting greetings and good wishes on the way.

"Winnie!" she cried and walked into open arms. "I'm so glad you came to my baptism."

"I wouldn't have missed it, Miss Stella. I'm thrilled for you. And thank you for helping me write my new novel. Researching a time period is easier when one can visit it in person."

"You're a writer?"

"I am, and it has been pure pleasure working with you. Look for my new book in the library, won't you?"

"*Mais oui*, I love to read. What's the name of it?"

"*Mississippi Charm*. And soon, I hope to finish another one about Queen Eleanor Talbot."

"Ah, from the book you received for Christmas, *n'est-ce pas?*"

"*Mais oui*. It's my most exciting one yet."

"Then, I must read it," Stella assured her.

⁂

Oliver combed the city for the bayou girl, but her whereabouts still eluded him. Discouraged and on his way back to home base, he received a summons to meet with Elder Wilson. Instead of his counselor's office, the messenger directed him to a different building.

Light from the holy cloud poured into the spacious stone meeting house. Between its windows on the left and doors on the right, exquisite paintings hung. Potted plants and wooden benches added to the inviting atmosphere.

Oliver allowed this calming space to work its magic on his agitation as he located meeting room number two. He paused to admire the arched walnut door, running his hands reverently over the smooth surface. All his significant experiences up until now paraded through his mind—fires, angels, devastation, miracles… and Stella. This door hinted at both *déjà vu* and a wonderful new chapter. He pulled it open to discover his dad, his stepmother and Elder Wilson, who greeted him first.

"Come in, Oliver. I think you know Elder and Sister Talbot."

Oliver chuckled. "Yeah. We met recently at Stella's baptism, I believe."

"Hello, son," his dad said, beaming.

Dad's so happy, now. Of course, it's the city of the Lord. How could anyone not be happy? Except me. I'll be a lot happier when I find Stella.

"Oliver," said JoAnne as they embraced.

"You look amazing. Dad, too. What's your secret?

"You'll soon find out," she said with a wink. "I'll be in the hall waiting for you when you're finished."

"Okay," he said. "See you soon."

"Have faith," she whispered and stepped out of the room and closed the door behind her, leaving Oliver alone with his father and Elder Wilson.

⚜

Late January 1880, the Mississippi River

Once more, Stella rapped on the heavy office door on the texas deck of the SS *Infinite but* heard no response.

A crew member passing by said, "If you're searching for the captain, he's up in the pilothouse." She thanked him, and he showed her the stairs leading up to the roof of the texas at the top of the boat.

I've never climbed up this far before. She admired the glass pilothouse framed with white wood, roofed with copper and topped with a brass finial. She had glimpsed it many times from the shore, but at close range, it dazzled. *Simple, yet très elegant.* As Stella approached the door, attempting to peer through the glass, it only reflected her image, the smokestacks with their brass crowns and the shimmering sky behind. She knocked, and the shipmaster called, "Come." Stepping inside, she pulled the door closed behind her.

"Captain?" she said. He pivoted toward her, with one hand lingering on the twelve-foot wheel, his extraordinary eyes speaking volumes.

~Come unto me, ye blessed, there is a place prepared for you in the mansions of my Father, though that can wait, daughter.~

Trembling, she dropped to her knees, overcome with awe in the sudden and complete awareness of His true identity. "My Lord *Jèsus!*" In an instant, the captain's uniform disappeared, replaced by a white robe and red sash, His head and feet bare.

"You did well, Stella, my star."

Waves of reverence and joy rushed over her. "How did I not know You before now?"

"Your eyes were not yet opened. But it is time."

Guilt crowded in and swept the joy aside. She lowered her head, unable to brave His overwhelming omniscience. "I have desired more than anythin' else to behold Your face, but now that I'm here, I…"

She stumbled in the telling while He waited with His customary infinite patience. "These hands that were meant to heal have taken a life. Sometimes, I think I shouldn't have fought him, but that would have been…" Gripped by shame and horror, she could not continue.

"I promised I would help you. I will also help you forgive yourself. Fletcher Hargrave lived a selfish life and grew ripe in pride and wickedness. Be at peace. You have been baptized in my name and are cleansed by the blood I shed for you." She lifted her head in rising hope. "You are mine, daughter. You are fulfilling your mission well."

"*Merci*, Lord. Thank you!" Her tears flowed as she bowed again in awe, gratitude and relief.

The gentle weight of His hand on her head brought immediate reassurance. "It is my joy to bless you. Now go and follow your deepest desires. When you and I are one, your heart is an excellent guide."

In deep reverence, she kissed His scarred feet, honoring the evidence of His sacrifice for her. Her loose and flowing hair served to wipe them free of tears.

୧ΦᏝᏋ୨

~CHAPTER 27~

Across the Chasm

"...the Son of righteousness shall appear unto them;
and He shall heal them, and they
shall have peace with him..."
2 Nephi 26:9, *The Book of Mormon*

2054, New Jerusalem, America

Oliver crossed the simple, light-filled room, shook Elder Theodore Wilson's hand, and turned to his dad. Rick grabbed his son's hand and shoulder in an enthusiastic man-hug. "Here we are again. Have a seat."

"Again?" Oliver questioned as they all seated themselves. The plain room emanated an uncanny familiarity—the way the heavenly cloud glowed through the skylight, three stools in a triangle, that 'otherworld' impression. He shook it off. "You mean... I *did* go back in time to meet Stella?"

"In a manner of speaking," said Elder Wilson. "If time were linear, this moment would be a few hours *before* your trip back to 1879 to meet Stella; however, time is not linear—it is fluid. All time is now for the Lord, as I'm sure you've read in scripture."

"Yes, but... I've never witnessed it."

"You don't remember witnessing it."

"Y-yeah."

"We do not make a habit," the senior elder continued, "of multiple trips into the past for couples. We utilize that power to help people reach Zion, wherever and whatever that might be for each of them. The occasional exception may be justified if both purposes are served in the process—courting *and* gathering Israel."

"And," said his dad, "those who covenanted in pre-mortality to find each other on earth, as you did, are typically born into the same time period. Less hassle."

"But in my case? Our case?"

"In your case, Stella made a special request in pre-mortality, and the Lord sent you to retrieve her from the past. He truly is the best matchmaker. Better than any dating app's algorithm."

Oliver was too distracted by this new intel to appreciate Dad's humor. "What was her request?"

"She wanted to bring her friends out of darkness and into the light of the Lord. She has fulfilled that desire with your assistance."

Elder Wilson said, "As a side note, other couples who didn't connect in mortality may use the Millennial period to do so. That may or may not require a bit of time-skipping, but rest assured, those who wish to have an eternal companion and qualify for one, will be provided for, one way or another."

"And Stella was provided for me." His gaze slid out of focus, thinking of the remarkable girl who dropped out of the past and into his life.

"You were provided the opportunity to win her over," the counselor said. "Just as Cami had, Stella has her freedom to choose."

Oliver couldn't help grinning. "I think she's open to the idea. Wait. You know about Cami? Can you tell me how she's doing? Has she changed?"

Elder Wilson exchanged glances with Rick, who gave a slight nod. "The policy is that someone else's spiritual development is between them and the Lord. Since she was your wife, however, I can tell you that she has passed from mortality into a spirit prison of her own making and is, by her own choice, closed off from the light."

"There is hope for her, of course, through our Savior's amazing grace," said his dad. "You are always welcome to pray for her. It isn't over, yet. For now, though, let's just concern ourselves with Stella."

"But I can't find her. Not anywhere."

"That's because she was sent back to her time."

"Back to…? But why? I didn't have an opportunity to say goodbye. Or… talk her into staying." In that moment, Oliver received the confirmation he'd prayed for. He knew that convincing her to stay was exactly what he desired more than anything. "Okay, I'm trying not to panic, here. How can we fix this? Could I go to her? I didn't… I don't remember meeting her before. We had to get to know each other all over again. and I don't feel that…"

"Yes?"

"I don't believe I was given a fair chance to make a go of it."

His dad raised an eyebrow. "You've been given three chances."

"So, three strikes I'm out? Hang on a sec. The first two times haven't technically happened for me, have they?" He looked back and forth between the two older men. "Didn't they happen *after* this moment in time?"

"That is *technically* correct," said Elder Wilson, eyes twinkling in approval, boosting Oliver's resolve.

"And as long as *she* remembers, I believe it'll happen, this time," he said.

Elder Wilson sighed. "Very well. We'll have you meet with Brother Torrez, the Portal-Mission Counselor, for training and briefing on what to expect when you pass through the portal. You'll be assigned the same helpers, issued some appropriate clothes, given a proper shave and a decent haircut..." He continued his instructions, but Oliver's attention veered at "pass through the portal."

This is going to happen. Am I dreaming? I don't **think** *I'm dreaming. That means I'm going to her. I'm actually going!* That realization tingled all the way to the tips of his fingers and toes.

The two elders suppressed their amusement as they watched Oliver's aura explode like fireworks through a thick fog. They rose to their feet and Oliver followed suit.

"Go back to the office building," Elder Wilson instructed, "but as you face my door, the portal access room is down the hall to the left, second door. You can ask around if you get lost."

"Thank you." He shook each man's hand with far more zest this time. "Thank you, Elder Wilson. Thanks, Dad."

"You're welcome," Rick responded, punching him lightly on the upper arm. "Now go get her."

"Yes, sir!"

Once Oliver vacated the room, Elder Wilson said, "Much different than last time we met here, wouldn't you say, Rick? Do you think I showed the right amount of reluctance?"

"It was perfect. He'll laugh someday when he finds out how he fought it the first time. He didn't know her then, and now he does. And of course, she prepared him for the idea. I'd better grab JoAnne and pop over to the steamboat before he does. We'll check in with you when we return."

⸺❦⸺

Late January 1880, the Mississippi River

Oliver stepped into an empty room and glanced back through the portal, expecting to see the glowing white room he had just left. *It's gone.* The same blue walls around him were visible through the large metal and white stone ring balancing without visible support. *That is so cool! How does it do that?* He examined it all over before refocusing on the mission.

Exiting the room, he found himself in a hall of doors, no label on any except the one marked "Captain," and no one around. *This place is deserted. Wasn't I supposed to have helpers? Pretty sure Elder Wilson and Brother Torrez both mentioned that I'd have helpers.*

~Look for them. ~

He gave kind of an embarrassed chuckle and said, "Thank you, Lord. I'll do that."

Oliver straightened his tie, then headed for the door with a small window in it. Success. *Hello, I'm on a steamboat. Oh, yeah, Stella mentioned that. Possibly Brother Torrez did, too, but I may have been a little distracted.*

He took advantage of this majestic perch to marvel at the view of the Deep South on a cold, clear day. *Mmm. Fresh air. People are talking somewhere, but no one's in sight. Must be on a lower deck.*

As he reached the bottom step of the wide staircase, he stood still another moment, hand lingering on the hefty banister finial, savoring the sensation of a world before cars, sirens, computers or lighted signs. A flock of birds zipped across a glorious sunset. This dirty brown shoreline wasn't as pretty as New Jerusalem, but it cheered his spirit.

So did the soft, mellow song resonating somewhere downriver. Investigating the deck, Oliver scanned the passengers for one face—one scarred, dear face in particular.

He found the woman he hoped would be his bride reclining on a deck chair beside his parents and rushed over. "Dad, Mama Jo, you look like you belong here. Hey, may I steal this young lady away from you? I've been searching for her everywhere." And without waiting for an answer, took Stella by the hand and helped her to her feet. "You're here."

"I'm here."

And without so much as a "Pardon me," Oliver took her in his arms, murmured, "Spectacular," and kissed her deeply.

"He doesn't appear to need helpers at this point, does he?" said JoAnne.

"Yes, I'd say he's doing a thorough job of it all on his own," Rick teased, and she giggled. "I think you two should go for a walk," he said a little louder. "We'll be here, should we actually be of use. Ahem."

"What? Oh, sorry..." He kept his arms around Stella, turning only his head. "Did you say...You're my helpers?"

"Of course, silly boy," said JoAnne. "Who else?"

"Go on, son. Take her for a romantic stroll."

"Yes, sir!" Closing in for another quick kiss, he said, "Shall we take a turn around the ship? We have a few things to discuss, don't we?"

"*Oui,*" a breathless Stella agreed.

***

The young couple disappeared past other passengers scattered around the deck. Rick said, "They remind me of when Allison and I were young. Not to take anything from you, Jo, but... I miss her so much."

"Of course you do. How could you not? I'm anticipating a joyous reunion with James at the Second Coming." She sighed and leaned back.

Rick reached across the space between their chairs and took her hand. "You've been good for me. Thank you, Jo. And thank you for loving my children, despite their varying degrees of acceptance."

"I'm sure they'll eventually comprehend, as I did, that our marriage was for the greater good."

"It took me a while to grasp it myself," Rick admitted.

"I cringe at how I didn't trust my Savior, at first."

"But you learned, as I learned, as our children will learn, that we are safest in His perfect care." He stood and tugged on her arm. "Let's go for a walk, too."

The river breeze lifted JoAnne's hair as she complied, as if a child were behind her, playing in the salt and pepper sausage curls.

"It will be glorious to rejoin our eternal companions," Rick said, tucking her arm through his. "But until then, let's appreciate the gift of companionship we've been given, as well as our current mission's success." He smirked and jiggled his brows.

"These two young people will be quite happy. I'm sure of it. Wait. You told them that we'd be here when they returned."

"We have plenty of time before they wander back. Besides, it's not *that* big of a ship. We may run into them. Or, we could teleport," he added with a grin.

"Let's just act like normal mortals," JoAnne said, winking at his teasing. "It's a lovely evening." As the stars came to life at a languid pace in the twilight, these two missionaries for the Lord Jesus Christ ambled along, recounting the blessings of the day. By the time the two couples crossed paths, most other passengers had vanished, and the wall sconces cast pools of warm light over the deck.

"So?" Rick asked Oliver as they met again.

"So, yeah, Stella agreed to marry me."

Exclamations from Rick and Jo accompanied hugs and congratulations.

"Hey," Oliver said, "are we going back to New Jerusalem, now? I'd like to explore this boat and this time period, first, if that's okay."

"We have to ask the Shipmaster," JoAnne said.

"Oh, yeah! The Shipmaster," Oliver said, glancing at Stella. "I wanted to meet him. Could that be arranged?"

"I believe He's in his office, now," said Rick. "The stairs are over here."

"That portal is phenomenal," Oliver said as they followed Rick's lead. "Can we all go through it at the same time, or…?"

"We don't need the portal," his dad responded. "So, when the Shipmaster gives the OK, you and Stella will use it, and we'll meet you in New Jerusalem."

"You don't need it?"

"Not anymore, and someday, you won't either."

"Wow. How does that work?"

"Well, since all time is 'now' for the Lord, when people are translated, they learn how to slide in and out of it unaided. If the Lord directs, that is. We don't do it for entertainment."

"You're twinkled?" He stopped and gawked at them. "Of course you are. That's how you suddenly looked older out on the trek from Utah, and younger when I came back from West Virginia. And how JoAnne seems so young, too. I thought maybe it was the water, but I haven't noticed any miraculous properties."

"That's my boy," Rick teased. "Can't pull a thing over on you." They all laughed and commenced climbing the stairs leading to the hurricane deck. "The water will, in fact, gain healing properties at the Second Coming, but no, 'twinkled' doesn't mean translated. It means resurrected 'in the twinkling of an eye.' We're not resurrected yet. Translation is the stage between mortality and immortality. It's a paradisiacal state."

"Still, this is huge," Oliver marveled. "Is it happening to a lot of people, or are you more special than I thought?"

JoAnne answered, "It's happening to quite a few individuals, now, so they can fulfill some specialized 'Last Days' missions from the Lord. There's still a lot of work to do."

"Wow. That's so cool!"

"Cool?" Stella asked.

"*Magnifique,* with a little *chic* thrown in*,*" Oliver clarified. "But yeah, back to the Lord. If all time is now, then the Second Coming is now. Jesus would already be here."

"He's been here all along," Rick said, "but most people don't exercise their faith enough to see Him."

"Then, why have the Second Coming if He's already here?"

"Everything in wisdom and in order, son. We need the element of time to *prepare* to meet Christ at the Second Coming, which is, in effect, His grand entrance. The veil will be drawn back like a curtain on a stage, revealing the scene that is already set up *behind* the curtain. In this case, it's Jesus and all the saints from history with him."

"Wow. Big stage," Oliver joked.

"As big as all the earth," JoAnne said, "and the removal of the veil of darkness and blindness will reveal Him as He is—a very 'hands-on' kind of God."

Rick added, "As Creator, Director, Producer, Author and Finisher, the Beginning and the End, He has been with us every step of the way. I guarantee it."

"I know He has been with me," Stella said.

"So, Jesus is here, now?" Oliver asked, half serious, scanning the otherwise empty texas deck.

Stella and JoAnne slid sideways glances at each other. Rick said, "Of course." He knocked on the captain's office door. *Reminds me of the first time I met my Savior face to face. I'm so happy for him.*

"Why can't I see Him, then? Why can't everybody?"

The Shipmaster called, "Come!"

Rick opened the door for Oliver and said, "Open your eyes." After dipping his head to the Lord, he closed the door reverently. "Let's give them some time."

~CHAPTER 28~

Confessions

"Blessed be the God and Father of our Lord Jesus Christ, Who hath blessed us with all spiritual blessings in heavenly places in Christ… that we should be holy… without blame before Him in love."
Ephesians 1:3-4, *The Holy Bible*

January, 1880, the Mississippi River

Rick escorted his stunned and humbled son to Oliver's state room, left exactly as it was the day Stella's father shot him. "This was your room. It's where you'll sleep while you're here."

Oliver poked around, asking questions about various items, before finding a tooled leather case. "What's this?"

"That's your Christmas present from the Shipmaster."

"A Christmas present from Jesus?" He reverently held the case, turning it over and around. "When was this?"

"December twenty-fourth, 1879, a week before your death."

"Wow, Dad, this is incredible."

"Open it."

Oliver pulled out the brass telescope. "Cool." He expanded the instrument, took it to the outer door and peered through it across the river, adjusting for clarity. "I can only see some lights and the stars. This makes me want to go ashore, tomorrow, and explore."

"Read the card."

"There's a card? Oh, okay… 'To the man who had the vision to see beyond the horizon. Best wishes for a wonderful future.'"

"I read that card over and over after you were murdered," said Rick. "It helped. It was a promise from the Lord that you *would* have a future—that it wasn't over. JoAnne always says that when bad things happen, it isn't over, yet, and that Jesus is in charge. Still, it helps to have it in His own handwriting."

"Jesus wrote this?"

"Just for you. Well, maybe for me, too."

"Incredible." He reread the note before asking, "What did He give you?"

"You mean besides your life back? The Book of Lehi."

"The Book of… Wha..? You mean the lost one hundred sixteen pages?"

"The very same."

"Spectacular. Can I read it?"

The four of them, Rick, Jo, Oliver and Stella, spent a few more days on the SS *Infinite*, running several errands for their beloved Shipmaster. Oliver joined the others in a happy daze, loving this fabulous experience and helping wherever and however he could with his "for sure" sweetheart.

One errand, however, was left up to him and Stella alone. "Oh-leh-vehr," she cooed, taking his arm as they once again strolled along the main deck.

That captured his attention. He adored how she pronounced his name. "*Oui, ma chère?*"

"JoAnne told me that you and I were shoppin' for weddin' rings before Henri stopped us."

"Is that so?"

"*Oui.* So… could we do that again?"

Amusement, excitement and pure love bubbled up inside him. "I think that could be arranged. Besides, they have to be cheaper here than they are in my time."

"Cheaper?!" Stella protested.

"Cost less money, I mean. But there's this—all jewels in any Zion community are now donated to the decoration of temples, so you wouldn't be keeping it."

"Ah, *oui,* that's right," said Stella, pensive for a few moments before brightening. "Then let's find the biggest ruby they have, and it will wink at us whenever we walk by our Lord's house."

"That's my girl."

2054, New Jerusalem, America

When the loving couple passed through the portal, they carried the Christmas gifts from the Shipmaster—Oliver's telescope and Stella's treasured portrait of her mother. She also sported a stunning fifty-five carat, rose-cut ruby in a gold setting with a coordinating filigree band on her right ring finger, as the prophet Joseph and Emma Smith had worn their rings, signifying the sacred covenants made with the same hand.

At the first opportunity, Oliver took Stella to visit the temple overseer's office. When she presented their offering, it was accepted with solemn thanks.

"This is a top-notch specimen. May I ask where you acquired it?" asked the manager's assistant who took their names and assessed the gem.

Stella said, "In Memphis, Tennessee."

"Do you know when the ring was made?"

"We believe the stone may have been cut sometime in 1879," said Oliver. "It was purchased Wednesday, January 14, 1880."

"It's in pristine condition. Do you have the receipt?"

"We do."

The assistant accepted the paper. "This receipt is also in perfect condition. How…?"

"Well…" Oliver said, tightening his arm around Stella's shoulders, "Time is a funny thing."

He sent a significant look to the assistant, who dipped his head in acknowledgement, recorded the information, filled out another receipt and handed it over.

"The Lord thanks you for your contribution."

"He is quite welcome," said Oliver, as he took the card and passed it to Stella.

"We're so happy to give it," she added. They walked hand in hand out of the office and into the clear, heavenly-lit day.

"Do you miss the ring, Stella?" Oliver asked.

"*Mais non,*" she replied. "It was too big and heavy. This little band is *parfait* for me. So perfect." She held up her hand to admire the narrow gold ring. "And it thrills me to add somethin' so *magnifique* to the Lord's house."

"I'm glad," he said, "although *I* think your whole life has been a contribution to Him and His work."

She snuggled into his side. "But it is small! And I will always want to give more. We can never repay Him, *n'est-ce pas?*"

❧

Oliver, Stella, Rick and Jo served in various callings and assignments in New Jerusalem while the new convert prepared to receive her temple endowment. The temple here was a long way from its completion date and Brother Torrez nixed the idea of speeding forward in time to be married there. They could have traveled to another temple in 2054, of course. There were plenty of houses of the Lord all over the world.

However, Oliver desired to share *his* world with Stella after visiting her world. "Wouldn't that help her understand me better?" he asked. He waited with all the patience he could muster as they deliberated, relieved when both Elder Wilson and Brother Torrez granted permission.

As soon as her leaders cleared her to receive her temple endowment, and with recommend in hand, she and Oliver passed through the portal once more. They arrived in the Talbots' hometown a few days after their original departure for Church Camp. That way, the neighbors wouldn't notice anything peculiar, and the house was still habitable.

He and Stella were instructed to use their power of intention to pass through the portal into his childhood home. Rick and Jo welcomed them upon their arrival. And right there on the console were their phones, keys and cards.

Rick said, "I hate to say 'I told you so'."

Oliver laughed. "And I hate to say you were right, but you were. Pretty slick."

"Always, always follow the Spirit's promptings, whether it makes sense or not."

They drove Drew's car, the only one left behind, to a rental agency to acquire another one. Rick drove Jo and Stella in the rental car to the condo, and Oliver drove his absent brother's vehicle home.

So eerie to be here alone after all we've been through. He wandered through the house like a displaced ghost. Turning on the lights, he stared at the mess they left when packing in such a hurry to leave for camp. *I should straighten up this place, but does it matter with the destruction coming? We'll all go back to New Jerusalem in a few days, anyway.*

He walked to the still-new sliding glass door, replaced only months before they left for camp. Moving aside the curtain, he gazed at the clouds gliding by. *I'm going to be a husband again, but this time will be different.*

"My cup runneth over," he said aloud. "Thank You, Father. And thank You, Shipmaster." With a swelling of gratitude, he viewed his immediate environment with a fresh perspective and cleaned with commendable fervor.

⁂

Stella enjoyed Oliver's delight in showing her around town. She ooh'ed and ahh'ed at appropriate times, but after her exploits, past and future, she faced it all with composure. Most of it, that is.

She did *not* enjoy what Oliver called a movie at a theater complex. Loud and large with too much happening too fast for her comfort, and nearly impossible to understand, it jarred her nerves. She spent most of the time covering her ears and cringing. And though he said he wanted to watch it, he showed compassion by taking her back to JoAnne's home early at the slowest speed traffic allowed, since cars were too fast for her, too.

The flushing toilets at Jo's place were another matter. *I have never* heard *of such marvelous wonders! And I love these magnifique mountains that show no signs of tumbling down. Glorious.*

Through all these experiences and the wedding preparations, doubt gnawed at the back of Stella's mind and infected her joy. Three days before their sealing appointment in the Payson temple, she and Oliver strolled together under the stars near JoAnne's condo.

"Oliver, I must ask you something."

"Sure."

"Ember was loved and respected by the women. I didn't see anyone look down on her or any of the other women because of their color."

369

"Of course not. White people are frowned on, these days, more than dark ones. Ember was one of our protectors as well as a terrific leader. If we had run into a white-hater gang, she and the other 'sistahs' would have spoken for us, though who knows if it would have made a difference."

"Truly?" She digested this information awhile before asking, "Could you... could you fall in love with a negress?"

"First off, we don't use that label anymore."

"*Non?* What do you call them?"

"We call them people, although I did have a few friends who called themselves black, and a woman I knew at the theater who referred to herself as a brown girl. But I couldn't fall in love with a black or brown or green or any other color of woman, because I fell in love with you."

Stella grappled with her doubts. In her time, dark people were treated worse than animals, and she could not fully comprehend the change in society's acceptance of them. Her feelings of inferiority, born of an abusive, dismissive family and underscored by what she now knew of her heritage, manifested themselves in the painful declaration of, "I'm afraid... I cannot marry you."

⁘

Oliver attempted to stay calm after Stella's bombshell announcement, but a little desperation did surface. "N-no. You can't leave me again. You have already left me three times by my count. Twice you died and once you disappeared. Tell me what you're thinking, and we'll work it out."

She remained silent. He put his hand behind her neck and coaxed her toward him, until their foreheads touched. "Stella, talk to me."

She turned away as if in pain, and Oliver, dejected, released her. Wringing her hands, she said, "You don't know what I really am."

"No?" he said, skeptical that she could surprise him at this point.

Her sweet face twisted with worry. "*Non.*"

"Guess you'd better tell me."

She inhaled as if gathering courage. "When I died, a great crowd of my ancestors greeted me. I thought I was purebred *Acadienne*, so it surprised me to be attended by many different… people. Some Spaniards and Indians, too. I know that they are all righteous men and women, otherwise, they wouldn't have been in that beautiful place, but it means that I have black blood. It must have come through my *père.* He always treated me with contempt, yet he couldn't have been any better himself in God's sight. In any case," she said with a sad shake of the head, "If you can't love a black or even a brown girl, then—"

Relieved, Oliver snorted in an unsuccessful attempt to keep from laughing, and though he stifled himself when he saw her shocked face, chuckles kept popping up into his reassuring words. "My dearest love, it makes no difference to me whatsoever. Really. It doesn't matter. In my time, before the destruction, we called that diversity."

"*Diversité?*"

"*Oui.*" He gave her a little shake. "I'm pretty sure your blood is as red as mine." He cocked his head sideways, attempting to meet her eyes, but she evaded him. His sigh smacked of pain and humor both. "Look, Jesus sent you to me. Or sent me to you. Well, both, I guess. Whatever. We are perfect for each other. You're perfect, even with a thousand different colors of ancestors and all your scars."

"But all my scars have not been on display, so you don't know. I have one from the day you died, too." Her troubled expression gave him a stab of pain.

"Oh, Stella." He pulled her closer. "We've had *beaucoup* trials, haven't we? And you still carry the evidence. I look forward to kissing every last one of your scars. Now, could you not give me any more shocks? I'm not sure I can take any more, right now. You wouldn't want *me* to slip off into the Spirit World. For the second time, I understand, but who's counting?"

Stella wrapped her arms around his ribs, laying her head on his chest, while he enfolded her in his grateful embrace.

"Oliver?"

"*Oui,* my love?"

"What happened when you passed to the other side? Who did you see?"

"I don't remember dying."

"Ah, *mais oui,* of course. I joined your journey before that could happen. I wish... I wish I could not remember that day."

"Do you want to tell me about it?" he asked.

"I… *non*."

"Did you kill me?"

"*Mais non*! It was my *père*!"

"Hm. Nice guy. We didn't accidentally bring him with us through the portal, did we?"

Stella's wide-eyed shock dissolved into giggles. "Oh, Oliver! What a thing to jest about!"

"Say it again," he whispered.

"Say what?" Her whisper matched his.

"My name."

"Oh-leh-vehr."

"I love how you say it." He kissed her fully before settling back into an embrace. "Stella, it's my turn to confess." She tightened her arms around him and waited. "I've been married before." She didn't move or speak. "Stella?"

"Elder Wilson told me. And he made it plain why you are *not* married anymore."

"And you're okay with that?"

"Oui."

He breathed another sigh, this one of relief. *Thank you, Father. Thank you for this woman. Help me love her the way she needs me to. Help me be the man to take her through eternity.*

She raised her face to his and he bent his head to briefly claim her lips again before nestling her face into his neck. He leaned his blond head on her dark one, content.

***

"Let's begin, shall we?" asked the sealer, none other than Elder Theodore Wilson himself. He stood at the head of the altar in a cheerful glow. With two of his brightest proteges making eternal covenants with each other, how could he let anyone else do the honors? His greatest joy lay in helping others to succeed, and he delighted in these two superstars.

Stella and Oliver sat on a pretty loveseat, with Rick sitting on a chair beside the groom and JoAnne sitting beside the bride.

"It's customary for the sealer to impart some useful advice to the new couple." Theodore found it a challenge to focus on what he had prepared to say. Part of being translated meant that he could view each person's radiance, or aura, and theirs filled the room with a happy, colorful lightshow.

After sharing a few obligatory pearls of wisdom, he decided to keep it short and moved to begin the sacred ordinance. "If you'll lead your bride to the altar, we'll begin."

Radiant, Oliver complied.

When they were settled and ready, Elder Wilson continued. "Brother Oliver Michael Talbot take Sister Estelle Vèronique Rubidoux by the right hand…"

Kneeling across the altar from this incredible woman in a sealing room of the Payson temple, Oliver heard the sealer speak of blessings of unsurpassed magnitude, while light filtered through the stained-glass windows, dancing all around them. The Holy Ghost whooshed over him, asserting that this marriage would last forever, and that celestial-grade spirits attended the ceremony. Losing himself in Stella's eyes, he could see both their convoluted journey up to this moment and far, far into eternity.

As they made their way to the Celestial Room, Oliver said, "Mom was there in the sealing room with us, did you know?"

"I saw her," said his dad. "Many other spirits, too. I suspect that some were Stella's ancestors."

"I can't wait to see Mom again myself."

Stella put her arm around his waist, settling under his protective arm, saying, "And I look forward to meetin' her in person."

Entering the Celestial Room, the four Talbots found a grouping of empty chairs and settled in, still chatting in hushed tones about the sacred experience in the sealing room.

I'm grateful, Father, for the privilege of being sealed to my dearest love and of having so many spirits of family members here. His one sorrow lay in the fact that some mortal faces were missing. Brooke's attitude remained the same, and the twins had their own assignment to complete. They were called to gather the worthy from Russia into cities of Zion there.

Oliver caught the wistful smile on his stepmother's face. *She's probably feeling a little left out.* He whispered to Stella, "Keep Dad company for a minute. I'll be right back."

He led JoAnne to the light of another exquisite window. "Thanks, Jo, for being here, for loving Stella, for helping me." He ran out of words. "For everything."

"Of course, dear boy. I love you. And this is part of why Heavenly Father assigned me to be with your father. It was part of the plan."

"Yeah, 'The Plan.' The Lord is an excellent planner, right?"

"He's the best."

"Thanks, Mama Jo. You've been great. Um…" He stalled, embarrassed. "I should confess something."

"What's that?"

Oliver put an arm around her shoulders, gave them a squeeze and whispered in her ear, "I love you, too."

"Oh, Oliver. Thank you. That means so much to me."

"I'm glad," he responded in a low voice. "A wise man once told me that loving more people doesn't divide love, it multiplies it. So, I put it to the test. Turns out it's true. Who would've guessed?"

Jo kissed him on the cheek, and arm in arm they rejoined the others.

~~~⋅⦿⋅~~~

~EPILOGUE~

The Shipmaster Comes

*"The Lord hath redeemed His people;
And Satan is bound and time is no longer.
The Lord hath gathered all things in one.
The Lord hath brought down Zion from above.
The Lord hath brought up Zion from beneath."*
Doctrine and Covenants 84:100

Time Is No More

The last few weeks before Christ appeared to all in stunning glory, Rick and JoAnne were still involved in their work of ministering. The quakes were much more severe. In some ways, the land died as wars, fires and devastation were rampant. Human suffering reached its peak, and most evildoers killed each other off. The Lord's followers, protected by Him in much better circumstances, nevertheless held onto their faith with both hands as they labored to build holier communities.

Christ directed the last-minute preparations for the Big Reveal, appearing to the relative few who were worthy of receiving Him and who were busy gathering others to many cities of Zion all over the world.

Feverish activity continued as the Lord's people worked around the clock to finish building the Mount Zion temple in New Jerusalem, as well as more homes for the influx of people directed to migrate to Christ's

Holy City. And every day, more arrived, thrilled to escape the worst tribulation and ready to help.

Finally, finally! The grand epoch, the beginning of a new era in the history of this world, foreseen and prophesied of for millennia, occurred. All of Heaven exploded in singing and blasting of trumpets.

The veil over the earth evaporated. The wicked still in mortality dropped like flies, unable to withstand the intense glory of the Son of God as He descended in full view of the entire population. Enoch's Zion people, as well as worthy souls from all ages attended Him.

They met the mortal saints, whose joy became so overpowering and their focus so fully upon Christ, that they were lifted in transfiguration to join the heavenly, ecstatic celebration high above the earth while it transformed into its paradisiacal, terrestrial state upon one united continent with one united Jerusalem.

Intense, magnificent joy and fellowship of Christians from all ages joined to celebrate earth's glorious graduation. The fervor of supernal excitement and praise for God exceeded all in this, the ultimate "Hallelujah Chorus."

Rick and JoAnne, in anticipation of a joyous reunion with their eternal spouses, said their final goodbye, sharing one last kiss.

"Our time together flew by, didn't it?" he said. "And now it's over."

"I'm sure somewhere, in the vast eternities, we'll cross paths. God bless you and your family forever!"

"There they are!"

Through the vast multitude of returning saints, Allison, still in spirit body, and James, resurrected, found their way to Rick and JoAnne in a great flurry of introductions, hugging, kissing, handshaking, tears and jubilation.

They were joined by Oliver, a very pregnant Stella, Drew and David and their spouses—sisters they found in Russia—and several grandchildren. The throng grew ever wider, as many more friends, trek buddies and loved ones joined them.

Allison turned her undivided attention to Rick and said, "I wanted to tell you first. It's time for me to be resurrected."

He broke into a huge grin. "Hey, everyone!" The immediate crowd quieted, their attention on him. "Party at the cemetery in Mapleton, Utah, or what's left of it! Allison's getting resurrected!" Cheers and laughter, over and above the high-intensity joy, permeated the sparkling stratosphere.

⁂

Stella sat with Oliver and their young daughter in the vast, glowing congregation many months later, absorbed in her own meditations, waiting for the Lord to appear, ever the main attraction. Her gaze wandered out a window over the inner city of New Jerusalem, launched by mortals and continued with the help of angels. *Back in the bayou, I could not have imagined such sights. This comforts and thrills my soul.*

The choir sang, "Our New Zion," a recent composition. As she listened, Stella surveyed the crowd,

379

contemplating the miracles which brought her here. Her sweeping glance halted on a man in her direct line of sight looking right at her.

He tipped his head to her, then directed his attention to the dais as the choir finished.

Henri is here. Only those who are worthy can come. He appears to have a spirit body. What does he remember? Do I dare seek him out? And is Hélène with him? She couldn't tell for sure with so many people between them, blocking her view.

The first speaker welcomed them and spoke of the incredible blessings of living in that current time. "Although," he said, "that is surely a misnomer, since time has become immaterial. Perhaps I should simply call it the Reign of Christ. And speaking of Him, as we love to do, it's *time* to hear from Him." He flashed a giant grin and returned to his seat.

The Savior appeared front and center. No sound, not a whisper. He did not open His mouth to speak, yet His voice vibrated her soul with a special message meant only for her. Later, Stella wrote in her journal:

"He knows us. He knows me as no one else could. I asked Oliver what he received, and his experience did not match mine. Each person there must have received a personal message. I could have listened for hours."

After the last "Amen," Oliver took their little girl, walking and talking at nine months, for a stroll. Children here progressed faster than in the previous realm. Stella watched them walk off, tiny hand grasping one finger of a big hand, and her heart sang praises to *Jèsus* for her precious little family.

She scanned the crowd and spotted Henri and Hélène approaching.

⁂

Henri Boudreaux dropped to his knees a few feet in front of Stella. "Forgive me," he said.

Hélène said, "Henri?" He hadn't told his wife everything, so of course she had questions.

"I'll explain later, *chère*. For now, let me get through this. Stella, my little sister, and Ruby, my angel, my soul aches for the trouble I caused you. The hatred, the knife, the alligator. Both times."

"Both times? What do you mean?"

"I saw it all in my life review, as soon as I passed through the veil. You battled a *caïman* in our happier childhood, too, because of me. I'm sorry for ever'thin', and I want to thank you for your kindness to me when… when I had lost all hope. Forgive me, *s'il te plait*."

Stella shook her head, and Henri sagged in sorrow. "No, Henri. There is nothing to forgive. *Jésus* has healed us both, and I am grateful."

Hope and joy fluttered inside him.

"Let mortality be a forgotten dream," she added, extending her hand to him.

He lifted his gaze to her hand, then to her face, the face of that very angel who had shown unwavering kindness to his five-year-old self. *I thank You, Jésus, that I can see her again, just as she was then.*

381

Since his spirit hand couldn't grasp her semi-mortal one, he rose to stand before her. The regrettable past melted away, no longer wedging itself between them.

"*Merci*," he said, his face crumpling, and Hélène rushed to put a comforting arm around his waist.

"Why don't we find a place for Stella to sit," she said, "then tell me all about this." The three moved to a small, wooded area equipped with four benches forming a square. In the center, colorful, jubilant birds splashed in a white stone fountain.

Henri took turns with Stella telling their strange story to a rapt audience of one. When they fell silent, Hélène said, "And now it's my turn to thank you, Stella-Ruby. He told me all about his angel, but I didn't know it was you. What a good friend you have been to both of us!"

"I didn't know my angel Ruby and my sister were the same person until I passed from mortality. The second time. So strange to remember two lives—one as a miserable boy on the shrimp boats, evolvin' into an angry man who blamed everyone else for his troubles, and the other filled with love, family, integrity and peace. Peace in our home and in my mind."

"I can recall only one dream-vision about our happy childhood," Stella said, "and not the rest of it, because the veil is still partially with me, but I'm thrilled to know that it happened, just as you say."

"It was the best."

"I'm so glad."

In silence, they watched the feathered fiesta in the birdbath. Stella motioned to a familiar figure leaning against the farthest tree of the little grove, whose face shone with love and admiration.

Oh, I know him. He and his père came to the trial and the jail.

As the man approached, Hélène said, "We want you to do our temple work for us. We've been waitin' ever so long."

"I'm sure we'd love to," said Stella, and reached out to the newcomer. "Here is my husband, Oliver. This is Henri, my brother, and Hélène, his wife and my dear friend."

No flicker of recognition came from Oliver who simply greeted them and said to Stella, "What were you saying before I joined you? We'd love to what?"

"Perform priesthood ordinances for them."

Oliver brightened as he sat beside his wife. "Of course! We'll make it a double date."

"You are showin' your century, Oliver," Hélène said. "I've no idea what you mean."

"It means that as two couples, we'll do something enjoyable together—first, the temple ordinances, then we'll grab a bite to eat."

Henri laughed. "Spirits don't eat mortal food, not even Terrestrial, splendid as it must be."

Oliver said, "That's okay. We'll have a blast anyway."

Henri exchanged a questioning glance with Hélène, then caught Stella leveling a stern look at her husband.

Oliver, duly contrite, said, "We would love to be proxies for you, as you make sacred covenants with our Lord, then we'll all take a stroll, basking in the joy of friendship and love."

"Much better, amusin' man," Stella said, "though a trifle overdone. Where's Ruby?"

"Ruby?" Henri asked.

"Our daughter," Oliver said. "She's with my brother David and his wife, Kate. They love her almost as much as we do."

"I look forward to meetin' her," Henri said, mustering his courage to comply with a prompting from the Holy Spirit. "Oliver, I want to thank you for bein' there in the jail and… at the gallows, you and your *père*. I didn't understand at the time, but now I do. You wanted to give me hope in *Jèsus*, which I have, with my whole self." He put his arm around Hélène.

"You're welcome, though I don't remember doing it. If it helped you, then it was a good thing."

"I was full of anger at the time that I … killed Stella, but I do know that I caused you great pain, and *je suis désolé*."

Oliver dipped his head. "Thank you."

"Of course, there's nothing I can do to repay—"

"No need. Jesus paid the debt, right?"

"*Certainement*. His grace is purely amazin'."

Oliver grinned. "And we can all use some more amazingness, right, sweetheart?"

"Always," Stella responded.

"*Mais oui*, always," Henri said. "I wanted to ask you, Stella, if you have done my birth mother's work?"

"I have, but…"

"She hasn't accepted it, yet?"

"She hasn't healed, but as soon as she does, I'm sure she'll accept it, and all will be well."

"I hope so. I'll keep prayin' for her."

"*We* will keep prayin' for her," Hélène added, putting her arm through his. "But in the meantime, let's get our savin' ordinances done, then we can work on your *mère*."

Oliver said, "Then let's go make the appointment yesterday, already."

Hélène shook her head and said, "I think we would all do well to master the Adamic language. It will make understandin' you *much* easier."

Their laughter bubbled up and floated down the path behind them on their leisurely way toward the Mount Zion temple. The tiniest little girl Henri had ever seen on two feet toddled towards them, with a young couple hurrying to catch up with her. *Must be David and Kate.*

Stella crouched low with arms opened wide to receive the excited child.

"Mama, Mama! I saw our wooby on da temple!"

Afterword

Decades ago, I heard someone postulate that those who leave mortality without finding their eternal companion could possibly end up with someone from a different time period. I thought it sounded reasonable and have since spoken to others who believe that it's true. That concept has percolated for all these years and has finally emerged in this book, which is not pure doctrine. It is romantic and spiritual science fiction.

This story goes beyond those elements, however, for it is in effect a love letter to all those who overcome, as it says in many verses in the Book of Revelation in the Holy Bible. Those who overcome sin, the pain of abuse, rejection or their poor upbringing, for example, and have taken upon themselves the name of Christ, will receive so much more in the eternities than they ever lost in this life.

Will future trials, disasters and plagues be just like this book? I don't believe so, no. They are only some possibilities chosen to serve the story. I think reality will surprise us all.

J.E. Gunther

Glossary And Pronunciation Guide

Acadienne—(ah-kay-dee-EHN) A female Acadian/Cajun.

Adieu—(ahd-YEW) 'Goodbye', literally, 'To God,' as in "I leave you to God while we are apart."

Bayou— (BYE-you) Similar to a river, but may flow slowly in either direction, depending on the tides, may have brackish (salty) water, and has many "threads," forming a maze of waterways.

Bien—(bee-EHn) 'Fine,' 'okay,' or 'all right.' The 'N' here is practically silent, being up in the roof of the mouth and sinuses, instead of on the tongue. When English speakers say a word that ends in 'N,' they tend to elongate the sound, holding the tip of the tongue on the hard palate behind the upper front teeth. The French and Cajun French do not, in most words, unless it's a double 'n,' as in Acadienne.

Bienvenue—(bee-UHn-veh-NYEW) 'Welcome.'

Bonjour—(bohn-ZHOOrh) 'Good day' or 'Good morning.'

Bonne chance—(bahn SHAHNS) 'Good luck.'

Bonsoir—(bohn-SWAH) 'Good evening.'

Boscoyo—(boh-SKOY-yoh) or 'cypress knees' are protrusions growing from the roots of cypress trees that grow directly in the swamp water. The knees resemble posts or buttresses, and may be the way the roots get oxygen, being constantly submerged.

Boudin—(boo-DAn) A French sausage adapted by the Acadians and Creoles to suit the available ingredients in the region. It would generally contain rice, pork or sea creatures, onions, herbs and spices. Some used alligator.

Caïman—(kahee-MAHn) Alligator. It appears to have been mainly used in the Terrebonne and Lafourche regions. (Cut off the 'n' in the sinuses as in the word Bien.) *Caïman* oil—see Gator oil.

Cadeaux—(kad-OH) Gifts.

Catgut—strong cord made from dried animal intestines, usually sheep, cows, goats or horses, but not cats, despite the name. Probably derived from *cattle gut*.

C'est bon—(seh-BOHn) 'It's good.'

Certainement—(sehr-tehn-MUHn) 'Certainly.'

Chapeau—(shah-POH) 'Hat.'

Chene—(SHEHN) French for 'oak.' It is a bayou and a populated area west of the Atchafalaya River.

Chère—(Cajun=SHAH, or French=SHEHrh) 'Dear,' or 'Precious'—an endearment. *Pl.* Chères. **Cher,** *m. Pl.* **Chers**. Also means 'expensive.' Stella uses this word to describe new shoes, for example. (The 'r' is breathy, like an 'h' but short.)

Chirurgien—(sheerzh-YEHn) 'Surgeon.' See Bien.

Choupique—(SHOO-pick) French spelling of a Choctaw word for a certain species of mudfish, namely the Bowfin, *Amia calva*, considered by some scientists as a throwback to the Jurassic period. Related to the catfish and the gar.

Cocodrie—(koh-koh-DrhEE) A more common word for 'alligator' in Louisiana, related to the word Crocodile, Greek in origin. Variant spellings: Cocodril, cocodri.

Couillon—(coo-YOHn) Crazy, stupid, foolish. The 'n' is only a nasal vibration. See Bien.

Coupable—(koo-PAH-bl) Guilty.

Crotte—(KRAHT) *pl.* **Crottes**—(KRAHT, no S) Nasty person. Literally it means a pile of feces, but if the shoe fits…

Désolée—(dez-oh-LEE) *f.* 'Sorry,' (spoken by women), and *m.* **désolé** (dez-oh-LAY) (spoken by men.)

Dupleix— (doo-PLEH) Stella's mother's maiden name.

Esprit—(ehs-PREE) Spirit, cleverness and wit.

Et—(EH, usually, or EHT in front of a word that starts with a vowel sound.) 'And.'

Eucharist—the sacred symbols of the Savior's blood and body. Communion, for Catholics, is the sharing of the Eucharist.

Excusez moi—(eks-coos-ehm-WAH) 'Excuse me.'

Fais-do-do—(fay-doh-DOH) 'Party.' It can also mean sleep, because the children were put in a back room to sleep while the adults partied. It is a corruption of *fête de Dieu*, or festival of God, held on Saturday. All the family attended, but of the women, generally only the unmarried were allowed to dance.

Fille—(FEE) 'Girl.'

Flux de bouche—(FLU duh **BOOSH**) Chatter. Literally 'mouth stream.'

Gator oil—Fat rendered from alligators repels mosquitos. Also written as Caïman oil.

Georges—(ZHOrzh) French form of George.

Grand-mère—(grahn-MEHrh) 'Grandmother.' More formal than Mamère.

Grand-grand-mère—(GRAHN-grahn-mehrh) 'Great-grandmother.' Cajun French.

Hélène—(eh-LEHN) Stress the 'N.' French version of Helene, Helen and Ellen.

Henri Boudreaux— (ahn-REE boo-DROH) Hélène's husband.

Houma—(HOH-muh) 1. Indigenous tribe of Amer-Indians; 2. The town named for the tribe.

Hurricane deck—an upper deck of a steamboat, underneath the texas, if there is one, and over the main deck.

Il est couillon—(EEL eh coo-YOHn) 'He is stupid.'

Il est mon frère—(EEL eh moh FREHrh) 'He is my brother.'

Il y a pas d'quoi!—(EEL ee ah pah dKWAH) 'There's nothing to it!' or 'It was nothing.'

Je m'appelle—(zheh mah-PELL) 'I am called...' or 'My name is...'

Jean—(ZHOHn) *m.* French equivalent of John.

Jeanne—(ZHEHN) *f.* French equivalent of Jean, Jane, or Joan.

Jésus—(ZHAY-zoo) French pronunciation of Jesus.

Joie de vivre—(zhwah duh VEEVr) Zest or joy for life.

Labadieville—(LAB-bud-dee-vil in today's world, but in the mid-1800s, it would have ended in VEEy) A small settlement on Bayou Lafourche.

Lafourche—(lah-FOOSH) A long bayou and one of the parishes it runs through.

Lagniappe—(lahn-YAHP) A little extra thrown into the bargain; a freebie.

Ma petite—(mah-peh-TEE-T) *f.* 'My little one.'

Magnifique—(mahn-yee-FEEKh) Magnificent, "wow" or wonderful.

Mais non—(may NOHn) Literally 'But no,' or 'Of course not.'

Mais oui—(may WEE) Literally, 'But yes,' used in place of 'oh, yes' and 'of course.'

Maladie—(mah-lah-DEE) Sickness; malady.

Maman—(mah-MAHn) 'Mama.' The 'n' is only a vibration in the sinuses. See Bien.

Mamère—(mah-MEHrh) Cajun French for 'Grandma.' Ma mère, separated, means 'my mother.' As a comparison, English-speaking Southerners often nickname a grandmother "Mama…," filling in the blank with her first name. Family members called my great-grandmother "Mama Belle."

Manglier—(mahn-GLEHrh or mahn-GLAY) Medicinal Groundsel bush, rare in Stella's bayou.

Merci beaucoup—(mehrh-SEE boh-KOO) 'Many thanks.'

Mère—(MEHrh) 'Mother.'

Mi cara es tu cara—'My face is your face.' Spanish. In other words, 'We look alike.'

Moi—(mwAH) 'Me.' Older Louisianans even today sometimes end a sentence with 'Moi' or 'Me.'

Mon ami—(mohn ah-MEE) 'My friend."

Mon Dieu—(mohn DYEW) 'My God.'

Mon petit—(moh peh-TEEt) *m.* 'My little one.' The last T is not pronounced, but is more of a glottal stop.

Mon poulet—(moh poo-leh) 'My chicken.'

Monsieur—(muh-SYUHrh) 'Sir' or 'mister.'

Moustique—(moo-STEEK) *pl.* **Moustiques,** same pronunciation, with no 's' at the end: 'Mosquito.' Another version is Maraguoin, which is not as easy to explain how to pronounce. The whole word is in the sinuses.

N'est-ce pas?—(nehs-PAH?) 'Isn't that right?'

Non—(NOHn) 'No'. English speakers tend to end a 'no' with a bit of a 'w' sound, but this ends abruptly in a nasal vibration. See Bien.

Oui—(WEE) 'Yes.'

Parish—Divisions of land in Louisiana similar to counties.

Pas de quoi—(pah duh KWAH) 'You're welcome,' or, 'No problem.'

Pauvre ti bête—(Pove tee beht) *f.* 'Poor little thing.'

Père—(PEHrh) 'Father.'

Pirogue—(PEE-rhOW) A Cajun canoe carved from a single tree trunk and painted, great for navigating shallow Louisiana swamps and marshes.

Plaquemine—(plahk-uh-meen) 'Persimmon.' Name of a Louisiana town on the west bank of the Mississippi River.

Pour quoi?—(pohrh KWAH) 'Why?'

Rubidoux—(ROO-bi-doo, the 'doux' more like the double 'o' in 'look,' though some simply say it as "oh".) Stella's last name.

Sacre bleu!—(sah-crheh BLEW) 'Good Heavens!'

Sainte Jeanne—(suhnt ZHEHN) a fictional village in Terrebonne Parish.

Sainte Marie—(suhnt mah-rhEE) Holy Mary

S'il te plait—(seel teh pleh) 'Please,' informal. Literally, "If you please."

S'il vous plait—(seel voo pleh) 'Please,' formal.

Ta mère—(tah MEHrh) 'Your mother.'

Tante—(TAHnT) 'Aunt.'

Texas deck—top deck or level of a steamboat, shorter, lengthwise, than lower decks. Not capitalized. Named for the state of Texas, which achieved statehood in 1845, the same year the deck was added to many new steamboats. The crew may or may not have had offices there, but the captain surely did, and the pilot house either sat on top or in front of it.

Thibodaux—(TIB-uh-doh) Parish seat (capital) of Lafourche, located in the northwest corner of the parish.

Tout d'suite—(TOOt SWEET) 'Quickly.' As a directive, it means 'Hurry up!'

Traiteur—(treh-TUHrh) *m.* A healer; *f.* **traiteuse**—(treh-TOOS). Not to be confused with a doctor. Bayou folk at that time didn't trust doctors, who were "English," so local people filled in, especially those talented in inspiring confidence and faith. Many remedies healers prescribed were herbal or practical, but prayer was, and still is, their primary tool.

Très beaux—(trheh BOH or BOOh, as in "look") *m. pl.* 'Very beautiful.'

Très belles—(trheh BEHL) *f. pl.* 'Very beautiful.'

Très bien—(trheh-bee-EHn) 'Very well.' See Bien.

Voilà—(vwah-LAH) 'There it is.' Used to suggest the appearance of a wished-for or worked-for thing. I say Ta-da rather than Voilà, but to each his own.

Vraiment—(vray-MAHnt) 'Truly.'

Explanatory Notes

~Preface

Page ii: "...for God all time is now..." See Ecclesiastes 3:15 in *The Holy Bible*; *Doctrine & Covenants* 38:2; and Alma 40:8 in *The Book of Mormon.*

~Chapter 1

Page 4: Oliver sarcastically references the Tardis, also written as TARDIS, which is an acronym for 'Time and Relative Dimension in Space,' the time/space machine in the popular British Science Fiction TV series *Doctor Who*, which ran from 1964-1989. From there, as of 2024, it has refused to die, being reincarnated as comic strips, books, a TV movie, and re-imagined TV/Internet series and specials.

Page 5: "… that skeptical question from scripture: 'How is it possible that the Lord will…?'" See 1 Nephi 3:31, *The Book of Mormon.*

Page 7: JoAnne mentions "Reproving with sharpness." See *Doctrine and Covenants* 121:43.

Page 9: Oliver says, "Maybe we'll get more of the story of Aminadi…" See Alma 10:2, *The Book of Mormon.*

~Chapter 2

Page 21: The undertaker asks, "Coffin?" His question was a legitimate one. The choices at that time were a coffin—a six-sided box, or a casket—a rectangular box. The popularity of coffins faded out, and caskets became the norm. Paupers or the unidentifiable with no one to pay for a box were generally buried in a wrapping of some kind.

Before the Civil War, the dead were cleaned, dressed, displayed and buried by the family. Many were photographed sitting on a chair with the family. The war presented the difficult problems of, one, its massive body count, and two, the corpses were often unrecognizable and therefore impossible for those burdened with them to find the families thereof. Embalming methods were also invented around that time period.

All these factors led to the custom of employing a business to *undertake* those things that families used to do for deceased loved ones.

~Chapter 4

Page 39: Cami's invasion of the men's restroom. As they say, truth is stranger than fiction. I borrowed this true experience from a friend's son's unfortunate situation.

~Chapter 6

Page 64: "…never thanking or paying her at the time of service…" Paying a healer immediately was and still is considered bad form, negating the special prayer the healer offered on behalf of the sick, thus "gifts" given in the next day or two expressed thanks without unwanted consequences.

Page 66: (Bottom of page) Jacques said that Hélène "was lookin' pretty peaked." Peaked—(PEE-kehd, not peekt) Sickly. A common expression in the South. From the past participle of the obsolete verb 'peak,' meaning to shrink, waste away or look sickly.

Page 68: "…fawn-colored feminine footwear crafted from alligator belly." Alligator belly leather is tanned to white, and can be dyed any color afterwards.

~Chapter 7

Page 89: The phone call in the truck: "Tweedle's here… Hey, Dee, hey Dum…" Tweedledee and Tweedledum are the round twins in *Through the Looking Glass*, by Lewis Carroll, 1871. Since the Talbot twins' names both start with "D," they call each other Dee, Dum and sometimes Tweedle.

~Chapter 11

Page 138: "Press Forward, Saints." *Hymns of the Church of Jesus Christ of Latter-Day Saints*, 1985, #81. It is not in the public domain, therefore it is not quoted.

Page 146: "… seal righteous judgments upon the wicked." See Alma 14:11; 60:13, *The Book of Mormon;* and *Doctrine and Covenants* 103:3.

Also on page 146: Rick counsels the saints "… to count it all joy." JST James 1:2, *The Holy Bible*.

~Chapter 12

Page 158: Doctor Grant asks, "Are you aware that she once recommended a tisane of dog scat?" Idea gleaned from *Gumbo Ya-Ya, Folk Tales of Louisiana,* Saxon, Dreyer and Tallant, 1991, Pelican Publishing Company, Gretna, Louisiana, p. 439. Side note: Gumbo ya-ya means "Everybody talking at once."

~Chapter 16

Page 216: Stella says, "I see a devastatin' battle in that field across the bayou. It will happen in a very few years…." Labadieville was the site of a Civil War battle called The Battle of Georgia Landing, fought in October 1862, though in reality, it was fought on both sides of Bayou Lafourche. More info may be found at www.nps.gov/civilwar/search-battles-detail.htm?battleCode=la005

~Chapter 20

Page 267: Search online for "secret queen of England, Eleanor Talbot" if you are not familiar with the story.

Page 270: "We sorrow for the sins of the world, and weep for joy. *God* weeps for *us.*" See 3 Nephi 28:38 in *The Book of Mormon,* and Moses 7: 28-40 in *The Pearl of Great Price.*

~Chapter 23
Page 295: Fiona says "Bless her heart." There's a misconception about this phrase. It can be a snarky comment, but it can also be a kind thing to say, depending on the speaker's intent. Fiona is kind and means this in a kind way.

~Chapter 25
Page 324: "Her name is Ebunoluwa…" Nigerian for "God's gift" or "Wake up rich."

Page 325: "Come, Come, Ye Saints," *Hymns of the Church of Jesus Christ of Latter-Day Saints,* 1985, #30. Public domain.

Page 326: "And should we die…" Ibid.

Also on page 326: "God Be With You Till We Meet Again," *Hymns of the Church of Jesus Christ of Latter-Day Saints,* 1985, #152. Public domain.

Page 331: The Church of the Lamb of God. See 1 Nephi 12:14.

Page 333: "God Be With You Till We Meet Again," *Hymns of the Church of Jesus Christ of Latter-Day Saints,* 1985, #152. Public domain.

~Chapter 26
Page 341: Oliver wonders what drawers are. They were the usual women's underwear in the 1800s and before. They were split in the middle, so removal was not necessary to do one's business. One simply had to *draw* them apart, finish up and *draw* them closed. I'm assuming her new "drawers" *weren't,* and she had to

learn to manage them, just as you would if you received underwear you weren't used to. *wink *wink.

~Chapter 27

Page 360: Rick says, "…but no, 'twinkled' doesn't mean translated. It means resurrected 'in the twinkling of an eye.'" See 1 Corinthians 15:52 (42-54) in *The Holy Bible.* It speaks of being resurrected "in the twinkling of an eye."

Rick also says, "Translation is the stage between mortality and immortality. It's a paradisiacal state." See *Teachings of the Prophet Joseph Smith*, p. 173. In older editions, see p. 170.

Another quote by Joseph Smith which pertains to this story is in that same book and is found in newer editions on p. 196. It mentions that translated beings are meant to serve missions.

For further understanding of the three main degrees of existence beyond this life, see *Doctrine and Covenants*, section 76. This as well as all other modern-day scriptures and the Bible can be found at https://www.churchofjesuschrist.org/study/scriptures.

Family Trees

Stella's Family:

~Lucille "Lulu" Dupleix (doo-PLEH) and her sister Celié "Celié" Dupleix are the daughters of Édouard and Charlotte Gouin Dupleix, of Sainte Jeanne, Terrebonne, Louisiana. Charlotte is the daughter of Ettienne and Delphine Gouin. After Édouard died, Charlotte married René LeBlanc, the only child of Jean and Antoinette "Nettie" LeBlanc. René and Charlotte had no more children.

~Estelle "Stella" and Georges are the children of Paul and Lucille "Lulu" Dupleix Rubidoux; therefore, their grandma Charlotte's second husband, René LeBlanc is their step-grandpa, and Nettie, René's mother, is their step-great-grandmother. Henri is Stella's half-brother.

~Jacques LeBlanc is Nettie's great-nephew, by marriage, being the son of her husband's nephew, not that it matters, but now you know.

Side note: Nicknames were so common in that era and area, and so overused that people often forgot the birth name. Some nicknames had little relationship to the birth name.

Oliver's Family:

Oliver, Brooklyn or "Brooke," David and Drew are the children of Frederick "Rick" and Allison Jones Talbot. Allison passed away from pancreatic cancer, and Rick married JoAnne "Jo" Kramer Gephardt. Jo's first husband, James Gephardt, passed away from Parkinson's.

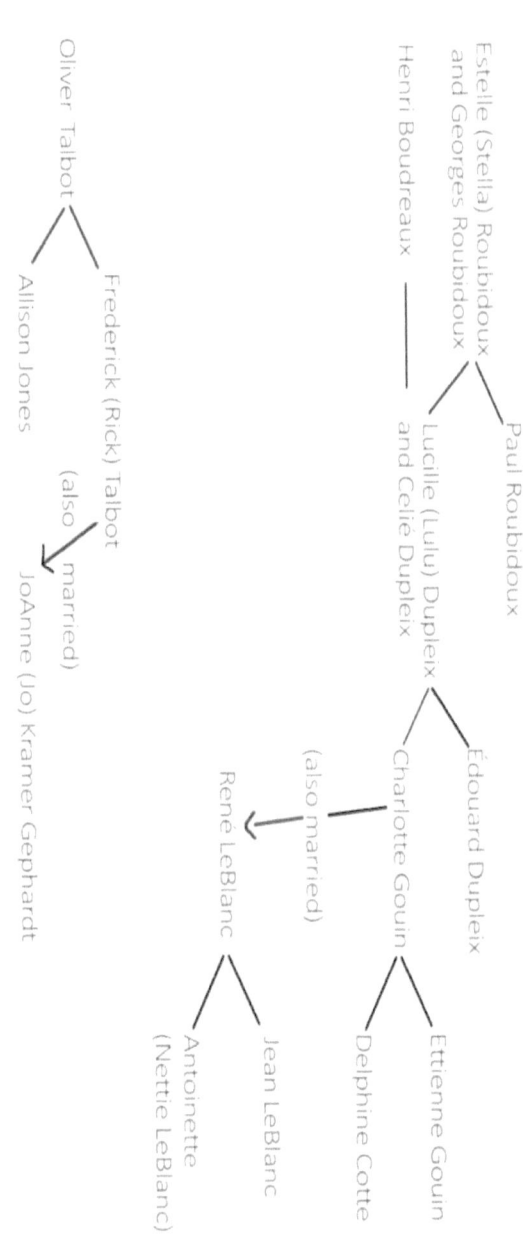

Estelle (Stella) Roubidoux
and Georges Roubidoux

Paul Roubidoux

Henri Boudreaux

Lucille (Lulu) Dupleix
and Celie Dupleix

Édouard Dupleix

Charlotte Gouin
(also married)

René LeBlanc

Étienne Gouin

Delphine Cotte

Jean LeBlanc

Antoinette
(Nettie LeBlanc)

Oliver Talbot

Frederick (Rick) Talbot
(also married)

Allison Jones

JoAnne (Jo) Kramer Gephardt

~Scriptures Quoted in This Book~

The Holy Bible—the King James Version.

The Book of Mormon—Another Testament of Christ. It is a record of some of the Lord's "other sheep not of this (the Jewish) fold (who) shall hear my voice..." See John 10:16 in the Bible, and 3 Nephi 15:15-24 in the *Book of Mormon* itself, which was prophesied of in Isaiah 29:11-14 and 18, and in Ezekiel 37:16-19.

The Doctrine and Covenants—A collection of revelations given in the 1800s, mostly to the Prophet Joseph Smith of the Church of Jesus Christ of Latter-Day Saints.

The Pearl of Great Price—Ancient and modern documents translated and/or produced by the Prophet Joseph Smith. These are: *Selections from the Book of Moses*; *The Book of Abraham; Joseph Smith—Matthew; Joseph Smith—History;* and *The Articles of Faith*.

All of these can be found at
https://www.churchofjesuschrist.org/study/scriptures

Chronology of Events for *Divine Portals*

(All the puzzle pieces in order. Chapters noted)

Date	Original Timeline	Changed Timeline
		(Due to the Talbots preventing Stella's death, and Stella rescuing Henri.)
May 1857	Stella is born to Paul and Lucille (Lulu) Dupleix Rubidoux. (Implied)	Henri, 5, is rescued and given to Nettie and Lucille to raise, along with Georges, 2, and soon-to-be born Stella. Paul/Phillipe is banished. (Chps 15-18)
Sept 1860	Sisters Lulu and Celié are killed. Henri, 8, is sent to work on a shrimp boat. (Chps 3+15)	Lulu and Celié live.
Oct 1862	The Battle of Georgia Landing, Labadieville, Louisiana. (Historical fact. See Chp 16 note.)	Stella, Winnie and JoAnne help in the aftermath of the Battle of Georgia Landing, when Sebastien is mortally wounded. (Chps 14+16)
1864	Nettie takes Stella under her wing and tutelage. (Chp 3)	
1874	Stella leaves home to live with Nettie. Nettie dies. Stella becomes the healer for Sainte Jeanne. (Chps 3+6)	
1876	Henri returns to Sainte Jeanne, marries Hélène.	Henri and Hélène are happily married. (Implied in Epilogue)

403

	They are not happy. (Implied, Chp 6)	
July 1879	Hélène dies, and Stella flees Henri's wrath. (Chp 6)	
Sept 1879	Stella finds work with Dr. Grant in Plaquemine. (Chp 12)	
Oct 1879	Stella tries to trade her services for a steamboat ticket on *SS Daybreak*, but has to return to work for Dr. Grant and save her money. (Chp 14)	(Before Henri is rescued) Rick and Jo find Stella on the steamboat *SS Daybreak* docked at Plaquemine. They buy her ticket and tutor her. (Chp 13)
Oct-Nov 1879	Oliver finds Stella at Dr. Grant's office. She agrees to join the Talbots in charity work aboard the *SS Infinite*. (Chps 2+20)	Stella, Winnie and JoAnne work together in charitable service. (Chp 14)
December 1879	Oliver and Stella continue their courtship as they fulfill service assignments. They become engaged at the Christmas gala. (Chp 19)	Oliver and Stella have separate assignments, then meet at the Christmas gala. (Chp 19)
Early January 1880	Oliver and Stella continue their courtship. (Assumed)	Oliver and Stella continue serving in humanitarian assignments and begin their courtship in earnest. (Chps 20+21)

Mid January 1880	Oliver and Stella are happily engaged. (Chp 2)	Stella goes from New Jerusalem in the future back to the SS *Infinite.* (Chp 26) Ditto Oliver, who proposes to Stella. (Implied in Chp 27) They return to New Jerusalem in 2054, and are sent to 2049 to be married in Payson (Chp 28). All of this avoids his death at Paul's hand.
Late January 1880	Oliver and Stella are shopping for rings. She is killed by Henri. (Chp 2)	Oliver is killed by Paul. (Chp 21) Stella is sent to 2053. (Chp 22. See Late 2053 in this chart)
Early February 1880	Henri's trial and hanging. (Chp 14)	Henri kills no one. There is no trial.
------	Span of 97 years.	
1977	JoAnne Kramer Gephardt is born.	
1993	Frederick (Rick) Talbot is born.	
2019	Oliver Michael Talbot is born.	
2043	At age 24, Oliver marries Cami. (Chp 4) Brooklyn, 20, marries and starts a family.	
2044	Oliver and Cami divorce. Rick and Allison sell their theater, send the twins on a mission, then serve as Family History missionaries. (Chp 4)	
2046	Allison dies. (Chp 4) An earthquake sends much of southern Louisiana into the ocean. (Chp 23)	

2048	Rick marries JoAnne. (Chp 5) An earthquake damages central Utah. (Chp 7)	
June 2049	Humble people in tune with the Holy Spirit go to camps of refuge. (Chp 7)	Oliver and Stella are married in the Payson Temple. (Chp 28)
2049 to 2053	Societal collapse, foreign invaders, deadly plague. Massive fires, earthquakes, tsunamis, etc. Temples close temporarily. Campers are relocated. (Chp 10)	
Late May 2053	Talbots are sent to Diamond Fork and find son David and company. They leave for Missouri. (Chps 10 + 11)	
Late Aug 2053	Rick's trekkers from Utah arrive at New Jerusalem in Missouri. (Chp 11)	
Sept 2053	Oliver is assigned to go to West Virginia; Rick and Jo are sent to Africa. (Chp 11)	
Dec 2053	Mount Zion is raised up. (Chp 25) Severe climate change causes temperate weather. Stella is sent to join Oliver on his westward trek from WV to New Jerusalem in MO. Stella has pre-empted Oliver being sent to her time, so he does not know her. (Chp 22) She is killed and healed. (Chp 24)	
Mid January 2054	Oliver brings a group of West Virginians and those they gathered back to Missouri. Oliver receives the assignment to go to 1879 to meet Stella. (Chp 1)	Stella arrives in New Jerusalem with Oliver's group from West Virginia. Stella is baptized by Oliver, and is sent back to 1880. (Chap 26) Oliver follows. (Chp 27) They go to 2049 to be married. (Chp 28)

		They make their home in New Jerusalem, 2054. (Implied in Epilogue)
2056	Had Stella's death (either time) been the end, little Ruby would not have been born. (Assumed)	Little Ruby is born. (Implied in Epilogue)
20??	Christ's Second Coming, and the earth changes to its paradisiacal or Terrestrial state. (Epilogue)	

Acknowledgments

~~First and foremost, to my Heavenly Father and my Divine Portal, Jesus Christ, who told me years ago through the Holy Ghost, "You were put on this earth to create, so get busy." However, I cannot do much without His help. "Of myself, I am weak…" All glory be to Him! I felt guidance and hugs from the Holy Ghost all through the writing of this story. It was a gift to me that I'm so happy to share.

~~To my eternal companion, R.J., who has stuck with me through thick and, for a while, extremely thin. He has been supportive of my creative endeavors for 48 years and provided me with a laptop computer to facilitate this project. Thank you for your patience and love. You're a peach, and you know it!

~~To Sadie, who asked me to trade handmade dolls with her. Since dolls have personalities, I started seeing Stella/Ruby as I constructed that doll and decided to write about her. Thanks, Sadie, for the inspiration to take up writing, again.

~~To alpha readers Audrae Rogers and Judy Brailsford. Thank you for your encouragement and good criticism.

~~To beta readers Kim Harman (without whom I would never have finished this book), Jerroleen Sorensen, Linda Butler, Jesse and Celeste Fisher and Angelique Conger. Thank you for supporting me and this project enough to spare some time out of your busy, busy lives to read it and give an honest opinion. And thanks to the ANWA Time Spinners for their invaluable advice.

~~Extra thanks to E. Levario, proof-reader.

~~And finally, to Nephi Anderson, who published *Added Upon* in 1898 and who inspired me with his vision of Zion. I want to meet him someday in the real thing.

Questions for Readers

1. What appears to be the main reason in this book that people leave their church or their faith right before the End Times destruction? What is the main reason in the scriptures for apostasy? What is the most common reason people leave or never join, now? Is it the same?

2. Rick indicated a struggle with impatience, and JoAnne a tendency toward tears, even as translated beings. Do you think translated/paradisiacal beings are flawless?

3. If you, or someone you love were murdered, would you be willing to go back in time to rescue the perpetrator? Why or why not?

4. Why was Oliver required to witness Stella's murder? Why were he and Rick required to participate in Henri's trial and witness his execution and burial? What good did it do?

5. Why do you think the Shipmaster was in such a hurry to dismiss Stella after her first interview with Him? For my thoughts on this, please see the blog entitled "Veil-Ripping Faith" on my website, SecondAdvent.Life.

6. Was JoAnne deceptive in telling Stella that they would go back in time to help Hélène? Was Hélène benefitted? Why didn't JoAnne tell Stella they were first helping Henri?

7. Stella did not cooperate graciously with Oliver when he cautioned her not to visit the spot where she was murdered, then insisted on going with her. He thought, "What's gotten into her?" Any ideas on what her issue was?

8. The Shipmaster cautions Stella to use desire wisely, because it's very powerful, as in that old saying, "Be careful what you wish for." Have you experienced the power of focusing on what you desired? Did it end well?

9. When Oliver's West Virginia group reached New Jerusalem, they asked their guides why so many people camped at the base instead of coming to the top. The answer was, "Because they already receive what they desire." Any ideas about what they were already receiving? What stops *us* from moving forward?

10. Why was Stella sent back to 1880 after her baptism? Did it help her? How? Besides becoming engaged to Stella, how did it help Oliver to follow her?

11. Does my vision of End Times, Jesus' appearance and life in New Jerusalem come close to yours? If not, how do they differ? I encourage you to sign up for my email newsletter to receive Stella's Millennial Journal, which explores life in New Jerusalem more fully. See #1 on the next page.

12. Do trials bring you closer to God? Or do you blame Him for letting you suffer? Do you ask, "Why me?" Or do you ask, "How can I grow from this?"

13. What are some ways to get along with and even love someone you would not have chosen to live with or near? This could include stepchildren, neighbors and church members.

14. How many "divine portals" have you found in this book?

Invitations to Readers

Please feel free to:

1. Sign up for my monthly-ish email newsletter and receive an appendix to Divine Portals in a Word document. It's called "Into Eternity—Stella's Millennial Journal," which explores her experiences during Christ's reign on earth and tells the rest of the story of her alternate childhood. It's about the size of a normal chapter.

   Go to www.SecondAdvent.Life and scroll to the bottom of the page. Click on "Connect" under my photo to add your email address.

2. Pass along your copy of this book to others or tell them how to find their own!

3. Send questions, suggestions and comments through my website, SecondAdvent.Life. Scroll down to the bottom of the home page and click on "Connect" under my photo. Look for clues on that same website and in the newsletter about the next book, another story about finding one's eternal companion after death.

4. Write your own faith-based sci-fi, supernatural or speculative novel. I wrote what I like to read about, and I'm hoping to find more stories about being in God's hands and trusting Him in these Last Days.

5. Follow me (as J.E. Gunther – Author or JEGuntherAuthor) on social media. I have a wide variety of interests, including the uniqueness of living in these Last Days before Jesus comes again. You may also find clues to my future books.

About the Author

Sprouted in Texas, rooted in Utah, J.E. Gunther has been a food server, actress, director, costumer, playwright, composer, mother, grandmother, gardener, poet, quilter, all-around artist, and now, ta-da! Novelist. She and her husband R.J. have four kids, six grandkids and a bossy chiweenie named Ollie. She was baptized a member of the Church of Jesus Christ of Latter-Day Saints at the age of twelve after an earth-shaking witness of the truth of the Book of Mormon. She loves talking about, writing about and singing about Jesus.

Photo of R.J. and J.E. courtesy of Breanne Weber, Breannelizabethphotography.com

Photo of the doll that gave her the idea for this book taken by the author. More about the Stella doll and the bossy chiweenie on SecondAdvent.Life.

...God will be merciful unto many; and our children shall be restored, that they may come to that which will give them the true knowledge of their Redeemer.

2 Nephi 10:2

www.ingramcontent.com/pod-product-compliance
Lightning Source LLC
Chambersburg PA
CBHW022348020726
47500CB00002B/177